I0700658

THE 11TH PLANET'S PEACEMAKER

THE BEGINNING OF WISDOM

ALETA MAREE

The beginning of wisdom is this:
Get wisdom, and whatever you get, get insight.

Proverbs 4:7

1

ANOTHER DAY! ANOTHER DOLLAR!

I HAD BEEN WORKING my way up in a research and development company that I had joined less than six years ago. After landing an internship with the International Communications Department, I completed my Ph.D. in Accelerated Metaphysics and found my way into a highly secret organization in the intelligence field. My current job responsibilities were to collect and review data and any other evidence that pointed to abnormal communications.

The part I never told anyone, when they asked, was this included both inside and outside our world's borders. Behind closed and secure doors I was being paid to intercept alien life-form transmissions. I had a team of remote viewers and talented cyber security scientists and engineers to help me accomplish these objectives.

On that particular day, I had just finished my progress report with the Secretary of Defense under the watchful eye of several assigned National Security Officers. I was quite content with my grasp on reality about how our security and monitoring controls were performing. My final and strategically planned oxymoronic statement to my well-dressed and pressed superiors was, "As far as our data can conclude, this incident was isolated and explainable. There is a conspicuous absence of solid evidence to indicate that we are not alone."

Satisfied with my delivery of this important message, I shook everyone's hand and found my way back to my home away from home – my work office, of course.

As I was rocking back and forth in my high-backed brown leather chair, I was peering out my oversized picture window that overlooked the tallest, treeless mountain in the United States. I was wondering if I should have disclosed the circumstantial evidence that my team had just uncovered the day before. I knew that it would be criticized with great scrutiny. I knew that "feelings," even if they were scientifically based, were not enough data to take action one way or another. So I sat on it, with hopes to investigate my remote viewers inklings, when we had more time to do so.

This is when I saw it.

A slowly moving triangular shaped structure cascading across my view with the backdrop of the magnificent Snake Mountain. Its metallic shimmering shape shined like a diamond in the clear blue sky. The hot summer sun beat down on its foreign luminescent composition. I could hear the occupants in the offices next to mine gasp as their realities were shattered by the view outside their window.

Oddly enough, for some reason I felt calm and collected because deep in my soul I knew they would come, some day. The joy in my heart was hard to conceal because I knew I would see him again.

As I sat there in silent wonder a voice began to sing through my mind.

"I was chosen to meet Your call. I train so that I can stand tall. I answer, because of Your love. Worthy are You, our Conductor above. I trust without sight. Reaching for the light. Even if pursuit of right is a fight. His final gifts outweigh this plight. I strive to do no wrong. I will sing His special song."

A deep understanding of what this arrival meant was being played back through my brain. This forgotten song gently carried me to the beginning of my story where the training for my new interstellar role had unknowingly begun.

It all started with one weird night in my dark bedroom when I was four years old.

2

FIRST CONTACT

———⌇———

ON THAT PARTICULAR four-year old evening my mom had just finished tucking me into bed. The clock turned to 12:32 a.m. It was way past my bedtime after celebrating my sister's eighteenth birthday. Time had slipped by, unnoticed, due to all of the singing, dancing, and eating we had been doing to celebrate her big day of becoming an adult. When my mother looked at the clock on my bedstand; she grimaced and murmured, "Don't fear little one, because He wants to give us the Kingdom."

I looked up at her with wide blue eyes in hopes to get a better idea of why she said these foreboding words, but my mom just patted me on the head and leaned down to kiss me on the forehead. As she raised up to leave the darkened room, she gently whispered, "Have sweet dreams little one."

I remember how my eyelids became heavy as soon as my mother left. My mind drifted off into a peaceful slumber when a cool wisp of a breeze brushed my cheek. It felt like the soft caress of fingertips.

Jolted awake, I suddenly became aware that there was something in my room, watching me. In utter panic, I threw the blankets over my head and began to hyperventilate within my bedcover cocoon. As I listened to the dead silence of my room, an intermittent humming began to tickle my ears. The different tonal sounds increased in volume and then echoed throughout my room in perfect synchronicity. It sounded like a harmonized symphony. I didn't understand all of the words, but I did comprehend the last few that ran through my head.

"Do not be afraid. We come in peace."

After several moments of inner self conflict I slowly pulled the covers off my head. The night light highlighted three shadowy figures that stood about 2 ½ to 3 feet tall. I silently cringed with the realization that there was actually something there. While taking deep calming breaths, my unwelcome visitors stood there in silence and waited motionlessly for me to collect my thoughts. I could tell they were communicating to each other through different pitched hums.

As my curiosity overcame the fear, right on cue, these somewhat concerning apparitions slowly floated over to my bedside table, as if they were on a silent steady conveyer belt. As they got closer, I could see that they wore hooded robes, similar to the ones that you see the creepy little Jawa creatures wearing in the classic 1970's Star Wars movies. The night light shimmered a few rays of light on their faces. Hidden underneath was a light gray almost non-existent nose, a small slit where lips should have been, and giant almond-shaped eyes that reflected the dim light back towards me.

Most normal people would have yelled and run down the hallway to get away as fast as possible, but these robed strangers enveloped me in peace. I wasn't sure if this was a good or bad sign, but my first impression, from my immature perspective was that they were non-combative observers. They seemed genuinely curious about me. One of the taller creatures reached out a pale four-fingered hand with the palm side up. I remember staring at it with wide-eyed fascination. When I looked up under its hood, to my surprise, this particular entity had bright blue eyes. As our gaze locked, I was unable to move. Without any physical word exchange, I knew it was asking me to give it my hand.

When I broke the spell that it had me under, I sucked my arms tight against my body to protect them from the alien's grasp. The three figures in my room had a hum conversation between them and backed up a few steps. The song sounded like the "Ssssss" of a pissed off diamond-back rattlesnake that we sometimes saw while walking the desert trails in late spring. After a few moments, I was able to understand three distinct words from the chatter in the room.

The whisper in my thoughts hummed, "Sing special song." As they continued their display of soothing sounds, there was a calm voice in the back of my brain.

"It will be okay."

As I relaxed, the words of a song that I was not familiar with started to float through my thoughts. The sweet melody brought me to my favorite place, like I had been magically transported there.

My mom and I sat on a piece of driftwood watching the ocean's blue and green waves rhythmically lap at the wet, brown sand. A brown and white Western sandpiper skipped along the shallows of the steady stream of a white fluff of foam at the edge of the depths of this magical seascape. Oddly enough, as my mother sat next to me she was humming the same song gently under her breath. The sounds of the gentle waves caressed my thoughts. It reminded me that my fears of the unknown needed to be washed over with warm, comforting peace.

As my vision cleared and I returned to my current reality, the black-robed figures were still patiently waiting at the edge of my bed. A three-word message tickled my thoughts.

"Come with us?"

The blue-eyed alien floated closer and offered his hand, once again.

This time I threw off the covers, planted my bare warm feet on the cold tile floor, and delicately placed my fingers into its long gray palm. I could tell that my actions pleased them as their hums increased in volume.

With a flash of light, the outline of a hidden door in my closet suddenly appeared. Once inside, I realized it had been transformed into a bright hallway that had several doors running down both sides. Each door was a different color and had different shaped door handles. In between the doors were colorful and vibrant framed photos that had unrecognizable figures that were in motion. The room was magnificent and full of so much beauty that I forgot that I still firmly grasped an alien's hand.

The entity stopped in front of an orange door. Then its long-fingered hand turned the ox-head shaped knob. In one swift movement the blue-eyed alien quickly pulled me through leaving the other two smaller aliens behind.

3

AN INTERGALACTIC INTERVIEW

THE WORLD WITHIN was full of brilliant colors and magical landscapes. At first glance, it reminded me of my art class where we would create pictures of multi-colored butterflies floating over bright green meadows of flowers. There were orange and green valleys that sloped down to purple sparkling lakes. The alien, of which still had my hand firmly in its hold, allowed me a moment to take it all in.

While standing in the entrance of the orange door, a giant butterfly with a wing span as tall as me floated by. It had huge sparkling blue eyes and tufts of white hair that made it look like it had horns. As it beat its wings over the fields of flowers beside us, my long blonde hair wisped into my eyes. I couldn't help but gasp out loud, "Oh My God."

I could feel my tour guide watching my reaction. It tipped its large bulbous head to one side and without moving its lips I heard it whisper, "Pretty cool, huh?" Then it began to tug me down an orange sandy pathway through the tall grass.

Along the way, there was a sparkling purple stream that cut through the valleys. Patches of odd-looking trees with pom poms on top of their sprawling branches dotted the landscape. The well-traveled path that we followed, snaked through the lush greenery. Every once and awhile there was a pure white marble structure that had an alien-looking figure carved into them. As we rounded the corner of this strange new world, my new friend squeezed my hand. It was as if it wanted to assure me everything would be okay, but nothing could have prepared me for what I was about to see. I shook my hand free from its grasp and slapped it over my mouth to contain my excitement.

"No way. They are real?"

In the knee length grasses, glowing white unicorns were playfully bucking in the distance. The herd of unicorns had flowing manes and tails that dragged on the ground. Several babies were resting in the fields. All I could see were their tails swishing up and down in the gentle breeze. Every once and awhile I could see their cute little heads, with nubs of a horn, pop out of the grass. The stallion of this herd was magnificent in stature as he carefully checked the air for unforeseen dangers. These mystical animals were definitely what I would have expected, if they had actually existed.

I quickly babbled to my guide about my favorite movie. It was called the "Last Unicorn." The creature, of course, already knew this and stood there motionless. As I soaked in the beautiful scenery, its thin slit of a mouth would periodically upturn, as if it was feeling my emotions of wonderment and awe. I remember thinking to myself, "I don't ever want to leave this beautiful place."

As if it heard my unspoken thoughts, my new alien friend pointed over to a small outcrop of smooth basalt-looking rocks that overlooked the glorious horned equines. We sat in silence, until the multiple suns above my head began to fade behind the distant horizon. As the last rays of light diminished, it was as if its hypnotic hold on me was broken.

Suddenly, I realized that I had a group of gray aliens soundlessly observing me. I think they were intently studying my reactions to this new world that I had been introduced. Having seen alien abduction movies in my short lifespan and as their intensity to examine me escalated, I screeched out in panicked verbal words, "What is this? Why am I here? I think I want to go home now."

For several seconds they stared at me with wider than usual pitch-black eyes. I could tell they were concerned by my reaction. My chaperone gently pressed a hand up to the small slit where its lips should have been and gave me a recognizable shake of its head from side to side. It then pointed to its big bald head and said, without moving its lips, "Don't talk. Just think. It will be okay."

After taking a deep breath and using my thoughts, I inquisitively asked, "What is happening? Is this a dream?"

My patient attendant took a deep telepathic breath and slowly blinked its blue eyes as it turned to look at all of the witnesses surrounding me. As I waited for the answers to my questions, the creatures did what I could only describe as a relieved response to my willingness to explore the unbelievable. They all began to hum like a swarm of bees.

When I heard a calming, "Let me explain."

The entire group of observers followed us up a path that led to a big blue door. It had an eagle head knocker. Once inside we passed through rows and rows of books. Eventually we ended up in a room that was filled with an oversized wooden round table. Behind the table, one entire wall was filled with stained-glass windows that were decorated with mythical-looking creatures.

When we all took a seat, one by one, the aliens in the room introduced themselves to me. Their names and the descriptions of the positions that they held were too difficult to actually pronounce, so I was glad we were telepathically communicating. I found out that my alien mentor had a name that I could actually verbalize. His name was Henoch. Henoch explained that he had been tasked to watch certain souls in the universe.

"The soul stays with you. Each minute, every day, month by month, for years, there are a series of tests and trials to determine your place in the future. At the end of each soul's story, they either go to the good place or the bad place." I remember feeling Henoch internally cringe when he said "bad place."

After a slight pause, Henoch looked into my eyes and pointed a long ET-like finger to the ceiling of our extraterrestrial conference room and emphasized, "Our Conductor is from above and He is watching all of us." Then he pointed to all of the souls sitting around the giant circular table.

"We are employed to help Him find 144,000 righteous souls to help us with His call."

He took a deep telepathic pause and said in an ominous tone, "There are bad things in the universe that if given certain parameters can interrupt and possess us; if we let them." When he mentioned "us" he pointed at me and the others at the table, once again.

"We call these bad things the Nero. Your planet calls them the Beast."

By this time, the song, "Comfortably Numb" by Pink Floyd, my sister's favorite song to listen to 24/7, was pounding in my head. Everyone in the room, started to bob their heads as if they were hearing my thoughts. After the last lines of the song trailed off, Henoch finally got to why I was there.

"We are part of the management chain that is looking for certain characteristics within each soul to be part of a special community. We are hoping that you would be willing to be part of this testing phase."

Dumbfounded by all that was happening. I sat there in silence.

When I didn't ask any more questions, they began to sing their special song. As they sang it, they encouraged me to join in. We practiced the song, over and over, and for some reason it reminded me of my mom. When I finally had the words memorized, Henoch nodded his head with approval.

"Remember it, as if your life depends on it."

Then I woke up in my bed. When I peered at the clock on my bedstand, it read 12:32 a.m. No time had passed. And I remember announcing to the room, "Wow, weird dream!" as I promptly fell back to sleep.

In the morning, as I rubbed the sleep from my eyes and stretched my arms high above my head, the song from my dream was heavy in my thoughts. I began to hum the tune under my breath. It made me feel warm and calm as I remembered the beautiful places my new alien friends had shown me in my lucid dream.

However, as the minutes, the days, month by month, and years passed by and Henoch never returned to my dreams, I forgot the song that I was asked to remember. I became comfortably numb to the possibility of different realities outside of what the human race was willing to accept.

4

THE SONG OF SAJAN

A FEW YEARS LATER our family moved out to a six-acre farm along the Yakima River. On the other side of the property there was a deep irrigation canal that started a half a mile up river from my house and ran all the way to the nearest town, which was eight miles away. When the water was drained out of the canal, my older brothers would let me join them. We would always end up covered in mud after we sloshed around in the muck looking for fish and other treasures that may have been trapped in there.

As a kid, I adored the simplicity of the farm. I absolutely loved how the river rhythmically lapped at the grass covered edges. A few feet from the river bank, there was a dry tree trunk that had been captured from an earlier flood. The log was surrounded by a variety of wildflowers that had traveled downstream. When I was feeling thoughtful, the lonely log often called my name. I would prop myself up on the smooth part of the decaying chunk of wood and sit there in silence watching the beauty that surrounded me.

A few months into late spring, I remember one of these log moments very distinctly. That day there were several large red-and-black-winged butterflies nestling on the orange milkweed. There was also a migrating yellow finch that was cheerfully sharing its song. The tall pasture grasses were gently waving in the warm spring breeze. As I sat there in silence, taking in the peaceful setting, there was a familiar whisper that tickled my ear. It hummed, "Remember the song."

In that moment, I had no idea what that whisper meant, but I do remember seeing a big beastly catfish jump out of the water in the distance and how the splash spread out in all directions. As the ripples faded away I heard my dad's red diesel truck roar down our gravel driveway. There was something strapped down in the back. My father was yelling out his open window, "Come see what I got!" while waving for all of us to gather around.

Curious, I lifted off my nice warm log, put the hum out of my mind, and quickly walked over to join the rest of my family.

Moments later, two of my dad's work buddies pulled up behind his dusty farm truck. All three men were taking intermittent puffs off their newly lit cigarettes and joking with each other.

Dad called us in closer and told us that he had decided that we finally had enough money to buy the one thing we all had been asking for. Initially, my mom had a confused look on her face, but then she remembered the previous day's discussion about this important purchase. My two older brothers looked at each other with intense curiosity and excitement. With a toss of their cigarettes, each of the men began to swiftly work on untying the straps that were holding down the tarp-covered surprise.

With overflowing joy plastered across his face, my dad loudly exclaimed, "Ta da!" as he whisked off the tarp. I couldn't read everything on that box, but I did see the picture of two kids splashing in a big round blue swimming pool. My sister, who had decided to move out of my parents' house the year before, rolled her eyes at the lateness of finally getting a family pool. She was clearly frustrated and without saying a word she jumped into her car and zoomed away.

The rest of us worked all afternoon to setup the walls and insert the thick plastic liner. The joy that thrummed through my excited six-year-old brain was hard to contain and even though I had no idea how to swim, I couldn't help but dance in circles with my arms in the air singing, "Best day ever!"

That was about the same time that my mother let me know that it wouldn't be ready for at least a week. They had found out that a pool in our area required a fence surrounding it with a locked gate. Then she reminded me that they were leaving for a long weekend to celebrate their 20th year of marriage. When my parents left, my sister was guilt-tripped into watching me at night after she got off work. However, during the day, I was under the care of my sixteen- and seventeen-year-old brothers.

As the weekend ticked by and the pool sat empty, I was overwhelmed with uncontrollable infatuation. I found myself sitting in the middle of the empty shell dreaming about swimming in it. Eventually, after hours of nonstop whining, I convinced my brothers to just fill it up. That is when we dragged over four hoses from all directions of our property. When they grabbed their poles and trudged off towards their newly found fishing hole, they sternly told me to stay away.

As they fished all day, the water poured out of the hoses and quickly filled up my obsession with crystal clear water. The draw to watch the liquid creep up the sides was unbearable. Quietly and carefully I found myself straddling the pool ladder that was stretched on both sides of the large round structure. The water crawled up the side quickly, with each passing minute. This was when the vaguely familiar whisper returned.

It was a quiet "Ssssss" at first and then over and over the intensity of its command increased. Like a pesky horse fly buzzing around my ears, I tried batting it out of the air. In my attempt to rid myself of this incessant nuisance, I erratically turned from one side to another to see where it was coming from. Just before I tumbled over the side, it screamed.

"Sing special song."

As my unintended dive propelled me towards the bottom of the slick pool, I flailed in the deep depths and searched for an escape. My lungs quickly filled with water and just before I lost consciousness, a small gray four-fingered hand reached out to me. In my panic, I took it.

Instantly, I was back at the hallway that had the multiple-colored doors that I had dreamed about, a few years earlier. It felt familiar and safe as I peered into the alien's big blue eyes. My past memories came flooding back. The little gray opening, where his lips should have been, turned upward as if he was trying to smile. I could feel his joy telepathically wrap around me as he urged me forward.

"We need to get to class. You are going to be late."

When I tried to ask him questions, he waved me off and pulled me towards a blue door. Its knob was shaped like an eagle and Henoch quickly twisted and ushered me in. Within the confines of this space there were rows and rows of books. As we walked along the aisles of various genres, we stopped in front of an open room that resembled a typical classroom for learning.

Henoch caught my gaze and pointed at an empty desk. As he floated out of the room and closed the door, a giant screen in the front of the room unfolded and began to show a story about the different worlds that the Conductor from above had created and watched over. There were twelve according to the movie's narrator, whom suspiciously sounded a lot like the actor Morgan Freeman.

As this documentary played on the screen, halfway through, the mood changed. A white-robed eagle-headed creature appeared. He started to preach doom and gloom. His mannerisms reminded me of my pastor's most recent sermon about the Biblical book of Revelation. Except this alien minister sounded more like a Yoda impersonation from the Star Wars movie, especially when it warned, "In your Bible and ours, the qualities of the chosen can be found. The Beast, opposite is he."

He continued his wisdom, and loudly exclaimed, "This Beast has an evil heart. He will only show kindness when it needs something it does not have. The Lawless one has no innocence and has purposeful deceit. The Nero definitely does not believe in the Conductor above. And most importantly the Beast will not believe in the words of the Peacemaker Song."

I remember cringing in my seat; hoping that I never met this Beast, or this Nero, or whatever it was. He sounded terrifying. After the scary movie ended, another creature that looked a lot like Henoch, floated in through the door.

She was wearing a tight pink suit and white short-heeled boots that were laced up to her knees. She had a thick white belt that held a variety of tools. Around her neck was a neatly tied white scarf that hung down between her very small alien breasts.

Without speaking any words, she grabbed a chalk-sized tool and whipped it open. It became a long pointing stick with a laser-type end. Then she pulled up the words to the song that I had heard several times in my young life. She began to hum it. The song's mesmerizing tones wafted through the air waves.

As she sang it, for some reason, it reminded me of my mom. Hour upon hour, she tapped and explained the hidden meaning behind why it was so important to remember its words. Then when she was finished, we sang her Peacemaker song.

With a wave of her hand, the room transformed into a room that looked like my mom's psychologist's office. It had several bright pink chairs that were circled around a long couch. The windows were shuttered, but the atmosphere of the room was nice. For the next few hours she told me about the benefits and dangers of using my gifts.

At first, when I asked about my gifts, she dodged my questions by telling me more than once, "They will arrive when it is time. Dariann, you must have patience."

The time spent with my teacher felt endless, as she taught me her ways. After what felt like months of daily instruction, she gave me several tests, including questions on the art of hypnosis. The very next day, Henoch showed up at the classroom doorway and floated over to me.

"Dariann, it is time to go."

Instead of leaving through the blue door, he guided me outside the building. There were simple cut-out pathways that stretched out in all directions. Each of them were a different color sand, like a rainbow. Henoch selected the dark blue road and we began to walk quickly down this path. In the distance, I could see a long train-looking ship made of luminescent other-worldly materials.

As we talked about all that I had learned, I finally asked him, "Where am I going now?"

In his own silent way, he shared, "You will see. You have done well. Please don't forget me."

I could tell he was in good spirits as he waved me onto the shimmering train. Then he turned to go up the blue sandy path that we had just traveled. When I pulled myself up onto the train-like compartment, I was surprised to see another human-looking boy sitting there. He was staring straight ahead, clearly in deep thought. He had not noticed me. I took a seat, a few rows down from him, and blurted out.

"Hi! How ya doing?"

He jumped a few inches in his seat and scooted closer to the window of our weird transport. He appeared very anxious, but when he saw me and my concern for his well-being, he quickly calmed down and nervously waved in my direction. It was almost like he wasn't sure I was real.

Luckily, when I shyly smiled at him, he beamed back at me with his mesmerizing green and brown eyes. His skin was light brown and he had wavy dark hair that reached past his ears and ran down his neck. His intense gaze made me feel warm all over and fluttery in my heart. As we stared at each other in awkward silence, trying to figure out why each other was on this train, we found ourselves in a full-blown laugh session. Within moments, we had tears streaming down our faces. Once we got our breath back, I asked if I could scoot over closer, so we could talk. He just nodded and patted the seat next him.

I jumped up, plopped next to him, and said, "Hi, again. I'm Dariann."

"Hi Dariann. Nice to meet you. I'm Sajan."

I remember cocking my head sideways like a confused puppy and thinking to myself, "Did he just say, 'Satan?'"

When he laughed out loud and quickly added, "Not Satan. Sajan, silly. There is a HUGE difference. Look it up."

Relieved for his clarification, but also slightly concerned that he had just read my thoughts, I slumped down in the chair for a long conversation with this stranger. We engaged in quick and out of breath excited banter on the places we had been. Almost immediately, I felt like Sajan and I were going to be friends. For some reason, I could tell he felt the same way. As we discussed the different experiences we had been exposed to during our visit to this magical land, the train floated silently along an invisible track. Sajan told me he had been there several times. He explained why he was so jumpy.

"I just got back from a scary part of Amaranthine. It was the part where Reptiles from Planet #12 settled." When he said Reptiles, he shivered.

My eyes must have grown wide with fear, because he quickly

added, "They are supposedly civilized and good now, but they still terrified me."

As we continued to get to know each other, I realized that he was a few years older than me. I also found out that he had been coming to the planet for specialized training for almost a year. I hit him with a plethora of questions. And even though we had differences in our age, he was thoughtful and patient as he answered them. He seemed genuinely interested in helping me understand the secrets of Amaranthine. As we talked, it felt like time was standing still.

Eventually, I noticed strange new sights come and go and without even asking him Sajan explained.

"The train travels on a figure eight pattern and we call it the Eight Train. It infinitely stops in all twelve sections of the planet." Then he started to hum the Peacemaker song.

After a few verses in, I joined him.

Our voices created a harmonious pattern and the joy within me brightly burst out. When we finished with, "I will sing His special song," we started to giggle out loud. That was when he leaned over and gave me a gentle shoulder bump. An electrical current of warmth shot through me. The hair on my arms stood up. When I looked at his bare shoulder, I realized that he had a sideways infinity tattoo. After a few more shoulder bumps, back and forth, we sat in peaceful but awkward silence as we stared out the window.

Familiar communities began to remerge. On our third pass through, I realized that one particular location was familiar from a long-lost memory. Without thinking, I instinctively reached up for the orange pull cord so that I could get off the train.

The train silently came to a halt and the herd of unicorns looked up in unison as the doors slid open. I began to stand up and move to the aisleway. Sajan didn't follow me, but he did wave back and forth like he was waving away an annoying fly. Then he shyly murmured, "I hope I see you again Dariann."

When I waved back, I thought to myself, "I have this feeling we will."

It was as if he had read my mind, because his smile grew so wide that I could see huge dimples in his cheeks. His warm gaze enveloped me like a fuzzy blanket that had just been pulled out of the dryer. With one last glance into his bright green and brown eyes, I stretched my foot over a shiny glowing step that led towards the baby unicorn that was frolicking in a field a few yards away.

Thinking I was stepping onto lush green and gold pasture, I aggressively moved forward. But instead of hitting grass, the metal steps of a ladder became visible. As I fell with a splash, I was suddenly floating on the bottom of a slick pool with the cool blue water surrounding me.

My hair was floating to and fro with the pressure of the water against my head. There was no sound. No fear. Just a weightless longing of the peace I had just witnessed – for what seemed like years of my life. I swayed with the water's movements, with unfocused open eyes, as my memories of the place that I had just left tickled my thoughts.

With a sudden jolt, a hand jerked me out of my peaceful slumber.

I don't remember my brother grabbing my limp torso or dragging me out of the pool. All I remember is how my mind spiraled through a colorful tunnel of colors that plopped me back into my body. As I became aware of the reality that surrounded me, I was that six-year-old awkward farm girl, once again. Only a few moments on Earth had passed by.

As I recovered from my drowning, I discovered that I had a distinct scratch and bruise on my shoulder. It was shaped like a sideways eight. When I traced the injury I felt comfort and safety. It reminded me of the experience that I had on the train with a boy named Sajan who sang a familiar song.

A few days later, I remember looking up the word Sajan to see what it actually meant. Just like the boy in my dreams had said, it was distinctly different than the meaning of Satan. The Indian meaning was "loved one." The Hindu meaning was "good man." Sajan seemed like all of these.

My parents grilled me and my brothers when they got home. I tried to tell them about my dream, but they just patted me on the head and blamed my hallucinations on my drowning. When I showed them the scar on my shoulder and explained that it was an infinity tattoo, they just blamed it on the fall. My brothers were grounded and the pool was drained. When I told my mom about the song, she didn't remember it.

As the months and then years of my life ticked by, learning to live on Earth overshadowed my dreams. The training, the song, the mysterious boy, and the significance of the infinity tattoo slowly faded away too. Eventually all that was left was a locked away memory in my unconscious thoughts.

5

WE ARE NOT ALONE

THE NEXT SUMMER our family packed up the big blue van and drove over to the Oregon coast to see Aunt Bee and Uncle Gee. This was an annual family fishing trip that all of us looked forward to. However, one of my favorite activities while there was collecting the giant yellow banana slugs that resided in their backyard. The slugs looked like little aliens with retractable antennae.

To top off that fun activity, my cousin Fanny, who was a few years older than me, was the coolest cousin ever and every time we visited I treasured every moment that I could get, to hang out with her. During this particular visit, Fanny was excited to tell me about what she had heard, one late evening, while hiding behind their kitchen island. She explained that her dad was visited by some men in dark suits. They wanted to talk about something that they called, "The Incident in Nam." I was a bit confused on what that meant, but she quickly reminded me that her dad was a Merchant Marine in the Vietnam War.

She dragged me to her room and we snuggled up on her bed. After a few moments of consideration on what she was willing to share with me, she took a deep breath, and stared into my eyes.

"My dad was slowly cruising up a narrow, but deep canal of murky water to deliver supplies to another ship. While cautiously creeping along, he and his crew were surrounded by an orange pulsating glow above their heads. As they looked up in awe and shock, the vibrating orb floated there for five seconds, and then zoomed off at incredible speeds. It was nowhere to be found."

I remember gasping out loud and I could tell by the inflection in her voice that her story was going to be frightening. Fanny paused, gave me a sideways glance and asked, "You okay?"

I remember erratically nodding my head up and down. Which encouraged her to continue her story.

"At the same time, a few hundred feet ahead of them, my dad said he spotted an enemy warship that was hiding out in the long reeds. A green orb suddenly positioned itself over the hidden ship and began to strobe at it with a rainbow of colors. When the enemy started to fire all of its guns at it, the orb fired back with a single beam of bright green light. POOF! The ship was destroyed in seconds. Shards of the once intact threat exploded in all directions as the smoke, fire, and shrapnel flew up hundreds of feet into the atmosphere. My dad's vessel and crew fell in the water."

When my cousin said, "POOF!" and threw her arms in the air, I jumped and my heart raced. I looked up at her to see if she was going to pinch me and tell me she was just joking, but she looked very serious and continued her story.

"I could tell when my dad paused and looked at the three men sitting around our kitchen table that he didn't really want to believe what he saw that one dark night in Vietnam. But, he continued his story, and told these guys, 'When I fell into the water a bubble surrounded me. I was able to breathe, but I could not move. I could see flames and burning embers through the murky water above my head. When the chaos subsided, the unidentified flying object passed over my head and the bubble that encased me popped. When I finally broke the water's surface, there were different colored orbs monitoring the wreckage.'"

When I sucked in my breath, Fanny gave me another concerned look.

"That was when the agents looked at each other and then asked my dad if he remembered what color the lights were. He told them, 'Just before they converged and shot off into space, he saw at least six different colors. Blue, orange, teal, purple, red, and white.'"

I just sat there in shock. It felt like I knew this story somehow.

That was when I asked her, "Did he see them again? Did he report it?"

Fanny let out a big sigh and explained, "No, he never saw them again. But all of his men had the same experience. When they got back from the war, they were told not to talk about it. Ever."

I remember how she nonchalantly shrugged her shoulders. I think she was trying to lessen the scariness of the conversation that she had just shared with me, because I remember her saying, "My dad didn't want to talk about it because people would think he was crazy. But, then again, who wouldn't be a little bit crazy after being in such a terrifying war."

At that moment, Aunt Bee called our names to have her famous homemade three-cheese and macaroni casserole. She always put a delicious, perfectly cooked bread crumb and butter mixture on top. As we skipped to the kitchen with great anticipation, I remember thinking to myself, why was it so important to hear his story now and why were they so interested in the color of the orbs flying around?

But I didn't have the time to ask Fanny about that, because I was too busy stuffing Aunt Bee's delicious casserole in as fast as I could.

6

THE COFFENBURY DIMENSION

LATER THAT AFTERNOON, we packed up the car and went to a place called Fort Stevens National Park. It was a few miles past Astoria, Oregon on the Pacific Ocean. We visited a magical place called Coffenbury Lake. The lake had a sprinkling of rustic picnic tables surrounded by tall Ponderosa Pine trees. You could walk around the lake and explore several areas along its banks, but the best part was a tall sand dune that the kids would climb up and then run down as fast as they could. Everyone that tried to conquer the dune usually did a fancy jump into the lake when they reached the bottom.

My cousin and my brothers spent hours running and jumping throughout that day. I was afraid of the water and sat at the picnic table watching them play. Eventually, my cousin plopped down beside me and asked in a silly voice, "The water is warm. The sand is divine. Why not try it just one time?"

I peered up through sweaty brows and confessed, "Kind of scared of the deep water."

She insisted, "I will go first. I will be in the water when you jump. I will catch you." Then she grabbed my hand.

Feeling the pressure of pleasing her, I clasped onto her hand tightly and begged, "Promise?"

She grinned as we climbed the big sandy dune.

As I waited for my turn, the warm grains of the slope pushed between my toes. I buried them deep below the surface. I remember nervously wishing I could bury my entire body in the sand, so that I wouldn't have to face the scary depths of the unknown. Fanny encouraged me along and when it was my turn she gently pushed me forward.

Without even thinking, I spun out on the soft substrate and yelled the entire time as I clumsily wobbled back and forth down the slippery slope towards the doom below. When I reached the bottom the other kids were clapping and cheering as I raced by and flung myself towards the lake. Just before I hit the water's surface, I remembered that I left Fanny at the top of the hill.

Pure panic set in as I entered the murky water. The cool water enveloped me from all sides as the quietness of the lake dragged me down towards the bottom. Just like my uncle's story a bubble of air encircled me. I was projected towards a spiral of water that looked a lot like a fast-moving whirlpool. The waves of this wormhole moved me forward towards a shining bright light. After what felt like minutes, I abruptly stopped several feet from a rocky platform. The bubble surrounding me did a loud pop, that echoed throughout the chamber.

There were creatures on both sides of me that resembled the ads that I got with my sea monkey experiments as a kid. They were pink with three long antennae's coming out of their heads. It looked like they had crowns. Their faces were human-like, but their bodies were scaley and they had a row of fins across their backs. Paralyzed from fear, they each grabbed one of my arms and lifted me up onto the platform. I choked and gasped as I cleared the water that had breached my airways. When I shook the excess water out of my hair like a wet dog, I looked around the room with a mixture of panic and awe.

The pink sea monkeys stood there on flippered appendages staring at me like I was the alien. Then they slowly slipped back into the slick-looking surface of the water surrounding me. Their long fin like appendages were hanging onto the edge silently waiting to see what was going to happen. One of them had a three-pronged teal-colored staff that had the number "6" hanging down the side of it.

Along the other edge of the platform was a human looking female figure sticking out of the water. She had bright gold wrapped up her arms and down her fingers. It looked like the pattern of the jewelry was displaying the number "3" in the design.

She had several gold and diamond necklaces layered down her neck. Her torso was covered with a snug black leather-looking material that reminded me of a warrior. Her long gray hair was braided neatly down her back. The bottom of the braid floated in the water behind her. When she pushed past the water's edge, I could see that she had a shimmering green and gold scaled fish tail.

Up on the platform, there were four figures on rock shaped thrones made of some kind of crystal or polished quartz. Each of the thrones had a distinct sideways eight etched into the back rest. I instinctively reached across my body and traced my own figure eight tattoo.

One of the creatures had the features of a lion. It had a long, shaggy brownish-red mane that trailed down its back. It's eyes were light brown, with a dark center that looked into my soul. He held a red-handled six-foot tall staff. Near the top of the staff it looked like there was an "8" etched in the stained teak wood. A long delicate chain hung below the red handle that read, "Amartv." He spoke no words, but I knew he had many questions based on his body language and the intensity of his glare.

One of the other beings looked like an ox. She had a long snout with a large, wet black nose. Her cheekbones were well-defined and were set below two bright shining eyes that looked like diamonds. Each arm was covered in shaggy black hair that ended with an ox-type hoof. She had large black wings stretched out behind her. Around her neck were two orange braided necklaces with dangling charms. One of them said, "I Am #7." The other, which was hanging between the crack of her large hairy breasts read, "Faith."

The third being had the coloring of a bald eagle, except its large beak was pale green. Instead of fingers, the creature had brown-feathered limbs with long sharp talons. He was holding a thick, old-fashioned leather book that had a golden clasp holding it sealed. He was impatiently tapping the top of the brown book with four of his pointy nails. As he alternated their touch across the soft binding, I noticed that he had four thick blue tattoo-like words on each claw that read, "Proud to Be #2." He had a thick silver necklace that said, "Gyaan." His small black beady eyes focused on the fourth being in the room.

She was actually human-looking. She had pure white skin and bigger than usual dark blue almond-shaped eyes. Her bleached white hair flowed up and out onto the floor. She had a large gold cross with the number "10" etched on it. She had several of her kind, surrounding her.

Their white frocks were neatly braided behind them. They each had bows and a leather quiver of arrows strapped to their backs. All of them wore some kind of snug shiny gold suit that looked almost like skin. My mind kept racing back to "The Lord of the Rings" movie and how these figures reminded me of the wood elves. I was half expecting the character Legolas, played by Orlando Bloom, to come around the corner. With that thought in my head, the wood-elf creatures all started to laugh, like they had read my mind.

As they continued to laugh from my unspoken joke, the lion figure slammed his wooden six-foot staff on the rock, like a gavel in a judge's courtroom. As this loud boom echoed throughout the chamber they all started to chant, in unison.

"Worthy are You, our Lord and Conductor, to receive glory and honor and power, for You created all things: by Your will they exist and came to be."

When they finished, I backed up a few steps and almost fell off the rock platform.

The pure white woman nodded at me.

"Come."

The weird part was she never moved her lips. I heard her request in my thoughts. She directed me to sit on a blanket that was directly below the four throned figures. I quickly sat down and gave her my full attention.

"I'm Intelligence, the leader of the Sisterall race. We have traveled far to connect with you. We have entered a new stage of the interview process. We have heard good things about you."

I was surprised by her praise, but not knowing what to say, I quieted my thoughts and prepared to listen. She explained that I would probably forget most of what she was about to say, but that she wanted to plant the seed for when they come back some day. She took a quiet mental breath and waited to see if I had questions. As I considered her words, I realized that she was careful how she explained her kind and purposely excluded "people" as a descriptor. I looked into her giant blue eyes and waited for her to continue.

She nodded her head affirmatively to signal that my choice to remain silent was the correct choice. Then she gazed from one side of the room to the other as if she was looking for approval to proceed with the discussion. When her long blond hair wisped across her eyes, she reached a noticeably longer than usual limb with four fingers up towards her pale white face to tame the loose hairs back into place. Her appearance suddenly reminded me of a long-forgotten experience that I had when I drowned in the pool in my backyard. With wide eyes at this impossible coincidence, I sucked in my breath, and waited for her to continue.

"We think there might be a big storm coming to Earth."

As she waved her long white finger across the room, she explained, "We sit on the Interstellar Contact Council and the Conductor has told us that He has decided it is time to intercede with the human species. We have been watching Earth for hundreds of years, and it is time to unseal the truth and begin the interview process for the 11th Planet's Peacemakers."

As my mind grasped for some sense of what was happening, many questions surfaced that I was not sure how to ask. The eagle figure, which stood to the right of Intelligence, suddenly spoke up, as if it had read my mind.

"We have no desire to harm you, we just wanted to give you a heads up that we will keep in touch with you as you grow up. We will show you what a Peacemaker does. You will, of course have a choice to join us or not. When the time comes." He pointed to, and then continued tapping, the leather book that he held in his feathery arms.

"We can't tell you all of the details of our future meetings, because it is not the right time for you to know. But we will be nearby watching you. There will be signs of our coming."

The Ox woman playfully snorted, "Have faith."

As my mind whirled out of my world, they all began to calmly call out the words of my forgotten song.

"I was chosen to meet Your call. I train so that I can stand tall. I answer, because of Your love. Worthy are You, our Conductor above. I trust without sight. Reaching for the light. Even if pursuit of right is a fight. His final gifts outweigh this plight. I strive to do no wrong. I will sing His Special song."

As they finished the words a slight tingle of recollection, that I had heard this before, floated through my mind. I had a picture of a young boy on a train cross through my thoughts and then it was gone.

I looked at the eagle creature named Gyaan and thought to myself, "What kind of signs?"

As if he heard my question, he shook his white feathery head from side to side and I thought I heard, "You will know when it is time." And then he looked at Intelligence as if he had asked her a question that I could not hear or understand.

Intelligence nodded at him and turned to me with great urgency. Her hidden wings fluffed out behind her and I gasped in surprise.

"There will be twelve on the Interstellar Contact Council. There are twelve points of entry. The key is in the doors. Dariann, you must remember the song."

A weird warmth enveloped me as my confused brain started to remember a past dream that described a potential path for my life. As I rubbed the fading tattoo on my shoulder, a small gray alien with big blue eyes floated into my sight. The creatures on the thrones started to move around and look at each other as if something big was about to happen.

That is when I felt a violent tug at the back of my shorts. Fanny was aggressively pulling me out of the depths of the lake. As I reached the surface I gasped like a guppy that had jumped out of its bowl. She pulled me up and out to the side of the sandy shore and asked if I was okay. Embarrassed and confused, I gave her a classic thumb up and groaned. For the rest of that day I sat on a towel, with my knees hugged up close, contemplating what I had just witnessed. As the seconds passed by, I began rationalizing what I had seen and heard. Then I convinced myself, "It was all just a dream."

Back at Fanny's house, we ended up sitting quietly in her dark living room watching our favorite science fiction show, "Star Trek," of course. Following a brave moment by the captain of the ship and after several awkward tries, I finally mustered the courage to ask, "Hey Fanny, do you have a second to talk?"

She looked down at me, back at the TV, and then got up and turned the control knob to off. She grabbed and squeezed a nearby throw pillow to her chest and asked, "What's up kiddo?"

After taking a deep breath, I stammered, "Is Coffenbury Lake haunted?"

With wide-eyed amusement she coughed.

"What? Why would you say that?"

I described what happened at the lake and I could tell by the look of disbelief and worry on her face that whatever I was saying did not make sense to her. She shrugged it off and told me that I must have been drowning or something. Then she exclaimed, "Thank God I was there to save you," just as she got up and turned the TV back on. She ignored me the rest of the night.

The next day we went back home. I wrote down the dream in my new purple spiral bound notebook. I even wrote down the words to the song that they chanted under Coffenbury Lake.

Then I vowed to never talk about the experience again.

7

BLUE BALLS OF LIGHT

A FEW MONTHS LATER my cousin came to visit us at our home in the Pacific Northwest desert. The climate there was completely different than the Oregon coast. We didn't have anything cool like yellow banana slugs or sandy beaches to run our toes through. For some reason my cousin avoided me the first few days of their visit. It was like she was scared to be alone with me.

Being younger, I constantly bugged her though and eventually she did pull me into my bedroom to talk. When she closed the door she whispered, "Something happened after your visit. I think you should know."

Then she proceeded to share how she and her dad, who was a park ranger for the Fort Stevens National Park, saw something weird. In a quiet voice she shared that her father had decided to take her along while he was doing his regular late-night rounds of the park. Part of that routine was driving around Coffenbury Lake before cruising along the coastal areas to check for anything or anyone that shouldn't be there.

"Just as we were turning to leave the park entrance we saw bright blue lights above us. He thought they came from the lake and said a couple of cuss words. He thought it was fireworks, at first. Next thing we knew the orbs were traveling out of the park towards the Pacific Ocean. They were moving really fast. We chased them to the beach."

I could tell she was freaking out, because her breathing had increased and she was pacing back and forth in my room.

"When we couldn't go any further, without driving into the ocean, he stopped the truck. He got out to investigate the lights. I could tell my dad was trying to rationalize what he was seeing, because he started mumbling that maybe they were helicopters. However, when he cussed again, after they started to move south and then north, super-fast and without any noise, I could tell he was struggling to explain them."

Before I could ask a question, she continued to spout.

"Then, just like that the blue lights suddenly blinked off and back on. And from out of nowhere the hovering orbs of light were joined by several white, teal, purple, and black spheres. They twinkled for almost five minutes. Then all of the lights plunged into the water. Several helicopters showed up. When this happened, my dad briskly shepherded me to the truck and we quickly sped home. As soon as we got home, he called a few friends in the military to report the lights."

Thinking the story was over, I actually raised my hand, but she waved me off with a violent shake of her head.

"Then it got really weird. Later that night, two guys showed up at our door. I, of course, snuck out and listened to everything they said." She gave me a quick wink.

"They interviewed him on what he saw for over two hours, then they told him to not talk about it and asked who else saw it. My dad was super careful not to mention that I was with him. I could tell he didn't want to drag me into the report that he knew they would be preparing. Two days later, two more men dressed in dark suits showed up at our door. They required me and my mom to leave the house while they interrogated my father. I never heard any details of that discussion, but after their visit, he never spoke about it, even when asked point blank."

My mouth must have still been open because she reached over and popped it closed. She assured me she didn't tell her dad about my experience and then proceeded to give me her advice.

"I believe that you saw something, by the way, I am sorry I doubted you! Sounds like you better listen to Intelligence."

Completely lost on what she was talking about, I looked up at her with questioning eyes.

"Dariann, I have no idea what those blue balls of light meant, but it had to be a sign of something to come, right?"

As I sat there in numbed silence and Fanny stared deep into my eyes, the whisper of the eagle and the white winged angel, that I saw under Coffenbury Lake, tickled my thoughts.

"There will be signs of our coming. You must remember the song."

8

OMAH

───❧❧❧───

AFTER MY COUSIN'S visit, I decided to pull out my purple notebook and look over my past scribblings. Although the words on paper were mine, the person that wrote them sounded like an alien and over time, the excitement of Fanny's experience and Coffenbury Lake was overtaken by everyday life.

I was constantly distracted with more important things in my life. My mom got really sick and pre-teen life consumed me, as the pressure to fit in was overwhelming.

The next summer my parents decided to forego our usual trip to go see Aunt Bee and Uncle Gee. Instead, as fate would have it, they decided we would start a new adventure at a camp site in the Deschutes National Forest that was nestled around a lake in the middle of Oregon. This change in vacation plans cemented my ability to remember my strange experience inside Coffenbury Lake. And not having Fanny there to remind me, helped tamper down the triggers I had used to remember the song.

There were multiple campgrounds that wrapped around the large lake. It was densely populated with old growth pine trees. Several clutches of yellow cedar trees and tall maples with colorful leaves, dotted the landscape. At the north end of the lake, there was a lodge that had a small restaurant and a gift shop that offered a plethora of candy. An uneven, but well-traveled, 3.2-mile dirt path wrapped all around the entire lake. When I was released, after setting up our campsite, I immediately walked the trail.

When I got back from my forest trail adventure, I found out that each evening there was a big roaring bon fire and a discussion about the surrounding area. My mom wasn't feeling well that night, but my dad promised to take me after I asked if I could still go.

Later that evening, Dad and I took our spot around the hot, crackling fire that the camp host had prepared in the park's community event area. Our tall, slender leader for that night took a deep breath and a dramatic pause and asked the crowd, "Who here believes that we are not alone?"

The guests looked around to see who was going to raise their hand. I was surprised to see my father wave his wildly in the air. He gave me one of his silly parental grins and then shoulder-bumped me so hard that I slipped off the hard wooden bench. When he pulled me up off the forest floor, his playful laughter echoed across the lake.

The host pointed at my dad.

"Well folks, these woods are heavy with bigfoot sightings and many people in this world believe that these hairy, tall creatures with big feet are actually a disguise for little green men."

As everyone burst out into laughter, he caveated that with, "Well actually little gray men."

He explained how the locals believed that the big footed hairy monster in the woods is actually a peaceful creature and only shows up when there are people that he needs to give an important message to.

"They actually have a name for him, they call him Omah. The first sighting recorded of a sasquatch in this area was actually behind a cluster of yellow cedar trees – so the name stuck."

He paused just before he did a silly dance move that indicated that he thought he had made a clever joke. However, his statement made the hair on my arms raise up to full length. I immediately tucked myself up against my father. He reached over and hugged me close to his side, as the camp host continued with a speculative tone.

"The few people that claim they see or hear these creatures believe they have been chosen for some kind of special purpose."

At that exact moment, there was a distant howl in the woods and everyone looked around. I shivered and whimpered as I tried to suppress a desire to let out a deep gut-wrenching scream. My dad squeezed me tighter and looked down with one of his big brown eyes and whispered, "You okay?"

I lied and gave him a wide-eyed nod. Then I unconsciously crossed my arms and brushed the tattoo on my shoulder with my fingertips.

The camp host jested, "No worries folks, I am pretty sure that was not Omah."

Then he quickly moved on to talking about the actual visible wildlife, like northern flying squirrels, the majestic bald eagle, and the elusive white-tailed deer that roam in the area. He also caveated that the howl we heard was probably a gray wolf. Then he went on a rant about how beavers were Oregon's state animal. Which led into a long discussion on the history of the lakes that were located in the Deschutes Forest and what kind of fish they were stocked with. My dad immediately perked up. He was an avid fisherman.

However, all I could think of was Omah and I searched the woods for any sign of his existence. When I shivered again, my father whispered, "Don't worry, they come in peace." Then he refocused back on the fish discussion that the host was babbling on about.

After a few minutes had passed, my dad began to quietly whistle. I don't think he knew what he was whistling, but as soon as he started, I was startled to know that I remembered the words to a forgotten song buried deep within my mind. It was the notes to the song written in my purple notebook.

The hum of his whistle floated through the air and across the crackle and pop of the fire. I sat there mesmerized as the words of the song flowed through my mind. I began to sing it under my breath.

Just as I finished saying, "I will sing His Special song," like a shock from an electric fence, I remembered a dream from the past where there was a bright hallway with many doors. One of these doors was dark brown. It had a bow and arrow etched above its ape-looking door handle.

When it opened the landscape looked very much like the park we were camping in, except there was something behind a clutch of yellow cedar trees. A hairy tall creature was staring back at me. In that dream, I was terrified. I closed my eyes and held onto this memory. I should have run away from this unknown danger. But I didn't. When I finally opened my eyes I was sitting around our campfire, all alone. The whistle was no more. My dad was no longer present.

Like a frozen frightened rabbit, I sat there staring at the fire. The crickets started to chirp and the melody from the lake frogs became a rhythmic song. At first it was very peaceful and safe, until I heard the shuffle of big feet coming my way. Not wanting to look, out of fear for what I would see, I continued to stare at the orange and yellow coals that crackled in the dying fire.

With one last shuffle and a grunt, directly across from the waning fire, a pair of shaggy legs appeared in my line of sight. My eyes slowly traveled from the long-haired legs up to the big brown eyes of a patiently waiting bigfoot. He had a quiver of arrows tucked up over his shoulder. He reminded me of Chewy from the movie "Star Wars." The furry creature just stared back at me for a few seconds and then without moving his lips, quietly said, "Hey, I'm Omah. I'm number five."

Oddly enough, I felt calm as I convinced myself that it was, "Just a dream after all."

When my overly stimulated brain didn't respond, he added, "I need to give you a message from above." Then he pointed up to the night sky, which was full of millions of twinkling stars.

Shocked, I whispered, "Are you an angel of God?"

He growled out loud. Took a dramatic pause, and then like he had listened to the camp hosts talk that night; without moving his lips, he sarcastically joked, "No, I'm just a messenger."

The focus on his giant brown eyes intensified as I tried to comprehend what was happening. He stared back into mine. After a few seconds, he slowly pushed a message into my brain, "Have you seen unexplainable beings and places in your dreams that test your sense of reality?"

He emphasized "dreams" like he was playing along with some kind of punchline to a joke that only he understood.

I sucked in my breath and blurted out, "Ummmm. Let's say yes."

He tapped his head with his huge fuzzy hand and requested, "Use thoughts. Not words."

When I considered the words that I had written in my purple notebook, I hesitantly thought to myself, "So like Henoch and the aliens I met on that weird planet he took me to?"

The beast in front of me grimaced, I think it was a sasquatch smile. He telepathically mumbled, "That's good. You saw them and understood them?"

Still speechless, I just nodded, "I think so. Maybe. I don't know."

Clearly amused, he silently communicated, "I am pretty sure you have heard this story before, but I will start from the beginning, just in case."

Relieved that the mind games were over, I straightened up and focused on this ape-like creatures thought transfer.

"There are others that are not from Earth. There is a council being pulled together that will be comprised of all twelve of the Conductor's creations. We call it the Interstellar Contact Council or the ICC. This ICC will determine who will help lead their tribes to the new world, if that time becomes necessary. All of the 144,000 individuals have been selected, except for the human race. The ICC has found 12,000 humans, as possible candidates, for the intergalactic program. We call these selected few Peacemakers."

Omah paused for a few moments, stared at the fire, and then continued his message.

"To be a candidate, the individual must be approved by an ICC member, have a good heart, are kind to all, are innocent and without deception, believe in the Conductor, and most of all must sing a song that no one else can sing. We believe that there is good and bad in all of His twelve creations. However, by doing the right thing, our candidates will find themselves on a path to immortality. They will find life in infinity."

When he paused I tilted my head slightly sideways and quickly asked, "So is the Conductor the same as God?"

I could tell that Omah was thoughtfully considering my inquiry and after a few moments he asked a question to answer my question.

"Are you familiar with what you call the Bible?"

After I nodded, he added, "Some of the first scriptures in your Bible provide this Truth. One of my favorite human Bible verses says, 'In the beginning, God created the heavens and the earth.'"

Omah pointed to the stars and gently said, "Heavens," then he pointed to the ground and said, "Earth. We call Earth the 11th planet in my world." When I didn't respond he continued his lesson.

"Another Truth to support your question is found later in your Bible which actually says something like this, 'All things were made through God and without God nothing was made.'" Then the furry monster in front of me, gave me a wink.

With wide eyes I found myself staring at him with disbelief, as he peered into my soul, around the crackling fire. When the situation was feeling slightly awkward, he explained, "If you didn't figure it out yet, you are being assessed for a Peacemaker role." Then he lifted off the log. Just before he lumbered away, he whispered a warning my way.

"Remember the song, Dariann. Your immortality depends on it."

I remember raising my hand, like I was in school needing to ask a clarifying question about the problem to be solved, but he continued to quietly shuffle away, until he slowly dissipated into the darkness and shadows of the trees.

My attention was drawn back to the red and yellow embers of the fire that was still in front me. As I sat there in mesmerized shock, there was a whisper from across the quiet tree line, from somewhere far, far away that said, "Don't be afraid." And as I closed my eyes super tight and joked, "I don't believe in fairies."

My dad was suddenly there, with me, and he explained, "They come in peace." It was as if he was there all along and was finishing up a story that had an important lesson to teach.

When we were back at the campsite, all tucked into our sleeping bags, I was restless. Omah's words rang through my head. His voice kept saying over and over again.

"You are being assessed. Remember the song."

So instead of questioning it, I hummed his song, and immediately fell into a deep sleep.

9

PRACTICE MAKES PERFECT

F OLLOWING MY BIZARRE camping trip I immediately wrote down some of the things that I had learned from Omah in my purple notebook.

However, as the weeks ticked by, every-day human life distracted me from the terrifying concept that I was possibly being observed for some kind of assignment that was out of this world.

My sister surprised my parents with a shotgun wedding as soon as we got back from Suttle Lake. Three weeks later she moved to Texas to start a life with her new husband. Two weeks after that, both of my brothers moved across the country to attend college. Then the day before my eighth birthday, a few hours after I sang her the Peacemaker song, thinking it would save her; my mom peacefully passed away in her bed from stage four cancer. When the social grieving process ended and everyone stopped coming by, our usual loud and obnoxious home life had suddenly become just me and my dad against the world.

That year our neighbor sold their house and another family with two kids moved in. One of the kids was named Madison and she was just a few months older than I was. She was awkward and sort of weird, just like me. Maddy was way more outgoing than me though, and she always pushed me to do things I normally wouldn't do. We became best friends right away.

Maddy and I spent most of our waking moments together. We rode our horses pretty much every afternoon. We both had pet chickens. We both loved to fish with our father's. But most of all, we both loved music. We even wrote lyrics for the annual Christmas talent contest, that my school hosted that year. The show included all of the schools across the Tri-Cities.

Maddy and I spent hours pulling together rhyming words and the chorus for our duet. We practiced it for days. When the big event came, I was absolutely terrified. But Maddy was so brave as she grabbed my hand and pulled me up on the stage. As they were announcing us to the crowd, she whispered just before we started our song, "This is our song Dariann. This song represents our trust and friendship with one another, forever."

Out of tune and as loud as we could, we sang:

"The day before Christmas Eve when Santa's working hard, the children write out lists to give to Santa Claus. The night is coming close, the children will rejoice, when you're asleep in bed, you'll dream of all the joys. For now it's Christmas day and you'll awake to see pretty presents wrapped in bows, and tied so naturally. We wish you a merry Christmas, we wish you a merry Christmas we wish you a merry Christmas and a happy new year."

When we finished my dad was on his feet obnoxiously clapping and yelling. My visiting brothers and sister were slumping in their seats, like they were incredibly embarrassed to be alive. We didn't win the big prize, but the best part of that night was when my new friend had said the words, "This is our song Dariann. This song represents our trust and friendship with one another, forever." And even though Maddy was definitely my best friend. I never got the courage to tell her about my weird dreams.

One evening, at one of our frequent sleepovers, Maddy and I had just finished watching the 1984 movie "Splash." The character named Allen, played by Tom Hanks, meets actress Daryl Hannah, who just happens to be a mermaid named Madison. The storyline triggered my memories about past experiences that both entailed a splash into some water and a few lucid dreams. After several quiet moments following the music and credits of our movie, Maddy quietly asked, "You okay?"

For some reason I instinctively reached up and rubbed my shoulder, where the infinity tattoo had been placed when I fell into the pool so long ago. I had learned the hard way that talking about my out of this world experiences were usually not well-received. I was very nervous to mention the several strange past encounters with creatures that are believed to not exist, just like Allen's mermaid love interest.

With her big blue eyes, she urged me to spit it out. After several seconds of silence, Maddy got up, turned off the TV and settled back into the cozy blanket she had wrapped around herself. I could tell she was not going to take silence for an answer.

I blurted out, "How would you feel if I told you I met an alien or two?"

Her mouth popped open in surprise. She began to nod up and down without making any noise. Her blond hair fell over her face several times as she dramatically, but nonverbally asked for me to continue. With her engaged enthusiasm, I was suddenly compelled to tell her everything.

With one deep breath, in and out, I whispered, "When I was six years old, I drowned in a pool and was transported to an alien world where I learned special skills. They trained me how to use my mind to talk to other beings that are not from Earth. And then I met this boy on a train, while I was there. He reminds me of Allen and Madison's relationship in the movie we just watched. Except I don't think Sajan is a mermaid."

She burst out laughing, like I was making stuff up. But that didn't stop me.

"Sajan was so smart and he helped teach me about the planet. I felt connected to him immediately. I really miss him." Then out of nowhere my cheeks spontaneously felt hot.

Until that moment, I did not realize how much I enjoyed sharing time with the boy on the train. As Maddy tried to comprehend what I was telling her, I immediately distracted my blushing cheeks by telling her more.

"I even saw mermaids and unicorns. I was told one of the worlds has flying horses."

I was surprised at how calmly she listened to my ramblings about otherworldly beings. She never uttered a word. Although, every once and a while her eyelids would flutter erratically. It was like she was so mesmerized by my voice that she had forgotten how to blink. As I listened to myself talk, it felt like I was standing outside my body looking in. But that didn't stop me from blurting out, "Later, I even learned how to hypnotize people."

Maddy snapped out of her trance and gave me a quizzical look.

"Why would you do that?"

I quickly explained.

"Seeing an alien for the first-time freaks people out. Hypnosis helps calm them down. But don't worry, I haven't hypnotized anyone, yet. I doubt I can really do it."

When I was finally done telling my interstellar tale, she jumped up and down and practically yelled, "Totally believe you. Maybe you should try to hypnotize me? Practice makes perfect, I hear." Then she giggled so loud that she snorted.

Without a second thought I agreed.

"If you are up for it, I would like to try."

She shook her head with incredible enthusiasm as I racked my brain to remember the process that I was taught by my out-of-this-world teacher. We collected our blankets and pillows from the living room floor and moved to my bedroom. After shutting my door, I patted the mattress for Maddy to come lie down. She skipped over to the side of the bed, threw her arms in the air and flopped over backwards.

"Let's do this."

I dimmed the lights, closed the dusty vinyl blinds, and flipped on the fan above my bed. After taking a few moments to flip through my purple notebook, I realized I had left the instructions inconveniently in my memories. Pushing that aside, I pulled up my squishy bean bag to the side of the bed and focused on her instead.

"Are you Comfy?"

Maddy gave me a big grin that reached both sides of her face and confidently declared, "Yep!"

Not exactly knowing what I was doing I started to hum, incoherently, under my breath. After a few seconds of humming, I quietly whispered to myself, "I can do this."

"Let the nervous energy in your fingers and toes flow out of your belly button. Let it float out into the atmosphere."

Maddy sputtered with laughter and opened her eyes. When I nonverbally closed my eyes dramatically, she did the same. Using a low, even tone I crooned, "You will start feeling very relaxed. The softness of the mattress will gently pull you into a deep sleep."

When her eyes popped open, once again, I pointed to the fan above our heads. She moved her chin up off her chest and looked up.

"Listen to the hum. It sings a song of peace and tranquility."

Within moments and to my surprise, Maddy fell into a deep trance. Her blue unblinking eyes were completely focused on watching the whir of the fan blades.

"Hey Maddy, you good?"

She didn't respond and my self-confidence in what I was doing quickly diminished in the darkness. At that exact moment, a blinding white light burst through the gaps of my closet door. Then the bi-fold doors opened and closed in a slow and creepy way. Feeling completely freaked out, I pleaded, "Maddy, wake up. Wake up now!"

But she didn't. Instead, she just stared at the fan's rhythmic rotations. She had drool dribbling from one side of her mouth. As I pondered what to do next, a voice from my past entered my thoughts.

"This is not the way, Dariann."

As I turned towards the closet, Henoch glided over to the side of the bed, tapped his long thin finger against my infinity tattoo, and without words he projected his disappointment.

"You better fix this. This will not look good on your scores."

I jumped back, like he had hit me with the shock of a defibrillator.

In my panic, I tried to remember the checklist that my well-dressed alien teacher warned me about. Henoch stared at me with intensity. As if a light bulb in my brain turned on, I quickly realized that I had not sung the Peacemaker song or provided the key words to wake her out of her hypnotic state.

As the uncontrolled fear boiled up and out of me, Maddy became agitated and popped up off the bed. Like a classic horror movie where the demon possessed character slowly rotates their head in ways that are not physically possible, her gaze flitted our way. I could tell she had spotted Henoch, who had perched himself up on the side of the bed.

Before I could intervene and explain the situation, she uttered a high-pitched squeak of terror. With Spider Man agility, she rose from the bed, opened my bedroom door, and ran to the locked front door. Within a millisecond she had managed to slide open the lock and run out of my house. She was bawling and yelling, "NOOOOOO!" at the top of her lungs.

I ran after her.

She didn't get very far though. When I found her, she was attempting to open a door that didn't exist. The worst part was we had a 10-foot-tall wall of prickly Oregon grape bushes that lined that side of the house. I grabbed her shoulder and shook it.

As she turned towards me I noticed that her eyes were glazed over, like a zombie. She stared past my eyes at something that was sneaking up on her in the distance. She let out another shriek and pulled from my grasp. I looked at her with deep-seated helplessness as she kept crouching down on her hands and knees trying to climb through the prickly barrier. Her arms started to get streaked with scarlet red scratches from the thorns.

At the height of my fear, about not getting my friend back, I projected my thoughts to her through the airwaves which hummed, "I strive to do no wrong. I will sing His Special song. It will be okay. Please wake up Maddy."

Instantaneously, Maddy straightened up and crossed her arms across her torso.

"Ummmm. Why are we outside?"

I remember breathing a huge sigh of relief. Wherever she was, she was back. When I asked her if she remembered anything about the experience. She gave me a "You are crazy look" and laughed it off, even though her arms were clearly bleeding. I quickly realized that from the time I turned off the lights to the time I woke her up outside, she didn't remember anything at all. She certainly did not remember Henoch propped up on my bed.

When I returned to my bedroom to talk to the little alien that had observed my mistakes, he was gone.

As time passed by and when the movie for the sleepover was "Splash" again, I asked Maddy if she was messing with me and actually did remember a small gray alien in my bedroom. As if she had been triggered with a scripted response, she defensively exclaimed, "OMG. Don't be a weirdo Dariann. I have no idea what you are talking about." Then she shrugged me off and immediately changed the subject.

It was almost like she had been hypnotized to forget the events of that day, Henoch, or any of my conversations about the special skills that I had been gifted while visiting a faraway place called Amaranthine.

10

ONLY IN MY DREAMS

OVER THE MONTHS and then years that followed, glimpses of Amaranthine only appeared in my dreams. I never saw the little boy called Sajan again.

Like a classic conundrum, I was faced with accepting or rejecting the reality of my dreamscape each morning. After a while, I convinced myself that it was easier on everyone to just call all of my weird rapid eye movement mishaps, dreams. Others around me didn't look down on me when I did. It was okay to talk about dreams, as long as I didn't believe that they were real.

So during my first year of high school, I embraced it and focused my frustrated energy on normal human teenager-related activities. That year I tried out for volleyball and actually made the team. Having no experience with this sport, I read everything that I could about the physics of perfectly spiking a ball. I paid very close attention to the coaches advice. And because of my obsessive desire for distraction from my supposed destiny, I worked my tail off to be the best player I could be. At the end of each practice my face resembled the red-faced characters in the Willy Wonka and the Chocolate Factory movie that danced around to silly songs. One of my teammates even started to call me Oompa Loompa. But I didn't care because there was something extremely satisfying about slamming a volleyball down on the opposing team's court and scoring a point for the win.

Later in that year, I also joined a local karate dojo. It was easy and effortless and I loved the discipline and repeatability of practicing Katas. It brought me peace as I worked towards moving my skills from a white belt to a yellow belt. And for a little while, the physical aspects of these two sports kept me distracted from the knowledge that I was being subjected to most nights in my dreams.

When I had completely embraced the fact that Henoch, Omah, and anything else not accepted on my planet were simply dreams; fate grabbed ahold of my plans and pushed me down a path that I normally would not have gone.

During the spring quarter registration, I was accidently enrolled in a creative writing class. Our first assignment was to journal every morning after a good night's sleep. Our teacher explained, "Sometimes our dreams make excellent science fiction compositions."

So as instructed, each morning I would immediately write down what I had seen in my dreams. Mrs. Belgard, my creative writing teacher, was fascinated by my imagination and was constantly encouraging me to continue with my science fiction stories. At the end of that quarter I won a young author's contest. I'm guessing if they knew where I was getting my ideas, I would have been drugged and institutionalized.

A few weeks later he appeared in my dreams.

As usual, the Eight Train was full of other bewildered students that I had never met, but this time I saw a familiar dark-haired, brown-skinned boy a few rows ahead of me. I remember how excited I was by the possibility of seeing him again. But this boy was much older. He was rubbernecking out the window taking in the fascinating sights. As much as I tried, I could not contain myself, as I jumped up and skipped over to his row of chairs.

"SAJAN?"

He jumped several inches into the air. His wide green and brown eyes took me in and then the biggest smile stretched across his face, when he whispered, "Dariann?"

Then, without waiting for any kind of response, he stood up, scooted through the rows of seats, and bear-hugged me so hard that I lost my breath. We settled back down into our cushy seats and took in each other. After a few awkward moments, I announced to the cabin, "Dang, I missed you. How long has it been?"

"Nine years, four months, and twelve days."

As he said this, he looked deep into my eyes and my cheeks immediately felt hot. I was a red-faced Oompa Loompa all over again. Sajan turned away to let me compose myself.

As time passed, the occupants on the train silently dispersed to the different locations along the Eight Train's tracks. I, however, was not interested in ever getting off. For what seemed like hours, Sajan and I talked about what had happened over the last nine years, four months, and twelve days that we had been apart. Sajan told me about the different sections of Amaranthine that he had visited over the years. He also confirmed my earlier suspicions when he told me he was seventeen years old. Ironically, he must have been concerned about my thoughts on this, because he quickly asked, "I know I'm old is that okay?"

Without a second thought, I whispered, "I don't care how old you are Sajan, as long as you are good person." Then my cheeks turned bright red, again.

He did a nervous cough and quickly changed the subject. He told me about a place that had the most amazing animals. After a deep breath, he hesitated, like he wanted to tell me more, but instead he looked out the window and pointed.

"See?"

Someone at the back of the train had pulled the stop cord so that they could disembark. Outside, just a few feet from the window, was an incredibly tall five-legged creature with black and white zebra-like markings on four of its legs. It was reaching up with a giraffe-like neck into the trees above it. As I looked closer, I was able to see that the fifth leg was actually a long kangaroo-like tail. The unusual creature was using its tail to help balance itself in a stretched position so that it could get access to the out of reach blue and pink leaves. Just as we passed by, I could see that it had a long black tongue that jetted out and grasped the leaves back into its mouth. It had a swollen nose like a Saiga antelope and two black spiraling horns coming out the top of its big bug-eyed head.

My eyes must have been bugging out of my own head, because Sajan gave me a warm look.

"So cool. I know. That is like an Okapi, but a little bit bigger and weirder. I love this place so much."

I couldn't break my eyes away from his intense stare and my cheeks flashed red again. The joy of his love for this place bubbled out of him and enveloped me in warmth and kindness. He had a knowing look on his face, like he was reading my thoughts.

"I feel the same. Each and every time I visit Amaranthine I am overwhelmed with its beauty – like it was the first time I had ever witnessed it. I just love all of the amazing animals here. I am so blessed."

As I looked at him not knowing what to say or do, he shared, "I have visited every section of Amaranthine, except one."

Before I could ask which one, Sajan reached up and pulled the thin red cord. The train hovered to a standstill and my heart skipped a couple of beats – because I thought this was the end of our journey. However, Sajan lifted up off the chair and reached down for my hand.

"This is the one. Want to check it out?"

I looked at his hand and then at the outside world. A flying creature fluttered by the window that looked a lot like a horse. Sajan caught my eyes and lifted up one eyebrow.

"Have you ever seen a Pegasus herd before?"

With a quickening of my heart beat, I swiftly slid my hand into his and he guided me off the train. When we stepped onto the grassy plain, he gently explained, "This is Evania. It means peace."

After a few steps through the tall wavy grasses a red sandy path appeared. As we walked along the natural-made trail, the Eight Train silently moved on.

Sajan continued to stare at me because my mouth was wide open in wonderment of the beauty of Evania. The lush grass landscape was interspersed with gigantic trees. The tree trunks were as wide and tall as the great Banyan trees of India. Each of them had multiple full-size trees growing out of them that touched high in the sky. Perched on several of the branches were a variety of colors of horses. Their feathery wings were delicately folded on their backs.

Lost in my thoughts, as I wondered how they could stand up there without toppling off. I realized that their hooves had the same gripping capability as a mountain goat. A few of the younger foals were effortlessly jumping from branch to branch playfully nipping each other. The adults however, were quite focused on the bipedal creatures inching up the path. A brilliant black stallion with black wings snorted, stretched out one wing and then another, before gliding to the path a few hundred yards ahead of us.

Without even thinking I crooned, "Well, Hello handsome."

Sajan and the shiny black horse responded, at the exact same time with, "Well, Thank you." Then they both snorted in unison.

My attention turned to Sajan with a questioning look.

"I read about this. So not only do they fly, but they talk too."

I let out my breath in disbelief, but sure enough the black beauty clopped over to us and said, "How ya doing? I'm Aster" and then he let out a loud whistle of a noise that stirred up the rest of the herd hanging out in the trees. They immediately fluffed out their wings and flew down to join us. The chatter was overwhelming.

When Aster let out a loud trilling noise that stopped the excited herd in their tracks, he went on to explain the lay of the land.

"The training facility can be reached through the ocean. I would be happy to show you where the transport platform is, if you like. The teachers pick you up on the other side."

I had absolutely no idea what he was talking about, but Sajan just kept nodding affirmatively and after a few moments he respectfully declined his offer to take us there. Then Aster asked if we wanted to meet his herd. There was no way I could have pulled Sajan from that offer and we decided to stick around for a bit.

Aster introduced us to his mate. She was a young white mare with a black mane and tail. She was noticeably with foal. Aster was beaming with pride when he introduced Star. She was a little shy and kept swishing her long full tail from side to side. Her white feathery wings hung just above her big bulbous belly. We found out that this would be their first baby. They had already picked the little foal's name. It was going to be Nova, whether it was a boy or a girl. Star snickered a little.

"I know it will be a girl, though."

Aster proudly snorted and then pointed us to the north of Evania and told us about the cottage that was there for visitors. His last words, before he flew back up to his tree house was, "Enjoy the wild life. They are quite friendly."

After a few hours of watching the flying horses graze and flutter above our heads, Sajan gently grabbed my hand, and we trudged down the reddish pink sandy path that Aster told us to follow.

The landscape began to quickly change as we moved forward. Grassy plains were replaced by rocky terrain. As we walked towards the sounds of crashing waves, smaller trunked trees became more plentiful. Oddly enough, the sand below our feet, began to look pink. When we reached a thicker part of this forest, we had to weave in and out of the trees. That was when we suddenly heard a loud "pop pop pop."

Slightly concerned, Sajan took a stance of protection as the "pop pop pop" sound began to surround us. At first it was behind us every couple of minutes, then to the left, then to the right. Then the rustling of the undergrowth began. When we looked for the culprit, it moved so fast that we could not get a visual. All I could think about was some kind of scary creature jumping out and eating us. I started to wonder if Aster had sent us into a trap.

After several terrifying moments into this nightmare, the unnerving pop sounds boxed us in from all sides. Sajan pulled me to the middle of a small clearing and we sat on a slightly raised, but flat basalt rock. He had a look of curiosity on his face that gave me a little bit of comfort.

"Let's see what happens."

Within seconds out from under the bramble poked a pointy noise and two long fangs. Panic rose in my gut, when the nose began to twitch back and forth like a rabbit looking for danger. Then a long leg with a white three toed hoof appeared followed by another. The sabertoothed deer-like creature slowly padded over to us and laid down beside us. It literally had huge fangs. Sajan dramatically sucked in his breath.

"It resembles a larger version of Earth's saber-toothed deer that lives in the Artic."

I was waiting to hear that he was just kidding, but his face was brutally honest and before he could explain his stance on this really weird looking creature, a two-foot, brown-feathered bird with the biggest beak ever popped out of the bushes. Sajan jumped up from the rock.

"Oh look, it's a Pooty" and then he released an excited child-like tee-hee-hee.

All I could utter was, "A what?"

Sajan went on to explain that a Potoo is a bird that he saw back on Earth during some of his travels. With a steady and even toned David Attenborough type voice he explained, "They have giant beaks that take up their entire faces. They make a weird noise like a ghost. My mom always called them a Ghost Bird, back home. They were rarely seen, but you could hear them. Usually at night. My friends and I call them Pooty Birds though."

This is when I realized that Sajan was from my planet. I had never bothered to ask him where he was from. This epiphany gave me so much unspeakable joy. It was as if Sajan could feel the joy emanating out of me, because he beamed right back at me.

When I vocally cooed, "So Cool," to the creatures surrounding us.

The Potoo Bird must have thought I was calling to it, because the goofy critter skipped over to me and laid its head on my shoulder. Its beak opened up wide and then it popped it several times. Sajan and I laughed out loud.

We spent the next hour with the little deer and the Potoo Bird. The deer snuggled at our feet, while the Ghost Bird's head cuddled in my lap. Sajan and I had effortless conversations as I stroked the silly bird's feathery neck. When the double suns of Evania began to set lower in the horizon, we reluctantly gave our new friends one last pat. Then we dusted ourselves off and continued our journey to a cottage that we had never seen before.

The deer and the Potoo followed us on the trail for a while, until they lost interest. Eventually, we found ourselves climbing up rocky terrain that crested over a cleared plateau that held a small cottage. The loud crash of waves could be heard in the distance. The cottage looked like a classic fairy-tale version of a white stucco house tucked into the woods. The door was painted bright red, along with matching red shutters on each side of the windows.

There was a small column of smoke dancing out of the chimney. Flowers of all kinds were growing around a small enclosed white fence that surrounded the house on all sides. The trellis that surrounded the gate had teal and white blooms hanging down both sides. Gigantic butterflies, the size of dinner plates, were floating from one flower to another. The sweet smell of nectar was overwhelming. All we could do was just stand there in awe and soak in the unbelievable beauty of the home that we would be hanging out in for the night.

As we stood there, something furry rubbed up against my ankle. A three-foot, bright pink creature with a naked pointy nose was looking up at me. It then stretched two-and a half inch-long claws around my exposed knees and wiggled its nose like a genie. Startled, I let out a blood-curdling scream and started to climb on Sajan's back to get away from this dangerous looking pink monster. Sajan chuckled.

"Watch out for the Pink Fairy Armadillo. They are pretty ferocious."

I stepped back a few steps behind Sajan and stared at the odd creature.

By that time the half pink and half white furred animal had rolled up into a tight ball. Clearly frightened from my yelp. Sajan leaned over and started to stroke its massive smooth armored back. It seemed to enjoy this attention, because the alien creature started to unfurl right before our eyes. Its beady red eyes fixated on me and took a few steps backwards.

"A What?"

Sajan pointed down to the half-naked fuzzy creature.

"That is a Pink Fairy Armadillo. They too, are from Earth. We used to call them sand swimmers because they can dig really fast through sand – like they are swimming in a lake."

And that is when I started to truly understand that maybe my dreams weren't really "just dreams" after all.

11

WELCOME TO EVANIA

THE PINK CREATURE awkwardly waddled away from us on its long-pointed claws. As we watched it disappear into the scrub brush near a well-hidden sand dune, the door to our cottage flung open and two figures appeared. They were dressed in what I could only describe as brightly colored orange and red Scottish kilts. They were waving at us as if we were gawkers at a fourth of July parade. Sajan and I looked at each other with a bewildered look and then we both turned and gave them a half-hearted wave back.

Even with our lackluster acknowledgement of them they began to squeal – much like the pissed off constrained pigs back on my farm that were receiving vet checks and vaccinations. Sajan and I took a few steps back when they proceeded to jump up and down. They were clearly excited to see us. As their pleated skirts shot up into the air, my cheeks turned beet red. These were things that I did not want or need to see. All I could squeak out was, "Oh my."

As I tried to keep my focus off the flopping and flipping of these overly exuberant outlanders, Sajan started to laugh out loud.

"Well this should be interesting."

Then he grabbed my hand and dragged me through the colorful gateway and down the cobble walkway towards the bouncy strangers. As we approached our cheerful hosts, they practically sang in unison, "Welcome to Evania."

The attractive white-haired blue-eyed boy, dramatically pointed to himself.

"Hello, welcome. I am Alaster. We are so happy to meet you."

The girl standing behind him punched one of his exposed broad and muscled shoulders. He had the same tattoo that Sajan and I had. Alaster dramatically turned to the girl that had fiery red-hair popping out from her small round face. With great warmth and gentleness, he radiated, "Oh, sorry. This is Davita. Mo anam cara." Alaster's long white braid flipped from side to side as he turned back to face us.

Davita perked up even more and beamed back at him and then us. Her cheeks were bright red. I had no idea what he said, but it seemed like it was endearing. Without waiting for a response from us, they waved us forward. We quickly found out that they were actually from Scotland. They were there for training, just like us. They had been there several times before. They knew we were coming and had been expecting us. They were tasked to help us get to the Evania Training Transport in the morning.

When Alaster explained with excitement, "But, we call it the ETT for short," Davita squealed like a pig and then exclaimed, "But in the meantime, we have prepared a gigantic meal for you."

She jumped up and down, looked at Alaster, and yelled, "Whoo hoo! We got friends."

Surprised by her exuberance, I jumped a few inches back and bumped into Sajan. He pressed his hand on the small of my back to steady me. Which threw me into a Willy Wonka and the Charlie Factory moment. When he saw my red face, he gave me a raised eyebrow and a cute little smile.

I had no idea how hungry I was until I saw the country-style table overflowing with all of my favorite foods. On one side of the feast, there were candied yams topped with browned marshmallows. A filet mignon with a big blob of garlic butter sliding down the side of it. Steamed broccoli was on the side. But the best part of this banquet was the dessert section, which was brimming with my favorite varieties of cheese cake and chocolate covered strawberries.

On the other side of the table was a variety of foods that were foreign to me. There were bowls of moving tentacles and large egg-shaped things that were cracked open. Inside it looked like they housed unformed baby birds. There were also several strange fish looking creatures and rolls and rolls of sushi. I was slightly befuddled on the differences in the food selections until I looked at Sajan. His mouth was open, and he was literally drooling as his eyes panned the delicacies that were on his favorite foods list. I think I even heard him whisper, "Balut, nom nom."

I didn't have the courage to ask what Balut was, but I did know it looked disgusting and I redirected my attention to my side of the table. With our mouths full of food, our new friends took the opportunity to tell us all about their lives back in Scotland. I was surprised to hear that they had actually met, for the first time, in Evania. I could tell that they were really good friends. They kept finishing each other's sentences and were clearly linked together somehow. Maybe even dating. Regardless of my first impression of them, Alaster and Davita were actually really nice. They were just a bit more extroverted than most and Sajan and I barely got a word in edgewise.

After dinner our hosts showed us around our new temporary home. From the outside, the cottage looked small, but once you walked in the door, the house was enormous. There were twelve individually themed bedrooms that were separated by long hallways. Each of them had their own bathroom and a small kitchenette. When Davita walked me to my bedroom door she vibrated, "Have fun." Then she bounced back to the kitchen.

My bedroom was literally a glass covered sun room. When I walked through the door it felt like I had walked outside into the garden. The room was full of flowers and greenery. To the right of the entrance, there was a dark mahogany bed with four decorative pedestals. Above the bed was a large silver ring that displayed a shimmery see-through curtain that was intertwined with multiple-colored green vines. One side of the curtain was pulled aside and I could see a teal bedspread and white satin sheets. Four matching pillows were propped up on top. Two large white rectangle pillows with black letters read, "SUBLIME," another one read, "PEACE."

I crooned to the empty room, "I couldn't agree more."

The wall that was to the left of the door had a fountain that gently cascaded down a series of rock formations into a large natural forming pond. There was a large pillowed bench that wrapped around its edge. I immediately shuffled over and sat down. Then I took a deep breath.

"How could this be any more perfect?"

That's when the cutest little yellow and brown shelled critter with green hair peeked up out of the water's surface. His bright blue eyes opened up wide and I could swear it had a goofy grin on its beaky turtle face. I, of course, waved at it and said, "Hello friend. I guess we are roomies tonight."

That's when Sajan knocked on the door. He looked baffled by my conversation with the room and quickly looked around for another occupant.

Without skipping a beat, I bellowed, "This place rocks!"

Then I pointed to the pond and my new found roommate. However, by the time his gaze found the pond, my little green-haired friend had disappeared below the surface. I just shrugged it off as the circular rings from his departure carried over its surface. After a few moments, Sajan taunted me.

"My room is totally better than yours. It is full of knowledge."

When I sputtered, "Are you calling my room stupid?"

Sajan beamed with excitement.

"Come see!" as he reached out for my hand to help me off the bench.

I followed Sajan down the hall. When we arrived in front of his door he flung it open and there in front me was literally, an old-fashioned library. The room was a large circle. When he closed the door, the space, where the door had been, was replaced with even more books. It was hard to tell where the exit was. He gently grabbed my hand and guided me to a large circular bed that had books already piled high from Sajan's earlier room exploration.

"This room has every book that I have always wanted to read."

He patted the bed and gave me a serious gaze, before asking, "Want to go for a ride?"

After backing up a few steps, I half-joked, "You are moving way too fast for me buddy."

He held up a control panel that had a bunch of multi-colored buttons on it. With a maniacal grin he asked, "Can your bed fly?"

When he innocently patted the bed again, I jumped up and down and settled in as Sajan flew his bed around the room. He was giddy as he reached the top levels of his room of knowledge. We spent several hours floating around his library exploring the different books that Sajan had always dreamed about reading. Eventually, he let me push a few buttons too.

The joy and excitement that crossed his face was hard to describe and I remember saying to myself as we floated towards the Ufology section, "Best dream ever."

As if he had heard my thoughts Sajan looked into my eyes and whispered, "Ditto," and gave me one of his shy smiles.

12

MO ANAM CARA

A S WE ZIPPED around his room for hours, we quickly realized that sleep in whatever dream world we had entered wasn't really necessary. I was also secretly concerned that if we did try to go to sleep we might actually wake up. I remember pondering the horror of this idea for several moments before Sajan saved my overthinking brain and distracted me with stories about his adventures while traveling his part of the waking world.

He described the different places he had been. I was surprised to hear that he had traveled to most parts of our planet. This answered several of my questions as to why he knew what a pink armadillo was and that saber-toothed deer, actually exist on Earth. I found out that his dad had died in a war and that his mom had raised him since he was a few years old. Her job required that she travel around the world and Sajan had no choice but to get dragged along.

I briefly shared that my mom had passed away at an early age, as well. As we talked about her, I started to squirm around from the memory of her loss. When Sajan brushed my hand and gently said, "I'm so sorry Dariann," I almost started to cry. After a few awkward moments of silently staring into his eyes, Sajan suggested that we go find Alaster and Davita. We found them snuggled up on a set of white fluffy couches that wrapped around a crackling fire. When she saw us, Davita jumped up, clapped her hands and yelled, "Hooray!"

Her red fuzzy hair was noticeably taller and wider as she dramatically shifted from one foot to the other.

She skipped over to the kitchen and filled up two cups of hot cocoa. There were marshmallows floating on top. When I nestled in and took a sip of the best hot chocolate, ever, I let out an impulsive, "Yum," then turned to Sajan and jokingly asked, "What the heck is Balut?"

Alaster and Davita were quite interested, as well, because they settled into the couch themselves and focused all of their attention on him. Sajan shrugged as if it wasn't that big of a deal.

"I discovered them during my travels to the Philippines with my mom a few years ago. Balut is a delicacy that I think originated from the Chinese traders back in the 1800's. It is a fertilized developing egg embryo that is boiled and steamed. You eat it from the shell. It looks gross, I know."

Sajan scrunched up his nose in disgust and quietly explained, "But I was so hungry that day when a good Samaritan handed me one on the street. The love affair has continued, even as I transitioned into an older and wiser man." Sajan wiggled his eyebrows up and down, and we laughed out loud, because not one of us in that cottage was over eighteen years of age.

We spent the rest of the evening sharing stories about our lives. It was confirmed that all of us spent our waking moments on Planet Earth. All of us had different cultures and beliefs. However, as we listened and learned from each other with respect and understanding, we realized just how small the Earth was and how connected all of us were. In this dream, it was very clear that we would be friends, forever.

Eventually, we were hungry again and found the country-style buffet. It had magically filled with all of our favorite foods, once again. This time, for my side of the table, there were breakfast type items that included grits with brown sugar, an egg dish called Dutch babies, and mounds of fresh fruits.

After another hearty meal to break the morning fast, Alaster and Davita announced that it was time to go. Before we headed out the door, Davita pointed at four medium-sized camo-colored backpacks. Each of them had our names in dark letters across the front of them. Below our names was "#11" stitched in big numbers. The sight of them gave me a bit of a nervous feeling in my gut. Camo, in my upbringing at least, meant war and seeing them made me realize the seriousness of this particular dream.

Sajan and I tentatively picked up our packs and followed our guides out the door. As we walked down the cobble walkway and under the flowered trellis, I turned back to look at the cottage. I whispered to myself, "I hope I see you again." I couldn't help but let out a great big sigh.

Sajan came up beside me and gave me a playful shoulder bump and one of his comforting glances, as we turned up the well-worn pink sandy route that led towards our ocean training facility.

Davita led us down the path. She had changed out of her colorful kilt and was actually in beige leather pants. She had a snug-fitting black top that made her look like a warrior. She carried her camo backpack confidently over her left shoulder. Davita's flaming red hair flipped from one side to the other as her golden-hazel eyes sparkled with enthusiasm. Although her pace was determined, she took the time to point out certain aspects of Evania's landscape or a creature that happened to cross our path.

The pink path was lined with tall grasses that waved in the gentle breeze of Evania's twin suns. On one misty portion of the trail, I was surprised to see yellow banana slugs crisscrossing our path. They reminded me of my cousin Fanny and the large slugs that we always collected back on the Pacific Ocean when I was a little girl. The coincidence of the resemblance was hard to overlook.

Alaster lagged behind us, as if he was protecting us from something.

The ocean waves were noticeably louder as we padded along. Within minutes we could see a tall sand dune in the distance. It had a red door fixated to the side of it. When we arrived in front of the sand door, Alaster popped up in front of us and pushed on a hidden keypad. He then pointed to a shimmering cleared off platform and a rock-type bench that was shaped like a figure eight. He surprised us when he used a commanding tone.

"Let's shake out our shoes and get ready for the pickup."

I slowly sat down in a bewildered panic due to my deep-water anxiety. Sajan scooted next to me and gave me a little bump with the side of his body.

"You good?"

I was too embarrassed to admit my fear and nodded. However, it was as if Alaster could feel my emotions.

"No worries. It's all good. I promise."

At that moment the dune that had been in front of us opened up like the story of Moses and the parting of the red sea. As the gap grew, there standing in front of us was my mentor, Henoch. He waved a gray spindly arm at me and telepathically teased, "Hey, did you forget about me?"

I gave him an uncertain wave and shrugged my shoulders from a loss for words. Henoch directed us through the sand dune tunnel that slowly dipped down through the ocean's surface, as he projected for all of us to hear.

"Welcome to the ETT."

The ETT was like a fully enclosed floating conveyer belt-type contraption. When we broke through the rough surface that was crashing onto the foamy pink beach, the view out of the tunnel became transparent. The fact that I was breathing air, convinced me we were within a protective bubble. There was a rainbow of colors under the sea. Every kind of plant and rocky-type structure in our way was magically avoided as we wound through them towards some unknown destination. As all of this was happening, Davita and Alaster were shockingly silent.

Some of the sea creatures that I saw seemed familiar. However, there were other oddities that were hard to describe like the armies of alien crabs that balanced on 20–25-foot stilts. Their beady black eyes and large claws waved back and forth, high above their bony shells. Their rough orange appendages clacked up against our protective transparent tube as they climbed up and over it. They were traveling in packs, definitely on a mission to the south. When the last one disappeared into the distance, Sajan mumbled, "Japanese Spider Crab?" It was like he was having an internal battle about what was real and what was not.

Surprisingly, Henoch looked over at him and telepathically announced to all of us, "Good Job, Sajan. This species of Evanian crab is related to Earth's Japanese spider crab population."

With uncontained excitement, Davita started to clap and jump up and down. Alaster brushed up against her shoulder, as if to remind her she needed to be quiet.

As we proceeded along this weird tunnel adventure, Sajan started to engage with the odd things that suddenly started to appear at the shimmering wall. One of them resembled a shark, but it was probably forty feet long and was very blue – like its surroundings. It swam around our enclosure and poked at the invisible membrane a couple of times. Feeling a bit more confident, I inched up to the wall.

Immediately this normal looking Earth-type creature disjointed its upper jaw and eyeballs upward that revealed rows and rows of jagged teeth. It then lurched forward at me, like the alien baby that jumped out at the actress Sigourney Weaver in the 1979 movie "Alien." I, of course, yelped and ran behind Sajan. Rather than saving me, he chortled out loud and announced to the room.

"Goblin Shark. Check."

Eventually our conveyer belt slowed down and I could see bright lights ahead. The end of the ETT opened up into a bright hallway that had a dozen doors running down both sides. Each door was a different color. The door handles were all uniquely shaped. In a flash of memory, I realized I had been in this place before.

When the words from a forgotten song started to "Sssss," through my unspoken thoughts, I began sing a song. When I got to the last few verses, the other three humans joined in and loudly exaggerated each verse, "Even if pursuit of right is a fight. His final gifts outweigh this plight. I strive to do no wrong. I will sing His special song."

Davita, Alaster, and Sajan were suddenly focused on me, as Henoch tapped his head from the loud human noises. Then we all started laughing after I realized they had heard my unprotected ramblings.

As we walked through the hallway of doors we passed by an orange door with an ox shaped gold handle. I paused just before I moved past it and impulsively stroked the features of the ox head. The memories of the magical creatures I had seen there were rushing back. I found myself suddenly longing for this forgotten knowledge. Sajan shuffled over to me and gently touched my shoulder.

"I love unicorns too." Then with a bashful gentleness, he added, "If we do good, we will be part of all of this, some day."

Henoch interrupted our tender moment and pointed at Sajan. "It is time to get ready. You don't want to be late."

Then my three Earth companions, trotted off to their classes.

Henoch pointed at me and then a blue door with a knob shaped like an eagle. That's when I thought to myself, "I have definitely been here before."

He nodded and replied, "Yes you have. Your class is right through that door, down the blue path to the library."

When I found my classroom, it was arranged like a dojo on Earth. I remember how excited I was to practice my already obtained karate skills within that dream. Each of the exercises that were placed in front of me to solve, seemed effortless. The Sensei seemed very pleased with my progress and when he released me for the day, he exclaimed, "Yoku yatta, Dariann."

I didn't know Japanese, at that time, but I was pretty sure what he said was good.

Henoch met us in the hall of colored doors and led us up to the red one. It had a growling lion head figure on it. The golden head had a large knocker that was shaped like a figure eight. Henoch reached his long spindly fingers toward the knob and guided us through. As we stepped back onto the ETT, I finally realized that each of these worlds had a connection to the Interstellar Contact Council members that I had met back in Coffenbury Lake.

This particular red door was connected to the world, Evania, which was under the watchful care of Amartv, the lion figure that I had seen at the lake, so long ago. I remembered that he had a red-handled staff that had the symbol that represented infinity. With this epiphany I slapped my forehead and loudly announced to the room, "Ah Ha! I think I'm finally getting it."

Davita and Alaster jumped a few inches away from me. Henoch's large blue eyes almost bugged out of his big bulbous head from the noise. Sajan, on the other hand, was distracted by what he was seeing outside the tube. Ignoring what I had just announced, he was talking to himself like he was working on a difficult math problem.

"Glaucus Atlanticus? Glaucus Atlanticus." Then he turned to Henoch for a clue.

"YES! That is right. Good job, Sajan."

Then Sajan pressed his face and hands against the barrier and whispered to himself.

"So cool!"

By this time I wasn't afraid of what resided outside our transport and I pressed my nose against the shimmering side, next to him. A two-foot bright blue and teal creature was floating by. It had several feathery type appendages. It was absolutely gorgeous.

Sajan murmured, "Back at home we called them blue angels, but they can deliver a very painful sting." He gave me wide eyes that implied he had received the kiss of this not so angelic sea slug. To make sure I understood his point, he dramatically called out, "Ouch!"

I remember rolling my eyes and thinking, "What a dork." Forgetting that everyone could actually read my thoughts, the entire room started to laugh out loud, except Henoch of course.

When we got back to the cottage, the country-style table was full of our favorite foods once again. After an early dinner we enjoyed a hot cup of cocoa by the fire and reminisced about what we had learned that day in training. When our excited conversations winded down and we all became noticeably tired, Sajan asked if I would walk with him in the garden.

"I want to show you something."

Intrigued, because I now knew that his special skills included plant and animal identification, I trotted outside behind him thinking he had discovered another Earth-like creature. Before I could ask what he had found, I stopped in my tracks trying to fathom the sight in front of me.

I had discovered through my recent studies of Amaranthine that on Evania there were several moons and suns. The last of the two suns were lowering beneath the western horizon. We could just see the second moon of three, slowly peeking up over the east. The glow from both celestial bodies were mixing together and creating a view that was comparable to a late-night Alaskan aurora borealis. The hues of purple, blue, and pinks were mesmerizing as they waved through the darkening sky. I'm pretty sure my mouth was wide open as I took in the colorful scene.

Sajan grabbed my hand and guided me over to a small bench that was located outside of my bedroom. A deep stream of water steadily flowed from the side of the cottage. I had not realized that my little pond actually extended past the house walls. Lily pads of all sizes and shapes were sprinkled on the sides of the stream where the water had slowed and allowed a calm place for them to flower. The dinner-sized butterflies were settling in for the night on the bushes that surrounded us. They were slowly fanning their wings up and down. My little turtle friend popped up out of the water with his big green head and blue eyes. I couldn't help but do a little wave and say, "Well, hello there. I will call you George because you look just like the Yeti from one of my favorite childhood cartoons."

Sajan chuckled for several seconds and then said, "That's a green-haired turtle. I have only seen one in my lifetime. They live in Australia."

As he educated me about this rarely seen turtle, I began to understand that animals on Evania were very similar to animals on Earth. I took a mental note to ask Henoch about that the next time I saw him. Sajan wrapped up his tutorial lesson on Australian turtles with a quick, "But that is not what I wanted to talk to you about."

He gave me a shy look and then averted his eyes back to George. After a few awkward quiet moments, he turned his body towards me and gently grabbed both of my hands. He took a deep breath and whispered, "Dariann, I really like you." His light brown cheeks were bright red.

"Gosh, I like you too Sajan. You have been an amazing friend to me, and you know all about critters and stuff. That is a giant bonus on my checklist of likeable attributes." Then I nervously giggled.

He did a little anxious cough to clear his throat and admitted, "Well maybe the feeling I'm having is a little more than that."

Then my cheeks turned bright red. When I looked deep into his eyes, I slowly nodded that I felt the exact same way. I didn't need to tell him how I felt, because he could read my thoughts and without any warning, under the bright blue moons of a world called Evania, the boy that I met on a train so many years ago gently leaned over and tenderly brushed my lips with his.

When we pulled apart, his eyes sparkled in the moonlight back into mine. I felt sublime and full of so much peace. Dream or not. I knew at that very moment my heart belonged to him. Forever!

I beamed at Sajan with the realization that I had found what Alaster had called Davita in our first awkward meeting at the cottage. I, too, had found mo anam cara. Sajan was definitely my soul mate. I leaned into Sajan and he wrapped his warm strong arms around me. And then I closed my eyes.

When I opened them again, he was gone.

Just like that, I was ripped from my dream and thrust back into a different reality. A place that suddenly didn't feel like home.

13

LOOKING FOR LOVE

A FTER HOURS OF trying to go back to sleep to get back to him, I peeled myself out of bed and threw on some clothes for school. I propped myself up on the bathroom countertop and haphazardly applied eye makeup and brushed my hair. It was hard to focus on the now as I thought about Sajan.

With dreams, I knew that if I didn't write it down, I might forget it, so I jumped up and grabbed my purple notebook. With my favorite blue pen in hand, I closed my eyes and thought about my recent experience in Amaranthine.

I began scratching out the details of my newfound friends. I laughed out loud, as I remembered my first impressions of Alaster and Davita when they greeted us outside the cottage. I wrote about my little green-haired friend, George. Then after letting out a deep breath, I furiously and meticulously detailed out everything that I had learned about Sajan. What he looked like. The animals that he taught me about. My cheeks burned hot as I remembered our kiss in the garden. The more I thought about him, the more I wanted to get back to him. As the minutes dragged on the more anxious I got, because I had been conditioned my entire life that his presence, the training, the memories of Evania were literally just a dream; that they were not real and part of me.

At one point, I asked the room.

"Am I crazy?"

However, just like a well-matched ping pong game, the other

half of my brain assured my nervous gut that, "I will see him again. He is real." I justified this feeling with, "Don't you remember how he knew what all of those weird animals were on Evania? It was because he had seen them on Earth."

With this epiphany, I jumped up, found my computer and started to search for a saber-toothed deer. To my surprise the deer, the armadillo, and even the large-mouthed Potoo bird, that Sajan dubbed Pooty, were actually real-life creatures on my planet. I remember shrieking quite loudly, jumping up and down, and yelling, "YES! They are real. He is real. He is from Earth."

Excitement bubbled up and out of me as I conjured a plan. Wherever he might be, I will find him. I hollered at the room, "Yes, I got this!"

In that same celebratory moment, with great disappointment I remembered that I had never asked where he currently lived on my planet. When I slapped my forehead and literally screamed, "IDIOT!"

My dad peeked around my half-closed bedroom door.

"You okay Kiddo?"

Surprised by his sudden appearance, I yelped, "It's all good, Dad. Having a bad hair day moment."

He ducked out of my room and walked away. I could tell he was not in the mood to engage in my teenage weirdness. There was no way I was going to tell him about what was on my mind, and he knew it.

School was difficult. As in, I couldn't concentrate on anything the teachers were telling us. As hard as I tried, all I could think of was Evania and the way that Sajan had looked at me after our kiss in the garden. Distracted by his memory, I scribbled on my notebook and whispered to myself, "How do I find him?"

When the bell rang and everyone shuffled out of the classroom, I slumped in my seat. Within seconds, Maddy came over to my desk.

"Hey, what's up? You have been way too quiet today." Then she flashed her baby blue eyes at me and demanded an explanation.

I looked down nervously and started to doodle on my notebook, again. Our hypnosis experiment nightmare flashed before my eyes, and I had no idea what to say. Then after a brief pause, all I could muster was a few silly song lyrics that were playing through my brain at that moment.

"Just looking for love in all the wrong places."

She giggled and started to hum the lyrics from the 1980 Johnny Lee song," Lookin' for Love." When she got to the chorus, she looked at me with a curious look and asked, "Are you looking for love in your dreams again, Dariann?"

I peered up from my doodling and gave her a little nod. An uncontrolled tear leaked out from the corner of one of my eyes. When the second bell rang, she gave me an exaggerated sad look, patted me on the shoulder, and sang, "Sometimes strangers turn to friends." Then without another word, she skipped out the door.

That night I did some major research to find a dark haired, green-eyed, boy named Sajan that lived on my planet. I had no last name. No parents' names. No specific location to search. It was incredibly frustrating and as if he never existed. And I realized that my only hope to find him would be in my dreams.

When I got back to Evania, I vowed to conduct an intense interrogation of my soul mate so that I could find him when the lights turned back on in the waking moments of my life. I pledged to turn that stranger in my dreams into a real live Planet Earth friend. After dinner and several shallow conversations with my dad, I quickly readied myself for bed. It was time to get back. It was time to turn the lights out and find mo anam cara.

That night, I tucked myself into bed and pulled the sheet and blanket up to my chin. Like every night, I recited the prayer that Mom had taught me. Each word had so much more meaning that night.

"Now I lay me down to sleep. Dear Lord, my soul, with you is complete. Guide me, Lord, through the night. Help me do the things that are right. No matter where I happen to go. I pray the Lord protects my soul."

Normally after reciting the prayer, it gave me incredible peace. Usually, I would drift off to dreamland quickly. But not that night. And after hours and hours of tossing and turning, I finally passed out.

In the morning, I woke up dreamless.

The rest of the week, each night, I called out to Henoch. I truly thought that the big-eyed alien would magically appear in my closet. I believed that at any moment he would reach out and grab my hand and take me to Evania.

But in my disappointment, despair and anguish, he never did.

14

LIGHTS OUT

THIS REOCCURRING NIGHTMARE happened over and over, each night, for months. I was baffled as to why I had been cut off from Amaranthine - why I couldn't go back to Evania. Every morning my tattered purple notebook looked back at me. The reminder of it waiting for me each morning was torture. One morning I threw it in the trash can and bellowed at the top of my lungs.

"I have no dreams. I'm done."

That was the same day that I dropped out of my advanced creative writing class.

Instead, I filled my obsession of finding Sajan and Evania with technology and science. One way or another I was going to find him. Whether it was on Earth or in another universe that humans had not discovered yet.

I buried myself in mathematical impossibilities, read every peer-reviewed article on quantum mechanics, magnetic anomalies, telluric currents, and attended every symposium I could find that tackled space exploration. In my senior year, I academically skipped past all of my classmates. But the pursuit of all of this knowledge and the application of it towards future possibilities came at a price. I stopped participating in sports, I avoided all social events, and literally only had one friend—Maddy of course.

A few days after my 18th birthday, when I stepped across my high school graduation platform to get my diploma, I was also recognized for obtaining my 2-year degree from the community college. My dad was so proud of me. Unfortunately, my brothers and sister couldn't attend my big day. After my mother died and with the 11+ years in age differences; I just wasn't that close with them. The trauma of my mom's death drove them far away from the farm. My brothers both lived on the east coast with their own families. My sister now lived in Europe with her husband and their five kids.

And even though it was only me and my dad against the world, he yelled so loud at the graduation ceremony, I was slightly embarrassed for him and for me. He had brought a bull horn. He blasted the ear drums of four rows of other proud parents in front of him when I shook the hand of the Principal of my High School. He did it again when Maddy walked across the platform. When she got back to her seat and we bear-hugged in the aisle, he did it again. Both Maddy and I almost peed our pants from my dad's obnoxious behavior.

Behind my dad were two men and a woman dressed in dark suits and hats. It was so weird, because they had on sunglasses. The only color you could see coming from these out-of-place individuals was flaming red hair sticking out from under the woman's black hat. When my dad blasted the horn for the third time and these people tapped him on the shoulder, I thought he was going to be escorted out of the building. Instead, they shook hands and were all friendly.

From a distance, I could tell that my dad was spilling his guts to these strangers about all of my accomplishments, because after a few seconds, he pointed at me and waved. The vibes running through my mind was a bit schizophrenic. On one hand I was anxious for his safety and on the other, I was proud that he had no fear of strangers like I did.

Later, after we moved out to the grass that surrounded the event center, these dark-clothed strangers hovered just out of sight. Or so they thought. I, of course, saw them immediately. I could feel their eyes burning a hole through my soul as they periodically peeked through the colorful purple and gold robes of the graduating students. When I asked my dad about the three odd characters that were behind him at the ceremony, he chortled at the memory.

"Nice people. They were very interested in your skills. They said they were federal government headhunters. They have been watching you, even before you started studying quantum physics, space travel, and international communications at the local university."

Feeling a bit creeped out, I gave my dad a lifted eyebrow scowl as he started to vibrate with uncontrolled joy.

"They are excited to see what you do next."

I remember feeling very uncomfortable when he told me this news. I wondered who "they" were. When I looked over at them through the crowds of graduated kids, the woman with red hair took off her glasses and winked at me. I cringed when I realized she had green and gold eyes behind her horn-rimmed glasses. They looked off, kind of like lizard eyes. As we locked gazes, I could swear I heard a whisper.

"Good job."

The whisper had a familiarity to it that reminded me of Henoch, and I looked around the masses with unrealistic hope that the short gray alien was there too. When I returned my gaze back to the red-haired lady, she and her black suit cohorts were gone.

A few months later, I started my studies at the university and I decided to enroll in a new class that had suddenly appeared in the course catalog. The curriculum claimed that the students would get to do a deep-dive on the scientific methods for discerning unidentified flying objects, black holes and thermodynamics. Luckily, our class was provided with an opportunity to access the Hanford's Laser Interferometer Gravitational-wave Observatory (LIGO) facility. I excelled on all levels related to my planetary scientific and extracurricular studies.

By the end of the year, I was accepted as a communications intern at the local research and development laboratory that was funded by the Department of Homeland Security (DHS). Ironically, the hiring manager and my new boss, was named Eris Cosbee. She was the red-haired lizard-eyed lady at my high school graduation.

On my first day at work, I was happy to see that my new boss had ditched her black suit for a brightly colored satin shirt and tan pants. She was incredibly friendly and visibly excited to have me as part of the team.

As I got to know her during that first week, she seemed like a good boss. She was slightly older than I thought, but she was very interested in my thoughts and ideas. She made it a priority to talk with me individually in her cushy office, at least once a day. Most of this time was spent talking about her general ideas, other research that related to our projects, and specific areas of concern that she could talk about outside of a secure space. That first week, Eris even got me connected with the Search for Extraterrestrial Intelligence team, after I asked if she knew anything about "SETI."

She explained that SETI had transformed into a group of telescopes and other monitoring methods of interstellar communications across the world. She told me about how a team was actually deployed to study the use of gravitational waves and neutrinos. Another group was being tasked with developing a more cost-effective way to setup our transmitters and our receivers to locate target star systems that might have intelligent life. And yet, another group was studying the advanced properties of sound waves and the ability to communicate in different ways.

When she said "different" I could tell there was more to the story, but that she couldn't share what she knew. She thought I would actually fit in better with a branch under SETI called CETI. Which I later found out was an acronym for Communications with Extraterrestrial Intelligence.

Needless to say, I was excited to be part of her team. However by the end of day two, I needed a stress therapy dog to calm my nerves. After an extensive search, I found an adorable mostly black, white chested, French Bulldog puppy. I named him Woola after my favorite science fiction alien character from the 2012 movie "John Carter." The Calot from that movie had a gigantic gaping mouth and ran at extreme speeds, just like my Woola. It was a perfect name for my little bundle of snorting, farting, and snuggling joy.

By the third day of work, I decided to reenroll at my local karate dojo to blow off some steam and get more balance in my life.

Back at work, each morning and as a team, we had a stand-up type planning meeting to discuss any new developments as they related to Eris's scope of work that she had agreed to complete for the government. The meeting always had three questions. What tasks are you working on? When will you be done with those tasks? And are there any areas of concern with those assigned tasks?

By the end of the week, I was feeling comfortable with the routine and learning about the role I was going to play as an intern for Eris.

On Friday morning, just before we started around the circle to collect project status, she cheerfully announced, "I am going to add one more question to our standup meeting." Without waiting for a response, she added, "I would like to know if you receive any ideas or thoughts about space travel or the existence of other worlds, outside of work."

I was first in the circle to report progress and when I got to the fourth question I announced, "I wonder if the Earth's core is a giant crystal and if the points of the crystal are portals to other worlds." Then I innocently shrugged my shoulders and flashed my pearly whites.

One of the cyber guys quickly raised his hand in the air like a schoolboy and sarcastically reported.

"Interesting development in the shower today, but I am sad to report, it is on a need-to-know basis."

Most of us coughed out loud and tried to stifle our laughter. Eris on the other hand was visibly annoyed.

"This is a serious question. We have an important role to play in this organization."

She took a deep breath, as if she was trying to gain her composure and then added some clarification to her request by saying, "There is no need to share if you don't want to, but sometimes great ideas are pulled out of the universe and hit you like train wreck at night. We are doing great things for humankind. They are relying on us to get this right." She pushed her glasses further up her pointed nose and then for some reason gazed at me with intensity.

I remember cringing a little inside. Not because of her weird gold and green eyes, but because I knew that the universe didn't want to share any ideas with me. The universe had abandoned me and unfortunately Eris appeared to be my only hope to find the answers I was looking for.

As that year passed by, I gained new knowledge about the tools being used in interstellar exploration and I discovered new friendships with super smart people. Eris was always by my side as I strategically planned and implemented experiments in her department. She assigned me to personally deep dive into a few aspects of Einstein's motion time dilation theories, the Drake equation, electromagnetic antigravity propulsion, the idea that Planet Earth was divided into twelve triangles, and even retrocognition and precognition ideas.

We even added a few tasks to keep an eye on other private sites that were collecting videos, pictures, and testimonials about unusual sightings across the world. Some of the more prominent and active sites included the National UFO Reporting Center (NUFORC) and the Mutual UFO Network (MUFON).

To give Eris credit, many of the ideas discussed seemed a bit crazy, but because our team had thrown them out there at the standup meetings, she wanted me and only me to look into them. The team appreciated her thoroughness and diligence when most in upper management would have called my team a little bit coo coo for cocoa puffs.

As I reported the results of my findings to her first and then to the team. Her line of questioning led me to believe that she was doubtful there was anything out there. At one point, I dreaded to do the research, because I knew she would debunk them in front of my peers. It was as if she got pleasure proving me wrong in front of the team.

But every once and a while I would get a win, and although she had strange eyes and was super tough on me, we did create several patentable items that had to remain in a highly classified environment. Unfortunately, this meant that I was developing and creating cool things that I couldn't tell anyone about. Including my overly inquisitive father or my best friend Maddy. My work environment became a love and hate relationship that I learned to compartmentalize.

On my graduation day from the university, Eris offered me a full-time position. I was only twenty years old. It paid very well. The job that she offered was sold to me as a critical position within one of the government's most secret institutions. I must have made them happy because they kept throwing exorbitant amounts of money at me.

It only took me a year before they offered me one of the highest clearances available and provided the opportunity to gain entry into Special Access Program Facilities. They told me they would provide me with the best technological solutions, tools, and people to pursue the truth about extraterrestrial life form communications; if I passed the background checks.

I will never forget the polygraph test process. I was shocked that I actually passed because one of the questions they asked was, "Do you believe in alien life forms."

Without overthinking the definition of "alien" I responded with a resounding, "NO!"

Somehow their lie detector machine believed what I said. I remember how pleased Eris was when she found out that I had passed. And that fact, passing this test, helped to convince me that it must be the truth. What I experienced and felt in my dreamworld must not have been real. That truth became cemented in my mind, as months of research and testing produced no solid evidence of the alien world or a feasible means to actually travel through space to habitable planet zones across the universe.

Any beliefs that I had at 15 years of age, waivered, and suffered an eventual death as the proof piled up against my hypothesis. My hopes of finding my beloved Sajan started to fade, day by day. I began to forget the song that the Amaranthine teachers and Henoch had ingrained into my soul. As time flew by, it was looking like it was going to be me and my dog against the world.

When I completed my master's degree and enrolled into a highly competitive program to obtain an Accelerated Metaphysics PhD, Eris encouraged me to focus my studies on paranormal type communications called Anomalous Research. After a little coaxing, I signed up for a class that was called "Remote Viewing." A part of me still had some hope in finding my alien friends and the curriculum sounded kind of cool.

Unfortunately, I quickly found out that I wasn't very good at remote viewing. I couldn't seem to concentrate on the target they were giving me. It was like there was a block in my brain and I was being stopped from projecting my thoughts outward. My professors and Eris discouraged me from taking the more advanced class after I had several failed attempts to pass the final test.

Oddly enough, that same week, Eris asked that I spend more of my time on researching space technology and communications. She implied that I wasn't spending enough time in this area and indirectly asked if there was more I could be doing.

After being passively reprimanded by Eris, I decided to quit my karate class at my local dojo, even though I was months away from an attempt to earn my black belt. My Sensei was very disappointed, but as always, he was very gracious and understanding. When I told Eris this development, she was very pleased with my commitment to her program.

About a week later, Eris pulled me into a sensitive compartmentalized information facility (SCIF). I was beyond nervous, because these types of facilities were only for the most secure National Security type discussions. Anything said in there never left. If it did, you could be fined exorbitant amounts of money and even thrown into jail.

However, without telling me anything super-secret at all, she recommended that I work with NASA on several components of a TOP SECRET space transportation and communications program. As usual, with compartmentalized information, I only had a need to know for a couple of sections. I was never privy to the function or overall construction of the different spaceships and or any other collateral uses of the technology that we were developing. However, she did share that the parts that I would be working on were related to some of my earlier work that I had done for CETI.

On my 25th birthday, I successfully obtained my PhD with honors. I was immediately promoted to a Program Director position. For some reason, the government decided that I was ready to manage their remote viewing and interstellar communications branch. Eris became one, of many advisors. I was given a secure lab full of really smart scientists and engineers and for the most part we were left alone. We were tasked with finding anything that was unexplainable beyond the Earth's atmosphere. This included unidentified objects and unusual or unexplainable communications.

My team consisted of three carefully selected and vetted remote viewers. These special people had been tested extensively on their abilities and benefits to the program. All three of them were kind of weird and overly sensitive to normal social situations.

I made it a priority to do everything I could to keep them happy. As I got to know them better, the thought that they could be classified as savants, crossed my mind. I discovered that they had better performance if they were fed their favorite foods, had a safe environment, and they had comfortable areas to think uninterrupted. I learned to give them their space and not put too much pressure on them. Eventually they would emerge with visions of interesting things that they had somehow magically picked up on.

Ironically, I had studied and even practiced some of what these seasoned professionals had mastered. I understood what they were going through and could relate to their trials and tribulations related to their focus tactics and finding vague targets. The ultimate goal, as a remote viewer, was to find things, usually thousands of miles away. Once the target was located, they would scratch out notes and sometimes draw pictures about what they could sense. The weird part was these remote viewers didn't actually have any details on what the target was. They did most of their viewing in a windowless secure area.

Two of the remote viewers that I had on my team were retired Navy intelligence officers. They had supported several wars around the world. The government had a special secret program, back in the 80's and 90's, that tasked them to find technology that our adversary was using. They had an 80% success rate. Which meant they pulled together enough specifics about the location that our special forces found it, and then either destroyed it or safely returned it back to the states.

The third viewer was a less-experienced older woman that was found by accident via one of our male remote viewers. Max was doing some side work to find a missing person for the police and found her instead. She was throwing suicidal thoughts out into the atmosphere and Max crossed their path. He reached out to her and they met. Then she joined the team after she was tested. She was still coming up to speed under the tutelage of the other two more experienced men.

The rest of my interstellar communication team was a bunch of introverted nerdy cyber guys. They happily manipulated their code to meet the hypothesis of the day. As long as I provided bucket loads of chocolate and checked in every once and a while they were in algorithm heaven. When an incident of concern was identified, we all got together and worked through protocol to try to figure out what caused it. Eris was usually lurking, either remotely via a secure channel or physically in our meeting room, to hear our conclusions.

Most of the time the concern was a false alarm. Which was usually associated with a military drill or an international miscommunication. When communication oddities were not able to be identified, my team usually got involved. Our remote viewers were usually able to discern the target as a satellite, an unidentified meteor, explainable atmospheric-type events, or in some cases space junk.

We also had access to any world-renowned volcanologists, cosmologists, oceanography experts, astrophysicists, and any other credible and willing participants across the world that we might need to help us investigate anomalies.

That same year I bought my first house. It was a cute 800 square foot two-bedroom house on Perkins Street in Richland. It was only a short drive from my office and it was close to my favorite Mexican restaurant called Isla Bonita. The house was a fixer upper and luckily my dad had a lot of experience in this area. After two months of ripping out cabinets, flooring, and a complete redo of the bathroom, Woola and I moved in.

Once we moved in, I saw my dad often. In fact, almost every weekend so that he could help me fix issues related to my house. Which we eventually started to lovingly call the money pit. However, my dad seemed to enjoy the money pit, because he was always whistling while we worked. Which was a big indicator of his happy meter. When he was feeling joy, he could not help it. Hearing him whistle always lifted my spirits.

Back at work, after a year of my team investigating communication anomalies, we only had a dozen incidents of concern that we couldn't explain away. When that happened, they were taken out of our hands and given to another division within the National Security Department. We were never privy to their findings because of a need-to-know clause. It was really annoying.

One Friday afternoon, my team and I had just finished up our quarterly review with high-ranking DHS management. Eris was in attendance, as usual, but for some reason she was dressed in her black suit and black retro hat. She was hanging on every word I was saying. Almost like she knew something and was going to jump in if needed.

However, when we provided the summary of our findings and we reported that all areas were explainable, she slumped back in her high-backed leather chair. With her weird behavior and wardrobe choices, I ran through the data we had just presented and wondered if I had missed something. When I looked her way, she gave me a slight upturned smirk. It was almost like she was reading my thoughts.

I guess I should have been happy that Eris was pleased about our results, but every time we reported, "nothing to see here," it frustrated me. Mostly because my hopes to find life other than the human race was dissipating. The evidence for alien life outside our world was becoming clear. And this particular day was the final nail in my coffin that made me realize that my silly teenage years were just that, silly.

After the out brief, all I could do was collapse into my cushy and overpriced office chair and feel sorry for myself. Like a frog in a slowly heating pot of water, I had been gradually convincing myself that Henoch, Evania, and most importantly Sajan did not really exist. While I was having my pity party and clearing off my desk to tackle another incident of concern from Colorado, Eris had unknowingly shuffled up behind me. She started to pat my shoulder, and I jumped several inches. Her gold and green reptilian-colored eyes found mine and without words, she gave me a nod of approval. Then she briskly walked away.

I thought I heard an unspoken whisper that said, "Good job," but this time I didn't look around for Henoch or any other imaginary creatures from my dreams. I just followed the steps of Eris out of the room.

When I finally dragged myself home, it was the usual flip through the home and garden channels, check my mail, and pet the dog kind of night. Woola was on my lap. His dark, shiny lips were vibrating with each breath he took. He was very relaxed. In fact, maybe he was a little too relaxed because he kept fart bombing me and giving me his satisfied silly dog grin. That's when the phone rang.

It was weird timing, mostly because I never get phone calls that late, or ever, really. Unless it's an emergency, of course. I certainly didn't have any friends to just chit chat with and I knew that Maddy, my only real friend, was on vacation in Australia. Annoyed, because I was betting it was one of those telemarketer calls, I picked up Woola's outstretched paw and moved him aside as I reached for the phone. Peering down, I remember being immediately concerned as I answered the phone.

"Dad, what's up? You okay?"

"Dariann, you better turn on the news? Sounds like you got some work to do."

I pushed off Woola, because he had jumped back in my lap, and found a local news station. The words "Breaking News," were flashing along the bottom. A guy named Ted was talking to the camera, but all I saw was the little imbedded window within a window that showed the blinking red and white lights of the nuclear power plant on the Hanford Reservation. This site was about thirty minutes from my house. There were multiple flashing blue and red lights on all sides of the reporter that were coming from the fire department, the local police, and the Hanford Patrol.

When Ted's videographer panned the skyline, you could see something coming towards them. Ted and the cameraman actually said, "What the hell is that?" in unison. When the lights that surrounded the circular cement steam vents of the nuclear power plant suddenly blinked out. That is when the cameraman started to cuss profusely and then the video cut out. A millisecond later, the TV went black.

When I mumbled in the phone, "Ummmm. That is concerning."

There was heavy breathing in my ear and then my dad uncharacteristically whispered, "Dariann, you need to go figure this out."

As I looked at the dark TV with unbelieving eyes I thought to myself, "Why me?" But instead, I said, "Hey Dad, gotta go to work," and then I hung up.

At that moment the TV feed came back up. In the camera frame you could see three bright orange orbs in a triangle formation that were flying super-fast over the site, in the opposite direction. The guy on the news was almost screeching with excitement. His brain was not comprehending the events that were unfolding in front of him. Within seconds, somehow, he had gained his composure.

"Well Leslie, all I know at this moment is that they flew over the hills from the direction of Othello at speeds witnesses said they had never seen before. The military has already scrambled several jets. I can hear a helicopter coming from the North."

I knew from experience that the triangular shaped orbs had completed several maneuvers that were not currently feasible with any known technology that we had today. The cameraman could not track them fast enough as they flew in and out of the frame from one side of the dark horizon to the other. Just as the camera feed cut out again, I saw that Eris was calling my phone. I immediately picked it up and without saying hello, she calmly said, "I am assuming you saw them. Relax tonight, but tomorrow is going to be busy." She didn't even wait for me to acknowledge her before hanging up.

And all I could say to Woola was, "Relax! Hah!"

The next day my team found out that multiple authorities were called in and that the system controls and cameras were being reviewed at the power plant. The nuclear operators were grilled on what they had seen and done during that night's shift. Several hundred people around the state were interviewed. Most of them had volunteered to provide their side of the story.

The white house administration had even been contacted to understand if any military operations and or foreign-related type drills had taken place that we were not aware of.

At the end of two days of intense and thorough investigation the preliminary results were in. Secretly the authorities had found that they had no way to explain what had happened. The public, of course was given the predetermined scripted message to ease their fears of an alien invasion.

In fact, that afternoon, Ted, the newscaster who had witnessed the ordeal first hand, was running interference for the government. He had already been convinced to change his thoughts about what he had seen.

"Well Leslie, it looks like another false alarm for alien life forms. We were informed by the National Security Division that we should not be afraid. They will be doing a thorough investigation and get back to us on what they find."

As an afterthought, he added, "These things take time, as you know."

Behind closed doors, my team and I knew what was being said. No one on this Earth, as far as I knew, could explain what had happened. While sitting at my desk, waiting for Eris's call to action, her conversation about the addition of the fourth question at our daily standup meetings floated through my thoughts. I flashed back to that day where she said, "This is a serious question. Sometimes great ideas are pulled out of the universe and hit you like a train wreck at night. We are doing great things for humankind. We have an important role to play. They are relying on us to get this right."

And for the second time in my life, I wondered who "they" were. Within seconds of this thought, the phone rang, and Eris excitedly announced, "They have exhausted all plausible explanations. It is go time. Stay tuned for more direction."

When she hung up without waiting for a response, I told the silent receiver in my hand, "They better hurry up."

Because the community was tight nit, the residents of Tri-Cities were talking, and they were freaking out. They were demanding answers. With the realization of what was ahead, I remember rubbing my temples and nervously chuckling to myself, because my reclusive, weird, and introverted nerdy team was their only hope and Eris knew it.

And with that thought in mind, a little flicker of hope stirred deep within me.

15

DÉJÀ VU

———⌘———

I T TOOK HALF a day for the DHS and NASA to draft up the statement of work for our team. Due to the nature of our highly sensitive and secretive work, they wanted to make sure that my team was only given the specific areas that we needed to know to get our investigation completed. It took another half day for Eris to pull the information that we could actually get access to. By that evening, I was slightly annoyed with their snail-like pace. I must have been exuding bad vibes through the air, because right before I left Eris walked in unannounced.

"Patience, Dariann. You and your team can get started in the morning."

Then, as usual, she walked out before I could respond.

The next day the approved investigative charter and a pile of files were waiting for my team, in the secure lab. My team was buzzing with excitement. We had finally been given the green light to do what we were all trained to do. We quickly got to work to try to figure out why there were unidentified orange orbs flying over a nuclear plant disrupting the power supply.

We all agreed we needed to have two standup meetings per day. The schedule that my bosses had constrained us to was aggressive and I knew that the results of our investigation would be highly scrutinized. And I needed to get this right. About two hours after giving the team time to review some of the files, we had our first standup meeting.

Immediately, my team started to grumble that they did not have enough information to discover the true nature of the orange orbs. They felt that my superiors were holding back critical information that they needed to know. Specifically, the findings of previous cases that my team had worked on that were ripped out of their control, when they had classified them as unexplainable. After a very unproductive and frustrating meeting, I excused the team and sought out Eris.

When I knocked on her expensive dark wood door in the executive wing of DHS, I noticed, for the first time, that her door had a gold inlay of a lizard head. As I studied it, a wave of vertigo and déjà vu hit me. I felt light-headed as I stumbled a few steps backwards. I suddenly had this strange feeling that I had seen this door in a dream.

Eris slowly opened the door. It creaked like one of those scary horror flicks, when the murderer with an axe jumps out. Instead of an axe she had a creepy look on her face. Behind horn-rimmed glasses, her weird eyes were stuck in a motionless stare as I pulled myself together.

"Dariann, I'm surprised to see you. Don't you have a big project to finish up. We have a lot of individuals interested in your findings."

I took a step forward.

"Yeah, about that, we need to talk."

She stepped back a few feet, opened up the door wide and ushered me in. She hovered over to her high-backed leather chair and scooted up to her bigger than life desk. It was of course made of the darkest most expensive woods you could find. Each leg, which I had never noticed before, was carved like a snake. As she shuffled papers on her desk and closed a few open drawers, she pointed to a stiff-backed puke green chair. I sat down and straightened up like my dad had just barked out, "Quit slumping before you stay that way permanently." Eris took a deep steady breath and folded her hands in front of her.

"So what's up my dear?"

Annoyed by her condescending tone, I took a quick breath, blew it out and asked, "What's really going on Ms. Cosbee?"

Her green and gold eyes started to blink rapidly.

"Can you please rephrase the question?"

Immediately, after asking me this question, she looked down at her desk as if she was seeing something that I couldn't. When she looked back up she looked composed, while she impatiently waited for my answer.

That was when her phone rang. She looked over at the black contraption that had a classic land line twisted cord handset attached to it. My brain spontaneously began to sing, "The telephone is ringing," which reminded me of the 1971 Alice Cooper song, "Under My Wheels." As I was jamming out in my head, Eris was trying to ignore her phone. But when it rang a third time she reached over and picked it up and quickly snapped, "Kind of busy Alice, it better be an emergency."

Alice, whomever that was, was practically shouting in the phone. Which made me spontaneously laugh out loud.

Eris scowled, hung up the phone, abruptly scooted out of her chair, and pointed at me.

"I will be right back, don't move." Then she trotted out of the room.

For some reason she closed the door.

After a few moments of silence, I became annoyed and started to feel a little defiant. I popped out my chair and started to saunter around her office. I was curious about Eris. She didn't socialize outside of her job, and I was thinking that maybe I could find some clues about what makes her tick when she wasn't stalking around my lab. Maybe I could find a soft spot in her thick as nails armor.

The floor to ceiling shelves were made from the same dark wood as her mammoth-sized desk. They were filled with all kinds of scientific journals and books. One shelf held glass etched trophies that outlined the accomplishments that landed her this big cushy office. The pictures on her wall were mostly pictures that had been taken by the Hubble space station years ago. They were cool, but not very personal. When I gingerly stepped behind her desk, I felt a tiny bit guilty. It didn't stop me from snooping though. When I shuffled forward, my shin hit the corner of an open desk drawer that she had failed to close upon my unexpected arrival.

I yelped and whispered, "Damnit Dariann, what the hell are doing?" and then impulsively reached down and rubbed my throbbing leg.

While down there, I couldn't help but peek into the open drawer. It was full of a variety of papers and small notebooks. One of them was a purple spiral bound notebook. It was the kind of notebook that you use in elementary or high school. And all I could think was, "Why would a highly educated and seasoned professional like Eris use a kid's notebook?"

But before I could investigate the notebook further, I was distracted by another discovery. With complete lack of emotional intelligence, I fell to my knees and reached for a single loose sheet of paper that was far beneath her desk. I was surprised to find a red winged butterfly with the number 88 on its lower wings. Eris had scribbled the words, "Found in Central and South America." The butterfly looked alien to me. I had never seen it before and I thought to myself, "Ha, she likes bugs, now that makes sense." I put the paper back where I found it and struggled to pull myself back to my feet.

That is when I noticed that under her large, unused desk organizer, another loose sheet of paper was sticking out. However, this time, there was a leg of a creature that looked very familiar.

As I battled with myself on how bad this was, a voice in my head egged me on by saying, "Don't be afraid. It will be okay." So, I reached down with incredible swiftness and yanked on the corner of the paper. I couldn't believe it.

There was a collage of creatures that I had only seen on Evania. There was a saber-toothed deer, a pink fluffy armadillo, and even a Potoo bird. When I flipped it over there was a goblin shark and a Japanese crab. Shocked and bewildered more than before, I quickly stuffed it back under the desk organizer and ran to my designated chair.

Within minutes, Eris returned. She resettled into her chair and smiled a sweet look that reeked of deception.

"So where were we?"

I took a deep breath and quickly decided to use her absence as my escape plan. I looked into her green and gold eyes and announced, "You know what, you are right, I need to get back to work." Without waiting for her response, I dramatically looked at my watch and explained, "I have a test that is timing out in a few minutes. My team was worried that we didn't have everything we needed to get this incident fully investigated, but I trust you to do the right thing Eris. So, I am going to go do what I do best."

Then I jumped up and briskly walked out of her office. As I left, I closed the door behind me. When I got back to my secure office, I put my head on my desk and had a conversation with myself.

"What just happened? Why does she have those pictures?"

But no answers came back. Just deafening silence and the whirring of my thoughts bouncing around in my brain. When I pulled myself together, I found my team, and gave them a well-rehearsed pep talk. Then I rummaged through my office and pulled up the materials from my remote viewing class. It was time to get back to work. It was time to figure this out.

At our second standup meeting of the day, to my surprise and disappointment, Eris was present. She was carrying a double wrapped and locked bag of secure documents under her arm. When it was her turn to give progress, she cleared her throat and straightened up.

"Dariann and I had a really good talk today." She looked at me with expectant eyes and I instinctively shook my head in a positive way to feed her facade.

"Dariann was right, you do need more information to do this investigation, so I have been able to gain permission to show you the results of a few of those cases that you started, but never finished. We also included a few other cases that you haven't seen yet. You can now use this information for this investigation."

My introverted team actually clapped their hands and gave intermittent appreciation for this information. Several of them walked over and shook her hand. I just stood back and watched the circus and hoped she would leave the room. Luckily one of my experiments, actually was timing out, and I had to leave for the computer lab. I could feel Eris's eyes burning a hole through my back as I scuttled out of her line of sight.

The next day, the team dissected the highly classified

information and integrated some of the tools, techniques, and tactics into the approach that we were using to investigate our strange orbs. There were the typical Project Bluebook type cases that all of us in that secret wing were very familiar with.

However, within some of the cases that our superiors allowed us to finally see, we discovered the answers to some of those mysteries. We read about what happened when the Apollo 11 crew turned off their video for two minutes when the crew landed on the moon. We discovered what was actually flying over the entire state of Arizona back in 2008. But the cases that were of most interest to my team were the incidents where several witnesses, which happened to be military personal of higher ranks, saw different colored orbs flying around supposedly well-hidden missile sites back in the 1970's and the 1980's.

Many of the root causes were attributed to secret purpose balloon experiments, an asteroid that our monitoring programs had missed, temperature anomalies, or in one case there was a large flock of whooping cranes that happened to reflect the lights in an ominous way. There were very few that could not be explained according to our most secretive element of our government. After careful review of all of this new data, our team decided to add a few new tasks to our plan to see if there were any similarities to our most recent orb fly by.

The mood around the different testing platforms was excitement and productivity. Every once and a while there would be an unrestrained, "Yes!" or the dreaded, "Oh Crap!" But overall, the team was in good spirits. It also helped that Eris didn't show up that day, which was a giant bonus in my book. We were making excellent strides towards discovering the true root cause of the mysterious orbs that seemed to cut off power to our critical energy generating station.

That night, while cuddling Woola, my phone rang once again. I was anxious to pick it up, because the last time I picked up this late at night, we had strange orange orbs flying around. But this time it was my cousin, Fanny. She was out of breath when I picked up the line.

"Dariann, I saw the news footage, those orbs, outside of the orange color, moved the same way as the orbs my dad and I saw so many years ago on the Oregon coast. Do you know what they are?"

Fanny knew that I couldn't tell her anything. But I gave her an honest vague answer.

"Not yet, we are working on getting to the bottom of it though."

She gave out a knowing chuckle and scoffed, "You mean like the bottom of Coffenbury Lake?"

I remember involuntarily gasping, because I had forgotten that Fanny knew about my experience at the lake. That she had believed me so many years ago. That she had told me not to forget. Fanny didn't wait for me to answer her question and whispered, "If I remember right, you are supposed to remember a special song."

Fanny quietly waited on the phone as I sat there in numbed silence. A whisper of the eagle and the white winged angel, that I saw under Coffenbury Lake, tickled my thoughts with, "There will be signs of our coming. Remember the song."

And I remembered that I had thrown all of my memories and the words of that song in the garbage over ten years ago. My notebook was no longer in my possession. After a few seconds of realizing my demise, I quietly replied to my faithful cousin, "Thank you for the reminder, Fanny. I wish I could remember."

Fanny's sadness for my loss could be felt through the phone line. She quickly changed the subject and asked me how Woola was. She knew how much I loved my dog. We had that in common. We truly and deeply loved our fur babies. After a few minutes of small talk, we said our goodbye's. However, her last parting words were, "Dariann, try to remember. I think it's important."

All I could choke out was, "Love you cuz. I truly appreciate you."

My professional integrity didn't allow me to talk to Fanny about what I was doing in the investigation, but I wished that I could, because she had seen these orbs in person. I felt like I owed her that truth at least. And I vowed to dig through the case files and see what the resolution was on my uncle's sighting that was closed so many years ago.

I went in early the next day, found the files that Eris had given us, and tried to find the file on the strange blue balls of light that had erratically flown over the Pacific Ocean that one late night. I flipped through each file folder and found absolutely nothing. It was as if it had never happened. I remember groaning out loud in frustration. Just as I was placing the documents back into the secure safe, Eris coughed behind me.

"Finding everything you need."

Startled and nervous by her appearance, I shut the safe door and twirled the lock to secure the files. As I turned around, I composed myself.

"Everything is going well. Thank you for your help. If you will excuse me, I have a test that is timing out in a few minutes."

Then, without waiting for a response, I turned my back on her and walked away.

16

NOTHING TO SEE HERE

⌒⌒⌒

BEFUDDLED BY MY weird reaction to Eris, I sat down on my rolling stool, placed my right hand on the desk, and began to thrum my fingers across my computer keyboard. My computer was turned off, but the tapping gave me solace. On the dark screen of my computer was a hot pink sticky note, that I had not placed there.

It had, "Need to talk ASAP," scribbled on it. Beneath the message, there was a set of numbers and symbols. After a few seconds of head scratching, I realized that what I was looking at represented a certain point in the Cartesian plane. They were specific coordinates to something or someone.

Using my remote viewing skills, I started to envision school-age children on roller skates going in circles. There was obnoxious music and a disco ball flashing above them. Then I saw rows and rows of different kinds of ice cream. I recognized that location right away. It was a place that I had worked, when I first turned sixteen to get a few bucks. Unfortunately, as my first job, it ended on a bad note when I asked for time off to attend the local Hydroplane races. My new boss didn't care that these boat races were one of the biggest events in my little town outside of the annual Sausage Fest that was hosted by the local Catholic church. After the owner of Baskin Robbins fired me, I remember being relieved, because I kept eating too much ice cream when customer traffic was slow. As that memory faded, a new vision arrived.

I saw several bistro tables under a small overhang that was

supported by two walls. There was a two-person swinging chair that was held up by thick chains. A coffee cup with a hummingbird drawn on the top of the foamy latte was sitting on a table. A man in all black was sitting there reading an actual paper copy of the local newspaper. I immediately thought, "Old guy. Black suit. This should be interesting."

Satisfied with my target, I grabbed my coat and purse and jetted for the door. I was headed to The Coffee Bean. The best coffee in town, in my humble opinion, and the only coffee place that put hummingbird art on top of their lattes.

When I arrived at the coffee shop, surprisingly, there was a slim, nerdy looking older man with glasses dressed in black at one of the tables. I had never met him, but I knew that this was my guy. I decided to order a coffee with a hummingbird etched on the top. I plopped it next to his on his table. I slid into a chair that was directly across from him.

"Who are you and why were you in my office?"

He nervously reached for his own cup and wrapped both of his hands around it.

"I was sent to give you information, please don't kill the messenger." He lifted his dark shaded glasses, so that his round black eyes stared into mine. He had a slight upturned grin on his face as if he was half kidding.

Dumbfounded by his words and royally confused by this development. I decided to take a sip of my perfectly prepared hot drink and stare back at him. After he squirmed a bit, I added, "You didn't answer my questions."

He straightened himself in his chair.

"I was told to give you this." Then he slid a thin double-taped yellow envelope across the table. Without saying another word, he grabbed his to go coffee cup and quickly walked to his car like he had set a short-fused bomb on my table.

I watched him drive off past the Rollarena Skating Center. When I refocused on the envelope, I wasn't sure what to do. My cyber friends had taught me to be paranoid in weird circumstances and this was super weird. So instead of opening it there, I grabbed the package and walked off the premises. I actually looked behind me to see if someone was following me to my car. Not knowing what I had in my grasp, I decided to wait until I got home to open it.

Back at work, I was distracted. I could not stop thinking about the unopened package in my car. I decided after our end of day standup meeting that I was going to head home early. The team was making good progress on our set of testing protocols. They didn't need me hanging around.

At home, I placed the package on the kitchen counter and patted it.

"We will get to know each other better later." I was nervous on what I was going to find. I needed some food and some Woola time.

Woola was very amenable to my wishes, and we cuddled up on the couch to watch a little mindless TV. Ironically the series we were watching was about time travel and the ability to bounce around in different dimensions. Although fascinating, it kept reminding me of the package sitting on my counter, so I turned it to the Animal Planet channel and watched a program about see-through frogs. Eventually Woola and I dozed off to the deep rhythmic tone of Morgan Freeman calmly talking about the rain forest and all of its endangered occupants.

What seemed like only seconds had passed, I heard, "Wake up sleepy head. Open the package. We need some help over here."

I was jostled awake by a voice that I had not heard in a very long time. Woola jumped off the couch and started to bark at the air. As I panned the room, there was nothing there. Just to make sure I asked, "Is someone there?"

Woola began a whole new series of French Bulldog barks, grabbed his bamboo bone, and snorted over to me like he had not seen me for hours. After giving him a few pats on the head and realizing I was having one of those night terror dreams, I walked to the kitchen and decided it was time.

I got out a pair of scissors and slid one of the blades along the well-tapped top of the unmarked envelope. As the contents dumped out onto my kitchen island, I jumped back like it was full of spiders. A key clanked across the island and bounced to the floor. Once again, Woola started barking at the air. But this time he ran for his fluffy dog bed, that I called his girlfriend. He curled up into a black ball and buried his head under the blanket.

After another shake of the envelope a single piece of paper floated out and landed on the counter. I gingerly picked it up and noticed that it had a picture shaped like a stop light but with more colors than red, yellow, and green. Each round circle of color had a messy hand drawn arrow to a number from 1-12. I had no idea what it meant, so I stooped down and picked up the key. It looked like a normal key for a door lock. Except there was a small picture of what looked like a snake or a lizard head on the handle portion of the key. Not having any idea what either item meant, I shoved them back in their envelope and went to bed incredibly frustrated.

In the morning, at our standup meeting, as we were going around the room to collect status, one of the cyber guys on our team nonchalantly mentioned, "Oh, I forgot to mention Eris dropped by last night. She wanted to make sure we had the final report results from the interviews, assessments, and investigations of the nuclear power plant personnel."

When he announced this, I was slightly surprised that she didn't give it to me directly.

"Well, what did it say?"

Thick with sarcasm, he announced, "It was the number four reason that they usually blame it on." Several of my team members chuckled under their breath.

After a few moments, he added, "They are saying the orbs were not related to the power plant. One of the operators screwed up and accidently hit a wrong button. That is why the power went out. The report said they fired the guy. His name was Homer something." A whole new round of laughter erupted.

When they were done, I looked at him.

"Seriously? Finding a fall guy was their answer."

He gave me a half-nod and a look that told me that whoever wrote that report wasn't really that interested in the orbs. They just wanted a reason to move past the incident. Regardless of this new information I asked the team to reconsider the data one more time, and then we went back around the table.

As my team tried to find new data-based reasons to explain the orbs, I could tell they were stressing out. Based on the other reports that we had recently become privy to, they had claimed that all orb incidents were related to reflections, misuse of rogue lasers, odd weather patterns, or something else that was unusual, but explainable. My team had no evidence or new findings to concretely say that the orbs were a national security risk or that they were extraterrestrial. They also agreed that it could have been any of the reasons that had been used to explain them in the past.

In the end, we pretty much decided that the new information that Eris had suddenly unearthed, made it look like the orbs could have been any of the past reasons that had been used to explain previous orb sightings. I was glad that Eris wasn't there with us that day. I knew the time was coming when they would want our final answer and we would have to give an update to the individuals that were way above my pay grade. I did one last look around the room.

"Are we saying we have no idea if these orbs have any kind of relation to the power plant outage?"

They all shook their head in agreement with my statement, except two of my team members. Max, my remote viewer, tentatively raised his hand.

"What's up Max?"

"So, I might have something. But as always, no concrete evidence, outside of my pictures and notes and general feelings."

Not wanting to disturb whatever focus and connection he was having, I quietly waited for him to continue. He was tightly holding the paper that had his chicken scratch on it from his most recent remote viewing session. After a few moments of awkward silence, he finally stuttered out, "When searching the coordinates of the orbs in the six reports that we finally got access to, I found some kind of connection. In fact, I heard a possible voice that needed help, maybe?"

He got this grimace on his face like he was realizing how weird his story was sounding. But none of us in that room were laughing, especially Ally, the woman that he had saved from killing herself.

When we didn't poke fun at him, he quietly added, "For example, the red and white orb incident that happened in September over

Ohio. In the recordings that I listened to; I kept getting 'I am number eight.' Then it would change to 'I am number one.' I know it sounds really weird. The special team that was sent out to investigate it said it was just a really bright star alternating colors in a freak cold weather pattern. But I am not sure after hearing those voices." Then he kind of cowered to the back of his chair expecting criticism. We all sat there contemplating this new information, when Ally raised her hand.

I nodded at her to speak.

"You know, I wasn't going to say anything, but I actually looked deep into the incident in Pennsylvania that happened in July. I listened to the actual recordings of the incident. I could have sworn I heard someone say, 'I am number one.' It was a white sphere that flew near the Washington-Dulles Airport. Our guys went to investigate the person that reported it, and they closed it out quickly afterward. They claimed it was just an airplane reflection against the clouds, but I am not quite sure that is the truth."

As they were talking, a memory of something about orb colors creeped into my thoughts. Then I looked up at the team and almost pleaded, "Please keep this to yourself. I need to figure out how to handle this new information."

Just as we were finishing up the meeting, Eris walked in. The team scattered to their sections of the Lab. Eris followed closely behind me.

"Anything new? They want an update tomorrow."

Aware that Max and Ally were just a few feet away, I offered, "Nothing new to report Eris. You will be the first to know."

I must have been convincing, because she did a few scans of the room and didn't press for any more information. However, she did turn to me and say, "I need to see you in my office 8:00 a.m. sharp, tomorrow. I would like to know what type of progress you will be reporting to my superiors." As usual, without waiting for a response she walked out.

That night I spent several hours pulling together as much as I could for the briefing that I was giving the next day. The secret elements would have to be added in the morning at the SCIF. When I finally made it to my bed, I was exhausted and fell into a deep sleep. Like the night before I dreamed that I heard voices. They were quite distraught and kept saying over and over again, "Did you open it? Do you understand? Do you remember?" But when I opened my eyes, there was no one there.

There was nothing to see.

17

ALIEN DISCERNMENT

<hr>

THAT MORNING I arrived early, completed the proposed progress report, and headed to Eris's office. I arrived at 8:00 a.m. sharp. Her door was closed. Annoyed, I reached up and then hesitated as I looked at the lizard figure on her door. I had that same feeling, as before, that I had seen it somewhere. Then Eris opened the door and escorted me in. When we got settled in our chairs, with clasped hands, she demanded some answers.

"Did you get that new report? What kind of conclusions can we expect from your team today?"

Knowing she would ask; I regurgitated my already prepared and practiced answer.

"As far as our data can conclude, especially with the addition of the new report, this incident was isolated and explainable. There is a conspicuous absence of solid evidence to indicate that we are not alone."

I was shocked when she said, "Good answer. I will see you at the briefing. Thank you, Dariann. Please close the door behind you."

So, I jumped up and skipped out of there as fast as I professionally could.

When my team and I showed up to the meeting. The room was configured like a high-level court room.

Seated on a raised platform were the Secretary of Defense, several National Security Officers, members of all of the three letter organizations, and of course Eris. Eris was dressed in her black uniform. They all sat in expensive leather seats. A matching cup of something was perfectly spaced on the long thin desk in front of them. The rest of us were organized in rows below them on a concrete surface in cold metal chairs.

When it was my turn to address them, I stood up and provided our results as scripted. My final and strategically planned oxymoronic statement to my well-dressed and pressed superiors was, "As far as our data can conclude, this incident was isolated and explainable. There is a conspicuous absence of solid evidence to indicate that we are not alone."

When I looked at Eris, she had a satisfied look on her face. Happy with my delivery of this important message, I shook everyone's hand and found my way back to my home away from home – my work office, of course.

As I was rocking back and forth in my chair, I was peering out my oversized picture window that overlooked the tallest, treeless mountain in the United States. I was wondering if I should have disclosed the circumstantial evidence that Max and Ally had just uncovered the day before, but I knew that it would be criticized with great scrutiny. I knew that "feelings," even if they were government-funded did not carry enough weight to take action one way or another. So, I decided to wait to disclose those particular findings, with hopes to investigate my remote viewers' inklings, when we had more time to do so.

I reached for the infamous envelope that was tucked into my locked briefcase and opened it back up. After pouring out the contents, I stroked the key and studied the color code stop light figure that was tied to the numbers 1-12. With an exasperated whisper I called out to the air.

"Please, help me understand this."

I was startled as a response tickled the back of my brain.

"There will be twelve on the Interstellar Contact Council. There are twelve points of entry. The key is in the doors."

I mumbled to myself, "If I only had that notebook." And just like that I knew what the key was for. I knew where my notebook was. The big question was, "Why did she have it? Which side was she really on?"

This is when I saw the slowly moving triangular shaped structure cascade across my view with the backdrop of the magnificent

Snake Mountain. The alien ship was a metallic shimmering shape that shined like a diamond in the otherwise clear blue sky. The hot desert sun beat down on its foreign luminescent composition. It pulsed a bright white light, all around the perimeter. I could hear the occupants in the offices next to mine gasp in awe as their realities were shattered by the view outside their window. Oddly enough, I felt calm and collected because deep in my soul, I knew they would come. The joy in my heart was hard to conceal because I knew I would see him again.

A voice boomed through my brain cells that said, "I am #1." My phone immediately rang, it was Max. He was out of breath. He had heard the message too and I told him I would call him right back.

I sat there in silent wonder as a familiar voice began to sing through my mind. "I was chosen to meet Your call. I train so that I can stand tall. I answer, because of Your love. Worthy are You, our Conductor above. I trust without sight. Reaching for the light. Even if pursuit of right is a fight. His final gifts outweigh this plight. I strive to do no wrong. I will sing His special song."

Then just as suddenly the bright white orb raised directly upwards into the clouds and disappeared. A whole new set of gasps and colorful language erupted from my hallway. Within minutes, those that had literally just seen this unidentified flying phenomenon in front of them, were already questioning their sanity. I shook my head in disbelief of their stigmatized brainwashing and got up and closed my door.

For me, I had a deep understanding of what this arrival meant. As I sat there watching the quiet, now normalized sky, my memories began to play back that forgotten song. It gently carried me to the place that I had written about so long ago. I remembered Evania. I remembered Henoch. But most of all I remembered every detail about Sajan. My heart quickened with the idea that even though I had failed to find him, that maybe, just maybe, he had found me instead.

But I needed my notebook, and I needed help. I called Max back and asked if he could meet in the secure Lab. As if he had no idea that there was a sighting just outside our building, he was quick to respond, "Absolutely boss, see you down there."

Just before I left my office, I rummaged through my desk drawers, found what I needed, roughed it up a little, and shoved it down the side of my pants. I made sure it was covered under my expensive suit jacket. Then I quickly trotted to the secure lab. After a few moments of figuring out what I was going to actually say to him. Max rolled his eyes.

"Spit it out Dariann. I know there is something big going on here." He pointed to the ceiling and said, "The color of the orbs means something doesn't it?"

"I think so. I need your help to figure out the key to the orbs. I need your help to do something that is sort of against the rules."

Without hesitation he excitedly replied, "Cool, what are we breaking into?"

I looked at him and wondered if he knew more than he was letting on, but I told him about the special visit I had at the coffee shop and that I was 99% sure there was something in Eris's office that would help us. We immediately went into plan mode and ended up deciding that I would hang out in the bathroom, while he dragged Eris to the lab to see an exciting new development that he had found. We knew that what Max had discovered would interest her and we agreed he should tell her his preliminary findings. Especially since a white orb looking UFO was flying above our beloved town at that very moment. We agreed not to share Ally's information.

When it was time to go, he exploded into maniacal laughter, politely pointed me in the direction of her office, and sang, "Let's do this." As we walked out the door he started to quietly hum the dorky theme song from the "Mission Impossible" spy movie.

We did a very unprofessional high five in the eerily empty hallway and I jetted off to the restroom directly across from her office. A few minutes later I heard Max knock on her door. When she answered, clearly annoyed by the interruption, he practically yelled, "Eris, I can't find Dariann, but I need to show you what I found thanks to your help with those additional files. Please can you come with me and check it out. I think it will help discern what we got going on out there right now."

Max actually dragged out the please like a two-year-old would.

There was a hesitation and then a slow, "Okay, Max. but I only have about fifteen minutes that I can spare." There was a slight pause, where I imagined her pointing to the ceiling, then the words, "I'm a little busy today."

As they walked by I could hear Max chatter on about his research. He was using incredibly complicated verbiage and discussing how he found just the right set of commands to perfect his script. He reiterated how her help was instrumental to his success. For an introvert, Max was talking her ear off. When the door closed behind them, I slipped out of the bathroom and practically ran to her office. I didn't waste any time and had the key ready to insert into the door's lock. It fit perfectly and I turned it and twisted the knob. I closed the door behind me as fast as I could.

I trotted over to the desk drawer where my purple spiral notebook had last been seen. Within seconds I found it and replaced it with a different worn and torn purple notebook that I had stuffed down the side of my pants. Oddly enough, I had a few of these notebooks in my office. It was as if my subconscious knew I would need them some day.

However, my hopes were that if Eris happened to look in there, she would think it was still secure. With a swift uncharacteristic ethical breach, I shoved my old journal down my pants and left just as quickly as I had come. When I got to my office, I grabbed my belongings and quickly left the building. The purple notebook was securely hidden in my locked brief case by the time I jetted out of there.

When I finally got home, I was worn out, but eager to dig through my notes. With the color codes stoplight figure and the corresponding numbers, I was finally able to make the connection between the color of the orb and the different planets that were supposed to be part of the ICC. There were twelve in all, however, Planet #11 had not been assigned a color, at least according to the stop light document that I had received.

As I read through each type of creature, I shuddered when I read that a warrior-type reptile-looking species was called the 12th Command. Their orb color was green. I scoffed at the irony that the color green usually represented good. I could not stop thinking about the stories in the Bible, and how evil the 12th disciple had been.

On a brighter note, I realized that Henoch was number one. His particular species, the Grays, was known as the 1st Command. Their coat of arms color was white. As I read on in my notebook, I remembered learning that the Grays had a special relationship with the Conductor, that no one else did.

With a quickening of my heartbeat, I realized that today's bright white orb over Snake Mountain was Henoch's Command. When I jumped up, raised my arms in the air, and yelled, "Whoo hoo! Thank you Jesus."

Woola jumped out of his fuzzy bed with a loud snort. Then he planted all four of his paws in a protective stance next to me and started to bark at the air surrounding us. The black fur on the back of his neck was raised. I reached down and gave him a pet on the head.

"You get him big boy."

And then I chuckled to myself, because today had been such a good day of enlightenment. The joy of visible proof was overwhelming.

But with all of this great insight, I still could not figure out what Eris's role was in all of this. Was she bad or good? Which side was she really on? Could I trust her – especially since she had my discarded notebook in her possession and never told me? As all of these questions crashed into my thoughts a wave of vertigo hit me and I stumbled to the couch and closed my eyes. Mentally depleted, I decided to stay there for a few moments. Woola jumped up his carpeted steps, nosed in between my folded arms, and put his cute little face on mine. I was out in seconds. To Woola's complete surprise and enjoyment, I never made it to my bed after I passed out on the couch. Somewhere around 11:11 p.m. I woke up to a voice in my head.

"Hey! You forgot about me, didn't you?"

When my eyes adjusted to the darkness, there standing in my living room was a 3-foot-tall gray alien with giant blue eyes. He gave me a really slow half wave and drawn out, "I'mmmmmmmm back!"

Ignoring the alien in my living room, I frantically searched the room.

"Where is Sajan? Is he with you?"

Henoch shook his large round head.

"Sajan is on a special mission. I'm sorry Dariann." Seeing my disappointment he added, "Just like Sajan, it is time to do the tasks that you were trained for. It is time to become what you were destined to be and that is a Peacemaker for the 11th Command. Do you want it? He held out a delicate gold necklace that read, "I Am #11." Then he placed it on the table beside me and Woola.

I looked at the necklace on the coffee table beside me.

"What took you so long? I had lost hope. It's hard being a clueless human."

His thoughts reached out to me.

"With the planet rotations, Planet Earth and Amaranthine are the closest to each other every eleven years. Some of the humans, possibly with help from some of my kind, are fighting the truth about other types of life forms. They built some kind of device that stopped us from reaching you. Our orbs have been trying to penetrate the shield for several months. All eleven of the planet commanders have been trying to provide signs that they were coming back by sending our observation probes. Some made it, but many were destroyed. We are all now just congregating at a safe distance to avoid their new monitoring systems."

Without allowing me any time to respond, he asked, "You got the notebook, right?"

I just shook my head affirmatively, because honestly, I was a bit shell-shocked that he was actually there in front of me. Just like the first time we met, when our eyes locked, I was unable to move. This time I wasn't frightened, as I embraced the vision of the Evanian oceans in his big blue eyes. When he blinked, it was gone and he continued his thoughts.

"I have a mission for you. It will be difficult, but I know you can do this. I need you to pretend that you never saw me and that you never got your notebook back. Definitely do not share that you know how to decipher the orb colors. We believe there are spies in our ranks that want to hurt our peaceful integrations between the old and the new worlds. I need you to find out why we can't get through. I need you to find the technology that they installed that blocks our communication attempts. Can you do this?"

I was still in shock that Henoch was there, in my living room, and I just shook my head. But, in my mind I whined, "Yikes, okay, not a great liar though."

He nodded at this and said, "Understand, just read the notebook, remember your training." Then he turned like he was seeing something that wasn't' there, said a few unintelligible words, and looked back at me.

"The portal is closing. Gotta go for now. Remember the song, Dariann."

As an afterthought he added, "Oh, Eris is connected with the 11th Command. She should be good but proceed carefully with that relationship. I personally can't stand her." Then he disappeared like a twinkling tractor beam had transported him out of my living room.

Woola somehow slept through this entire experience. He let out a big loud snort as his smelly French Bulldog gas bomb wafted up into my nostrils. I scratched him on the head and gleefully cooed, "Good boy!" as I processed what had just happened.

My life, as I had known it, was over. A new life was getting ready to start. And with that thought, I reached over and picked up the necklace, put it around my neck, and became a Peacemaker for the 11th Command.

Whatever that meant.

18

I AM #11

IN THE MORNING, I pretended that my life was normal. I took a shower, brushed my teeth, had my coffee, fed Woola, and headed to work. Just like any other workday. I did, however, tuck my new gold necklace under my professional looking high buttoned top, just before I entered my office.

Within minutes Max was at my door, impatiently waiting outside, while I finished up a non-emergency phone call with my dad.

My dad was searching for answers about what had happened, and I had to remind him that I was not at liberty to fill him in. On that particular day, it was especially difficult to say no to my father's questions, because it was the anniversary of my mom's passing and the day before my birthday.

As soon as I placed the phone back in its cradle, my phone rang again, and it was Fanny. I looked up at Max, put a finger in the air, and quickly told Fanny I would call her back when I had a second. She sounded disappointed, but understood.

Max started to fiddle with the papers in his hands. He looked up with intense expectation on the stolen artifact that he had helped me steal. I could tell he wasn't sure if he should ask. I waved him out the door and directed him to a secure space so we could talk more freely.

Once there, I took a deep breath and reluctantly lied.

"So the item was a notebook, although it was funny to reminisce through my childhood thoughts and dreams, it didn't really help with the investigation. I'm sorry Max, I wish I had better things to report back."

I could tell he wanted to know more. Lucky for me, he was well-trained in the protocols of the secret environment that we worked in. Instead of asking more questions about a mysterious item of mine that was in Eris's office, we sat in silence. Eventually, to fill in that awkward gap, he offered a status report.

"Well Eris had no idea. She seemed very pleased with my viewing. She even made me repeat what I had said. She was very interested in the number that I had heard. I did not share that Ally had heard numbers too."

I released the breath that I didn't know that I was holding.

"Thanks Max. I wish I had more to share. It does seem weird that she would have it though. I will look into that as well. I might even directly ask her and see what happens."

Max cringed like I had slapped him across the face.

"Now that I will never do. She is scary."

As Max turned to leave he mouthed, "Good luck boss," just before he closed the door behind him.

In the silence, I pressed my forehead on the top of my desk and moaned at the room. "Ugh! Time for Eris one on one time." When I lifted up I had to pull a rogue hot pink sticky note from my forehead, before heading towards her floor. Eris was standing in the doorway of her office like she was waiting for me. Without saying a word, she stepped aside and directed me to my usual stiff-backed chair in front of her desk.

"So why are you gracing me with your unannounced presence?"

I pointed out her window and did a blinking light hand signal. She frowned a little bit and then uncharacteristically said in a "Star Wars" movie Yoda impersonation, "Saw that, you did?"

Shocked by her sudden humor, I literally almost fell out of my chair after busting out laughing. I think it was more of a nervous hysterical fit, but Eris actually cracked a genuine smile.

"We probably better go to the SCIF. We have a lot to discuss."

To my horror, she lifted up from her desk and pulled open the drawer where my purple spiral notebook had been. She grabbed the fake notebook and tossed it across the desk at me and said, "I am thinking you might want this back now. I have been keeping it safe until you were ready to get back to the real work." She emphasized "real" like I hadn't been working my tail off for her and her superiors.

After I gave her a confused sideways glance, she pointed towards the door.

"Let's talk and walk. It is better to be on the move when talking about personal development topics."

As we walked towards the SCIF, Eris filled in the time with small talk. She asked how Woola was. She wondered if my dad had recovered from his mishap on the ice that broke his ankle back in February. She even asked me how Fanny was doing and made sure she pointed out that she knew Fanny lived in Liberty Lake, which was a few hours from my house. I was getting pretty paranoid when she started to tell me that she keeps close tabs on me and my professional and personal interests.

Within seconds of thinking this, she added, "It is good to really know everything about who is on your team, don't you think?"

To my relief, we finally arrived at the SCIF. We did our check in procedure and made our way back to a secure conference room. When we finally got settled, she jumped up and dramatically exclaimed, "Be right back. I forgot to grab something that I want to share with you."

As my paranoia meter ran up the scale, she returned with a folder. Within that folder there were two documents that read, "TOP SECRET" across the middle and on the back. She slid them across the table. Nervously, I grabbed the documents and tentatively opened them up.

"What am I getting dragged into Eris? Because I am slightly worried that all of a sudden, I have a need to know whatever this is?"

She didn't utter a sound. She gave me an encouraging and gentle nod towards the documents within my grasp. Then she lifted up out of her chair and walked out of the room to give me some privacy.

I spread the documents out over the table. One of them was a long-term strategic plan for communications related to

CETI findings. There were three parts to it. A narrative, a set of instructions, and a schedule of events. The second document was a list of data and correlating tools, techniques, and tactics.

According to the first document, approximately three years ago CETI had received communications from an unknown entity coming from a bright white orb. There was an agreement made between the government and the inhabitants of this orb. This agreement was not disclosed. But it did reference the title of another secret document that was dated 1952. It, of course, wasn't in the package that Eris provided, either. However, there was information that did specifically talk about a piece of technology and corresponding cyber scripts that was built to function as a filter for communications.

It went on to describe what the government would do if certain communications were received. I was disappointed to read that one of the scenarios actually directed this tool and unnamed special team to block certain signals from space. It listed twelve locations that were identified as open portals on Earth. I was surprised to read that Coffenbury Lake was one of them.

I quickly realized that someone in the government knew there was other intelligent life forms in the universe and for some reason they were using this particular technology to deter them from communicating to the people on my planet. When I read through it and got to the last page, it had a list of components and the teams that were working on that technology. I was dumbfounded to see that my name was on two of them. These were the special assignments that I had been working on when I first joined the government.

I thought I was going to throw up when I finally realized that I had been working against myself all of these years. I had been part of the reason that Henoch, the Interstellar Contact Council, and maybe even Sajan couldn't reach me. To top that new knowledge off, Eris knew too. She knew that Coffenbury Lake existed. I had specified every detail of that experience in my notebook. I remember putting my head on the desk and burying my head in my arms in frustration.

This is when Eris cracked the door of my room and walked in. She was carrying two small white cups of liquid with her.

I remember thinking to myself, "No way in hell am I taking a drink of that."

Instead, I quickly pulled the documents together and put them back in the secure folder. I scooted it across the table.

"Why now Eris? Why are you sharing this with me now?"

She took a deep breath and for the first time in our working relationship she looked slightly shaken. She flicked her lizard like eyes at me, then back at the secure door, and said, "I am number eleven."

All I could utter was an exasperated, "How?"

She looked relieved that I believed her.

"I have been working on both sides. I am a double agent, and I used your notebook to gain the government's trust so I could understand what they were capable of. I had no idea they were using your developed technology to actually block out the entire ICC, until recently."

When I looked at her with a suspicious look. She slid back into her seat and gave me a defeated look.

"I need to know all that you know. I am not sure I can trust you Eris. Especially after you stole my notebook, set me up to block Henoch, and then when he suddenly breaks through, you come clean." I left out the part that Henoch had actually said she was on our side. I needed to hear what she was going to say. When I took a deep breath and let it out, I uncharacteristically grumbled at her.

"You are going to have to convince me that you can be trusted."

She shook her head and lowered her gaze to the document secured in the envelope.

"When the ship flew over today, I immediately went down there to see why Henoch had made such a display for all to see. I didn't realize the connection to the previous night's events with the orange orbs over the Columbia Generating Station. That was when Faith's group had disconnected the device that was blocking communications."

Eris stopped to take a drink of liquid from her cup and catch her breath. She was talking incredibly fast. I was struggling to keep up, but with this new information and the long night of studying my notebook the night before; I realized that orange represented the 7th Command. The Leader of that group was named Faith. I remembered that she looked like an ox. As this knowledge swirled through my thoughts, Eris had started back up and I did my best to listen to her words.

"After I went in there with all of my questions as to why they were pissing off the ICC, that was when the people in charge gave me this file. They told me they were working for someone else that was willing to help humans fight their wars. They told me they had a better offer than what the Grays were offering. They knew that you had meticulously pulled together specific sightings and events that led up to your strong relationship with Henoch and the others. I didn't realize, until that moment, that they no longer trusted Henoch or the ICC. I was surprised that they were sharing this information with me."

My unhappy glare was received, because she cringed.

"When they told me to hire you to support CETI, they knew I had the notebook. They wanted it, but I told them the only way I would bring you in was if I was the only one that would have access to it. But this morning, they directed me to give them the notebook. It wasn't an ask; it was an order."

Knowing that she didn't have the notebook at that time, I squinted at her.

"So did you give them my notebook?"

She let out the breath she was holding and confessed, "Not exactly, I told them I would, but when I got to my office, I realized it was gone after I flipped through your decoy. I was pretty sure you had it. Max was so nervous and out of character yesterday, I knew there was something nefarious going on." She gave me a nervous glance.

"You do have it, the actual notebook, right?"

Ignoring her question, I shot back, "I am still not sure I trust you Eris, even if you are connected to eleven."

That is when she straightened up and looked me in the eyes.

"How about I show you. Let's shut down that technology that got you this job. Let's prove that we are ready to be Peacemakers for the 11th Command."

I reached for the hidden necklace that Henoch had given me. His thoughts rang through my mind, "Oh, Eris is connected with the 11th Command. She should be good but proceed carefully with that relationship. I personally can't stand her."

I couldn't help but agree with Henoch's last statement, but I wanted to give Eris the benefit of the doubt.

"Alrighty then Eris. Let's do this."

19

WISDOM AND SACRIFICE

———— ∞ ————

THE REST OF the afternoon, Eris and I made a plan to decommission the secret technology that was put into place to filter and potentially block communications with other life forms. While we brainstormed ideas, she told me the truth about the orange orbs that had flown over the nuclear power plant a few days earlier.

"Faith was able to get in under the defense mechanisms that the government had put into place. She flew in through a portal that was close to Othello. There is an abandoned Air Force Station that had been used for general radar surveillance and housed aircraft control and warning squadrons. It was closed in the mid-70's and forgotten. Once Faith's fleet of orange orbs got in, she travelled with lightning speed across the white bluffs hills and directly towards the nuclear power plant. That is when she deployed her signal that shattered the physical device that was blocking the ICC's transmissions."

I sat there in shock as my antisocial and aloof boss spilled her guts. As she talked, I also found out that DHS was already repairing the module that Faith broke. Eris shared that they had a plan to have it fully back up and operational by the end of the week. Which in government terms meant at least a month or two.

As we finalized our plan, I realized she was very well versed in what the other side was doing. I was taken by surprise when she asked, "Can I let them know that you were contacted by Henoch and that you were concerned with him reaching out to you. That way I can get you a badge. They will think you are on their side."

I shook my head slightly, and thought to myself, "Yikes, okay, not a great liar though."

By the time we ended our meeting, we each had special tasks to complete before the morning.

My task was to hopefully reach out to Henoch and get more information on his plan going forward and to let him know what was going on. Her task was to get me special permissions to visit the site where the device had been placed. She had to convince her superiors that I was in fact on their side and ready to help them with their mission.

When we left the SCIF we donned our facades and vowed to not tell anyone about what was really going on. I rushed to my office and grabbed my things. I needed to get some fresh air. My afternoon with Eris was suffocating. When I made it to my car, I put my head on the steering wheel and took a few deep breaths to calm myself down.

That is when there was a tap-tap-tap on my window. I jumped a few inches off my seat and quickly looked out the window. Outside, was a man dressed in all black. He had a weird hat and dark sunglasses. It was the same slim, nerdy looking man that had met me at the coffee shop a few days earlier. He put a familiar hot pink sticky note on my window, pointed at it, and then quickly walked away.

When he disappeared around the corner of the parking lot, I opened my window just enough to snatch the note. Once again it said, "Need to talk ASAP." There was a set of numbers and symbols below the words. I slowly read the numbers and symbols to myself.

As if some kind of magic was happening right there in front me, I saw a cone-like concrete structure that was at least 80 feet tall that looked like a giant fingernail. It was a few hundred feet from a swift and wide body of water. Several people were floating by in multi-colored kayaks. There were dozens of geese and their goslings resting in the lush park grass under the shade of giant cottonwood trees. I quickly realized that my target was near the Columbia River down in the Howard Amon Park.

I did a little celebration in my car as a feeling of overwhelming self-confidence flowed over me for actually finding my target twice in a row. I drove the five miles through the city of Richland to an old office building, now known as the Fingernail.

When I pulled into the parking lot, just behind the Fingernail, I saw the thin man peeking around the sixty-ton cement structure that is used for park events throughout the year. He waved me over and I briskly walked towards him. I looked behind me, several times, to see if anyone was following me. At the same time I was thinking, "I sure hope he isn't an axe murderer. I'm being pretty stupid right now."

When I got there, without speaking any words, he waved me over to a bench on the other side and offered me a place next to him. I opted to stand. Just in case I needed to run.

The man sat down and fumbled through his hard-backed lockable briefcase. When he finally found what he was looking for, he handed it to me and whispered four words, "Shred it when done." Then he walked away. I remember just shaking my head and thinking, "This guy really needs a life." Then I headed home for some much-needed dog therapy.

Woola of course was more than happy to oblige me his unending affections. We cuddled for a few minutes, then I changed my clothes to a sweatsuit and threw in a frozen spaghetti and meatball dinner. Once again, I was anxious to open the man in black's package, whatever it was. Its presence weighed heavy on my mind, but I found reasons not to open it. After a few back-and-forth battles in my brain, I eventually decided to pull up my favorite network series and snuggle with Woola a few more hours.

Just as the final scene of "Yellowstone" was playing out and several of my favorite characters were getting blown up or shot at, Henoch arrived. I remember grumbling, "Great timing my friend."

"They all survive and make it to the next season." He gave me one of his mental teasing jabs and closed and opened his blue eyes to emphasize his spoiler alert.

After grumbling, I turned off the TV and lifted the sleeping dog off me and walked to the counter where the large envelope was.

"Got something today in the spy guy mail. Want to help me open it?"

He hovered over and tried to peer over the kitchen island. I couldn't help but mumble, "Do you need help little fella."

Henoch just pointed at the package and telepathically hurled back, "Just open it already."

I sliced open the seal and poured out the contents a little haphazardly, considering it was coming from some strange guy in the park. Two pages fell out. It was in a color-coded table that had eleven different rows. It was similar to the other data that this guy gave me, but this time there was a third and fourth column. One of the new columns had random numbers and letters. The fourth column had numbers that ranged from 2 to 200. When I turned the page so Henoch could see it from under the counter, he extended his long bony finger like an "ET" movie remake and announced, "That one is me. Where did you get this?"

When I looked down at the listed item he was pointing at, the first column had #1, the corresponding second column had the color white, the third column listed 667Cc, and the fourth column said 200. I looked at Henoch with a confused look. He didn't have to read my mind to know that I had no idea what this meant.

"That is my planet. We call it Zeta Reticuli, but the people from Earth call it Gliese 667Cc."

I gave him a nod and then pointed at the papers.

"And the fourth column, with 200 listed?"

Henoch reached up and snatched the papers from my hands and started to study them.

"I have no idea."

Henoch was completely absorbed in analyzing the document in his hands. After a few minutes he actually mumbled to himself.

"Where is Cozbi? His planet's information is missing?"

At first, I thought he meant Eris Cozbee and I shuddered a bit thinking that she was a giant lizard in disguise. In a flash, I thought that maybe I had somehow misunderstood Henoch the night before when he said Eris was number eleven, but I didn't push that thought over to him. I kept that one to myself, at least, I thought I did. Henoch was so enthralled with the papers; he wasn't paying attention to what I was thinking. After a long-distracted pause, he finally explained who Cozbi was.

"He was commissioned to lead the 12th Command shortly after we discovered humans. He isn't listed on this paper."

Relieved to hear it was a male leader and not Eris, I took back the papers and scanned page 2. It looked like it had been cut off when the thin guy copied these files for us. I did push that thought over to Henoch and he became noticeably calmer. Although it could have also been that Woola had found his long thin fingers and Henoch was giving him the best scratch of his life.

Eventually Henoch and I talked about the plan that Eris had proposed to destroy the blocking technology that was encoded into their servers. I also asked him if he knew that Eris was a double agent. When he paused a few moments and thought about this new information, he shook his head and said, "Sounds about right."

With that doubt out of the way, I pressed Henoch for more information about the mission ahead of me.

"I was hoping to understand how far and wide this technology was and if it extended across the planet. Do you know?"

Unfortunately, all Henoch knew was that communications had been sporadic for several years, but he wasn't sure to what extent. He flippantly added, "If I was a betting alien, I would say that it does extend past the Pacific Northwest. Faith was the first to make any real progress in breaking through here, but now we are all on standby in a safe zone waiting on you."

When he said this last part, I was slightly concerned that they were waiting on me. After a few skipped heart beats, I pulled myself together.

"According to Eris, the humans are fixing the broken devices that Faith's ship had temporally destroyed. Our window to continue our open communications will be short if Eris and I are unable to take it down from the inside." When I said, "the humans" I cringed a bit. I was human after all.

For the first time in my young life, I felt like I was teaching him something. It was a weird feeling to have such an advanced being look to me for help. He must have read my thoughts or felt my anxiety because he gently began to hum the Peacemaker song.

I sat down on the corner of the couch and put my forehead in my hands to take in the hum of his words. When he finished singing, without looking up, I said, "Sort of like the old Proverbs saying in the Bible, 'The beginning of wisdom is this: Get wisdom. Though it cost all you have, get understanding.'" When he didn't respond, I looked up and over to where he had been standing.

He was gone.

Too tired to think or care anymore. I crawled over the arm of the couch and wrapped my arms around my sleeping dog and fell into a deep dreamless sleep beside him.

20

WHY DID YOU LEAVE ME HERE ALL ALONE

THE NEXT MORNING, I went directly to Eris's office. For the second time in my life, her office door was open and when I poked my head through the opening, she waved me in with actual enthusiasm.

She was dressed in black attire. Her loafers were propped up on her desk. It was really odd to see her relaxed and actually have a personality outside of her hard-core work ethic. For some reason this behavior made me nervous.

After I closed the door and before I could settle into my chair, she blurted out, "I got us in. I told them that we met in the SCIF and that I felt you were ready to help us out with our mission. I let them know that I filled you in on the parts that were broken and that you confirmed that those were the ones you developed for us. I just got an update on the physically damaged equipment. It won't be fixed for a few weeks, but they believe you can verify that the data collection servers are still okay. We are headed out there today."

I remember choking a bit on my own saliva, because I was suddenly terrified.

"Seriously, just like that?"

She shrugged and said, "Just like that," as if what we were being tasked to do, wasn't a big deal. She pulled her shoes off the desk and gave me an inquisitive stare.

"I got my tasks done, what did your friend say? Did he share what their next steps would be?"

The intensity of her gaze bored into my soul. I was thankful she couldn't read my thoughts.

"He didn't have a plan – or at least he didn't share it with me. He said they were on hold in some kind of safe zone. He did say that their efforts, 'Appeared to work.' Which is why I could speak to my friend last night."

Suddenly confused, I asked her, "So they didn't contact you? I would have thought they would since you are..." Then I stopped because we were not in a SCIF or Special Access Program Facility. Saying, "#11," outside a SCIF would more than likely break some rules when it comes to National Security. It almost felt like Eris was trying to trap me. So, I just left it at that and kept quiet.

Surprisingly, Eris answered my question.

"I must have missed their calls. I was in the SCIF most of the night getting ready for today's exercise. I never went home." Then she got a disappointed look on her face like she was upset she missed her chance to meet her alien mentor, whomever that was. I knew it wasn't Henoch based on his comment that he couldn't stand her. However, she quickly recovered from her apparent sadness and began to push me for more answers.

"What else did he say? Did you tell him what we are planning to do today? Who else are they trying to reach?"

I pointed to the door, shrugged my shoulders, and quietly explained my unwillingness to disclose answers to her questions.

"We need go to the SCIF if we want to talk more about this area."

I could tell she was not happy with my response. Luckily, just before she was going to suggest we head down there I was saved by the ring of her phone. When she picked it up, she didn't say hello. She just listened and then responded with, "Yes sir."

She jumped up and advised, "Time to go. Our escorts have arrived." Then she guided me towards the parking lot. Her demeanor changed to her normal cold and thick-skinned self. She didn't say one word on the walk to the car.

Per Eris's instructions, I dressed in blue jeans, a comfortable cotton top, and closed toe shoes. She believed that the location of the communication blocking technology could possibly be in areas that would require dosimetry and special monitoring. I was hazmat trained, but absolutely hated the suit. I could feel the sweat dripping down my back as my minor claustrophobic triggers ran through my thoughts. We jumped into her black Tesla with tinted windows and headed out towards the nuclear power plant.

As if she had read my thoughts, she nonchalantly offered, "By the way, we won't be donning any advanced personnel protective gear where we are going."

When we reached the first security checkpoint, we were escorted by two black sedans. One in front of us and one behind us. The windows were so dark that I couldn't see who resided within.

We moved past what we call the 300 area and traveled on the only two-lane road that allows access to the east entrance of the nuclear designated area. Along the way I saw the familiar flat, treeless desert landscape. It was dotted with green 100-year-old sage bush. There were oceans of yellow cheat grass waving in the hot breeze. Along both sides of the road were sturdy barbed wire fencing to keep unwelcome gawkers from accidently entering a radioactive zone. To the left of the road was the tallest, treeless mountain in the country. From a distance it looked purple as it loomed above the slowly rolling landscape. The mighty Columbia River was to our right. After a 30-minute drive through the Hanford area, we arrived in front of a giant blue building. The locals called it the Smurf building.

I was surprised that the sedans held eight men and women that were dressed in black. When they all piled out with incredible grace, I noticed that they all wore dark sunglasses and had on cape-like long leather coats like you would see in the 1999 movie "The Matrix," starring Keanu Reeves. All of them had some kind of modified street baton attached to their belts. Their over-the-top garb – especially since it was in the middle of summer in the eastern Washington desert made me even more anxious. Eris handed me a special entry badge and a Thermoluminescence dosimeter for radiation detection.

She whispered, "Remember, don't talk, just listen and follow my lead," as we stepped out of her car.

One of the men closed in on us and silently checked my badge for legitimacy. He nodded at Eris, and she gave him a smirk that told me she knew him personally, which made me slightly suspicious. After she composed herself, he nodded again and as a group of ten we all walked over to the door of the big blue building. One of the dark-clad women pulled up a small door that exposed a secure omni-type lock keypad. Five of the black caped individuals surrounded her while she punched in the code, like I was going to jump her and break in like a superhero.

Once again, I couldn't help but think Matrix movie type behavior, and I started to quietly wonder when "The One" (aka Neo) was going to arrive. Eris could tell I had lost myself in my thoughts and nonchalantly bumped her shoulder against mine.

"Oh sorry Dariann, this ground is a bit uneven."

Electrical currents coursed through the point where she had touched me like a defibrillator machine had been discharged into my arm. The message was received, and I refocused on the task at hand.

Inside the building was a labyrinth of rough looking hallways. Some of the wiring, in the ceiling, was hanging down. There was a thin, but uniform covering of sand on the floors. We had to wind ourselves through broken chairs and office-type debris. It had that creepy horror flick feel. I kept wondering if one of these black caped figures was going to suddenly turn on me and cackle out loud, "Surprise! We are here to dispose of you."

However, the shock of Eris's glare was still fresh and so I pulled my dork self together and followed my captors to my demise. After about five minutes of walking through the Smurf maze, we arrived at a fully enclosed plexiglass door. Upon entering another highly protected omni lock device, the environment beyond was spotlessly clean. There was a desk with an old lady typing at her keyboard.

When she looked up her small black eyes pierced into mine as she sized me up. Without a word, she pointed towards another big metal door that looked a lot like an impenetrable brushed steel bank safe. The same black caped locksmith that got us through the first two omni locks stepped over to the big spinning door lock, turned it back and forth and then the entire side of the wall opened up.

Inside was an array of equipment and twelve wall-sized screens that had images of Earth projected on them. A few of the screens had high-definition views of places that looked like vacation spots. I didn't have time to study them, because the people in black, along with Eris, aggressively escorted me down a bright white sterile-type hallway to a large computer server room behind another plexiglass type omni locked door.

Once inside, I could see racks and racks of computer servers. The environment was being controlled by a high-end temperature and air quality system that was backed up with an even more expensive uninterruptable power supply system. One of the people in black silently directed me to a specific set of racks and pointed at them. Eris walked over and said, "Well this is it. This is the one that those weird orbs tried to destroy."

I stepped in front of it, stared at it, and then realized I had no tools to unlock the server cabinet door. I turned to ask for some, when there in front of me was a rolling cart full of every computer repair kit item I could ever need to fix the technology that the 7th Command had just worked so hard to destroy.

I looked at Eris and coughed a little. She immediately started to bark out orders, "Bring us a couple of rolling chairs and get out of our way. This could take a while. I will stay here with her. Why don't you all go check out the video feeds and make sure nothing happens while we are in here." Shockingly, they jumped at her commands. As soon as they located and rolled in our chairs, they headed out, and locked the door behind them.

"Dariann, we got about an hour, let's do this."

As she stood in the view of the camera that was perfectly placed to watch the server room, I quickly undid my badge and pulled out a small green computer chip that Eris and I knew would disrupt any of the devices that were blocking communications to and from our friends in the sky. The night before I had personally tested it, to make sure it would do what she told me it would do. As I unscrewed the server door and pulled out the component, the irony was thick as I put in a device that would destroy the very thing that had got me in this position that I was in that day.

After fifteen minutes of checking and double-checking; I had the chip inserted into the server and the outside buttoned back up. With a silent nod to Eris, we left the tool cart and two rolling chairs and headed for the door. The door was of course monitored, and it clicked open when we stopped in front of it. Outside, our entourage of black caped observers were silently waiting for us. Eris gave them a thumbs up. Then we traveled down the sterile hallway, through the plexiglass door, and out into the big room that housed the giant screens and other equipment for monitoring whatever they were monitoring.

My escorts quickly rushed us through, but not before I took a nice long look at the wall-size screen on the East side of the room. It was a live view, of a large lake that was about a mile inland from the Pacific Ocean. There was a large sand dune with a plethora of kids that were climbing up and then running down and jumping into the lake. I immediately recognized Coffenbury lake.

When I saw it, I looked at Eris. She had seen it too and knew exactly what I was thinking. Her green and gold eyes flicked from me to the screen and then back at me. She gave me a nod that only I could have seen. I knew we would be talking soon in the SCIF about it when we got back.

The ride back was oddly quiet. When we passed through the last security check point, the two black sedans turned off and went towards the 300 Area. As they disappeared in our rearview mirror, the realization of what we had just accomplished weighed heavy on me. When we pulled into the parking lot, I opened the door and threw up. Eris stood back and observed from afar.

"Maybe we should regroup tomorrow? I am curious what your friend will say when you tell him about today's events. Let's just meet at the SCIF at 8:00 a.m. sharp."

When I opened the door to my house, Henoch was cuddling Woola on the leather couch. Oddly enough the TV was on, and an old musical show called, "Hee Haw," was playing. I actually yelped, which caused Woola to start barking at me. The irony was thick, as I stood there and stared at my dog protecting a small gray alien on my couch, in my house.

When things settled down, I filled him in on everything that happened at the Smurf building. He listened very carefully. Every once and awhile I could tell he had concerns with what I was saying by the consternation in the air waves. When I finished my story, he seemed surprised, but relieved.

"It worked? Great Job Dariann!"

Then he paused, and said with a serious life or death tone, "I need you to concentrate on my voice in your thoughts and then I need you to remember how to communicate with this." He pointed to his big bulbous head and projected with urgency, "All the time, from here on out."

I gave him a thumbs up and sent him a mental message that said, "Like this?"

He nodded.

"Perfect! That is the only way we will communicate from here on out." Then Henoch told me to pull out my worn and torn purple spiral notebook.

"It's time to review a few areas. Let's start with the Interstellar Contact Council. What do you remember about the ICC?"

Surprisingly, I remembered quite a bit about the Interstellar Contact Council. As I read my notebook, I penned in the new knowledge of the colored coat of arms for each planet and their corresponding ruling party. Henoch reaffirmed my thoughts that Planet #11 wasn't part of the ICC, yet.

Henoch also had to remind me that the 3rd, 6th, and 9th Command leaders were from water-based planets. When I stumbled to remember what they looked like, he joked, "It sounds like your cyber communications team and the 9th Command would get along swimmingly. Except my alien friends look a bit like an Earth creature called an Octopus. Their coat of arms is purple."

Having never seen these creatures, I imagined a purple octopus with eight arms tapping on a computer keyboard.

"They really would be an awesome asset as a hacker."

After we both chuckled through the air waves, Henoch switched to a more ominous topic.

"Do remember the warning about the Nero. We have to keep sharp so that we don't get deceived."

When I didn't quite understand what he was talking about, he explained, "There are old texts from all of the different planet belief systems that actually call out some type of Lawless one. Many, within the human race believe that the book in the Bible called Revelation describes the same type of beast. But they call it a sea beast and an earth beast."

As I sucked in my breath, I couldn't help but say out loud, "Oh dear God."

Henoch tapped his head, to remind me to not use words, and then he agreed with me.

"Actually Yes, we call him our Conductor." Then he did a telepathic sarcastic blink with his blue slanted eye before saying, "Remember the song? We stand against the Nero. It is important to always remember that, too." We took a few moments and sang our Peacemaker song. When we finished he nodded and then we moved on with my lesson.

"Amaranthine is our new world per the Conductor. The ICC has made it a top priority to collect all of the different species that reside on their home planets and transport them there. At first, we tried to separate the different planets to reflect their home worlds, but some of those creatures, like the unicorns and our winged horse friends, found homes in different parts of Amaranthine."

"The Eight Train touches on all of the different sections of Amaranthine. It gives the travelers on the train choices to visit all of the worlds, if they want to. This is why Earth has representations of some of the animals that are in Evania and in the ocean that Sajan recognized."

"As you know, Sajan is from Earth. One of his special skills is biology and he was able to make those connections when he saw the different creatures on Evania. Each planet, including my home world has duplications of the same types of creatures on Amaranthine and vice versa, if you want to get technical about it."

When Henoch said Sajan's name, it was like a punch in the gut. I really missed him. Unfortunately, I forgot that we were sharing openly through our brain waves. Henoch nodded with understanding.

"I can open a channel if you want to hear from him. He is a

couple of galaxies over, but thanks to your efforts today, I can actually reach him tonight. Should I make that happen?"

The joy in my heart burst out and covered Henoch in a blinding bright blanket. I didn't have to answer his question with words. He already knew what I wanted by my unconstrained feelings.

"You got it Dariann. You deserve some answers." Then Henoch walked to the other room.

Woola and I watched him leave. My one-person kind of dog looked longingly after Henoch, even after he was out of sight. He must have liked his long fingers scratching his fuzzy white belly. I looked down at him and said," Well that was weird. Now what?"

We cozied up on the couch and impatiently waited for Henoch to return with Sajan. When I heard, "Why did you leave me here all alone," I realized that the TV was still blasting "Hee Haw" skits. The 1969 song, "You Were Gone," rewritten by Buck Owens was flashing across the screen.

I couldn't help but purse my lips and cry out, "Yep, yep, yep," as the off-tune country pair of farmers sang, "I searched the world over and I thought I found true love…."

When the two farmers made the fart sound, Woola scooted in closer and did his classic French Bulldog stalker stare deep into my eyes. I patted him on the head.

"Not you stinky little buddy, I know you wouldn't leave me here all alone."

As minutes turned into hours, eventually both Woola and I passed out on the couch. When I reached stage four rapid eye movement sleep, I heard a little cough in my mind. When I popped up, there was Sajan, standing in my kitchen. He had the biggest grin on his face.

"Oh my God, is that really you?"

He shimmered a little bit as he moved his hand to wave a quick "Hello."

Then he said, "Sort of, it's kind of an energy telephone system. It uses some kind of sound technology that reaches a certain frequency that is set up for you and me to talk during REM sleep. Henoch set it up for us. In theory, it is just you and me in here. It can only work when you are in la la land though. So, I had to wait until you fell asleep." He winked at me like he was kidding, but I don't think he was.

Sajan was dressed in a head-to-toe Jesus-looking kind of robe. He had on a wide brown belt with several weapon-type items clasped to it. His dark hair was longer than I remembered. His eyes looked sunken and tired. I was full of so many questions and I blasted him with one right after the other.

He told me as much as he could, but he was definitely holding back. As the night ended and the morning sun started to come up, Sajan turned and talked to someone that I could not see. Then he whispered, "It looks like I need to cut our call short." Then he laughed, because we had been on the phone for at least five and a half hours.

Just before he left the call he quietly explained, "I have been assigned to the 12th Command. I am helping with the biological aspects of the mission. I was given the task to make sure that any animals not already on Amaranthine, get collected and readied for transport. The ICC leader in charge of this mission is named Cozbi. He is pretty strict and cold. He isn't very fun."

When I coughed out, "Is he the lizard man?"

Sajan grimaced and said, "Sort of, more like a reptile with a...."

But before he could finish, I hit my forehead with the palm of my hand and said, "I forgot to ask Henoch earlier, is he related to a lady named Eris Cosbee? She spells it C–O–S–B–E–E."

Sajan squinted his eyes and pursed his lips, like he was really analyzing my question.

"No, my boss's name is spelled 'C–O–Z–B–I.' But he has actually talked about one of his agents on a special mission. I think her name was Eris. He said she was a pain in his tail. In fact, he is always talking about her incompetence. She is supposed to be helping us with breaking through some technological advances that were put into place. I guess she isn't doing a great job with the rescue operation. What was her name again?"

But when Sajan said "rescue," I perked up with great curiosity.

"Ummmm. Rescue? What's happening? I must have missed the memo."

That is when I was jolted awake by a barking dog as my connection to Sajan faded into the waking world.

21

BLACK MAGIC WOMAN

FRUSTRATED WITH MY dropped connection to Sajan, I decided to pretend that my life was normal. I went through the usual routine to get ready for work, patted my dog on the head and gave him a pep talk about being a good boy. Then I slowly headed into work.

I knew that Eris would have a lot of questions and for the first time in a long time, as crazy as it seemed to admit it, I felt more confident about my role in all of this weirdness after talking with Henoch and Sajan.

Eris must have seen me coming from the parking lot, because she was in front of my office door. She looked slightly anxious, which was really odd for my unemotional and somewhat cold-hearted boss. Without any words she nodded towards the stairwell that led to the SCIF. I silently followed her.

When we were settled into a secure room, she let out a long-held breath and said with much urgency, "Well, what did Henoch say? What is the council's plan?" She said Henoch with what I could only describe as loathing.

Taken aback from her more blunt than usual approach and by the way that she emphasized my friend's name, I took a deep breath and told myself, "This doesn't feel right. She should have her own mentor relationship, like I do with Henoch. Why is she so worried about the council's plan."

So instead, I hurled the conversation back on to her.

"Eris, he didn't tell me the council's plan, only my part in the plan. Just like we were trained to do. Why was Coffenbury Lake on that screen yesterday?"

Totally ignoring my attempt to deflect our talk about the council, her eyes squinted like a chameleon getting ready to strike its prey with its long sticky tongue.

"Right, so what is your part in the council's plan?"

This is when I realized that I was being played. She was using me and my notebook for information to learn more about what the Interstellar Contact Council was up to. While she impatiently waited, I thought to myself, "Why the big façade to fix the blocked connection yesterday?"

As I replayed the day trip to the Smurf building and the overkill of caped figures to escort us around, I remembered how she unintentionally smirked when interacting with them. Then how she quickly composed herself. She wanted me to believe she was on my side. She wanted to test my relationship with Henoch. Maybe even see if I would turn to the dark side that she clearly was dabbling in. As all of this was whirling through my thoughts, I remembered Henoch's mentoring to keep my thoughts protected – so that those that do know telepathy don't tap in.

Eris was still squinting almost like she had constipation, so I guessed she was trying to impinge on my brain. Her horn-rimmed glasses kept trying to slide down the bridge of her nose. Rather than getting pissed off that she was trying to read my mind, I started to titter instead. The look on her face was priceless. She opened her eyes wide and practically whined, "What is so funny? Are you going to answer my question?"

I reached beneath my shirt and dramatically pulled out my necklace that said, "I Am #11."

"I have given you years of dedication and commitment for the cause. Where is yours?"

Eris dropped her eyes and began to unbutton the sleeve of her expensive white silk shirt. She pulled back the smooth fabric and exposed a cryptic green design that when she rotated her forearm and faced it towards me it looked like she had the Draco constellation tattooed on her arm. Below this visual of the stars it read, "I Am #12."

As I looked at it, all I could utter was, "Check mate Eris."

She took a deep breath and tried to peer into my eyes.

"I can explain. Please let me explain."

I was impressed with her display of desperation. This was the first time I had ever heard her use the P-word. But by that time, I was confused, pissed, and ready to bolt. I pushed myself away from the desk and walked out as fast I could, without running. Once out of the SCIF, I ran straight to my office. I grabbed my things, skipped down the stairwell, and jetted out to the parking lot. I knew what was next and I needed to make an interstellar phone call. One way or another.

Before I got home, Eris had called multiple times. Luckily, I had the automatic text messaging app that let her know I was driving and would call her when it was convenient. In my book that would be never or ever, but she didn't need to know that. As I zoomed down Van Giesen Street to my little house off Perkins, I said the words to the song that he had taught me and then started to project my thoughts into the airwaves.

"Henoch, I need you. Henoooochhhhh, I really really need you."

When I pulled up and opened the front door, Henoch was propped up on the brown leather couch with the remote control pointed at the TV. His other hand was gently scratching Woola on his fuzzy white chest. Woola's head was sideways across the alien's lap with his legs dangling off the couch.

"Oh, Thank God."

Henoch shook his head from side to side, put down the remote, and pointed to his big gray head.

"Please don't speak so loud, I have a headache."

I grabbed a chair and quickly filled him in telepathically, of course, on what had just happened. He shook his head when I told him about Eris showing me her arm tattoos.

"Oh geez, I'm sorry, I knew she wasn't #11." Then he added, "I thought she was part of #12, under Cozbi's watch. But I'm not sure. She just drives me crazy and Cozbi for that matter. He is always talking about his disappointment in her performance."

I remember looking at him, and then slapping my own head.

"Damn, you are right, you said she was connected with the

11th Command. Not that she was #11. Well, I found that out the hard way today and that lizard lady is not happy with me." I slumped into my chair as my mind raced in a million different directions. As I played back the conversation between Eris and I, I kept getting hung up on her comments about being a double agent and also part of #12.

"Hey Henoch. Does it seem strange that Cozbi wouldn't let Sajan reach out to me all of these years?"

Henoch calmly explained, "My understanding is that he couldn't reach you. At first it was the distance from your planet. They were on the other side of the universe. Then when they got into range, they couldn't reach anyone on Earth. That is what Eris was supposed to be doing and why Cozbi was so angry with her. Or at least that is what he kept telling the ICC."

After a brief pause he added, "What an amazing coincidence that you worked with her though."

When I looked up at him, his blue almond eyes were pointed upward in a sarcastic gaze.

After a brief silence, Henoch transmitted, "You know what might happen now, right?"

Without hesitation, I groaned, "Yep, they are going to cut us off again."

Henoch shook his head in agreement.

"Let's see what happens tomorrow, but if we go dark, it is time to meet the 5th Command. Do you remember who and where that is?"

I rushed to my bedroom, grabbed my notebook, and read out loud quietly to myself.

"Fifth Command, brown coat of arms. Their planet of origin is Keplar-69c. At one time, there were a lot of them on Planet Earth. Most of them decided to move back to their own planet thousands of years ago as the human race spread out across the different continents. They communicate through telepathy only. A few still remain on Earth. Their leader is named Omah." And that is when I remembered him and our brief discussion by the fire at Suttle Lake. Luckily, I hadn't named the specific location in my notebook. Which meant Eris wouldn't know where he lived.

From the bedroom, I pushed a few words towards Henoch, "I remember. Big fella. Slightly stinky."

He joked back, "No worse than this little black fella beside me that just cut one loose."

As I laughed and put my notebook away in the safe under the bed, Henoch rushed to say, "Be careful with Eris. I don't know what she is capable of. I will confront Cozbi and see what he knows. I will let Sajan know you said hello."

As I turned the corner of my bedroom to discuss the possibility of a phone call with Sajan, again.

Henoch was gone.

That night on the local news there was another "Breaking News" headline scrolling across the screen. Ted, the news guy, was explaining to the viewers that he now had updated information about the strange occurrences that had happened over the nuclear power plant.

Ted was interviewing one of my superiors on live TV. Eris's boss was wearing a dark suit, minus the leather cape. I could tell he was clever with his words and within moments he had the male journalist eating out of his hands. When they recapped what others and I had personally seen, the man in black quickly found ways to disprove the sighting. Clearly he was saying everything needed, to gain the public's trust.

"There is absolutely nothing to worry about. The government has it all under control. You can trust us."

He continued his lies with big words to try to confuse the audience from the true facts. When pressured about the orange orb that Ted admitted he had seen, my boss's boss dropped his shoulders, like he felt bad and announced, "We were reluctant to admit it, but the orbs were part of a new military technology that we were testing."

After a brief pause, he added with a chuckle, to invalidate the people that actually saw and reported it.

"The bright white orb that some claim they saw over Snake Mountain was attributed to a conjunction of Venus and Jupiter.

When he said this part, I scoffed at the TV. I was shocked that he would even mention the white orb event at all. When Ted finally cut through the gaslighting tactics this smooth talker was deploying, he actually asked a good question about why the power went out.

"It was a glitch that has been fixed."

Ted, not quite convinced, he asked, "And how do you know for sure that it has been fixed."

The man in black looked pleased that Ted asked this particular question and confidently stated, "We have made several personnel changes to make sure that incompetency never enters our ranks again. Including the firing of our Program Director and several of her team members."

And that was when I knew I had been fired and that I probably wouldn't see Henoch in my living room again. My phone started to ring off the hook, but I couldn't find the courage to pick it up. So instead, I lifted off the couch and packed a travel bag for me and my therapy dog. As I packed our things, I actually started to whistle. When I was done I looked at Woola and crooned, "I'm a stressed-out mess. You are going to be a busy boy."

Moments later Max called, this time I picked it up and I murmured into the phone.

"Hey Max. I am so sorry. What a nightmare. How are you holding up?"

He paused and then uncharacteristically started to sing into the phone.

"She's a black magic woman. She is trying to make a devil out of you." It was sung to the tune that sounded very similar to the 1968 Fleetwood Mac song called, "Black Magic Woman."

Not knowing what to say and after a long silent pause between us, he whispered, "I can see that they are coming for you. You need to move. I can keep them busy in all the wrong places."

As the kindness seeped through my phone line I whispered, "Thank you my friend. Stay safe Max. Change is coming. I will get in touch when I can."

After several quiet thoughtful moments, I hung up and left my phone on the coffee table. With one final look at Woola I told him, "Ready or not, here we come. I sure hope Omah is home."

Within 10 minutes Woola and I were gassed up and on the backroads to Suttle Lake, Oregon.

22

THE FIFTH COMMAND

SURPRISINGLY, IT WAS a very uneventful road trip along the back roads of Washington State that took me through Goldendale. I traveled right by the Maryhill Museum and the concrete replica of Stonehenge that Sam Hill had dedicated to World War I casualties. Then I jumped across the Columbia River at Biggs Junction and took Highway 97, as far as I could, through the middle of the state of Oregon. I played my favorite soundtracks from Rush and AC/DC.

As the songs randomly played, they mirrored my hysterical emotional mood swings that went from telling myself I was going to be okay to loud head-banging sorrow. As I worked through my emotional rollercoaster, Woola slept the entire time. I was pretty proud of myself; I didn't cry once.

Five hours later, one quick trip to a rest area, and a grocery run in Sisters, me and my well-rested therapy dog arrived at the entrance of Suttle Lake. We found our way to the Link Creek Campground. The park was pretty empty. I was thankful that I found one of the more private first come first served camping spots. It was next to a natural running stream that flowed into the lake. I was also thankful that I had my camping gear in the back that I had forgotten to take out after the last trip to Priest Lake.

Woola was well-rested and excited to protect me. He kept bristling up and barking at anything and everything. After several rounds of trying to settle him down, I remember telling him under my breath, "Wait until you meet the big hairy monster that will be coming your way soon."

At least I hoped. I wasn't sure how to call Omah.

When the light of the day fell to darkness, I lit a small fire in the provided pit. Luckily the previous occupant had left me some chopped wood. There were large cut off logs to sit on and I grabbed a doggy blanket for Woola to sit on at my feet. The crickets were chirping really loud. I could hear the small stream trickle down to the lake. Every once and awhile I could hear a kid scream bloody murder because it was time for bed. The waft of delicious BBQed steak dinners tickled my nose. It was about that time I wished that I had s'mores materials. The desire to nibble on a perfectly roasted and toasted marshmallow was overwhelming. As I watched the crackle and pop of the coals of my fire, the soothing hum of the bullfrogs filled the air. I sat there mesmerized by their sounds when the words of a song flowed through my mind. I began to sing it under my breath.

Just as I finished up the last verse of the Peacemaker song, Woola began to growl as the tufts of hair on his lower back stood straight up. It was so dark; I couldn't see anything, and I tried to quiet the disturbed black beast at my feet. That was when I heard the familiar sound of shuffling big feet coming my way.

With one last shuffle and a grunt, directly across from the waning fire, a pair of shaggy legs appeared in my line of sight. My eyes slowly traveled from the hairy legs up to the big brown eyes of a patiently waiting bigfoot. He stared back at me for a few seconds and then without moving his lips, quietly said, "Hey, I'm Omah. I'm #5. Nice song." Then he smiled a big toothy big foot grin.

A normal person would have shrieked and rushed off to tell the camp host about the monster, but not me. Instead, I enthusiastically projected back, "Nice to meet you, #5. I am #11," as I held back the frightened dog.

After a slight pause he shared, "I'm glad you are on our side. I am glad you remembered the song. There is good and bad in all of His creations. However, by doing the right thing, we will find a path to immortality." Then he looked up and pointed behind me.

"You might know these two?"

As I turned to look towards the darkness of the lake, there coming up the path was a tall man with white flowing hair. On his upper torso he had sturdy armor with gold décor that ended at his waist. It shined in the light of my fire. His khaki-colored pants were loose fitting and were tucked into his khaki leather boots. He had a quiver of arrows that poked up over the top of his shoulder. He was holding the bow loosely in his right hand.

The woman that had been walking behind him, suddenly pushed him aside and started to run up the path. Her fiery red hair was popping out from all around her round face. She wore a similar outfit, but instead of bows and arrows, she had a sheathed two-handed Scottish sword that flopped back and forth as she quickly moved towards my campsite. Without any sound, she squealed in my brain, "OMG, It's Dariann. Geez Omah, you said it might be dangerous and to come prepared."

Omah grunted, which I realized was his only verbal way to laugh. Then I heard him float over the airwaves, "Surprise!"

Woola couldn't sit still, he uncontrollably jumped out of my arms, ran forward, planted his four six-inch legs in the dirt and gave the biggest series of barks that he had ever given in his life. He sounded like a little chainsaw. As I jumped up to constrain the terrified dog, the next thing I knew, I was being crunched in a bear hug by my friend Davita. A few seconds later, Alaster came up from behind her and gave all three of us a hug. As we group hugged and my dog licked all of their faces, a joy, that I had not felt for a very long time, bubbled up and out of me as I thought to myself, "Damn, I missed you guys."

Forgetting the important lessons that Henoch had just taught me, they heard my thoughts, and said together, "Ditto."

Then we all jumped up and down from the overwhelming excitement of our reunion. I am pretty sure Woola peed on me.

Back around the fire, Omah shared with me that he was the designated teacher to get all of us to the final stage of our training. He told me that I needed to move my campsite to where the other students were training. It was safer and away from the other humans.

"They are not ready for us, yet."

He raised up from his log and began to leave. Just before he disappeared into the blackness he chuckled, "See you in the morning."

Davita and Alaster stayed with me that night at the Suttle Lake campsite. I wasn't ready to let them out of my sight. Woola immediately warmed up to the new members of his pack. Alaster and he became quick friends, especially when Alaster found his special itchy spot just behind his pointy ears. When the morning light arrived from the east, my friends told me that I would need to leave my car at the park.

Alaster explained, "We will move it later; no cars where we are going." Then they helped me pack up and move to the designated training area, which was supposed to be deep in the forest.

We traveled down well-worn dirt paths, past a summer camp called Camp Tamarack. It had a stable of old tired pack horses and lots of wailing kids. A mile or so later, we turned on to a barely visible deer trail that led straight up to a rough rock face. When we couldn't go forward anymore, Alaster turned and looked at me, "Does this feel familiar?" as he pulled down an invisible latch that exposed a numbered keypad. But instead of punching in the code, he turned and gave me a serious look.

"Before I can let you into my kingdom you must forfeit your phone. Omah has strict rules on cell phones or any external contact while we are behind his magical walls." Then he put out his hand and waited for me to hand it over.

I reached out and slapped the palm of my hand against his.

"I have a cyber background Alaster, I left it at my house knowing they would probably track me."

He nodded with approval and put in a few numbers to the keyboard. An enormous wooden door appeared. It had a golden ape-looking faced doorknob. The number "5" was etched into the wood above it. Davita reached up and knocked three times.

"Open sesame."

When nothing happened. She started to laugh.

"You don't really have to say that, but it makes me laugh every time."

Alaster scooted her out of the way and turned the golden knob. When it opened, he just rolled his eyes and playfully pushed

Davita through. When I hesitated, she grabbed my hand and pulled me through behind her.

The camp looked normal enough, outside of me just walking through a magical door. It looked like it was surrounded by large outcroppings of basalt that reached up several hundred feet. The old growth Redwoods reached high in the sky and surrounded us. In the middle of the camp there was a large stone campfire. It was surrounded by makeshift log chairs that were arranged like an amphitheater. It had enough seating for at least 100 people.

When I looked up, I projected for all to hear telepathically, "How do the humans not see this from the sky with radar, heat sensors, and or satellite monitoring?"

That was when Omah poofed into the scene from behind a tree and communicated, "The ICC has a few tricks up our sleeve to stop any nosy #11's."

Woola, who had been such a good boy up to that point, started to bark like crazy at the tall, hairy and scary monster. Then he ran directly towards Omah and sat down at his feet. He looked up with his big brown eyes. I think Woola actually had a doggy smile on his face.

Omah couldn't resist his cuteness and bent down and patted the dog on the head while saying to me, "We have technology to keep them and the others out. It was agreed that each of the ICC members would be allowed safe zones or secret grounds on each planet. We call them our quiet places to think. I have one of the last ones that no one knows about. Outside of Henoch, of course. He has been sending me the Peacemakers from #11 that he knows are on our side. That is why you are here."

As I processed what he was saying, I nodded my head like I knew what he was talking about. But honestly, I was sort of freaking out. This was getting serious. What about my family and friends that I cared about. Will they be safe?

Omah shook his head like he understood my thoughts.

"We will talk about this topic later." He looked over at Davita and explained, "For now, let's get you settled in."

Davita excitedly announced, "You are in our taigh, sister."

When I tilted my head sideways in confusion, she explained, "It means house. It's where you will be sleeping." She grabbed my hand and dragged me down one of the many trails that were etched in the ground that exited the community fire pit area.

We walked about a quarter mile when I started to see the taighs she was talking about. There were at least 30 small cabin-type homes sprinkled in the forest. Each of them had an outside picnic table and a fire pit. They looked like your basic KOA kind of campground setup. When we arrived in front of Cabin #11, I reached up and traced the numbers lovingly and thought out loud, "Love that number."

Davita vibrated with excitement as she pulled me through the cabin door. She explained that each taigh was equipped with three to four bedrooms. Each bedroom had bunk beds. The kitchen was small, but fully stocked, all of the time. Then she crinkled her nose.

"We only have one bathroom though."

In the center of our cabin there was a large round glass-topped table with a wooden spinning carousel the size of a wine barrel top. She pointed at it and announced to the room, "Not as cool as Evania. Food doesn't just magically appear. They have to buy it and we have to cook it too. At the moment, it is just the three of us in here. However, Omah thought there would more in the next few days that would need to bunk with us."

When I was settled in, we all sat around a warm crackling fire outside of our cabin. Omah eventually joined us. He described the history behind his training camp and how it was brought to life. As we talked, I found out that Davita and Alaster had already graduated, and they were actually teaching some of the others.

When I asked how many were at the camp, Omah seemed forlorn when he grumbled, "Only 42 so far." When he got up to leave and just before he disappeared behind a tree, he projected to all three of us, "The first thing I need is that car hidden. They will be looking for it. How you do it is up to you."

We all looked at each other and grimaced. We had no idea what the plan should be to dispose of my beloved car, of which I had named Bessie. After a moment of silence, and going against everything Omah had just told us to do, Davita squealed out loud.

"But first, we eat s'mores." Without any arguments from me,

she jumped up and grabbed the deliciousness out of the cabin.

While overeating sticky and burnt marshmallows, we spent about an hour brainstorming a location to conceal my dependable and trusty old Bessie. It was Davita that finally lifted up off her log and began to jump up and down with the final piece of our plan.

"I got it! I got it! We can take Atlantis."

Alaster nodded and added, "Cool!"

Having no idea who Atlantis was, Davita turned and ran into the woods. Within minutes I could hear the telltale sound of a motorcycle coming down the path. Davita was on a camouflaged blue and green Yamaha TTR250 four-stroke off-road motorcycle. When she stopped a bit too fast in front of us. She revved the engine a couple of times, and then shut it off. In her thoughts, we heard her lovingly say, "Atlantis you are braw."

We finalized the plan and code named it "Bessie."

Alaster walked me back through the door in the stone wall, down the deer tracks, and past the screaming kids at Camp Tamarack, to pick up my car. His last words to me were, in his best Scottish accent, "Haste Ye Back, Dariann."

I remember looking up at his piercing blue eyes and saying a quiet but unsure, "Thank you?" Then I jumped in my car and zoomed out of the park.

As directed, I drove Bessie past the Camp Sherman campground into Sisters, Oregon and left her on a secluded back road a few miles outside of town. I even tried to hide her with a few downed tree branches and some loose underbrush. After I locked up my car and mumbled, "By my sweet Bessie. See you soon," I had to walk half a mile to our planned meeting spot.

Davita had somehow beat me there and was waiting at our designated trailhead meeting spot. Her hair looked like an 80's flashback. It was so fuzzy and big. She had an elated look on her face. She held out a matching half helmet for me and a set of Bluetooth-type earbuds. Personally, it felt a little Harry Potter-ish and I remember thinking, "With that wild curly hair of hers, she could be Rubeus Hagrid."

That is when I heard her words floating in my head, "Works for me, I loved that character and you do seem a bit lost like

Harry was in that movie scene." Then she aggressively kicked the bike rest back, popped up on the blue camouflaged motorcycle, and tapped the seat behind her.

"Well come on Harry, Omah has a lot to teach you today at school."

As we zipped along the concealed deer trails and avoided busy hiker hot spots, I held on tight as Davita wildly zigged and zagged along the forest floor. Eventually a different outcropping of rough basalt hills and mountains became visible. In the distance, we could see Alaster. He was waving us over, but for some reason, he was using sign language to tell Davita to cut the engine. We walked the last few hundred feet pushing the heavy motorcycle up and through the open door that Alaster had already opened. We popped out the other side into our safe and secure forest paradise.

Woola, clearly feeling more at ease, was in the arms of Omah with a classic French Bulldog grin. Omah was busy scratching my dog around his black chin and down his white puffed out chest. They were sitting around a stoked fire with a bunch of people I didn't know. Alaster guided us to a bench.

"We had a bunch of new recruits show up today while you two were out for a joy ride. We are up to 97 now."

His blue eyes sparkled when he gazed at Davita with respect and admiration.

"I'm glad you are okay, mo chridhe."

Her cheeks turned as red as her fiery messed up hair and then she scooted next to him, shoulder bumped him and said in her best Scottish accent, "Love you too, m'eudail."

I didn't need to know Scottish Gaelic to know what they were saying to each other. The pangs of longing and jealousy rose up in my gut. After a brief moment, I pushed it back down, protected my thoughts from others, and told myself, "Sajan will find me one day."

Then out of nowhere a man with deep dark skin, black eyes, and long dark dreadlocks that were interwoven with colorful beads, stepped out from behind a redwood. He was dressed in a brown leather outfit and he had on dark steel toe work boots. He had a thick leather belt wrapped around his waist that hung down almost to his shins. He had two 18-inch sheathed swords on each side and an Indiana Jones bull whip curled up and secured to his right hip. He had a stance of surrender and exhaustion, like his journey to reach us had been difficult. When Omah saw him, he raised up his fury arm and waved the stranger over.

"Welcome Noach. So glad to see you. Please take a seat and we will get started."

Moments later, Omah did a grunt to action, gently placed Woola in my lap, and loudly announced to the group of individuals from all over the world, "My friends, it is time to get ready for the upcoming war."

With that, 98 souls sat up straight and focused on the leader of the Fifth Command like our lives depended on it.

Which of course, it did.

23

TRUTH REVEALED

<hr>

IF I DIDN'T know Omah, like I did, I would have said he was scary while taking on his academic role. His demeanor as a command leader was strength, sagacity, and slightly unapproachable, as in you did not want to interrupt the big hairy beast when he was instructing you.

Through his teachings, we learned about the people in black that resided all over my planet. I was surprised to hear him say, "At first these special people were selected to be observers only." Especially since Eris had taken such a prominent and active position within the government.

He went on to explain, "When the interplanetary agreement was made with Earth's government in the 50's, the people in black were carefully chosen by the ICC in the early 60's and beyond to make sure that Earth's leaders were following the rules. Since then, the eleven different planetary commands have been interviewing candidates for the Peacemaker role. The Conductor instructed the ICC to find 12,000 individuals, per planet. Under the direction of the ICC, the people in black were then tasked to discreetly train and test the Peacemaker candidates that would eventually be the face of the 11th Command." Omah waved his hand over the crowd of students.

"Congratulations, you are in the last stages of training and testing for this important role."

The students looked around at each other and then back at Omah.

"One of the Peacemaker's roles is to help implement the

Conductor's plan; which is to gradually expose humans to the existence of other life forms and our plans to populate Amaranthine. As the ICC identifies those that will go to Amaranthine, the Peacemakers will help shepherd them there. However, certain things have to happen before we can execute the Conductor's plan. We have to wait for the right time to tell them the truth."

My mind was whirling. I had so many questions. It seemed like what Omah was describing had similarities to what was in the Bible. It was a verse out of Daniel 12:4.

"He said to me, 'And now Daniel, close the book and put a seal on it until the end of the world. Meanwhile, many people will waste their efforts trying to understand what is happening.'" After remembering these words, I was suddenly terrified and thought to myself, "Is this the end of the world as we know it?"

Almost uncontrollably, I raised my hand in the air.

Omah ignored it.

When people started to look my way versus at our tall hairy instructor, he turned towards me, swept his hand over the other 97 people sitting there and complained, "We can hear your questions, Dariann. Can you please just wait a few minutes and let me get through my spiel?"

Everyone nervously snickered. I, on the other hand, was horrified. I had forgotten that most of these folks knew how to control and project their thoughts. So, I did an intentional, "Ooops, sorry," towards the crowd and closed off my overactive telepathic channel. Then I scrunched down and tried to disappear from the attention that was focused on me. Woola even started to growl as if he could feel my anxiety.

Omah grunted.

"No apologies needed; we will help you understand. Those were good questions and thoughts. And yes, our Conductor above did leave clues about certain signs to watch for in certain historical artifacts, including the human's Bible." Omah continued his history lesson with an exasperated tone.

"There is bad news that I must share. We have found that some of the people in black have gone rogue. They were supposed to only take direction from the ICC, but a few have become confused about their purpose and have turned against us. We will need to discern each of these individuals one by one."

Omah took a deep breath that made the hair on his chest dramatically wave back and forth. In the airwaves I felt sadness and weariness for the human race. He began to remind us of the training that most of us had received while on Amaranthine. He also reminded us that some of the animals from Earth had already been transported to the twelve different countries that resided there.

"However, there are still a lot of people and animals that we need to find and prepare to transport, just in case things get out of control on Planet #11."

When Omah turned towards me, he looked into my eyes before saying, "A few of our selected few are already on special assignment. Including Sajan, Dariann. His ability to identify and relate to animals has made him an invaluable asset to help us with our animal collections across the planets. He is helping Cozbi of the 12th Command at this very moment to make this happen."

There was a slight pause before he announced, "It is time for all of us to hear and understand the truth. As Dariann pointed out, there is a war coming. We will need to train hard to get everyone here, ready for what is to come. Starting tomorrow morning we will begin intense training exercises. Alaster, Davita, and a few others will be helping since they have officially graduated. I will need all of the help I can get with our short timeline." Omah looked specifically at me.

"Some of you need a little bit more of a crash course in this stuff." His gaze hovered on me, for a few seconds, before he looked up towards the sky.

Based on his body language, you could tell that Omah was being contacted from something or someone not sitting around our firepit amphitheater. He nodded to the sky with some kind of invisible acknowledgement and then I could swear I felt a sense of joy and excitement coming from him.

With one final look at me, his final words before he lumbered away was, "We must be strong, courageous, and brave so that we may lead others to safety. Some of you have been there, some have not, but ultimately our goal is to move as many good souls to Amaranthine before the end of this world comes to pass. Rest tonight. Tomorrow will be difficult, but rewarding."

We all watched the big hairy beast walk through the forest and disappear behind several large redwoods. When he was gone, I squeaked at Alaster and Davita, "End of this world?"

But they just shrugged as the entire circle of people erupted with chatter, handshakes, and in some cases hugs for those that had not seen each other for a while.

I put Woola down and he immediately raced around the ring of fire to sniff, snort, and meet every single person. It appeared that there was not one person that could resist his big brown eyes and silly dog happiness. We spent the next few minutes talking to new people and getting to know their stories. There were people from all across the world. They spoke different languages. They had different cultures and beliefs. But there were no enemies at that fire. It was a ring of friendship and camaraderie to obtain success at meeting a common goal. We were Planet #11's only hope and we bore that knowledge with heaviness and gratefulness. With our new telepathic skills sets, we had a common language and understood each other deeper than any words could have expressed.

Eventually we made it around the circle to where Noach was sitting. Alaster let him know that he would be bunking in Cabin #11 with us. Noach seemed pleased to be in our little group. When Davita had recommended that we all roast marshmallows around the fire, everyone cheered out loud. By the time I had shoved my second gooey marshmallow into my mouth; all 98 of us broke out into song. We sang a revised version of our song, in unison, as if we had practiced it all day long.

"We were chosen to meet Your call. We train so that we all can stand tall. We answer, because of Your love. Worthy are You, our Conductor above. We trust without sight. Reaching for the light. Even if pursuit of right is a fight. His final gifts outweigh this plight. We will strive to do no wrong. We will sing His special song."

Just as we finished the last verse, I saw Omah emerge from the tree line. He was lumbering down the path. His thought patterns were definitely blocked, because I didn't hear him arrive or receive any announcement. I don't think anyone else saw him. As I watched him come towards us, I was surprised to see that behind Omah was a very thin man walking in his shadows. He was dressed in a bulky robe type outfit. He had a hood up and over his head. From what I could see from the distance, it looked like he had dark skin and long brown hair. He had a long staff that he was leaning on as he walked. I remember thinking to myself, "Is that Jesus?"

The people that circled me must have heard this unintentional release of thoughts, because a couple of people perked up and started to look too. When Davita saw the two individuals coming down the path, she actually shrieked at the top of her lungs and started to jump up and down. It reminded me of the first time I had visited Evania with Sajan and we met the wild-haired Scottish girl that had become one of my best friends.

Then it hit me like a ton of bricks, "Is that Sajan?"

And with that thought, the caped man flipped off his hood like the character Luke Skywalker did on Temple Island, which is actually a real place in Ireland, when the character Rey finally finds him.

Sajan beamed as he projected his thoughts across the people standing around the fire. He didn't filter it and it was totally directed at me.

"Did you miss me?"

And all of the 99 soon-to-be warriors hummed with happiness, like a well-connected bee swarm, as I ran as fast as I could to jump into his arms.

24

THE 99 WARRIORS OF THE 11TH COMMAND

FOLLOWING OUR EMOTIONAL reunion, Alaster and Davita joined us, and we slowly walked back to Cabin #11. Woola of course loved Sajan. We did a quick tour of the tiny cabin and the first thing Sajan asked was, "Where is my magical food table and my balut."

Davita and I crinkled our noses in disgust as we recalled what that was. After we joked around a bit, Sajan changed out of his Jesus garb, and all four of us cuddled up around the campfire. It reminded me of our time at the Evania cottage that the four of us shared so many years ago. We took turns updating Sajan on the different events that had been happening since we had last talked. When it was Sajan's turn to share, he seemed reserved and somewhat reluctant to say what his mission was or how it was going. I made a mental note to ask him in private what was really happening in his world.

He did quietly offer, "I am seeing many different worlds that I thought only existed in the movies. My new boss is definitely a manager-type versus a servant leader. He dictates the rules, daily tasks, and always expects perfect performance. If you mess up, his temper is horrible." You could feel the frustration in his thoughts.

Davita and I both exclaimed, "Oh no.".

Sajan quickly rebounded and explained, "There are some good parts of the assignment too. I get to work with all kinds of really cool, never seen animals. We have been collecting and transporting them to Amaranthine. It has been a fascinating experience."

About that time, Noach was walking up the path. When he got

153

there, we encouraged him to pull up a log and sit with us around the fire. When Sajan asked him, "Hey man, what is your story?"

Noach took a deep relaxed breath and pushed out, "Jeezum Pees, man. Crazy. My story is crazy, but good man."

As we laughed at his response, I remembered that Jeezum pees was a similar expression to "OMG." Which made his accent even more entertaining. That's when Noach pulled out a rolled-up dooby and a lighter. He fired it up and took a deep drag. The boys straightened up in their seats as the strong smell of ganga wafted across the slowly dying orange glow of the fire. Noach closed his dark eyes and grumbled with joy as he took another hit of the weed.

"One Eyed Jamaican. Delightful."

He gave Alaster and Sajan an animated look and then he offered the smoking cannabis to Davita.

"Ladies first."

She busted out, "I am already silly, I don't need it, but thank you." She looked around the circle of fire with a paranoid look like she had already taken a puff.

Then he pointed at me, "How about you?"

I cringed and thought out loud, "Allergies! Can't do that stuff. It makes me think I have mushrooms growing on my tongue and once I saw a talking flying horse."

Everyone started to laugh, because we had all seen the talking, flying horses of Evania. Just about that time Omah arrived at the campsite. He looked at Noach and the joint.

"Seriously Noach. Why do you need that stuff?"

And Noach gave him a sideways glance and a dramatic wink. With a very relaxed Jamaican grin he teased, "Mi Nice."

Omah grunted and looked around my circle of old and new friends.

"I wanted to let you know that we are going to have a special guest tomorrow. We will start at daybreak. Please get some sleep." Then he did an "I'm watching you" kind of stare at Noach and lumbered away.

We all groaned and pulled ourselves from the mesmerizing grasp of the dying and smoldering coals of the fire. Noach, ignoring everything Omah had just said, gave us a little wave.

"I'm off to see what happens in the woods at night." He stumbled off towards the community pit fire.

Alaster stood up and put out his hand to Davita. Without a sound, she placed her hand in his. He affectionately pulled her up and they walked back into our cabin, hand in hand.

Sajan looked over at me and said with a whisper, "I'm afraid to go to sleep. What if I wake up and you are not there again?"

When I sent him the exact same thoughts, he stood up and put his hand out, just like Alaster had. I immediately bypassed the hand and jumped into his arms. We held each other for several seconds in a firm hug. When we finally broke apart Sajan gently brushed my long blonde hair out of my face and murmured, "Dang, I missed you."

And all I could say was, "Ditto," right before he reached down and brushed my lips with his. The electricity from his touch made the hair on the back of my neck stand on end. I didn't want him to ever let me go.

The next morning came fast. Davita and I ended up bunking together since we had Noach in the house now. She was banging around our bedroom getting ready for a busy day of training. She was chatting about how she was the teacher now and how she was going to be really tough on the students like her instructor had been on her. As I listened to her banter, I couldn't help but remember how patient she was with all of my overabundant questions when we walked the sandy path in Evania to reach the ocean ETT that took us to our classrooms. I knew, based on that positive educational experience, that she would be an amazing teacher.

When I emerged from the bedroom, Sajan was sitting in a chair facing my door, reading a book about advanced telepathy. He peeked up over his book and raised his eyebrows and telepathically surrounded me with, "Good morning sunshine."

Everyone in the room chortled, except Noach, who telepathically said, "Yow man, mi luv yuh tuh."

Sajan popped up, went down on a knee in front of me and asked, "Dariann, would you give me the pleasure of walking you to your class?"

Davita yelled, "Aww, how sweet."

Alaster yelled, "Good one man."

Noach shook his long dreadlocks with approval and called out, "Walk good."

Sajan and I took the long route to the community firepit. The path was a well-worn dirt path that traveled along the edge of Black Lake. I was incredibly nervous. Omah's pep talk, from the night before was ringing through my thoughts. As if feeling my emotions, Sajan explained, "The final classes are a mixture between pure exhaustion and enlightenment. Each student's experience will be different, depending on their gifts. What you learn will change your life, forever."

Then he added, "Well, at least it did for me."

For some reason I shivered, and Sajan wrapped his arm around me. He gently whispered, "Don't be afraid. It will be okay. They come in peace."

But all I kept hearing through my thoughts were the last few words of my ailing mom just before she passed away from pancreatic cancer. With her last ounce of strength, she had reached out with her bruised and bony hand and grabbed mine. When she looked into my eyes with a clarity I had not seen for many weeks, she gasped, "Dariann, to have transformational change there is always sacrifice." Then her soul passed on and I was left holding the hand of her empty shell of a body. At that time, as a young girl, I had no idea what she meant.

Today the meaning of her wise words hit me like a freight train. I realized that over the next few days, I would be given knowledge of who I am and what my purpose would be going forward. I knew that this knowledge would come with great sacrifice.

Sajan, as hard as he was trying, was unintentionally wrapped up in my thoughts and when he stopped and held me in his arms, I started to sob. The tears that I had been holding back, for years, flowed freely out of my eyes. They splashed down my cheeks and all over his shoulder. And without words, I knew that Sajan was there for me, for all the right reasons. I knew that he loved me. In that moment, I knew that I loved him too.

He must have known I needed to get control over my emotions, because after a few more moments of his tender embrace he quipped, "Walk good?" What do you think that silly Jamaican was talking about?"

After wiping away the snot dripping out of my nose and several moments of overanalyzing Noach's words I whispered, "I like to think it means as we walk forward on our journey that the person wishing you to 'Walk good' would like it to be a good journey. But if I remember correctly, it technically means, 'See you later.'"

Sajan pulled me in, gave me one last warm hug, and took a step back.

"That response is exactly why you were chosen to be part of the 11th Command Peacemakers."

When we arrived at the community pit, all of the students and teachers were gathered around Omah. Omah pointed his gaze at us and sent over the public air waves for all to hear, "You are late."

When I cringed from embarrassment. He felt the nervous tension spewing out of me and playfully waved us over. Omah provided an overview of what we could expect over the next few weeks.

As his instructions, and the subsequent question and answer session came to a close, he began to say, "Although all scenarios of how your training will go is not known," he stopped and looked in my direction. After making sure I was paying attention, he finished saying, "To have true transformational change, there will have to be sacrifices." Then he gave me a thoughtful gaze, before turning and disappearing into the forest.

Alaster and Davita moved to the front of the group and started to call off student names. When they were done, I was surprised to see Noach jump up on a log bench and do the same. There were two other instructors that followed him, that I did not know. When my name wasn't called, I looked up at Sajan as he looked over his list of students. The tender gaze that he gave me back, made me swoon.

"Looks like I get you today."

When our eyes unlocked, he jumped up on the log bench and announced, "Anyone that wasn't called, you are with me."

When the collective group of 99 students and teachers were paired up, we all gathered our things and moved down separate paths towards our classrooms. Just before we left the clearing, we heard the whisper of Omah blanket us with his wise words.

"Walk good and when you return you will be the 99 warriors of the 11th Command."

25

THOSE WITH EARS – LISTEN

S AJAN WAS UNUSUALLY quiet as we walked along with the other twenty students that were in his group. He held out his hands, palms down, like he was feeling the environment around us for just the right vibe. I kept my thoughts trapped inside my head, as to not disturb him and whatever he was focusing on. Unfortunately, a few of the other students were not as respectful. I was so focused on where we were walking, I didn't realize that we had come to a clearing in the dense redwood forest.

On one side of the clearing was a tall basalt rock formation. The multi-ton columns of lava formations were perfectly aligned, as if an alien had levitated and placed them there on purpose. When Sajan stopped in front of the castle looking structure, he waved his hand in the air and a keypad appeared. He punched in a few numbers and magically the wall slid to the left, exposing a tall, rounded entrance.

When I peeked over his shoulder, I could see smooth tunnel walls and a sandy floor. It was lit with the flickering wicks of what looked like computer-generated candles. At the end of the passage, there was a bright white light. I was so consumed with the tunnel; I didn't realize that Sajan had turned around. He coughed to get everyone's attention. When I finally looked at him, he had an impatient teacher-like look on his face, and I let an "Oops" slip out of my mostly closed mind.

Sajan addressed the class with a boisterous, "Good morning class. This is a skill simulator that will help you learn what your special gifts are. You are in my group because we are not quite sure what those are yet. I will help guide you through the process. But first I will let you in on a little secret and demonstrate what my gift is."

Sajan slowly walked out about 25 feet from us and asked that we stay very still. He placed his arms perpendicular to his body, palms down, and started to hum. Within seconds the butterflies that were not visible before, surrounded him and began to float in a circular pattern that looked very much like a tornado of floating beauty. He moved his pinky ever so slightly and they landed on the tree branches above his head.

Once again, he put his palms down and we could feel the hum vibrate through the atmosphere. It was as if he was communicating silent commands. The air around us was full of static electricity and invisible energy. That was when the bear, the cougar, and the wolf showed up. They padded over and laid down at Sajan's feet. Within seconds a moose, a family of deer, and a couple of squirrels peeked out of the forest underbrush. Just before they too were headed towards Sajan's location, the hum stopped, and the hypnotized prey ran back undercover.

Within seconds the bear and the cougar, shook their heads as if they were confused, and then they lumbered out of sight. The wolf hesitated and then took a few steps towards the stone still group of students. When Sajan shook his head no. It trotted off.

As the students began to whisper to each other about the miracle that they had just witnessed, Sajan lowered his arms and peered in my direction.

With uncontrolled amazement, I shouted, "OMG, you are fricking Snow White."

And the entire class busted out with laughter. After a few moments, Sajan explained, "It is what I have been called to do. I am honored that the Conductor has given me this gift so that I may help save them."

He seemed relieved to finally be able to show me his gift. I could tell this was what he had been keeping secret. And with great conviction to keep my unprofessional thought buttoned up inside of me, I couldn't help but think, "Damn he's hot." No one reacted, so I figured I was successful in keeping my thought discreet, but Sajan did make it a point to look at me and wink.

That day, one by one, the students disappeared into the skill simulator. They entered scared and unsure on what they would find. When they exited, they were electrified and impassioned. Many of them actually bellowed out loud, "When can I go back?"

Sajan always patiently replied, "Soon, very soon," and asked them to join the others around the fire that had been built in the center of the clearing.

When it was my turn, I was incredibly anxious. No matter how hard I tried to hide it, I knew Sajan could feel it. And against the normal teacher and student proper protocols, he reached out his hand and pulled me through the basalt entrance while saying, "Don't be afraid. It will be okay."

As we walked along the corridor of the tunnel, Sajan explained, "Each of our gifts emerge when you least expect it. I always loved animals, but I never imagined that I could call and control them. When Henoch started to come to me in my dreams, he told me I was special. That I would have a large role in the 11th Command, but honestly, I thought it would be more of a kick-ass kind of role, not animal husbandry."

As we closed in on the bright lights at the end of the tunnel, he let my hand go.

"I can't go in with you. This is your journey to take."

After one last look back at him, I moved into what I could only describe as a Japanese garden setting. There were multiple pagoda temples, water features, groves of bamboo, and even several ponds filled with multicolored koi. As I moved forward the ground turned to evenly spaced steppingstones that led to a rounded bridge with handrails. I stopped at the peak of the bridge and looked down hoping to see the fish, instead I saw a green-haired turtle. His blue eyes were full of delight, as his turtle beak pointed up at me.

When I called out, "George?" He nodded and then looked to the right. There was a snake slithering towards him from behind a grove of bamboo. Its tongue was flicking in and out like it was tasting the air. Then it dove into the water towards my little friend. Without thinking, I did a superhero jump over the side of the bridge and tried to land in the pond next to George. However, the moment when I should have splashed into the water, I was suddenly on a type of fighting platform that looked similar to the one I used to practice on in the karate dojo down the road from my house.

The snake had transformed into a human looking creature, but it had a reptile head. It was dressed in a gee. When I looked down, so was I. As if I was in autopilot, I readied myself for combat as the lizard lunged towards me. Effortlessly, I slapped down every advance that it threw at me. At one point, it was as if my combat partner was in slow motion. With one final blow, my adversary hit the mat and tapped out.

It lifted up its reptile head, flicked its tongue, and hissed, "Welcome to the team," then it turned and transformed back into a snake and disappeared into the same grove of bamboo. Slightly confused on what just happened, I sat on a bench overlooking the pond full of koi. Eventually, Sajan walked down the path and quietly sat next to me. After a few moments, he gently asked, "So, what did you learn?"

I slowly turned, until I was fully facing him, and wholeheartedly proclaimed, "I'm a badass ninja?"

He broke out into laughter.

"Makes total sense to me. You've got it all, Dariann. Brains, bravery and beauty."

And just like that, my badass ninja cheeks turned beet red, like an Oompa Loompa, once again.

When he grabbed my hand and guided me out of the simulator, we joined the others that were sitting around the smoldering fire.

Sajan loudly announced, "Great job everyone. My job is done here." After the clapping died down, he added, "Just kidding. My job has just begun. Tomorrow we will start intense training tactics in your special area. The simulator will provide the training and techniques based on your gift. The difficulty level will exponentially increase. It won't be easy. But always remember, we were chosen to meet His call. We train so that we all can stand tall. We answer, because of His love. Worthy is, our Conductor above. We trust without sight. Reaching for the light. Even if pursuit of right is a fight. His final gifts outweigh this plight. We will strive to do no wrong. We will sing His special song."

When he finished his pep talk, we all rumbled with exuberance and began to collect our things to go.

Omah popped out of the woods and added, "Yes Sajan, so true. Anyone with ears to hear, should listen. Those that listen will understand."

Then he looked directly at me and announced to everyone, "And tonight, we have a very special guest visiting us that will help all of us to better understand."

26

THE NERO

———∾———

A S WE ROUNDED the corner that led up the path towards the community fire pit, there was a lot of telepathic chatter and excitement wafting through the air waves. In the center, standing on a picnic table, was the mentor of my interstellar journey. He was surrounded by dozens of students, with their hands in the air, like he was a rock star. I could tell Henoch was feeling a little overwhelmed as the people surrounding him bombarded him with questions about the outside world. When he saw us, I felt a heavy sigh of relief transmit our way. Omah jumped into action and quieted the noisy crowd.

"Okay. Okay, everyone, please settle down and take a seat. We will provide Henoch with some time to brief us on what he knows and then both of us can take your questions."

The students quickly moved to the benches and sat impatiently to hear what Henoch had to say.

Henoch started to pace back and forth on the table. His eyes darted out and across the group of people that would be his leaders for the upcoming war. His shiny silver suit was snug against his body and his legs looked like toothpicks with shoes. I wondered if he was losing weight from the stress of whatever was going on out there. That was when Henoch began to hum.

As if instinctual, together we all sang the song, then out of nowhere Henoch did a telepathic projection. He showed us what he was seeing, like we were actually walking in his tiny little shoes.

The scene began in a large round dome-type structure. It was like someone had taken a huge white golf ball and split it in half and shoved it into the ground. We, as in through Henoch's eyes, were in the middle of the building. Large cathedral ceilings rose above our heads. There were nine other individuals sitting on or near throne-type chairs in a circular formation. One of the thrones had a strange contraption nestled on the seat. Another throne was empty.

As Henoch turned his head, an octopus-man looking creature appeared. Next to him was a female with long gray hair and piercing blue eyes. I barely recognized her, because she had legs, where a tail had been seen, while under Coffenbury lake. She was dressed in shimmering teal slacks, that flowed all around her. Intelligence, Amartv, Gyaan, and Faith were also present. These were the other four entities that were on the thrones that I met at the bottom of Coffenbury Lake.

Aster, the flying horse that I met on Evania, and Omah were present as well. At the far end was a reptile looking individual that I figured was Cozbi of #12.

In the middle of the circular thrones was a large gap between the seats that led up to a platform that had a podium for addressing the congregation. The rest of the building was equipped with row upon row of seats that wrapped around in a circular pattern, like a football stadium. As Henoch panned the thousands of individuals tuning into this important message, I realized that the stadium was divided into twelve different sections. There were thousands of souls in attendance to hear what the Interstellar Contact Council had to say. They were quietly talking amongst themselves. There were no humans present, that I could see.

Intelligence moved to the center platform and after a few seconds she looked at us, through Henoch's eyes, and then around the room.

"Good. We are all present. It is time to discuss some of the new developments and plan out our next steps. Just so you all know, Pelagic is listening in from her ocean home. Henoch will replay this message for the warriors from #11 that are training with Omah."

When she said Pelagic, I immediately envisioned the pink sea monkey creatures from Planet #6 that had helped lift me up on the platform at Coffenbury Lake. As my mind started to wander back to the memories of that weird day with Fanny at the Oregon coast, Omah personally mind-nudged me and said, "Shhhhh. Try to control your thoughts Dariann, and listen to what she says. It is important that you hear and understand this stuff."

The recording of Intelligence continued to play as he mentally reprimanded my uncontrolled ramblings. My classmates were noticeably annoyed with me as well. I took a deep breath and bottled up those individual thoughts deep inside of me and focused on what she had to say.

"We are seeing more and more corruption my friends. The original agreements with our planetary leaders are not being honored. We believe that this is what the Conductor forewarned us about. We have found that there are campaigns to shame and quiet those of us that are trying to speak against unethical behavior. On Planet #11, we are seeing that there is some dissention within the ranks of the people in black. Some of them have turned away from the ICC's direction. They have obtained information that they should not have. We believe they may have the answer to the hidden Beast."

When she said this, there were gasps and additional chatter all around her. After a few moments, when things quieted back down, she continued.

"They have even put technology in place that blocks us from communicating with each other and to the people of #11. The technology that Faith and Dariann worked to destroy will be back up and running within a few weeks. They are trying all kinds of gaslighting and psychological warfare to deter and control the people of #11 from knowing the truth about what is coming." She paused and took a quick mental break.

When she said my name, Sajan grabbed my hand and squeezed it. I felt like I was having an out of body experience and that I was actually in a dream. When he squeezed it again and I looked over at him. He was staring back at me with kindness and support.

Intelligence started to speak again.

"The end is coming. We have no way to stop it as the greed and selfishness of the bad are overtaking the good that we are trying to create on Amaranthine. We need to figure out what or who this Beast truly is. Our lives depend on it." The crowd surrounding her responded with quiet contemplative silence.

"It is time to collect the people that are worthy for our new world. We have done a good job with the other eleven planets, but it is time for the Peacemaker's in the 11th Command to ready themselves for the upcoming rescue efforts that we are foreseeing. We must save as many of the good souls that we can." Shockingly, she moved back to her seat without any other thoughts.

Then Cozbi, the reptile-looking creature stepped up to the white podium. Cozbi actually clicked his tongue, like he was taunting Henoch.

"The war is already here. I will win."

Since we were looking through Henoch's eyes, we could tell that Henoch was squinting with confusion. Then he broke his focus from Cozbi and swung his gaze to Intelligence, and then Omah. All three of them seemed confused by the use of words that Cozbi had started out with. Cozbi must have felt this weird vibe. His big green and gold eyes blinked sideways, a few times. And then, like he was reading off a prepared script, he clarified his statement.

"I will continue to locate the creatures that are on my list. I have found Sajan very useful in my efforts over these last few years to help with this important mission. We will be ready to win this war. I will sing His special song."

When he said Sajan's name, I automatically squeezed his hand. Then I checked the protection over my internal thought projections, because hearing Cozbi's praise affirmed the feelings I was having for Sajan. Not only was he super-hot, but he was a superhero.

Even Cozbi saw that Sajan was a great guy. And seeing Cozbi in the flesh and hearing that he didn't like Eris either gave me comfort. I had not realized my doubt around Cozbi's intentions, but I knew that if Sajan had seen something weird, he would have reported it to the ICC or at least to Henoch. When the large lizard man stepped down off the platform, Faith, the ox-like creature stomped up to the platform.

"We are training the chosen few, several forbidden skillsets, in case we need them for war. Our special operations team will be ready very soon." Then she snorted loudly and clomped back down to her seat.

Without moving, Gyaan, the eagle simply said, "Still researching The Book of Knowledge. I will report more if I learn something that will help us to identify the Nero."

Amartv, the lion-looking entity shook his long dark mane and announced in a loud roaring voice, "We are considering reactivating the monitoring system that was last seen orbiting Planet Earth."

When he said orbiting our planet, I knew that he had to be talking about the Oumuamua asteroid that was seen from the Pan-STARRS 1 telescope in Hawaii. Ironically, the Hawaiian name Oumuamua means messenger. I remember that incident clearly because when Max pinpointed it with his remote viewing, he got a weird reading. My team actually thought it might be alien technology because it was moving in a way that was not normal behavior for a comet or an asteroid. Plus, it was ten times as long as it was tall, which was not a usual trait either. But we were told by the governing bodies and supposed technical experts that it wasn't possible.

In fact, Eris was very adamant that the asteroid was no longer in our jurisdiction. Eventually it disappeared out of our range when it passed by Jupiter, and we were told to drop our investigation, immediately. Max was pretty upset, but I didn't give it much thought, until now.

Aster clomped up to the podium. His long black tail touched the ground, and it swooshed back and forth as he prepared to speak. After letting out a horsey-type trill with his lips he announced, "Star and I are preparing our warriors for battle. They will be ready when called." Then he shook his long curly mane and murmured, "Our little one is due within the next few weeks."

The Council members congratulated Aster. The section that held his horse-like representatives stomped their hooves on the concrete floors and let out horsey trills. Their overly exuberant reaction seemed as if the journey to have a child was difficult and that there was a hidden story not being publicly revealed.

When he stepped down, I found out that the mermaid leader

was named Maya. She provided a brief status report for the sea monkey named Pelagic and for the leader of the octopus-looking guy, which was named Caspian.

"We are continuing to monitor and analyze all data and evidence to help Gyaan find the hidden beast."

When Omah lumbered up to the podium, he loosely described his efforts to train the identified 98 warriors of #11 that were well hidden from the rest of the world. The ICC must have known about Sajan and that he was helping Cozbi, because he was excluded from the count. Omah was careful not to say where we were training. He also didn't mention that Sajan was actually with us at the Fifth Command training camp.

When it was Henoch's turn. It was weird because it was as if we were talking to the Interstellar Contact Council and the crowd, directly. He briefed the ICC about the efforts of my planet to block all communications. There was a lot of chatter between them about this unfortunate development. My name was brought up, once again.

"Dariann is safely hidden and is being trained to use her gifts. As reported out earlier, she helped us bring it down. Part of our plan forward will be to disable it again, if it comes back online, so that we can continue to rescue those that have been selected for Amaranthine."

After he said this, he turned to address Amartv.

"We should talk more. I think I might have a Plan B, if needed." Amartv shook his long lion-looking mane in agreement. With that, Henoch's recording of the council meeting ended as suddenly as it started.

The people around me, were eerily quiet as they tried to process what had just happened. For me, the biggest question I had was, "What the heck is this beast that everyone keeps alluding to?"

Once again, I must have been letting my thoughts slip out, because Omah stood up.

"Let me try to explain what the Beast means from the council's perspective. We have spent many years debating this concept and how to define it. The Beast isn't an actual creature or a singular thing as far as we know. It is the idea that bad stuff will rise and overtake good stuff, but it is possible that someone is behind this rise. We just don't know. That is what Amartv is trying to figure out by looking at all available ancient texts and even scripture from all of the planets."

When most of his audience looked confused, Omah added, "For those of you that have read the Bible or other ancient scripts, there are some words that talk about beasts. The Book of Knowledge calls out a similar beast called "The Nero.""

That was when Henoch jumped in.

"For instance, in the book of Revelation it describes this evil entity as the beast of the sea and earth. Both are bad, both aim to deceive. They feed off of each other. The Nero, basically has this same description. The Book of Knowledge tells us that it will take wisdom to lead to insight, which will ultimately help us to find The Nero."

Omah gave an exasperated grunt.

"We have been searching for a human, someone from Planet #11, with the insight to help find this beast. We believe that the Nero is on Earth. The Bible mentions the number 666, but we have no idea how to decipher what this means. At least that is what Gyaan is interpreting from The Book of Knowledge and other areas that he has thoroughly investigated."

When they finished describing the Beast, and after looking at Sajan with a bewildered look, I, of course, accidently blurted out, "So we are looking for Satan on Earth."

Everyone in the circle nervously looked at me like I was just kidding, until Henoch bluntly replied, "Yes Dariann, we are looking for something that is comprised of pure evil. Some kind of force that will do unspeakable things, maybe even destroy the human race to conceal themselves. It is described as something completely void of light."

When Henoch said the void of light description, Sajan let go of my hand and walked away. When I asked if he was okay, he just shook his head and acted like he needed some time to think. Woola followed him along the well-worn path out of the circle of curious students.

Eventually the question-and-answer session with Henoch and Omah ended and we were excused for the night. I immediately went to search for Sajan. I found him on a log by a little hidden creek that was just off the pathway. Woola had all four of his feet in the air. Sajan was petting Woola's white belly. I had him scoot over on the log.

"What's up?"

Sajan sat there protecting his thoughts from me, when he finally shared, "Cozbi was the one that approved me as a member of the Peacemaker team after you and I trained with Davita and Alaster. When you left that night, I was asked to meet with the ICC the very next day. They had observed my abilities with the animals in the ocean tunnel, through Henoch's eyes. Henoch believed in me and thought that I was gifted, and he validated my nomination."

When I nodded, he continued.

"However, there were reservations from some of the ICC members because I was so young. Cozbi was the final approval for me to be part of the 12,000 Peacemakers from Earth. In fact, he insisted that I be on his team immediately. He assured the ICC leaders that he would mentor me and complete my training."

I looked at him and said with a touch of jealousy, "And this is a problem, because…"

His cheeks got red, as he explained, "That is why I never reached out to you. I have been on special missions with Cozbi since I was seventeen." With a pained look, he continued telling me things that I was pretty sure were beyond my approved security clearances.

"At first I didn't want to be near him. He gave me some weird vibes, but when I couldn't find you again and the years went by, he convinced me that he would help me find you, if I helped him. So eventually I agreed. His one caveat was that all communications about what he was doing had to remain secret. He made me promise not to tell Henoch about some of the things that Cozbi was taking."

With that knowledge, I jumped up, grabbed his hand, and dragged him forward. We walked along a quiet path in the forest. Woola trailed behind us. Our thoughts were replaying what we had just heard and seen. I remembered how Cozbi's first words were, "The war is already here. I will win."

"You don't think Cozbi is bad, do you?"

Sajan immediately responded, "He might be a snake sometimes, but I think his intentions are in the right place. He specifically asked for my help because he knew I could control animals. We have been able to transport a multitude of amazing species of animals back to Amaranthine. I just don't see him being evil. Just a jerk, sometimes. If anyone is evil, it is that lady you worked for. What was her name again?"

I coughed out, "Eris. Her name was Eris. Ironically her last name is Cozbee."

Sajan quickly added, "My Cozbi can't stand her. He is always talking about how incompetent she is. He would check in with her often. Most of the time, when he came out of those meetings he was extremely pissed off."

That was when I abruptly stopped and faced Sajan.

"Wait. What? They talked?"

Sajan yawned, put his arms above his head, and casually answered, "Yep, they talked quite a bit. She was doing a secret project and was supposed to report back anything interesting. According to Cozbi, she was always late to the meetings. He was continuously complaining about her in the open. Then just recently, right before I came here, I heard that he fired her. Then she disappeared."

When he said this, I shivered just thinking about her.

"She is #12, right? How does she look so human. How can she just disappear?"

Sajan gave me a sideways glance and joked, "It is one of those weird conspiracy theories that is more than likely true, I suppose.

When I didn't respond he added, "I am not sure. I never met her personally. I thought she looked like the rest of their planetary species until recently when I heard she was on Earth working with you. That is the first time that I got really mad at him. All of these years he had told me he didn't know where you were. He told me that we couldn't reach Earth. When I confronted him, he explained that he couldn't tell me certain things. That you might even be involved in blocking the ICC from reaching the 11th planet."

When he said this, I nervously reached down and began to stroke Woola behind his ears. In a way, I did help block the ICC.

"After we talked at your house, Cozbi cut me off. That was when I threatened to quit, we were close enough to the council's headquarters that he sent me to talk to Henoch to see if I could finally see you in person. I was shocked when Henoch told me you were at a secret camp and that he would help me get there. Cozbi still doesn't know I am here. He still thinks I am at headquarters."

When he paused, he elaborated, "To be fair to Cozbi we have been traveling long distances to far away planets to collect unique animals all of these years, so I guess either way, it would have been hard to reach you from some of those distances." I could feel that he didn't want to talk about this topic anymore.

"As long as Cozbi is using his powers for good and you trust him, I am on your side. I am just worried there is more to this story than we know."

Sajan shook his head.

"I don't think so." Then he pointed to his head, like he knew things that others didn't.

That is when Woola let out a big jowly set of barks and ran towards a light brown rabbit on the path in front of us. The fluffy rabbit twitched its black nose and then scurried effortlessly into the brush, as my 6-inch legged dog zoomed after it. I actually called out to him several times, but he just kept going the opposite direction. I looked at Sajan and pleaded, "A little help, please."

He put out his hands, palms down and hummed. Woola abruptly turned and bolted towards us. He immediately sat at Sajan's feet and did a classic sit pretty stance that French Bulldogs are famous for. When Woola did this, it reminded me of the saber-toothed deer and the Potoo bird that we had met on Evania. As I pondered how sweet that moment was, I wondered if that whole experience was actually fabricated to impress me.

After playfully reprimanding my meat ball of a dog, Sajan and I headed back to the cozy cabin to hang out with our friends before another big day of training.

27

INSIGHT TO LOVE

WHEN THE MORNING rolled around, I was excited to learn more about my gift. I also got a little payback on Davita as I banged around in our room trying to get ready. After she grumped at me a couple of times, I finally cracked the door to leave. I half-expected Sajan to be there reading his book, waiting for me, but he wasn't. Quietly, I hid my disappointment and made a big cup of kape. Sajan kept calling it that and eventually I realized it meant coffee in his native language, which was Filipino. I also found out that he was fluent in twelve other languages. Two of them were alien.

When he told us this, around the campfire the night before, Noach asked if one of them was Dr. Doolittle, since he could control animals. It took us a while to stop laughing over that one. Just thinking about the joy that I had, laughing with my friends, triggered a few more giggles. Eventually I settled into the cozy couch with my kape in hand and a Woola at my feet. There was a warm fire crackling away in the fireplace, so I knew that someone was up.

Within minutes, Sajan quietly opened and closed the front door to our cabin. I could hear him say, "Yum, kape." Then I heard him pour himself a cup.

Woola jumped off the couch and snorted with each step, to receive a pet on the head from his newfound friend. When Sajan softly walked over to where I was sitting, I tried not to ask, but it snuck out and I murmured, "You okay?"

He took a deep breath and let it out slowly.

"I just spent some time with Henoch. We are strategizing how I can help with future efforts. I'm slightly nervous about it, but it is for the greater good. I get it."

When I raised my eyebrows for him to continue with the details of his meeting, he just shrugged and let me know that he couldn't say any more. I could tell it bothered him to keep secrets from me and so I tapped the couch next to me and he sat down.

His toes and my toes were touching as we sat on opposite sides of the couch. It felt like electricity was surging through the tips of our touching feet. We started to have a toe war, when Woola climbed up in his lap and saddled up. Which meant that he pushed his cute little black butt in between your legs and put his paw up and over one of your thighs. As he babbled to the dog, I could feel Sajan's stress leave his body as Woola shared his warmth and love with him.

After several minutes of protected quiet contemplation, Noach, Davita, and Alaster emerged from their bedrooms and began to bustle around the kitchen. Noach busted in on our quiet moment and boisterously said in his thick accent, "Gud Mawwin my friends," then he sat down in between us and gave us a big Jamaican white toothed smile. His dreadlocks bobbed from side to side as he looked at our intimate situation and asked, "What's up?"

With the sweet moment with Sajan gone, we grabbed a quick breakfast and headed out the door for a day filled with intense training, that would ultimately get the 11th planet ready for whatever was coming.

As we gathered at the community circle, Henoch climbed up on one of the tables and demanded our attention.

"This week will be full of some serious understanding and insight. Our goal is to get Earth ready as soon as we can." Then he took a long pause, like he was struggling with the right words to say.

When he uttered, "If we…" he stopped, did a sweeping look into everyone's eyeballs and nodded his agreement with something or someone and then finished his thought with, "If we, the 99 can save even one person we are doing the Conductor's good works. Let's work hard to meet his expectations." He did another acknowledgement to the Spirit in the sky.

"I will be here for another week to assess your progress. Next week we will decide if you are ready for deployment." Then he stepped down and walked away without taking any of our questions.

Sajan collected his twenty students, and we headed back to the basalt training simulator. One-by-one the students tentatively entered the tunnel. One-by-one they exited a little bit more powerful and self-confident in their part of the war that was to come. When it was my turn, I literally threw up from nervousness. The information from the night before was keeping my mind busy with thoughts about the Beast. I had this incredible desire to learn more about what had been collected so far, and to help find this allusive thing that everyone was looking for.

When Sajan interrupted me with a cough and an outstretched hand, he actually used his voice and asked in his soft Filipino accent, "Kamusta?"

It was weird to hear him, or anyone, talk after several days of being grilled to only use telepathy, but I responded back to his question about how I was doing with my actual voice by saying, "It's all good." When I grabbed his hand, it was soft and warm. A wave of happiness emanated from my heart, and I immediately felt warm in my cheeks. Sajan noticed and gently asked, "Are you sure you are okay."

I gave him a quick affirmative nod and thought to myself, "Dang, I'm crazy about this guy. I don't want to ever let him go."

This time he left me at the entrance of the tunnel. Right before he turned around to leave, he murmured, "Mahal kita, Dariann." When I looked confused, he smiled, knowing I had no idea what he had just told me, and mouthed, "See you soon."

As I walked down the dark tunnel, I pressed my fingers along the smooth rock wall. My fingertips pushed through the wall and dragged through the illusion. When I reached the opening of the tunnel it spilled out into the same Japanese style garden that I had experienced the day before. As I sauntered along the rock path that snaked by the different koi ponds, I heard, "You, over here, now."

I was surprised to see the same lizard type creature, from the day before, in the middle of the pond on top of a wooden bamboo fighting platform. He had on a white gee with a black belt tied around his thick reptile torso. There was a black and silver retractable Bo fighting stick attached to his side. The only way to get to the platform was to walk on basalt steppingstones that reached above the water's edge. As I tiptoed over to his location, once again, the simulator physically clothed me in a white gee with a white belt.

When I finally arrived at the platform, with a commanding voice he said, "Let's begin."

He proceeded to practice familiar karate kicks and punches while shouting, "Ichi, ni, san, shi, go…" I recognized these as the names for counting 1-10 in Japanese. Instinctively I crouched in the ready position and began to run through the martial arts movements that I had learned in my local Earthly dojo. The reptile-faced creature's tongue flicked in and out as we ran through simple katas. Sometimes he would yell, "Kiai" for extra emphasis. We practiced front kicks, round kicks, sidekicks, and back kicks for what seemed like hours. We also revisited the different stances and jabs, punches and blows.

When he finally stopped and bowed at me, we had made it through half of the twenty-six katas that I had learned in my earlier years. My new Reptile sparring partner nodded, pointed a clawed appendage at my waist and said, "Good start, see you tomorrow."

I was pleasantly surprised to see that my belt had changed from white to yellow. When I bowed at my Sensei and turned to go, a black and gold retractable Bo fighting stick had magically appeared on my belt. When I emerged from the tunnel, Sajan was sitting there with Woola waiting for my return.

He popped up while asking, "Better trip this time? Any questions?"

As the joy spilled out of me, I gushed, "So fun! I think I did good. Look at this cool fighting stick that I earned."

Sajan beamed with this news and gave me a little "Kiai."

The next day there were fewer students at the simulator. As promised, my training with the Reptile Sensei increased in difficulty. After running through the remaining katas, he squared off, and pulled his fighting stick off his belt. When he dramatically snapped it open, he yelled, "Kiai." Within an hour I had mastered the moves that he subjected upon me with the Bo staff. And although it was an intense workout, I never felt like what he was teaching me was beyond my ability.

On the third day, there were only three of us left in Sajan's class. I started to wonder what I was doing wrong and why I was being held back from attending other classes. That particular day I was feeling very confident and almost slightly bored with my Sensei's exercises. My mind started to wander as I openly thought about what move I was going to do next. The next thing I knew with a sudden sweep of my feet "Wham!" he had dropped me to the ground.

I was surprised, but not deterred and changed up my strategy. Within three moves, "Bam!," I was on the floor of the bamboo platform. After the third time, I put my hand up in surrender and asked what he was doing to overtake me. He took a pointed claw and tapped the side of his head.

"You make it easy to defeat you." Then he excused me.

As usual Sajan was there waiting for me outside the tunnel, but when he asked me if I had any questions, I couldn't ask them fast enough. When he finally found a break in my emotional outburst, I could tell he was disappointed in me.

"Dariann, you have to get this mind control thing under wraps or you will never be ready. You will never move on."

When I cringed with my incompetence, Sajan softened his stance.

"Let's work on it tonight in a special one-on-one session."

With extraordinary effort I protected my thoughts from him, and said to myself, "Like a date? Whoo hoo!"

Sajan didn't acknowledge my question, and with great self-confidence in my skills, I told him, "Sounds great!"

Back at the cabin all five of us sat around the dinner table talking about the day's events. Since I was the only non-teacher, I decided to sit back and let them decompress. Noach was particularly impressed with how one of the guys in his group was able to regurgitate everything he taught him on the first try.

Alaster went on a rant about a differing opinion he had with a student over advanced telepathy techniques. Davita simply exclaimed to the room, "My class rocks!" Then she pointed at me and sang, "Soon you too will be subjected to my teaching young Padawan."

When I mouthed the words, "Can't wait!" Alaster turned to me and asked, "So Dariann, how did your day go?"

Three of the four teachers at the table turned their focus towards me. Sajan glanced at me with an innocent look.

"Ummmm, okay. I guess. I am getting special attention from my teacher tonight. Evidently not as good as he had hoped." I nodded my head towards Sajan.

At first, there were no words exchanged as they looked at each other with knowing eyes.

Noach, in his kick-back Jamaican way growled, "Aye, right! Sounds boonoonoonoos."

Then without another word, the three of them lifted simultaneously from the table and headed to their rooms. Just before Noach closed his door, Woola slipped in. We could hear Noach talking to the nosy little dog in his heavy accent. After a shared gaze, Sajan tapped his wrist like he had a watch on and teased, "We better get going we don't want to be late for our date."

When I dramatically crinkled my forehead with self-doubt. He beamed at me.

"I mean training session on how to control that mind of yours."

He grabbed my hand and we meandered out of the cabin towards Dark Lake. After a brisk fifteen-minute walk, the forest opened up to a small clearing that overlooked the little lake. There was a firepit that had a neatly arranged pile of kindling and paper. Someone, maybe him, had laid out a thick red and black plaid blanket. There were several puffy pillows and a fuzzy red blanket draped across them. Propped up in the middle of the blanket, there was a bottle of pink wine. Two plastic glasses were placed beside a plate full of chocolate covered strawberries. My mouth must have been open in shock, because Sajan gently grabbed my chin and pushed it up. When he didn't let go and gently pulled me towards him, I thought he was going to kiss me.

Instead he nervously whispered, "Mahal Kita."

Slightly confused and caught off guard by his words, I pulled back and practically whined, "See you soon? Where am I going? Where are you going? Am I being deployed? I don't think I'm ready."

Sajan let out a full bellied roar of laughter. When he finally pulled himself together, he explained, "Sorry, it actually means something else. We can talk about that later. We have some work to do. Let's talk about why the Sensei sent you out of the dojo today."

When I shook my head affirmatively, he continued with, "I personally learned Taekwondo. One of the first things I was taught and had to grasp were the five tenants of the art form. They are courtesy, integrity, perseverance, self-control and indomitable spirit. Which one of these do you think you might be lacking." Then he did a playful tap to his chin, like he was thinking about it.

I quickly responded with, "Self-Control!"

"Good." Then he waved us over to a cleared off area where we could spar.

"So I want you to practice opening up telepathically and then closing it off. I will tell you how you are doing."

My mood perked up, and I thought to myself, "Sweet, sparring with my hottie."

"I heard every word of that. Was that intentional?"

When my face turned beet red. He gave me a sad face, but immediately said, "Let's try again."

We got into fighting position. One of the first rules of Taekwondo is that you bow at the referee and then at your opponent. With no Referee in sight, I bowed to the tall forest trees that surrounded us. Then I bowed to Sajan, and I opened up my mind to Sajan and said to myself, "Choku Zuki followed by a Mae Gen." Then, when we squared off with each other I closed off my mind completely and said to myself, "Psyche! I meant Gedan Barai followed by a Mawashi Geri."

Sajan moved forward and I did exactly the opposite moves that I had supposedly shared with him. When I actually hit him with a Gedan Barai, followed by a Mawashi Geri, he hit the ground like a ton of bricks. When he pulled himself up on an elbow, he grunted, "I think you got it. Perfectly delivered, assuming you were doing the opposite of a straight punch and a front kick?"

With great satisfaction, I announced, "Yep. Now can we get back to what Mahal Kita really means."

He got a mischievous look on his face, pulled himself up, dusted off the pine needles that were sticking to his shirt and blurted out, "It actually means I love you."

I sucked in my breath and made sure he wasn't kidding, before I blurted out.

"Jeezum Pees Sajan. That is not even close to see you later."

As we joked at Noach's way of saying OMG, we moved closer and closer until the tips of our shoes were touching on the forest floor. As we stood, face to face, inches away from each other, Sajan touched my nose with his. It sent electric bolts through my body that reached down to my toes. He moved a stray blonde hair from my cheek and kissed me gently across the lips. My self-control went out the door as my desire to hold him overtook me. I reached up and delicately clasped my fingers behind his warm neck and pulled him in tight. Then he gently placed his hands around my waist. We explored each other's lips, cheeks, necks, and then eventually our tongues touched in overwhelming passion. It was indescribable, as the warmness enveloped me.

For the first time, I saw and heard Sajan's unprotected thoughts and they were full of sweetness, kindness, respect, and love for me. I knew he felt the same way I did, because his desire for me had him losing his self-control too, as he kissed me with so much want and gentleness.

Eventually, we awkwardly made it to the blanket and Sajan fumbled with the fire until it was a dull roar beside us. He popped out the cork and poured us a couple of glasses of wine. We nibbled on sweet strawberries dipped in chocolate. He wrapped me up in the blanket and we chatted the entire time in silence as the crickets started to come out and the light from the last rays of light disappeared behind the Deschutes Forest mountainside. When Sajan gently pulled the glass from my hand and set it aside, I knew exactly what he wanted, and I wanted it too. He reached over and pulled me into his arms, and he whispered in my ear, "I Love you."

As I snuggled in deeper to his warm, soft embrace I whispered right back, "Mahal Kita Sajan."

There was no doubt about my understanding of this love we had for each other. I knew the importance of that night with my beloved Sajan. It was the beginning of wisdom. With it, I was ready to get insight to make sure that this love between us would persevere for infinity and beyond.

28

THE BOOK OF KNOWLEDGE

THE NEXT MORNING, I kicked my Reptile Sensei's butt. He didn't have a chance after the amazing tutoring that I had the night before. After about twenty minutes of pulling himself off the bamboo floor, he tapped out and excused me, forever. As I walked away, he said, "Yoku yatta," in Japanese.

I knew exactly what he was saying because my human Sensei used to say it to me all of the time. It meant, "You did really well." That was when I turned back to my teacher and bowed to him, one last time.

"Thank you, Sensei. I am grateful for your lessons."

When I looked down at my feet, I was overjoyed that my belt had finally changed from yellow to black. As I left the basalt training simulator, I jumped straight into Sajan's arms. I yelled into the forest, "I'm a badass ninja, for real."

Unfortunately, there was no one left to hear it.

Sajan peeled me off of him and gave me a celebratory peck across my lips, before letting me go.

"Great job Dariann. Phase 1 complete."

Then he reached behind his back and pulled out an original tanto Japanese dagger from his belt. When he unsheathed the double edged 9-inch weapon, I felt giddy. It was beautiful. I quickly snatched it from his hands and slid it into my belt.

"It's a gift from Henoch and me. Now let's get you over to Davita so you can see Gyaan's Book of Knowledge. I know that you have been keyed-up to do that."

When he said Gyaan, my mind flashed back to Coffenbury

Lake to the eagle entity that was tapping on a leather-bound book. I remembered how his beady black eyes bored into my soul. Not understanding how Sajan knew I was so interested in the book; I gave him a confused look.

As if he was reading my thoughts, once again, he tapped his head and grinned. When I grumbled and privately thought to myself, "Wow, I really sucked at keeping my thoughts protected from others."

Sajan cupped his ear and bantered, "What? I can't hear you?"

And I quipped right back.

"Exactly."

Back at the cabin, we had a quick snack and a Woola snuggle. When it was time to go to my next class, Sajan insisted on helping me get there.

"Davita's class is tricky. You might never find it."

We took a trail to the east of the community amphitheater. After about ten minutes of walking along a well-traveled path, we came upon a sketchy looking cabin that looked like it should have been condemned and ripped down.

The door was barely hanging on its hinges, and it was slightly propped open. Several of the windows were shattered and broken. Scraggly looking vines were wrapped around the entire house. There was a rough-looking pathway of cobble stones that led up to uneven steps and a sideways leaning porch. This time I opened up my thoughts to Sajan and joked, "I'm thinking a Japanese garden in a tunnel simulator is a better move for me right now." Then I pretended I was going to leave him and go back.

Sajan got a devilish look on his face.

"Watch this, then you can determine your next steps," and then he actually did an eyebrow waggle.

He moved to the cobble stone pathway and literally started to tap his right toe in a rhythmic fashion. When a small audible hum was heard, he started do a classic floor-sized piano scene, just like the one found in the FAO Schwarz toy store, from the 1988 movie "Big." I immediately envisioned one of my favorite movie actors, Tom Hanks, playing the 1938 Heart and Soul song by Hoagy Carmichael. As Sajan moved along the cobble stone pathway tapping out the notes to this song, I couldn't help but hum the tune and sway back and forth with him from the sidelines. When the last note played, the cabin transformed into the campus of the Trinity College of Dublin.

I had read about it briefly in college, mostly because it was one of the oldest and well-known landmarks of Ireland. Its library was estimated to have held over five million books throughout its history. The Trinity College Library was a legal deposit library which meant that every book ever published in Great Britain and Ireland could more than likely be found there. The Long Room in the Old Library of the Trinity College was actually on my bucket list of things to do before I died. The excitement of what stood before me was overwhelming. I think I might have been quietly vibrating as I stood there.

Sajan, after finishing his piano recital, stood next to me as this magical moment unfolded before us. He bumped my shoulder, feeling the happiness rise out of me.

"Want to go in? Or should we turn around and get out of here?"

As the joy escaped and emanated out of me, I grabbed his hand, started to drag him forward, and squealed, "Let's go." As we entered through the majestic doors into the insanely high ceiling building, my self-control, on a 1-10 chart was a solid zero.

The deep dark wood structure was over sixty-four meters high. It looked like someone had cut dark wood wine barrels in half and used them to decorate the massive ceiling. Along the sides of the walls were hundreds of thousands of books that were in perfectly spaced rows. Large wood beams lined each row perpendicular to the floor. They were etched with letters of the alphabet and or a numerical value to help those looking for books find them. There were white marble casts of well-known individuals at each section of the library. Large wooden ladders were attached to rollers that helped seekers reach the upper levels. At one point I felt like maybe the characters of Harry Potter were going to pop out and run by.

When I turned to Sajan he was beaming with joy and I remembered the flying bed in his room full of knowledge, back at the cottage in Evania. It was not a surprise, when he exclaimed, "Cool, huh?! This is one of my favorite places."

That was when Davita popped out from around one of the corners of a tall bookshelf in the back and shrieked, "Dariann! Dia dhuit. Failte."

I looked at Sajan for a translation.

"Hello, welcome, something like that," then he shrugged and turned to leave.

As I scurried over to Davita, she actually gave me a hug and guided me to where the other students had been studying. I was surprised to find eleven different colored doors with shiny gold handles along one side of the library. The students were kicked back in oversized seats, reading books. It sort of looked like they were lined up in front of each of the doors.

Davita explained, "They are waiting for their turn to enter." Then she grabbed my elbow and said, "You have to spin the wheel to see which area you will study next."

Quietly, I let her lead me to what looked like a five-foot tall "Wheel of Fortune" show wheel. It was propped up on a large wooden table that had eleven different numbers on it. The #11 was not on the wheel, yet. There was a two-step platform to reach the handle for spinning. The doors and this wheel-thing looked totally out of place in the Long Room of the Old library. Trying to discern the reality of my situation, I asked my wild-haired Scottish-born teacher, "Ummmm. Is this real?"

She shook her head, which made her hair fluff out even more.

"No, we are not in Dublin. However, when they asked me to teach, I was told I could have my classroom in any setting, and this is my happy place. This is just a simulation, like Sajan's basalt training simulator." Then she reveled, "I thought this would be kind of fun," as she pointed at the wheel.

"Want to give it a spin?"

With a little more enthusiastic encouragement from my teacher, I stepped right up, grabbed the chrome-plated metal handle, and gave it a strong spin. It whizzed around for almost twenty seconds before it landed on #12. Davita squealed out loud and the entire student body turned around as if to say, "Shhhhh." Then she gave a mental, "Ooops," turned back to me and whispered, "#12 is fascinating and weird, all in one."

Within seconds one of her students popped out of the big

green door and walked over to Davita. The girl looked like she was going to throw up. She gave Davita a horrified grimace, and then stepped up to the wheel to spin it again. I watched her grab the handle and when she touched it, the wheel only had the number #4 showing." She let go.

"Thank God. That last one was disturbing. I need some flying horse therapy in my life after that."

Davita shooed her off to a silver door. As the girl opened it, there was a lot of bright light and a rolling grass pasture with funny looking trees in the background. It looked like Aster, the pitch-black winged horse that I had met in Evania, was slowly coming into view. She waved at the remaining students in the library, gave an excited squeal, and then closed the door behind her.

Davita pointed me towards the tall green door. When I walked up to it, I realized that the gold handle was shaped like a lizard. Just above the handle there was a gold etched #12. After a few deep breaths of reassurance to myself that this is just a simulation; I quickly turned the handle, walked in, and shut the door behind me.

Like a well-scripted theme-park documentary ride, a Reptile from #12 appeared in what I could only guess was their coat of arms and colors that they wear for formal ceremonies. He was dressed from lizard head to lizard toe in silky green and white robes that draped along the ground. The creature had its claws clasped in a resting position of authority in front of the belt that held its robes closed. It quietly observed me as if waiting for me to start off the conversation. So, I said, "Hi, I'm Dariann."

Like a well-coded program, the instructor cheerfully responded. "Hello, Dariann. Let's begin."

Immediately, I lowered myself into a karate stance. When he didn't engage and actually turned away from me, I straightened back up. The misinterpretation of his words quickly lit up my cheeks with embarrassment. After several moments, I quickly trotted after him on the same dirt path that led up and over a tall sand mound. At the top, it was hot, dry, and gritty. Luckily, my host had a covered cabana that protected us from the heat of the three hot suns that I had counted as I walked up the dune.

Under the tent, there was a large outdoor green carpet that had the look and feel of real grass. There were two multicolored director chairs and a table in between. I was overjoyed to see that it had two glasses and a pitcher of water. My commentator had already taken a seat and was waiting patiently for me to do the same.

When I slid into my chair, the lizard flicked its tongue and looked at me with its bright green and gold eyes and said, "Hi, my name is Llanfairpwllgwyngyllgogerychwyrndrobwllllantysiliogogogoch. But, you can call me Goch." Without waiting for me to respond, he continued with, "We will be uncovering the historical background of my planet and why we are known as the 12th Command."

As he said this, I was still trying to figure out what the heck he said his name was and I thought to myself, "I need to ask Davita if all of the 12th Command critters have amazingly long names."

When the side of the tent opened up, there in front of me, like I could reach out and touch it, was a Reptile family hunting and gathering on a landscape that sort of looked like Africa. The lower life forms in this picture were weird, but then again, I had seen creatures on Evania that I thought were aliens. When in reality they were on Earth today.

My tour guide Goch, continued his well-scripted spiel.

"These are some of my earliest ancestors. Like most of the planets in our collective community, we started out as hunters and gatherers. As we learned to use more advanced tools and several of us found ways to hunt and gather food more efficiently, we quickly formed more advanced ways to communicate and live in larger groups."

The picture in front of me suddenly changed to a couple of white orbs. After spinning around in the sky, they landed and a couple of aliens that resembled Henoch stepped out on to the African-type plains of #12's planet. When it showed Grays and Reptiles shaking hands, Goch began talking again.

"When the Grays visited us several thousand years ago, we formed partnerships with them, and they shared their technology with us. When our population exploded, leaders of my planet were greedy and destroyed many of our habitats. They turned away from the Conductor's Golden Rules that all of us were supposed to abide by. We consumed most of our food on our planet after ignoring the Grays advice on how to sustain our agricultural farmlands."

The view in front of me changed from joyful families playing games together and teams of Reptiles working with advanced technology, to the Reptiles being confined to crowded cities, pollution, and scenes of suffering.

"When we started to explore other planets, some of our leadership was given a bad reputation. They used the advanced technology that they had been given to harvest species from other planets for food. This would include bovines from the Planet Earth and the earlier flying ancestors of Planet #4."

In the middle of this seemingly PG–13 movie, it turned into a horror flick when the screen started to flip through scenes of cows on Earth, eating peacefully on the sides of mountains. Suddenly they were on the ground dead, being mutilated, drained of their blood, and in some cases magically lifted by a green light on to a cloaked space craft.

When the scene changed to rolling waves of pasture grass, weird trees with big balls of leaves on top, and winged horses floating in the skyline, I gasped out loud. As suspected, the screen flashed up wingless horses flailing in their own blood. Horses of all ages were being corralled after having their wings sliced off by lasers. One by one, they were lifted up to the flying slaughterhouses above their heads. It was hard to watch and eventually I turned away. As I winced, and started to grumble about this newfound wisdom and horror about #12, Goch paused his discussion and turned to me and asked, "Did you have a question about this?"

His question actually made me jump, because I thought this was a recording. When I gave it a quizzical gaze and it gave me several impatient blinks back, I realized, "Holy cow, this thing is talking directly to me."

So, I coughed and asked, "Ummmm, where are you exactly, or better yet, where am I."

Goch sneered, "I am here, you are there." Then he pointed at my chair.

He finally added, "The way this works is I teach you about my planet from my simulator. We are not really together physically, but we can talk to each other and interact. I work with all of the new recruits this way. However, we have strict confidentiality when working in Omah's special sector. His location is actually off the grid. We have no idea where you are."

As I privately freaked out about this new revelation, I decided to be safe, just in case, and I opened up my mind and said, "Oh good, so he has no idea we are in Dublin. Whew."

But Goch never flinched at my supposed slip of thoughts. If he did hear them, he acted like I was just silently waiting for him to continue his history lesson. So he did.

"Planet #4 is known as the Pegasus Planet. My ancestors with evil intentions had decimated an entire race of them as shown on this recorded footage. Shortly after this event, we went to war with the rest of the ICC. Thankfully, they won that war and allowed those of us that fight to do the right things in life, to redeem ourselves. Eventually we were approved to join the collective. We were one of the last groups to join the ICC because of our past mistakes. Any questions?"

My mind was whirling with so many questions, but the one I blurted out to Goch was, "So what do you eat these days, Goch?"

With a flick of his tongue, he snarked, "Pretty much whatever the people of Earth eat. Anything new to the list has to be approved by the ICC. We live in communities that are protected from the sun and sand. We have learned to grow our own food. However, our environment is pretty much destroyed. This is why Amaranthine is so important to us."

Goch donned a forlorn look, as he stared at his clawed feet. Then he pointed to the sand dune and outlying areas that backed up his claims. Everything that I could see looked sandy and desolate. In the distance I thought I saw a white dome-like structure through the wavy heat of the desert-like planet. It resembled the place that the ICC meeting had been held, just a few nights earlier. We sat there in silence, until Goch looked up like he was talking to someone and then looked over at me.

"Your time is up. Thank you for your interest and understanding of the differences of our species." He gave me a nod and disappeared like an apparition in a good ghost story.

I walked down the sandy dune to the green door that appeared to float magically in a background of sand. I quickly moved through it back to Dublin and on to my next assignment.

On my second spin, I hit #2. Which was the jackpot, as far as I was concerned because this was the blue door. This was the world that I was most eager to explore. I would finally be allowed to open up Gyaan's Book of Knowledge and hopefully figure out some of the answers to my questions about the data that I had received from the man in black, back at my hometown. When I entered the blue door world it felt like I was walking into a section of The Long Room in the Old Library. It was full of all kinds of books that went from the floor to the ceiling. However, to the left there was a full-length stained-glass wall of an eagle holding the book that I couldn't wait to see.

As I waited for my instructor to arrive, I noticed that there were ancient rolled up scrolls and old leather-bound books with intricate gold clasps. I gingerly walked over and started to peek at some of them, when I heard a little cough behind me, I turned around with a guilty look.

My feathery instructor opened and closed her beak, then I heard, "No worries, you can look, you just can't touch them. I'm Gyaan's sister. They call me Arisanna. I am the ancient historian here. I understand that you have some specific questions about The Book of Knowledge."

I could hardly contain my enthusiasm as I blurted out, "So happy to meet you Arisanna. I can't wait to see what is in The Book of Knowledge."

She fluffed her large white and brown wings and did a little stutter with her beak before she said with a little titter, "Well you can't actually see what is in it, but I can show it to you." Then she pointed one of her taloned feathered hands at a large glass encased book. It was entrapped by several types of locks.

"Only a few can read the Book. Gyaan and I are two of a few that can, but you can ask your questions and I can try to explain the answer as I know it."

With a disappointed sigh, I explained the two documents that I had received from the man in black that had color coded stoplights tied to the planet numbers. When I said documents, she perked up with interest.

"When Henoch saw the second document, he knew right away that his planet was listed accurately. He also noticed that #12 was missing from the bottom. I think it was just a copy error, but I was curious if you knew what the numbered column meant that had 200 listed for Henoch's row of data."

Arisanna took a few minutes to consider what I had said and then inquired, "What is 'copy error'?"

Slightly surprised that an ancient historian wouldn't know what this was, I took a few minutes describing in way too much detail, about copy machine technology. At one point, I thought I had lost her, but after several moments of careful consideration, she simply said, "Thank you for this information." Like a computer's search engine, she began to spew out possible ties to my question.

"We have these papers. I can confirm that our two water planets are 62E and 62F in Earth's terms. Those are well known. As far as #12, my understanding is that the people of Earth have no idea that it exists, but #12's planet is named Raziah according to The Book of Knowledge."

Arisanna looked up into the air like she was running an advanced query. Finally, she looked back down at me with a confident look.

"Yes, this is all I know about this subject. I will let Gyaan know your questions and we will do more research to see if the 200 number, as it relates to Henoch's planet, is something we should be concerned about."

With that Arisanna pointed a talon at the door.

"It was nice meeting you. I hope we meet again."

Although disheartened at the secrecy around the book's contents, it felt good to provide what I knew to the ancient historian. I was hopeful that it would help. I completed the rest of the tutorials over the next day and a half. Each of them added a bit more knowledge to my toolkit as I progressed through Davita's program.

The days after that, I spent quality time with Alaster and Noach. Alaster taught me advanced telepathy techniques and concepts about radiofrequency communications. Noach taught me spy techniques and associated technology. I passed both of their classes with honors, or at least that is what they told me.

As the week wound down, I was feeling very confident with my progress. I just hoped that Omah and Henoch agreed. Ultimately, as ICC members, they had the final say on who was in or out of the 11Th Command. That afternoon around the community fire, as if someone had read my mind, Omah announced that graduation day had come. All of the students had passed. All had done very well. Everyone, including me, cheered out loud.

After several moments of celebration, Omah quieted everyone down.

"Tomorrow, after your breakfast, we will meet here. Your teachers will provide you with assignments. We will provide time to ask questions and get you what you need to ready yourselves for deployment in the next few days. In the meantime, please enjoy the rest of your time here. There are kayaks, hiking trails, and the simulators can be used as you please. This journey going forward will be difficult, but rewarding. Thank you for your service."

After a brief pause, he began to hum.

Instantly, like a well-connected bee swarm, 99 Peacemaker's hummed His song.

29

MAHAL KITA

<hr>

IN THE MORNING, the Peacemakers gathered around the community firepit to get their assignments. Henoch and Omah were both present and looked anxious, as they waited for all of the teachers to arrive. Davita and Alaster were unfashionably late. When they did show up Davita had clearly been crying. Her normal happy-go-lucky demeanor was nowhere to be found.

With their arrival, Henoch climbed up on his table and looked around the circle.

"It is time to spread the word to those that are ready to accept our new lifestyle. It is time to let them know that "It is time." Then he took a dramatic telepathic pause. Most of us laughed at his play on words. Then he got serious.

"Those that have an ear, let them listen. Find and spread your message of love and kindness. Save those that you discern are worthy of the Conductor's everlasting life on Amaranthine. Save those that will remember our song and protect its beauty. We will be deploying you all around the world, to different parts of the country. Your teachers will provide the assignments this morning. We will pair you up according to your gifts."

I was concerned when Henoch paused, found my gaze, and looked at me with sadness. Everyone standing with me started to look around at their now friends and wonder whom would be on their team. Then he continued his pep talk.

"I am worried we might lose contact at some point, so please stay on the schedule that we have planned. Please remember your pick-up locations in case we get to a point that we must evacuate earlier than expected. Please protect and memorize what is in your envelope. Tonight, we will burn them in a ceremonial fire to celebrate the end of the old and the beginning of the new."

Both Omah and Henoch started to hum our song. Once again, we all joined in. When we finished, Henoch nodded with approval.

"I will be leaving today. I hope to see all of you on Amaranthine someday soon."

He looked at Sajan and noticeably nodded at him with some kind of unspoken acknowledgement. Then he jumped down and left us all standing there in quiet contemplation.

As if on autopilot and with no obvious emotion, Davita passed out legal size envelopes to her original class of students, murmuring, "Congratulations. If you need me, I'll be at the simulator," and hurried off.

Alaster stood there confused and unsure if he should follow her. Deciding against it, he passed out his own envelopes and repeated the messaging that Davita had just delivered.

Noach did a little dance every time he handed his students the envelope. They were all laughing out loud and being quite obnoxious.

Sajan, on the other hand, presented his envelopes with a professionalism comparable to someone with high emotional intelligence. Except for when he got to mine, he walked over to me, handed me the envelope, winked at me and almost sang, "Congratulations beautiful."

It was a bittersweet feeling of joy and anxiety wafting over the 99 students and teachers. Having passed the program and officially becoming 11th Planet Peacemakers, we all understood the weight of our responsibilities and the dangers that lay ahead. Several of the students were pairing up and walking away from the circle. Before I could open my envelope, Sajan grabbed my hand.

"Let's take a walk and talk."

Woola trailed after us, as we moved down our well-known path through the trees and underbrush. Every once and awhile Sajan would do his little palms down thing when Woola wandered too far from us. Eventually we found ourselves in front of the basalt simulator. Sajan gave me a hopeful gaze and jested, "One last spin on the fighting floor? I gave the Sensei the night off."

Knowing exactly what he was talking about I nodded enthusiastically as we found our way through the rock tunnel and into my Japanese pagoda garden paradise. However, instead of my usual bamboo fighting platform there was a cozy couch, several fuzzy blankets, and even a fluffy dog bed for Woola to hang out in.

Sajan had even brought in some of my favorite breakfast foods and set them up on a long, tall table with two stools. The banquet spread was impressive, and I immediately thought of Evania and the magical wonders of that place. I knew that the end goal would be to return there one day. As we bellied up to the bar, we talked about everything, except what the next day would bring.

When breakfast was devoured, I nervously flipped the unopened envelope on the table from front to back. The desire to know my future became overwhelming and I lost all self-control. With vehement speed, I snatched his hand, and practically shouted, "What is going to happen tomorrow? Will we still get to be together?"

I could tell he was torn on what he could tell me. After a long pause and a long Woola, "Pfffffft," he finally replied, "I have to go back and pretend I want to be there. The only thing I really want is to be with you and this little fart monster at our feet."

We both laughed, until the words that he had spoken hit me, and then I started to sob. A big blubbery, snotty cry. By this time, he had moved over and was hugging me as my tears silently dripped on to his shoulder. We didn't need any words to pass between us, because our souls were already entwined, which made tomorrow even harder. When I got myself under control and looked up at him, He took a deep anxious breath.

"Henoch and I talked; he thinks I should take Woola with me when I go."

Having been well-educated on #12's history, I blithered through new found tears, "What if Cozbi eats him?"

Sajan couldn't help but laugh out loud, which actually got Woola's attention. My little dog raised up from his resting spot and put his outstretched paws up on Sajan's legs. He had one of his classic French Bulldog underbite smiles. If dogs could talk, I am pretty sure he would have quipped, "Sounds like fun boss." Sajan reached down and scratched behind his pointy ears and cooed, "I would never let the big bad lizard eat you buddy. I promise."

When he focused back on me he added, "That historical run down that you got in class was from thousands of years ago. The bad lizards are probably more civilized than the human race. I will get him to Amaranthine on the next available transport. It will be safer for Woola to be with me than with you and Noach. Oh, oops, spoiler alert."

That was when Sajan grabbed both of my hands and pulled me up into his arms and gently cradled me like a baby. He offered, "Let's talk about this mission business later, okay" as he bent down and nibbled on my neck. His long dark hair brushed against my cheek, and it made me melt into him.

He lightly tugged on my ear and then pulled back, wondering what my answer was going to be. When I moved forward towards him, he brushed my lips with his. He gave me a frisky gaze and then delicately placed me on the couch. He pointed to the spot next me and shyly asked, "May I?"

As I pushed the future out of my mind, I proclaimed, "Mahal Kita, Sajan."

And he whispered back, "Ditto. Dariann."

We snuggled, kissed, and talked for hours. Eventually Woola found his way up between us and started to snore. The next thing I knew Sajan was sound asleep too. I untangled myself from the man of my dreams and my beloved dog and found myself at the cleared off food table staring at the cascading streams that fell into the deep ponds. Colorful Koi were swimming along the banks with their big fishy lips in the air looking for food. After taking a few deep breaths, I quietly opened the envelope that held my destiny. There was one piece of paper inside. I was surprised to see that it only had four lines.

Line one read "Noach." Which I already knew from Sajan.

The second line had "Washington."

The third line had "0xFF" and the number "15."

The fourth line had a set of coordinates.

As I studied them, to remember them, before I had to burn them; Sajan snuck up behind me and wrapped his arms around me.

"Well, do you understand what that says?"

I shook my head and shuddered, "Yep, it means I won't be seeing you for a while. But why Noach?"

Sajan gave me a sideways look and teased, "We felt you needed to learn a bit more of the Jamaican language."

When I groaned, "Ha Ha."

He professed, "Noach actually has a special assignment in Washington State, it made sense to pair you two up. Since we are a bit short-handed in our Peacemaker ranks, we put you two together. Plus, I would prefer you have a bodyguard."

When I flexed my muscles and gloated, "Badass Ninja. Hello!"

He pushed on my bicep and gave me a dramatic, "Oooooh!"

I patted the stool next to me and he slid onto it.

"Is Davita okay?"

Sajan pondered my question.

"Davita and Alaster have different assignments, thousands of miles apart. She was obviously pretty upset about it."

I remember grimacing at Sajan, but thinking to myself, "I really need to stop feeling sorry for myself, those two have been together forever."

When Sajan and I headed back to Cabin #11 we could hear someone screaming from within. When we busted in to see what was happening, Alaster was on the floor and Davita was on top of him still shrieking. Noach was settled into a recliner watching the show. He had a look on his face that told me something big was up.

When Davita realized we had entered the room, she screeched again, scooted off Alaster, and flashed the back of her hand towards us. There was a gigantic princess cut diamond ring on her well-manicured wedding finger. Just about that time Omah arrived, clearly concerned about the loud noises happening in Cabin #11. When he figured out what it was, he did one of his classic bigfoot grunts and pointed a furry appendage at Sajan and quietly told him, "Your ride is here. Sorry." Omah swung one of his big brown eyes towards me and cringed a little.

Within an hour my emotions swung from the happiest to saddest time of my life.

As Davita and Alaster continued to celebrate their engagement, I had to watch my two most loved things in this world head towards a clutch of cedar trees with a sasquatch. Woola trotted along beside Sajan like I didn't exist.

Just before they disappeared, Sajan turned towards me and promised, "See you soon. We will call you tonight. Mahal Kita Dariann."

And then they were gone.

30

THE ROUND UP

AS PROMISED, I did get a secure call from Sajan. He and Woola were getting settled in. Sajan couldn't talk about his mission, but he did say that Cozbi liked the little dog. He quickly caveated Cozbi's like, as in friend – not food. Which made me laugh out loud.

After our call, I joined the other Peacemakers around the fire, one last time. We quietly hummed our song, as we one by one, dropped the envelope with our documented mission into the flames. We all turned in early, because in the morning we would be emerging back into the wild to fulfill our assignments. Not being able to sleep, I packed a few clothes that I thought I would need.

Davita had left me a bright gold high-necked top with a long ninja looking gold sash that fell past my waist. She had also laid out stretchy black leather pants. On top of those, was a pair of matching black arm sleeves. I wasn't quite sure it was my style, but I decided I would try it on at the very least.

Her words from the night before rang through my thoughts, "Might as well look good when you go kick the bad guy's ass." That was the same time that she suggested we dye my hair pink, just for fun. The color pink was my least favorite color choice, but it was a moment of weakness, and I needed a distraction from Sajan's absence. So, I agreed. As I slipped on the tight-as-skin, bright gold top, and looked in the mirror, I did not recognize the reflection looking back at me. However, if it had not been me in that mirror, I would have said that this girl did look like a badass ninja superhero.

Davita's gold top did look pretty amazing with my newly dyed blonde and pink highlighted hair. When I slowly opened the door to quietly make my way to a cup of kape, I was shocked to see Noach on a chair staring back at me.

I looked at him, panned the room, and then with pursed lips asked, "Ummmm. What's up Noach?"

He declared, "With Sajan malayo, I keep a close eye on you. Keep you safe for my bredda."

Then he ogled, "Nice outfit," with a friendly Jamaican tone.

That was when Davita and Alaster popped out and wanted to know what was going on. But, when Davita saw what I was wearing, she squealed to the room, "Oh my God. It's amazing!"

It was already lonely without Sajan in the room, but it was sure nice having friends there to keep me entertained. Eventually, Omah knocked on the door and timidly poked his head in. He let us know that it was time for Davita and Alaster to go. Behind Omah, were the two individuals that would be paired up with my friends. Omah backed out of the door and closed it, so that Davita and Alaster could say goodbye. Noach and I looked at each other. Then he offered an escape plan, with a wink.

"Let's go talk about our plan for our future missions."

As we passed by our two friends, I gave them a double bear hug as I wiped away a few tears that had escaped from my watery eyes. Just before we walked out the door, Noach turned and exclaimed, "Walk good my friends. Know that you are loved."

Noach and I sat at a picnic table and watched the group, being led by Omah, disappear behind the clutch of cedar trees. When Omah reemerged, he walked directly over to me and dangled Davita's motorcycle keys.

"She wants you to take care of Atlantis. Will you accept this mission?" Then he grunted with laughter, dropped the keys into my open palm, and walked away. Over his shoulder he commanded, "You two need to get out of here in the next couple of hours to meet your window of departure. Feel free to take Atlantis with you when you go."

Noach started to reach for the keys, and I closed my fingers around them.

"Not today bredda."

After a few friendly jabs at each other, Noach and I reluctantly lifted off the bench and prepared for departure. Within an hour Omah showed up at the door and asked if we were ready. He had already located and pushed Atlantis up to our door. We walked along the path that led to the basalt door exit. When Omah punched in the code to his magical keypad, he handed me a license plate for a car, two burner phones, and directed us out.

At the edge of his bigfoot kingdom he waved and stammered, "Change the license plate on Bessie. May your mission go great. I hope to see you soon." Then he disappeared behind a magical shimmering opening, that turned back to solid stone.

We walked the motorcycle out a few hundred feet and jumped on. We took deer paths out of the forest and popped up on to the main road. We zoomed past normal residences to see if Bessie, my car, was still in the same place. Luck was on our side; Bessie was exactly where I left her. She was a bit dirty, but still functional as I started her up and warmed up the engine. Noach switched out the plate and hopped in. We had decided that Eris and her government friends would be looking for me in a car like mine. If they saw a large black man with dreadlocks, they might leave us alone, at least for a little while.

Noach tapped his burner phone and sarcastically chortled, "Remember to use your voice."

I just rolled my eyes and warmed up my vocal cords.

"Okie Dokie, artichoke."

Then he surprised me when he sincerely said, "See you in a couple of days, my friend. Please, be careful."

I smiled manically at him, revved up the engine, kicked it into gear and zoomed off. I knew I had left him shaking his dreadlocks and making some kind of smartass Jamaican remark.

I took the same path back to the Tri-Cities that I had taken to get to Suttle Lake. The ride was exhilarating and exhausting all-in-one as the wind blew through my hair and I sped past slow cars with incredible ease. The small motorcycle took a lot of strength to keep it steady and the distance to my hometown was a little over five hours.

When I finally rolled in to the town where I used to live and work my entire life, I had to keep going another forty minutes to a small farming community called Eltopia. I had used the coordinates that had been provided in the fourth line of my assignment to figure out where I was supposed to go. I was directed not to contact anyone I knew through traditional means. Which meant no phone calls, no computer messaging, and definitely no social media. It was frustrating to be so close, but not be able to see my dad or Maddy. I really wanted to talk to my cousin Fanny and see how she was doing, but I couldn't. It was just me and Atlantis in some strange place on the top of a hill.

From a distance the house looked like a typical farmhouse. It had a large porch that wrapped around the entire building. Two white porch swings hung from each side of the entrance. The building was painted dark brown, but the front double doors were painted white. Tall private vinyl fencing ran along the property lines. At the end of a long driveway there were two extra-large automatic gates that had an accompanying keypad. Luckily, I knew the number and punched it in. Within seconds the two gates separated and swung inward letting me pass. It took me at least 2-3 minutes to wind up the driveway and park in front of the house.

As I was putting down the kick stand of Atlantis, a woman that looked a lot like Noach's grandma was suddenly on the porch. She was waving at me and then pointing to the right side of the building. Telepathically, I could hear, "Please Park in the garage. It is right over there."

I waved back at her and hopped on Atlantis. She must have had some kind of special technology that allowed cloaking of the garage, because as soon as I got within twenty feet of it, it appeared. An open door was waiting for me. Once inside, the door closed and another door opened. The lady that was just on the porch was waving enthusiastically. Her long dreadlocks were bobbing to and fro. She wanted me to follow her. So, I did.

She telepathically chattered my ear off about the farmhouse

amenities. She gave me the run down on the rules of her house and then showed me a 3rd story bedroom that overlooked the Tri-Cities. She even explained why the closet was full of clothes and shoes that were all in my sizes. Eventually, she introduced herself as Nesta. She knew I was coming and was excited to have the company. She took a long pause and looked me up and down. Then she shared the time for dinner and quickly left to let me settle in.

I was overwhelmed with exhaustion and opened my balcony sliding glass door. I sank into one of the cushioned chairs and let out a breath that I didn't realize I was holding. As I panned the horizon, I could see Kennewick's light Blue Bridge spanning over the Columbia River. To the west, was the towering Snake Mountain. Seeing them made me yearn for my dad and friend even more.

At dinner, Nesta told me her entire life story. She was actually from Jamaica, but did not know Noach personally. She explained that the property was settled in the 1870's and was kept up to date by the undisclosed owners. The house was meant to provide a safe place for the Peacemaker teams that were assigned missions in the Tri-Cities areas. As suspected, Nesta let me know that she used to be part of the active teams.

"I'm too old now, so I just help others that find this place. I have been waiting a long time to go back to Amaranthine."

She actually chortled out loud when she said, "I think this might be my year."

As she continued to fill me in, I realized that there were actually numerous rooms in the farmhouse. The anonymous owners had created enough bedrooms, kitchens, and bathrooms below the normal looking farmhouse to accommodate up to 150 people. Nesta boasted, "We have also installed a couple of exercise rooms, a movie theatre room, and a special playhouse area for the little ones. There are two others like this one in Washington State."

I remember casually thinking to myself, "So this is the house that will harbor the people that I rescue?"

Nesta answered my private question with a "Yes." Then she tapped her head and gave me a wise scowl.

"I am on your side, but be careful when you are out there.

Things have gotten nasty in the last few weeks. There are a lot of bad people that will want to destroy what we are building. They have started to round up good people for no reason, other than power and greed." When she yawned and started to get up, she pointed to a wall of keys.

"Feel free to use any of my vehicles. They have all been upgraded to help keep them out of your head and safe while you go on your missions."

Just before she disappeared, she casually pointed to the sky and mentioned, "Oh, and all phone calls come in at 8:30."

Before I could ask her more about these phone calls. She was gone. When 8:15 p.m. rolled around, I was sitting on the side of my bed, fully dressed, waiting for a phone call. Which was about the same time I remembered what Sajan had told me about interstellar phone calls.

"It can only work when you are in la la land though." He could only reach me through my REM.

So, I jumped under the covers closed my eyes and began to chant the Peacemakers song. Fortunately, within minutes I was fast asleep.

When I opened my eyes, sitting next to me was a shimmering version of the two most favorite things in my life; my beloved Sajan and a little black and white-chested French Bulldog. We spent hours talking and getting caught up. Woola kept trying to jump in my lap and saddle up, but of course that didn't work out very well. Eventually he sat in the corner and barked every 4-5 minutes with frustration. When Sajan started to scratch him behind the ears, he finally curled up in a ball on his lap and fell asleep. Sajan and I talked for hours until I woke up and lost our connection.

As the morning light filtered through my window, I pulled myself up and got dressed. After a quick breakfast from my chatty Jamaican cook, I grabbed the keys of a Toyota RAV 4 and headed back to the garage.

Nesta must have moved Atlantis, because Davita's beloved bike was no longer where I had parked it. As I walked along, lights started to turn on with my forward movement. I was shocked to see rows and rows of every kind of car you could imagine. Some of them were million-dollar cars that I had seen on TV. One of them was built by a local family that I had grown up with. They had sold the same type of car to a famous night-time comedian and there was an entire program about how fast the car could go.

When I found my boring gray Toyota RAV 4, I started it up and found my way out into the bright sunshine of Eastern Washington. My first assignment was to discreetly find my former team member, Max. His remote viewing skills were instrumental to the next step of my plan. Luckily, knowing Max and his tendencies made my task easier. When I was his manager, I paid close attention to what made my people tick and Max loved his quiet time at his favorite coffee place every morning at 7:10 a.m., before heading to work.

It was 7:00 a.m. and my first stop for the day was The Coffee Bean. I couldn't wait to get a latte with a hummingbird on top. I parked my car down the street at the local credit union and walked the few hundred feet behind the Baskin Robbins to the back entrance of the coffee shop. After scanning for dark suited people lurking around the coffee shop, I walked up to the window and ordered my favorite drink. I was incredibly happy that my appearance threw off the owner that usually greets me by name. When I got my coffee, I took a seat, sipped the sweet mixture, and waited for Max.

Like clockwork, Max pulled up in his blue Mazda Miata and sauntered over to the order window. His nose was buried in his phone, and he never looked around or up until he ordered. When his name was called and he got his coffee, he sat at the table next to me and started to fumble with his phone again. As I sat there quietly deciding how I was going to engage with Max, he mumbled, "Where the hell have you been and what did you do to your hair?"

Without looking at him, I used my best Jamaican accent, "Jeezum Pees, Man. Crazy. My story is crazy, but good man."

When I finally looked into his eyes, he sputtered, "Holy crap, what happened to you?"

As we sipped our perfectly roasted coffee, I told Max everything that I could and let him know that I needed his help to find a guy.

Surprisingly, when I told him this, he gave me an uncertain sideways glance.

"Seriously?"

That was when I turned beet red, like an Oompa Loompa, and clarified, "I need to find the guy in black that contacted me twice with important information. I need to pick his brain on what some of the data means."

Max was totally in, of course, and I gave him as many details as I could about the mysterious man in black. Max in turn, told me how bad things were getting in the world since I had left. He said that Eris was still in charge and that her black dressed cronies were wreaking havoc in the community and beyond. They had even started to segregate and round up people claiming they were a threat to society. When Max said this, his eyes started to tear up as he described his own situation.

"They also questioned my family and then they took my close friend, Gary, when he refused to answer their questions. I know he is not bad. I think they are doing it to scare me into submission."

As he told me this, I realized I needed to talk to the man in black sooner than later, and relayed this urgency on to Max. Then I added, "If you can, avoid Eris, until we talk again."

I wasn't ready to tell him that she could possibly read other peoples unprotected thoughts. I didn't think it was the right time to creep Max out about Eris, quite yet. Max promised to try to find the man in black as soon as he could, and we agreed to meet again at the same place and time.

When I left the coffee shop, I walked around the block before returning to my car and heading back to the safe house. I didn't want to miss my interstellar phone call, even if it was almost ten hours away. Back at the safe house, Nesta was in a frenzy and explained, "I am super busy getting things ready downstairs, can you check on my critters? Maybe take Henry for a ride?" Without waiting for an answer, she disappeared down a set of stairs. I could hear her humming the Peacemaker song as she descended.

I spent most of the day wandering around the backyard where Nesta had collected over a dozen chickens, several pigs, a couple of milking goats, and one very fat and old draft horse that I assumed was named Henry. Per Nesta's suggestion, I saddled up Henry and walked him around the property.

Henry only had one speed and that was walk, but it didn't matter. It was a beautiful day. The sky was clear, the sun was shining, there was a slight breeze moving through the pasture grasses, and the tall Sycamore trees that lined the vinyl fence slowly swayed back and forth. The clomp clomp clomp of Henry's feet was familiar and peaceful, and I cleared my mind of the worries that swirled there, and just enjoyed the ride.

That night, I had another wonderful conversation with Sajan. He felt that his mission was going well. Woola was adjusting to the changes, but that they would be transporting their rounded-up cargo and Woola to Amaranthine by the end of the week. I remember being relieved. The 12th Command's history still concerned me. You never know when someone is going to fall off the wagon.

Sajan and I, of course, teased each other a lot; cried a little, and even did an unsuccessful shimmering energy light hug in my room. When he hung up, I couldn't wait to see him again. Even if it wasn't physically him.

The next morning, I drove myself to The Coffee Bean to talk to Max about the results of his remote viewing on the man in black. I made sure I was at least ten minutes early. When I walked up to order my drink, I was surprised to see Max quickly getting in his car and leaving. He looked at me, shook his head in a negative way, and then peered towards the Les Schwab Tire Center across the street. Then he tapped his cup and gazed at the barista. When I turned to look at Beth, the barista, she was smiling at me.

"That guy, his name is Max, he got you this for free. Isn't he adorable. Have a nice day."

By this time Max was driving off. Shortly after he disappeared from my sight, a black sedan with dark windows pulled out of the Les Schwab tire store and zoomed off after him. Numb from this development, I grabbed my coffee, gave her a huge tip, and nonchalantly walked off towards the library.

When I got back to my car, I searched the cup for clues. After thinking that it was just a cup of coffee, I finally found a rolled-up hot pink sticky note under the sleeve that had familiar writing on it.

It read, "Welcome back," with a set of coordinates. Max had found the man in black and had already met with him.

Using my own remote viewing skills, I looked at the coordinates. I started to see a boat that was floating in the air. Behind it were dozens of loud-playing children that were weaving in and out of a gigantic wooden castle structure. The mighty Columbia River was on the left. East of the playground was a kid fishing pond that my dad had taken me to visit many times as a child. I knew exactly where to meet the man in black and I started up my inconspicuous car and jumped on to George Washington Way and headed for Columbia Park.

The 450-acre park runs parallel to the Columbia River for almost five miles. Every summer, in late July, we used to spend a weekend there watching the hydroplane races. The city of Kennewick even had a hydroplane hoisted up on a pole, as you come in to the park's entrance. The Playground of Dreams, was nestled in between the kids fishing pond and the Columbia River. At the roundabout there was a pretty cool Regional Veterans Memorial display.

I decided to take the less traveled Columbia Park Trail Road all the way down to the fishing pond. When I arrived, I checked for suspicious black sedans and other non-friendly type figures. I decided it was best to park at the east entrance of the playground. I walked the long way around the pond and found myself at a small dock. He was standing on the back side of a huge pine tree. I could feel his nervous energy as he peeked out at me. I wasn't sure if he even had the ability, but I sent a telepathic message across the air waves, "Are you alone?"

Shockingly, I heard a quiet and reserved, "Yes."

When I started to saunter over towards him, he did a double take on my new looks. It almost looked like he was going to turn around and leave, until I said in my thoughts, "Safer to talk this way. You never know who is listening."

He nodded, slipped his hand under his cape, and handed me an envelope. I quickly put it down the side of my pants and asked, "Is this all I am going to get from you?"

He nodded and I kept walking like I was looking at the geese that had settled near the shore. As he stepped out and started to walk away I projected, "Thanks for your help."

That's when he quipped, "Thank me later, if you know what I mean? They are rounding us up. We need help."

And I did know what he meant. And I telepathically reassured him, "I will find you. I promise."

On the drive back to Nesta's safe house, I took extra care to make sure no one was following me by taking the back roads of Pasco. Somehow I found myself in Othello, where my Aunt Patty lived. After several attempts to convince myself it would be okay to say hello, common sense gripped me and I jumped back on the main highway and headed to Eltopia. As I walked up to my room, I began to sing the Peacemakers song, and at the end I whispered, "Henoch, I need you. Are you there?"

By the time I had climbed the three flights of stairs, Henoch was sitting in the chair next to my bed. He had a bored look on his face, like he had been waiting for me a long time. I pulled out the envelope and exclaimed out loud, "Got something."

He grabbed his head and said, "Ouch. Quit screaming," and then reached out for it.

Without hesitation I gave it to him and he ripped it open with his long alien fingers. He poured it out in front of him and it floated to the floor. We immediately recognized the same format as the other documents that the man in black had provided, except this time he included the missing row of data that Henoch had asked about.

If a Gray could look shocked, that is the look that was plastered across Henoch's face. His small slit of a mouth was actually gaping open, and his big blue almond eyes were as wide as I had ever seen them. With a distraught tone in his thoughts, I heard him mumble, "I have to talk to Gyaan. I will contact you later." Then he poofed out of the room leaving me all alone.

Reminiscent of my earlier experience back at my Perkins home and Henoch's love for the TV show "Hee Haw," I started to hum "You Were Gone," by Buck Owens.

I made sure I did the "Pffffft" sound really loud as I fell back on my bed and sang, "You was gone."

31

THE MEANING OF ERIS

HENOCH NEVER RETURNED to fill me in on his sudden epiphany. But I did get my usual 8:30 p.m. call from Sajan. When he appeared, he looked nervous and kept looking over his shoulder like someone was going to crash our call. Woola wasn't with him. He let out a deep breath of relief when he saw me and then uncharacteristically blurted, "Hey, it's bad here. The crew is infighting. I can't find Cozbi anywhere."

When he tried to explain, his voice began to shake and crack.

"Dariann, I can't find Woola. I am so sorry."

I was in complete shock as I watched him struggle with this news. The tears that I was trying to hold back began to fall down my cheeks. I rubbed at them with frustration and anger, because there was nothing I could do. I had no idea where he was or how to help him and Woola. As I thought about my cute little loving dog wandering around a bunch of Reptiles, I started to dry heave. Visions of National Geographic documentaries and giant crocodiles attacking helpless water buffalo as they cross the rivers in the African plains danced in my head. I wasn't keeping my emotions under control, because about that time Nesta barged through the door while imploring, "What's wrong boonoonoonoos?"

When she saw Sajan, she backed out and closed the door.

Sajan called to Nesta and pleaded with her, "Please listen, I need you both to listen to me."

Nesta came back through the door and quietly sat down.

"Eris, the one from Earth, I just saw her. I don't know how or when she arrived, but she is here. I think she and Cozbi have been planning this all along. I knew he was hiding something—but this? I think he is the Lawless one that Gyaan has been looking for. You need to tell him."

As Sajan said her name, I knew immediately what had happened. Eris had read Max's mind. She knew I was back and that I had been meeting with the man in black. Somehow, she had found a way to Cozbi's ship.

Sajan took another deep breath, rubbed his hand through his dark hair with frustration, and whispered to himself, "OMG! Woola."

As all of this is running through my head, I said out loud to Sajan, "Did you contact Henoch or Omah? Do they know?"

He was shaking his head, but I don't think it was at me, when he turned back to me, he had fear in his eyes. Then it looked like someone was dragging him out of our call. That is when he temporarily fought someone off and looked deep into my eyes and quietly, but passionately sobbed, "Mahal Kita, Dariann."

Then I woke up and he was gone.

I shot up out my deep sleep and cried, "Noooooooooo!"

Nesta was sitting there beside me on the bed. She had actually been holding my hand and sobbing quietly as I made my call with Sajan. I was glad she had heard the message, because I was a hot-mess and immediately ran to the bathroom and threw up. When I pulled myself together, I found Nesta and Henoch downstairs.

They both looked incredibly sad when I walked down that final flight of stairs. I plopped into one of Nesta's old leather recliners and slumped back in defeat. Nesta walked over and draped a fluffy red blanket over my legs. I sat there silently looking at the crackling fire that Nesta had prepared earlier that evening. I had grabbed the envelope with the one piece of paper that possibly held the answers to my loss and despair. I was hugging it tightly against my chest in shock.

Henoch took a telepathic breath, saw that I had the envelope, and calmy said, "The paper that you provided clued us in on who was behind the deception. We truly thought Cozbi was being honest with us. We truly thought Sajan and Woola would be safer there. I apologize Dariann."

As seconds passed, my denial wore off and my anger bubbled up when I practically yelled, "How could one piece of paper from the human race be the one thing that clues you in on an answer that alien races have been looking for all of these centuries?"

Henoch shook his head and gently confessed, "Because humans were the ones that were foretold to find that answer. We knew it would be someone from the human race. We had to wait until there was someone that could tell us what that answer was. We had no idea that a hybrid of Homo sapiens and a Reptile could be the Lawless one. We were always just looking for a man. Not a woman hybrid, from the 12th Command."

Frustrated I cried out, "How do you know you have the right human anyways?"

Henoch floated over his thoughts on how this had happened. He explained how the final document that I obtained from the man in black provided the code that led them to Eris. That was why he left so suddenly. Henoch knew he needed to get it to the ICC, which included Cozbi, because he truly did not believe that Cozbi knew all of what was revealed. When the ICC saw the evidence, Cozbi actually mentioned Eris as the one they were looking for. He exhibited a lot of remorse and shock after he claimed he realized that it was her. After multiple hours behind closed doors to determine what to do next, the members of the ICC took a break.

Henoch ended his description of the meeting with, "When we met one hour later, Cozbi was gone."

As Henoch was describing all of this, I opened the envelope and began to look over the new data. In the 12th row it showed the four missing areas. The first column had #12, the corresponding second column showed the color green, the third column listed Kepler-666b, and the fourth column had 250. Above the fourth column were two words written in pencil that read, "Times visited."

I half-joked to myself when I read the new numbers, "As in Satan has visited Earth 250 times?"

I evidently was not doing a great job of holding my thoughts to myself because Henoch added, "Exactly Dariann. Humans described the 12th Command's planet with the numbers foretold in The Book of Knowledge and they have visited Earth 50 times more than my group has. That is why you see 200 in the times visited column for #1. Which as you know is me." He actually pointed at himself for emphasis.

I slumped back into the recliner and sarcastically sputtered, "How do we get rid of the wicked witch of the West? I want Sajan back and my little dog too." Then the tears of frustration that I was holding back came pouring out of my eyes.

As Henoch and Nesta watched me bawl my eyes out, Noach suddenly busted in from the garage and yelled, "But si yah! Small up yuhself," as he wedged his body next to mine on the one-person recliner. He wrapped his strong arms around me and gave me a big bear hug.

I squeezed him back as my eyes started to tear up for round two. I tried to hold them in, but one of them spilled down my cheek.

Noach scrunched me harder in his grasp and whispered, "Time to kick some ass Ninja Girl."

Behind Noach was a line of people that I did not know. I could tell they were feeling awkward based on their thoughts that they were sharing telepathically. I quickly found out that these were selected members for Amaranthine transfer that Noach went to recruit from the Seattle area. They were part of the 11th Planet Peacemakers. I could tell by the looks on their faces that they felt my grief and pain.

Nesta popped up and ushered them downstairs to the plethora of rooms, kitchens and bathrooms that were created by the Conductor, just for this purpose. Nesta had been training all of her life for this moment and she was ready to help in whatever way she could.

Noach finally moved after I complained of parts of my body going numb. Then he gave us the rundown on his adventures on the west side of Washington State. He was exhausted from the number of confrontations that he had with those trying to stop him from his mission.

He explained that the people on that side had been brainwashed to think the government was truthful. That the government would actually take care of them. So, when the government started to round them up, most of them went peacefully. They didn't question their motives, even when they started to put tattoos on the back of people's hands that would help the sorters determine where they would be shipped.

Noach finished his story by saying, "It was creepy. I think they were part of the menu, man."

Noach expelled an exasperated sigh, pulled out a dooby, lit it up and just before he took a giant puff, he said, ""Jeezum Pees, Man. Crazy." Then he pointed to the people that were still streaming in the house from the garage. He breathed out a plume of smoke from his lungs and finished saying, "My story is crazy, but good man." Noach had found good within all of the bad and he brought them back to help us.

Henoch left within the hour. He said he needed to regroup with the remaining members of the ICC and decide what to do. After he left, I tried to go to bed. However, no matter how hard I tried, I couldn't sleep. Instead, I did some research on the one secure line that Nesta had setup for me.

The first thing I did was look up the name Eris. I was shocked to find the following description from the online Collins English Dictionary that said Eris was, "A feminine name of Greek origin that means strife. They are known for their dark and mischievous side. In simple terms they are liars." Other searches were saying that based on mythology, Eris is the one who builds up evil war and commits great slaughter of the innocent." When I couldn't find anything related to the spelling of her last name, I typed in Cozbi, just for fun. I was sickened to find that the meaning of Cozbi was defined as a liar sliding away.

As soon as I read this. I threw up again after mumbling, "OMG! Please don't let them be the ones that eat my dog."

32

THE MISSION

A FTER A FEW more nervous heaves, I did finally pass out on
top of my bed after hugging my pillow and shedding a few
more tears. When I made it downstairs for some of Nesta's kape,
I was informed that Noach had already left. Nesta explained that
he needed to run a few errands in town and then he was headed
to the mountains near a place called Deer Lake. When I asked
her how long he would be gone, she shrugged.

"He will be staying at the Spokane area safe house collecting
others. I am not privy to the specifics."

When she said Spokane, I immediately thought of Fanny and
wished we would have had that conversation last night. Fanny
lived in the Liberty Lake area, and I needed to get a message to
her somehow. I wanted her to be ready to go if needed. I would
never leave her behind.

Nesta gave me one of her wise looks and crooned, "Just relax
Boonoonoonoos. We will save your Fanny." Then she tapped
her head.

With a pained look back at her I realized that, once again, she
had read the unprotected thoughts in my mind. But Nesta just
gave me a sweet grandma smile and then pointed to a piece of
paper that was on the coffee table beside the big leather chair and
crackling fire place.

"Noach wanted you to have that."

I plopped into the chair and grabbed the single piece of paper.
On it were three words and a set of coordinates. The three words
said, "Find them now."

As I read the coordinates and thought about his words, I

realized our schedule for our assignment was being crashed. The original mission called for 0xFF, which was a code name for finding 255 people in Washington. The 15 was code for the date 11/11, which was the date that a blue orbed ship piloted by #2 Commanders would be transporting us off Earth. Noach and I thought we had weeks to collect our targets and get them to the safe houses in Washington, but thanks to me we no longer had the luxury of time or secrecy on our side. Me going to Max and Max inadvertently spilling the beans to Eris, really messed things up. That is when I ran to the toilet and threw up, once again. When I got back, Nesta looked disappointed.

"I thought you were a badass ninja."

I looked down at the floor and brooded my mistakes.

She quickly added, "You got this Boonoonoonoos. You are more powerful than you think. Just believe in your training, the gifts that you have been given, and the love that you have for others. No one, not even the lizard-eyed Lawless one can take that from you." In her hand was a set of keys and she gently placed them in the palm of my hand and snickered, "You should take this one when you go."

With Nesta's pep talk in my pocket, I jingled the keys and told myself, "Nothing like a little joy ride."

In the garage, I found a brand-new Aston Martin DBX SUV that belonged to the keys in my hand. As I ran my finger down the side of it, the color made me think of Evania's oceans and the tunnel transport that Sajan and I took to class, so many years ago. The car's deep blues and greens flowed across its surface as I pulled it out into the late fall morning sunshine. The creamy beige leather interior hugged my body like a warm fuzzy blanket. It purred like a kitten, as I pointed it towards the Tri-Cities and gave it some gas. When I instantaneously reached the posted speed limit, I locked in the cruise control.

There were three extra buttons below the DBX on the dashboard. One showed a picture of big lips with their index finger over them implying quiet. The second button had four letters that read, "FSTR." The last button looked like it had a colorful robotic transformer on it like you would see from the 2007 movie "Transformers: Beginnings." The irony was thick when I thought about the beginning of that movie and the first contact from an alien species. I immediately started talking to my overcomplicated car.

"I probably should have asked for instructions from Nesta before taking you out of the garage. Hopefully, I don't need to touch any of these special features that you have."

I took the George Washington Way Road, through the center of Richland for several miles. When I pulled up to the parking lot of the USS Triton Park, I could see my contact peeking out from behind the top part of the submarine, known as the sail.

The retired USS Triton's sail was shoved in the ground, just above what the local folks call the Port of Benton. The flags placed beside it were gently waving in the wind like it was sailing on the ocean. My concealed contact was shy, and I stepped out of the car and walked over to him.

As I moved past and around the submarine exhibit, Max was there with Ally. They were in jogging attire. I couldn't help but let out a hearty chuckle, because I knew that they hated public displays of exercise, or any kind of exercising for that matter. It was the perfect disguise for my two nerdy ex-teammates. Max waved with the awkwardness of someone that didn't get out much in the social world. When I got over to him, he blurted out, "OMG, Dariann. I can't believe you got the message."

I kind of looked up in the air and shrugged my shoulders and vocally replied, "I gots skills Max." But secretly, I had already made a mental note to ask Noach how this meeting had been arranged so quickly.

Max was practically vibrating when Ally put her hand in his and quietly urged him to, "Just tell her what you saw."

That's when I put my finger up to my lips and pointed to my car.

"Let's get in the car and talk."

When all three of us climbed in the car, I got brave and pushed the first button with the big lips on it. The car adjusted up and down and then actually responded with a deep Australian male accent.

"Safe. No worries."

Like magic, the car became a soundproof room. We couldn't

hear one noise outside, even when the flashing lights appeared with a beeping garbage truck that backed in and emptied the trash twenty feet from us. Max slapped his hands over his mouth like he was going to shriek from the excitement of the cool car we were in. When he started to stroke the soft leather of his seat, Ally warmly peered at him, like he was a 2-year-old child, and calmly egged him on to tell me what he knew. I got the feeling she wanted to get out of there and away from whatever danger surrounded me. Max shook his head a few times in agreement.

"Okay, both of us did a remote viewing on the data you provided on a missing person and black colored dog." When I cocked my head to one side and gave him a confused look, because I never gave Max any data, he must have thought I was sad about Woola. Because the next thing Max did was nervously shove his glasses back up on his nose and whisper, "I'm sorry Woola's missing."

Without waiting for me to respond he spouted, "We both, basically saw the same thing. However, my vision was pretty detailed. I saw a large oblong-type structure. I kept seeing green lights. I am 99% sure it was in the air, flying. But not an airplane, if you know what I mean?"

He paused and looked at me to see if I was believing him, which I definitely was.

"There were strange upright non-human creatures that were all over in this flying structure. It felt like some of them were fighting each other. However, the target was in a hidden locked room."

After a brief pause, he asked, "Does the person that you are looking for have dark skin, dark longish hair, and greenish eyes? Because this target was yelling 'Woola,' like he knew your dog. He was also constantly pounding on the door that he was locked behind. He had a noticeable accent."

That was when the tear that I was so desperately trying to keep to myself, fell out of my eye. I aggressively wiped it away and practically begged, "That's him. Is he okay?"

Max shook his head.

"Yes, as far as I can tell."

When I looked at Ally, she shook her head affirmatively, as well. Then Max added, "Ally didn't pick up on the other vision I had. There seems to be another human on that ship. I think it is a female. She had short curly bobbed hair, glasses, and green eyes. She was really angry and barking out orders. I am pretty sure she was in command." Then he sucked in his breath and shivered, "OMG! Was that Eris?"

When I confirmed his suspicion, of who it was, I shuddered, "Yes it is. The Black Magic Woman strikes again."

Ally looked confused by my comment, but Max started to chuckle at my attempt to soften the blow about Eris being evil.

"I didn't see Woola, Dariann, but that doesn't mean that he isn't there. Like this car, they could have some kind of communication cloaking technology that we can't get through."

Trying not to cry again, I asked Max where he had gotten the data about the missing person. He told me that Beth, the barista at The Coffee Bean handed it to him. He didn't think anything of it, until now. He assumed it was me.

After a slight pause, I told them to go home. Pack a few things for a long trip. I also asked them to call in sick and avoid contact with anyone in black suits and capes. It was time to get my new friends out of here and to a safe place. The last thing I did, right before I dropped them off in a back street about half a mile from their car, was give them the coordinates and a range of time frames for pickup in the morning. It was another one of Max's favorite places – a quiet community garden off Union Street in Kennewick.

Just before they got out of the soundproof car I whispered, "Park, walk, and when you hear 'Jeezum Pees,' that will be your ride. Follow them. Don't talk until you are back in this car."

Without a word, they nodded and quickly jumped out of my car. By that time, it was 7:11 a.m. and against all of the alarm bells going off in my head telling me not to, I drove to The Coffee Bean drive through, and got myself a hummingbird latte. As I turned towards the local Fred Meyer store savoring the delicious coffee, I realized I had a black sedan with dark tinted windows on my tail. With way too much confidence, that I was just being paranoid, I pulled into the Fred Meyer grocery store parking lot, near the entrance that had multiple escape routes, and I waited to see if they would follow.

When they kept going and turned left towards the Beaver Bark Garden Store, I got distracted with drinking my coffee and listening to the lyrics of "Drops of Jupiter," which is a song sung by the band, Train. As this band played this classic 2001 song, my mind wandered to Sajan and Evania and the beautiful sunset where we shared our first kiss. When I started to sing out loud, "The best hummingbird latte that I have ever had," four black sedans came from every direction and boxed me in from all sides.

They sat there in their cars, blocking any escape. In my panic, I actually hit the hazard light switch in hopes that it communicated some kind of secret message back to the safe house. Instead, it did exactly what the Aston Martin creators intended, and it just made my cars lights blink, on and off.

After a full sixty seconds or more, a woman dressed in all black, including black boots and black glasses, stepped out and walked over to my car. She tapped on my window with her knuckles, like I was being pulled over for a speeding ticket. Even though she couldn't see in, when I looked up, she had pulled down her dark tinted glasses. Her green and gold eyes blinked sideways back at me. She had a wicked smirk on her face. I almost peed my pants from shock. I had never seen her eyes do that before, but it was definitely Eris.

After a few seconds, hoping the lizard lady would go away, I decided to let my tinted black window lower a few inches, so we could talk in the open. Not afraid of her anymore, I looked her in the eyes and stated, "No more games, I see." Then, I winked at her.

She looked like the cat that had eaten the canary. Which made me cringe, as I thought of Woola.

"This time, I win Dariann. You might want to turn off your car. Don't be afraid. I just need to talk to you."

With that, I heard chains and cables being attached to the back of my parked running car. A black tow truck, with a ramp attached to an enclosed black car trailer, was quickly reeling me into it. I immediately hit the soundproof button to the off position, and started to sing the Peacemakers song. As I hurried through the lyrics, I telepathically shot out into the airwaves, "Oh Henoch. Kind of in a pickle here with a hybrid. Black covered trailer. No idea where I'm going."

As the nose of my car popped up over the black ramp, I saw Eris getting into her own black car and speeding off. One of the caped black figures quickly jerked up the ramp and closed me in. In my dark prison, I turned the engine off, and talked to my overcomplicated car, once more.

"Nothing like being in the grasp of the devil herself. Sorry my friend."

When we arrived at Eris's evil headquarters, I heard chains and cables being removed, as the ramp came down. A familiar big burly man in black, directed me to drive out of the trailer, and stop at some imaginary line in the underground facility that they had taken me. Then he tapped my window and told me to get out. So, I did.

I was really curious what Eris had to say. I had worked with her for several years of my life. A few of those years I thought she was my friend. I was still struggling to believe that she was the one they called Nero. Deep down, inside my gut, I was open to some explanation and perhaps enlightenment, as to why she got this bad reputation.

The man in black directed me down a narrow dark tunnel to a green door that opened up into what I would call an interrogation room. It definitely had two-way glass. There was a shiny silver table, a couple of cold metal chairs, and a well-worn brown cloth couch in the corner. There was a bottle of water on the table. Just to the right of the couch was an open door that disclosed a simple toilet and pedestal sink. To the left was another green-colored door that led deeper into the facility. When the guy left through it, I tried to follow him. He, of course, just pointed to the table and dictated, "You wait there."

Not wanting to cause any trouble, yet, I sat on the couch instead. It looked way cozier. When Eris finally arrived after what felt like hours, she was actually dressed in a light gray pin stripe suit with a white silk collared top. Her short curly bobbed hair was pulled back in a tight bun. She even had on a light tone of pink lipstick. She smirked when she saw me lounging on the couch, and not at the table, waiting for her.

As she moved closer to me she snapped, "Wouldn't expect you to follow orders at this point."

As nice as I could, I tapped the couch next to me for her to sit. Surprisingly she did.

"Where have you been Dariann? You are hard to find. You left so quickly, and I have so much to tell you."

With all the strength I could muster, I politely told her, "I can't wait to hear what you have to say, Eris. I'm sorry that we didn't have that talk in the SCIF. I was completely spooked by what you shared there."

I must have been getting better at holding my true feelings in, because she let out the breath she was holding. After taking a swig of her bottled water, she finally responded.

"Oh good. Let's get started. You lost your mom at an early age, right?"

Shocked by her question about my mom's tragic death, I sat there in dumbfounded and unblinking silence. As usual, she didn't wait for a response and proceeded to tell me her life story.

I quickly found out that her mother was named Matilda. She was an incredibly smart scientist back when women were not necessarily appreciated for their knowledge. In the early 1950's, somehow Matilda had intercepted a foreign language over her transistor radio. Curious and well-equipped to grasp what she was receiving; Eris's mom eventually found a way to communicate back to the voices. That is when Matilda met her dad one dark night through the help of a green orb from space. Eris looked at the ceiling and then back at me.

"Their friendship turned into an intergalactic relationship."

She pointed to her eyes and gave me a dramatic unnatural sideways blink.

"Obviously, my dad was not human."

When I gave her a wide-eyed "holy crap" gaze, she appeared pleased that she was freaking me out.

"My mom died in childbirth and my dad didn't want me. So, my dad gave me to Cozbi to train in the ways of the 12th Command."

After dropping her truth bomb, Eris proceeded to give me a history lesson.

"In 1952, after several visible displays of alien existence – including a flight of one of Henoch's fleets over the U.S. White House; the ICC made official contact with Earth's governmental entities. The rules of engagement were codified. Twenty years later, Cozbi decided that he was going to assign me to Earth to help with the transition. His reasoning was that I looked human enough and I could blend in. I had to practice for over a year to actually blink like a human."

She did a quick demonstration of her ability to blink up and down versus sideways.

"When Cozbi was satisfied that I was ready to go undercover, he renamed me Eris Cosbee. I was tasked with keeping watch on Planet #11's government to make sure they kept up their side of the bargain. I was told to only report back to him. Eventually, I was in charge of debunking any kind of sightings that slipped through that were not approved by Cozbi. When we saw how gifted you were, we decided to hire you to help with that mission."

About this time, her story started to fall apart, especially when she explained the reasoning for becoming a double agent.

"Cozbi started to embrace the old ways and was using Sajan to collect animals across all of the planets for food, not for transfer to Amaranthine. After a while, Sajan knew what was going on and he decided to look the other way because he was afraid of Cozbi."

When she said Sajan's name and that his efforts had evil intent, I started to shake my head in disbelief. Her interlaced web of lies was confusing me, and I couldn't help but exhale dramatically, like I was being hurt by her words.

As if to feed my reaction, she added with an exasperated rattle, "I knew I needed to intervene and stop them. This is why I took command of Cozbi's ship and put Sajan in a safe room to protect the animals. Luckily, I am part human, Sajan had no control over me."

She did a dramatic pause and opened up her freaky eyes wide and said in her sweetest voice, "I saved him from Cozbi's twisted plan. I tried to save your little dog too."

With her news that Woola was dead, I tried to hold back my tears, but I couldn't, and they spilled out over my cheeks. I purposefully and openly communicated my thoughts for Eris to hear, "OMG, I loved him so much."

When Eris inadvertently let her thoughts slip my way, I heard her whisper, "Good job Eris," like she was mentally patting herself on the back. That was when I knew she was living up to her name and lying about her intentions. This moment was when I realized the real reason why the communication channels had been left open. She had planned on using me to trick the ICC.

I pretended to compose myself over the news of Woola.

"So where is Sajan now?"

She quickly responded with, "He is safely hidden off the ship away from Cozbi and any other animals that he could attempt to control."

As I processed her words, I felt a wave of relief wash over me. I knew this was a lie based on Max and Ally's earlier information about Sajan's location. Maybe the other stuff she was babbling about were lies too.

I opened up my thoughts, just like Sajan had taught me back at Suttle Lake, and projected to Eris, "I need to let Henoch know that he was right and that Cozbi is bad. I need to let him know that they were wrong about Eris." When she crinkled her forehead, I knew she had heard me.

For some reason Max's voice popped into my thoughts. It was asking, "Where are you?"

It prompted me to ask Eris, "What is this place?"

Eris, thinking I was buying into her deception, offered, "This is one of the facilities throughout the country where we bring those that are sympathetic to Cozbi or are resisting our new safety measures. Many of the original men in black are not complying with the new rules. We humanely keep them here, so they don't try to create momentum behind a conspiracy theory. We are also holding a few terrorists here, to keep the Tri-Cities area safe. We are using them as leverage to get critical information about their plans to combat us."

I must have looked lost, because she added, "This is war Dariann. Did you not know this?"

To keep her talking, I trembled like I was scared, and then asked, "So, what happened to Cozbi?"

She shrugged.

"No idea."

Realizing I needed to keep her talking, so I could find out as much as possible, I began to shoot questions at her as fast as I could think them up. I let my frustration purposefully bubble up and out of me. Like an out of body experience, I heard myself blurt out, "If this is true, why did you use me to develop technology that blocked the others? Did you know I was being recruited for the 11th Command? Why didn't you tell me earlier about this war? Why did you always steer me away from the data and evidence about finding other life forms if you were sent to help them assimilate? Why did you have my notebook?"

I could tell my questions were confusing her and after a few sideways blinks, she claimed, "You were smart, talented, and driven to find life outside of Earth's boundaries. You and your notebook were key to helping us find answers. I simply didn't tell you all of the truth, because I didn't know if I could trust you with that truth."

These brutally honest words, uttered from my old boss, finally told me who "they" were. It had been Eris and Cozbi controlling key figures in my government, all along.

She lowered her shoulders, looked down at her feet, and then said with deep disappointment like she was scolding a star pupil for making dumb choices.

"I had no idea that you would actually fall in love with the Lawless one. That was an unfortunate development."

I inhaled when she called Sajan this name. Her words struck an emotion deep inside of me that actually emerged as a growl like a protective mamma bear. Just as I was getting ready to emotionally unload on her, the big burly man in black busted through one of the green doors and held it wide open. I could see behind him a hallway with rows of locked heavy-duty doors. Each of them had a small prison-like window. Eris was visibly pissed by his disturbance. They had a private conversation telepathically, of which I overheard. Someone was breaking into the facility. They were having a tough time figuring out who or what it was. When the red lights and alarms started to flash I started to wonder if this drama was related to me.

Just about that time I heard a Jamaican accent float towards me, "Badass Kunoichi? Where are you. It's time to go now."

I started to laugh out loud and Eris turned towards me with a confused look, "What's so funny?"

I lifted off the couch, walked half-way to the table, and tilted my head towards the big burly man. Noach suddenly materialized behind the man in black.

"The truth is coming for you Nero."

She hissed like a snake and snarled, "I knew it. You were just stalling so they could find you. I hate humans so much. I will make sure none of you make it to Amaranthine."

That is when I gave her a Choku Zuki followed by a Mae Gen. She fell to the ground and rolled into a ball. Noach took down the man in black in one weird move to the back of the head. Standing behind him were several individuals that I did not recognize. They looked terrified, but relieved to be free from their prisons. Noach pointed down the hallway at the green door that led outside to the garage.

As I looked over at the locked door, it magically opened, and there standing in front of me, was Nesta in an actual ninja outfit. Her head and thick gray dreadlocks were completely covered in black leather and cloth. She had a curved katana–like Japanese sword in one hand. The enthusiasm flowing out of her made me temporarily stop in my tracks, especially when she crooned at me with her heavy Jamaican accent, "Hello Boonoonoonoos."

Noach pushed me forward and into the waiting Aston Martin. He ran around the front of it and popped himself into the driver's seat. Nesta guided the shocked prisoners to her car and zipped away.

Ahead of us, I could see the crack of sunlight and an opening garage door, as Nesta flew through the opening with the speed of light. When we arrived, the door was wide open, and our car bounced over the speed bumps and past the checkpoint gate. Noach immediately pushed the be quiet button. When we rounded the second gate a mile away from the checkpoint, he pushed the FSTR button.

The men that were supposed to be there protecting certain points of this secure road, were on the ground unconscious. When my eyes adjusted to the sunlit day, I realized we were out in the middle of the desert in between the two entrances of the Hanford site. There was nothing to see but sagebrush, sand dunes, and chain-link fencing with barbed wire on top. When Noach hit the transformer button, I was seriously expecting the car to magically transform into something cool, but it didn't. Noach felt my question, before I could ask.

"It basically makes our vehicles blend in like a chameleon does with the surrounding environment. They won't be able to see us from the air, as we go through town, and back out to the safe house."

As he said this, I realized that Nesta's car was literally invisible in front of us.

By the time we were back at the Eltopia safe house, Noach had filled me in. While I slept, Noach had made contact with the man in black, that had been providing me with data and information. He asked if the man would contact Max and give him a special assignment. He agreed and dropped it off at The Coffee Bean for Max to pick up.

"I was hoping that your meeting with Max would go a little better. Clearly it didn't."

That was when I cringed and admitted, "Well, I sort of went to The Coffee Bean after my meeting. Eris picked me up at Fred Meyers."

Noach gave me a pained look and sassed, "No sah, Dariann."

Then we both laughed.

When we finally pulled into the safe house, Noach and I were the first to enter. There were two shell-shocked and frightened individuals in the hallway. When they saw me, the looks of relief washed over their faces. Max and Ally didn't know any of the people at the house and thought maybe they were in the wrong place or maybe even the wrong side of the conflict they had embarked upon. When I asked how they got there so fast. Max pointed at the figure in the living room that was sitting in my usual leather chair by the fireplace.

"We almost didn't get in his car. You had told us to stay away from men dressed in black, but I knew that you trusted him and we figured it was your guy coming to get us early. I actually sent out a mental call to see where you were."

The thin man, dressed in black, had his feet up on the coffee table drinking something from a steaming cup. The table had a plate of Nesta's homemade chocolate chip cookies. When he saw me, he waved and actually looked at ease. Without his hat on, I could tell he had a marine-cut hairstyle. After a few moments of complete confusion, I finally realized that it was the mysterious man in black that had been helping me all along. He had retrieved Max and Ally early knowing that they would be next on Eris's list.

I sent him a heartfelt telepathic, "Thank you? I'm so sorry. I don't even know your name."

When he projected his thoughts towards me, he playfully said, "It was a good opportunity to make sure you didn't forget me. You can call me Milo." Then he grabbed a gooey cookie and shoved it in his mouth.

Moments later, Nesta and the prisoners crossed the threshold. When Max saw them, he actually shouted the code words that I had just taught him.

"Jeezum pees. It's Gary."

Gary ran across the room and flung his arms around his best friend. Noach and Nesta had not only saved me from my stupidity, but they had saved Max's imprisoned friend Gary, and a few other good souls too.

Feeling guilty about my failures in meeting the mission that the ICC leaders had given me, my feelings poured out across the room. That was when Noach gave me a sideways glance and proposed, "Maybe you better stay away from kape badass Kunoichi. Maybe try some of my Ganga instead?"

And the entire room was filled with kind laughter, even though I had royally screwed up our mission—twice, in less than two days.

33

THE 11TH PLANET'S PEACEMAKER

THAT NIGHT I slept like a baby that had been perfectly swaddled in a blanket. When it was way past breakfast, I finally made it downstairs to a large crowd of old and new friends. Max, Ally, and Gary were loudly replaying the previous day's events. When I looked over at Max he gave me a warm look and a classic thumbs up. Nesta and Noach were in the kitchen cutting up sandwiches and shoving them into brown paper lunch sacks.

It reminded me of my mom and how she had always packed my lunches in the same kind of bags. Every school day, when I woke up, she would be downstairs in the kitchen singing some kind of happy song, making my sandwich, and packing the fruit of the day. The memory didn't make me sad, it just reminded me of her and how much comfort I had when she took care of me, even when she was secretly suffering from Stage 4 pancreatic cancer. She was always such a strong woman. I liked to think I got some of my courage from her.

About that time, both Noach and Nesta turned to me, and Nesta crooned, "She sounds wonderful, Dariann." They both had warm and loving looks on their faces, as I inadvertently shared the sweet memories of my deceased mom.

This time I didn't beat myself up for opening up my thoughts and I whispered back, "She was a great momma."

When the sandwich making was done, Noach pulled me aside and directed me to a room, that had two executive-stye chairs that spun around and reclined. I was struggling with the knobs and doing playful 360-degree spins, when he asked, "I have good news and bad news. What would you like first?"

With one final spin, I grinned, "Let's do good news first. Why not?"

Noach went into great detail about how Eris, with all of her governmental power and control over the men in black, was setting up military style barricades to try to find us. They had started to deploy electromagnetic pulses neighborhood by neighborhood to disrupt the use of electronic equipment. They were then publicly declaring that it was some kind of terrorist attack. As they hauled people away, they blamed it on that.

"Her people are telling everyone to stay home until notified. This is making our ability to get into the Tri-Cities very difficult. They are starting to imprison anyone that questions or resists their curfews. We just received word from Davita and Alaster that her tactics are spreading around the world. She has way more control than we anticipated."

When he finished, I crinkled my forehead, cocked my head to the right, and retorted, "That was the good news?"

With an upbeat tone he jested, "It means you get to do your badass ninja girl stuff; I thought you would be happy."

I perked up with that thought.

"So we are going in?"

He shook his long dreadlocks up and down.

"Yep, and the first stop is your dad's house. Second stop will be Maddy's. Whoo hoo! Surprise."

Grateful for this news. I took a few more spins in my chair and sung, "Best day ever!" When I stopped twirling, and faced him, once again, I nervously asked, "So what's the bad news?"

"We are taking Atlantis back to Suttle Lake. Henoch needs us over there for something they are calling Plan B. We believe that the safest bet, to get us there in one piece, is by motorcycle."

As I remembered the brutal trip home from Suttle Lake on the saddle of Atlantis, I couldn't help but blurt out, "Yep, that is bad news."

Then I pulled up some positivity, took another spin, and stated to the room, "Let's go see Dadio."

Since my dad still lived on our families six-acre farm on the Yakima River, Noach and I chose a Nesta fully equipped side-by-side utility task vehicle (UTV) to reach him. This particular

Polaris Ranger Crew XP 900 was not your normal recreational vehicle. Nesta had bought the six-person version. It was fully enclosed and drove like a car on the paved roads. When Noach turned it offroad after we saw several black tinted windowed SUVs through our binoculars, our UTV tore through the sand and around the sagebrush like a race car. It also had the sound proofing option, along with a FSTR button, and of course the transformer button for camouflage.

Once we popped over the first of the twin bridges that crossed the Yakima River, we took a sharp right and dropped into the empty canal that ran along the road. It was deep and wide all the way to my dad's place. We were shocked that no one was waiting for us. I would have thought that would be the first place they would go to secure that leverage Eris was bragging about, at the hidden facility she thought she was going to imprison me in.

Noach stayed in the UTV inside the canal, and I climbed up and over the canal, across the one lane paved road, to my dad's wooden steps that he had built for me to catch the school bus, so many years ago. Our old round swimming pool that my dad had brought home when I was six years old, that almost killed me, was bent over. The blue liner was ripped and torn. As broken as it was, the pool still reminded me of the first time I met Sajan on the infinity train and how that spark of kindness that he showed me changed my life forever.

Without knocking, I entered through the back door and creeped along the hallway listening to the sounds within. I could smell a cloud of cigarette smoke wafting my way. It was weird being home and I hesitated to call out to my father. It felt like it wasn't real.

When I heard the telltale pump of a chambered shell from a loaded shotgun, I snapped out of it. My dad's voice nonchalantly floated over to me and warned, "Best you leave now, or else I will blow a hole through your head."

I started to laugh, just before I yelped, "Dad, it's me. OMG."

My father's voice cracked when he second-guessed himself.

"Dariann?" Then he quickly followed that up with, "Where have you been?"

When I poked my head tentatively around the corner with my hands up, he looked me up and down and yelled, "What the hell did you do your hair!"

After a flurry of hugs and an emotional reunion, we sat and talked for 28 minutes, because that is how much time Noach said I could have. Anymore, and he would be coming in Jamaican ninja style. I told my dad everything that had been happening in the last month, and as much as I could about the events that would be happening in the near future. When I told him I was a badass ninja and part of a secret society that protects others, his response was not what I was expecting.

He kept saying over and over again, "So proud of you baby girl. Mom would be so proud of you too."

When it was time to go, I pleaded, "Dad, please stay put, okay? I am leaving town for a bit, but I will be back and I will come get you." When I looked at the gun sitting on the table beside his favorite recliner, I quietly added, "Please don't go causing any trouble."

He shrugged like he would try to be good. Just before I left, my dad started to whistle the 1937 song, "Whistle While You Work," from the animated "Snow White and Seven Dwarfs" movie, just like the old days when we worked on my money-pit of a house.

As I tore myself away from him I mouthed, "I love you Dad."

Once back at the UTV, I found a distraught Noach because I had been 15 seconds late.

After a few strategic moves through the city of West Richland, we found Maddy at her house that night too. She didn't believe it was me until I started to sing the Christmas talent song that we had created together. When I was done I explained, "This is our song Maddy. This song represents our trust and friendship with one another, forever."

We proceeded to do a classic girly bear hug. and a squeal with uncontrolled happiness. I was glad Noach wasn't there to witness it. I told her what was going on and I told her that the little gray alien that she saw in my bedroom was actually real.

I was surprised when she shyly admitted, "I kind of remember him. He scared the bejesus out of me."

I also assured her that I would come back for her. She would know it was me because of our song. That was when she warmly hugged me a bit too tight, and told me that she loved me.

When Noach and I miraculously made it back unnoticed to our safe house in Eltopia, I was exhausted. We quickly went over the plans for the next day as I shoved some of Nesta's amazing grilled chicken and cornbread in my mouth. Nesta, Max, Ally, and even the man in black were there to hear the good news about the connections I had made with my dad and Maddy. I even saw Nesta jot down some notes when I started to whistle and sing the songs that were shared that night.

In the morning, Noach and I said our farewells and climbed on to Atlantis. We had limited space for any extras. Under his big jacket he hid his swords and bullwhip. I had my Bo stick and my Japanese dagger tucked safely in my belt. We were able to take a back way, through the small town of Othello, and avoid any checkpoints along the way. A few times we were forced to zip up a rough deer trail, but overall the trip went well. After a couple of detours to avoid questionable vehicles, we made it to the Suttle Lake area in less than seven hours.

We pointed Atlantis towards the same hidden doorway that we had left one week earlier. When we jumped off the bike and saw Omah at the cave entrance, Noach and I both gazed at each other as if to say, "Déjà vu weirdness, right here."

As we walked along the trail to the camp, Omah advised, "You two can bunk in Cabin #11. Please get some sleep. Big day tomorrow," then he actually gave me a weird look.

His last telepathic communication over his shoulder was, "The entire ICC will be here in the morning, except the 12th Command, of course. Henoch, Amartv, and I have a proposal for Intelligence to consider. Part of this proposal will depend upon you two and another that we will send for, if she approves it."

Noach and I dragged ourselves to our temporary home. We were relieved to find that someone had prepared a charcuterie style plate of meat, cheese, crackers, and other snack-type foods. After quickly stuffing in several mouthfuls of deliciousness, without any words, we disappeared behind our old bedroom doors and passed out. In the morning, Noach was already up and making coffee by the time I poked my head out.

"Good morning Boonoonoonoos. Kape?"

I didn't have to answer, he knew how addicted I was to coffee. When Omah knocked and then walked in, he had a hopeful demeanor about him. His usual lumbering step had a bit of an excited skip in it. He told us that they were ready for us, and we followed him out to the community fire pit area. The fire area had been covered up with a large platform that now had eleven chairs setup in a half-circle that was facing towards the east side of the amphitheater. I was shocked to see a crowd of creatures residing in the chairs of the amphitheater. When Noach and I came up with Omah, the chatter in the stands quieted down. There were representatives from all of the eleven different planets.

I realized the crowd included Peacemakers from Earth as well. Davita and Alaster were busy chatting to each other. I also recognized several others from our training classes.

Noach and I both sent telepathic "Jeezum Pees," across the air waves as Davita started to unprofessionally jump up and down with excitement to see us. Our other Scottish friend Alaster remained seated. He looked noticeably tired, and you could tell he wasn't his usual self.

To the left and right of our friends, were a variety of different creatures. They were all in their coat of arms colors. A small group of winged Intelligence-looking entities were up front in their gold armor. It was as if they were standing guard over the ICC.

Henoch's leadership group was peeking around trees in the forest with their big black eyes and creepy capes. There were eagle-looking creatures with blue streaked feathers on their heads. Their beady black eyes never left their leader, Gyaan. Behind them, there were half a dozen of Faith's leaders. The ox-looking fighters, with bright shining eyes, had on an orange triangular-type sash that hung around and down in front of them.

There were also two other large hairy individuals on each side of the council's chairs. One was male and one was female. They each had a set of bows and arrows across their backs and wore a brown armor-looking vest, that looked just like what Omah was dressed in. They both looked very intimidating and unapproachable as they quietly monitored the crowd and the forest grounds.

Finally, I saw Aster's trusted advisors, including his beautiful partner, Star. She was no longer heavy with foal. Their command represented all of the different types of colors that you would see in a herd of Earthly horses. However, their long wings of which were tucked up on their backs, were tipped with silver swords. They had silver armored plating protecting their face and on all four of their legs. I remember thinking to myself, "I can't wait to see the baby." And I saw Star push her nose in and out, with acknowledgement on her proud horsey face.

All of the chairs were occupied with a leader from each planet or a weird looking device that projected the leader of the planet being represented, except one.

Intelligence, the white winged elf-like entity with blue eyes, was standing in front of her chair staring at me and Noach. Getting the hint, we quickly took a seat up front and focused our attention on her. Intelligence slowly moved the gaze of her big blue eyes from me to Noach, as if she was judging our usefulness.

"You two are going to be great friends."

When she said this, Noach and I looked at each other and openly projected at the same time, "Been there, done that."

Intelligence beamed with warmth, as she felt our strong bond of friendship.

"The ICC has decided. We have a very important mission for both of you, but first you need some training." She then pointed to Faith.

Faith straightened up in her seat and snorted really loud, as her bright eyes focused on us. Noach and I jumped back a few inches in surprise. Faith quickly addressed the crowd by replying, "This is going to be so much fun."

The Council members began to laugh out loud. The others in the amphitheater, outside of the ox-like creatures, had no idea what Faith was talking about, but they started to join in with nervous laughter too. When Intelligence telepathically raised her voice and had to shout, "Enough," the circle immediately quieted down.

"I am not done."

Then she looked at me with her blue almond eyes.

"Dariann, I need you here."

She pointed to the chair next to hers and let me know, "You have been nominated as the leader for the 11th Planet's Peacemakers. Will you accept the final ICC member position?"

The crowd roared with lively chatter, clapping, stomping, and some vocalizations from Planet #11's section – mostly Davita. Like a frightened rabbit, I couldn't move. I think I may have projected openly, "Seriously?" because Intelligence and most of the Council members shook their head affirmatively.

Noach physically pushed me up to my feet and when I took my place in the circle of seats, another roar from the crowd erupted. While all of this was going on, all I wanted to do was throw up. The focus on me was nerve-wracking, and I realized how much I missed my little dog. Luckily before I could inadvertently spill any of my hysterical emotions on to the crowd, Intelligence called the meeting to order and gave each of the ICC members a few minutes to provide a generalized progress report for each of their tasks.

I was the last to be offered a chance to speak. When it was my turn, Intelligence encouraged me to talk about Eris and her evil plans on Planet #11. I relayed to the ICC and the crowd what Noach and I had seen on the ground while touring through my hometown. I quickly touched on the lie that Eris was spreading about Sajan being the Lawless one. I also told them that she claimed Sajan was helping Cozbi collect animals, from the different planets, for purposes other than transporting to Amaranthine.

With this new information, there were uncontrolled emotions coming from the crowd about both Cozbi and Sajan's role in the upcoming war. I left out that Eris had gloated about the death of my dog. I was still in denial. I wrapped up my short status report with, "I don't believe anything coming from that liar, so it is hard to know the truth. However, I do trust Sajan. I hope that you do too."

Intelligence gave a nod of approval and requested that certain groups break out and discuss strategies for getting their people collected and moved to Amaranthine, sooner than later. Just before everyone left, she suggested, "Let's sing our song and remember why we were chosen to be the planet's Peacemakers." Then there was complete silence, as we waited for the first word to be projected.

Instead, Aster's kind began a rhythmic tap with their horsey hooves. After a few reoccurring beats, Omah, Henoch, and their leadership teams began to loop a humming vibration. Gyaan started to tap his talons on the book in his hands, as his eagle leaders began to quietly pop their beaks, like the Potoo bird did on Evania. Amartv began to tap and drag his staff every fifth beat, as his lion bodyguards gently purred in unison. Faith just watched with diamond white eyes and then lifted a black hoof like she was conducting an acapella team. Then the first words floated over the crowd as Intelligence hummed, "I was chosen to meet Your call."

The entire crowd joined in and sang, "We train so that we can stand tall. We answer, because of Your love. Worthy are You, our Conductor above. We trust without sight. Reaching for the light. Even if pursuit of right is a fight. Your final gifts outweigh this plight. We strive to do no wrong. We will sing Your special song." When the last thump from Amartv's staff came down, the song ended, and intelligence excused the others except Noach and our new teacher, Faith.

We discussed the proposed and approved Plan B in general terms with the promise of more information to come. Intelligence's last words to me were, "Dariann, we know you can do this, especially with Noach by your side. Your other teammate will be here tomorrow morning to help."

I protected my thoughts, just like Sajan had taught me, and asked myself, "Was Sajan found?"

But I knew the truth. He was still under the control of Eris, or Cozbi, or both. The ICC had just informed me of this fact. Faith snorted impatiently and led us to the basalt training simulator. It was a bittersweet moment as we traveled down the rounded dark tunnel to the very same Japanese garden that Sajan and I had sealed our love for each other.

The remnants of leftover food, a cozy couch, and Woola's dog bed were still present on the fighting platform. Luckily,

Faith did a swipe with her hooved appendage and the entire simulation changed to a spaceship type environment. I could see the darkness of space and bright twinkling stars out of the large window, above the ships command center. As we slowly barrel-rolled, a blue and green marble looking planet came into view.

After a few moments it disappeared, and the white and gray surface of the Moon appeared. I quickly realized that we were on the dark side of the Moon. It was something that I had only seen in classified documents back in the SCIF's at home, under the watchful eye of Eris. Except the reality of the dark side of the Moon, at least in front of me that day, was much different than those pictures she deceived me with.

This Moon had abandoned alien-type structures and towers that reached high above its surface. This Moon had, at one time in its past, been occupied. My mind began to wander back to all of the times that Eris tried to insert doubt into my mind about other life forms in those closed-door discussions. For years she had been replacing my gut feelings and my gift of discernment, with doubt and gaslighting. She strategically and intentionally made me question my sanity about the things that I had experienced outside of Earth.

When the anger and frustration started to seep into my thoughts and spill out over Noach and Faith, she stomped her foot and snorted, "The past is the past. Pay attention. This is a simulator of Amartv's secret monitoring system. It was used for passive surveillance. It was actually discovered by Earth, several years ago, after the cloaking technology malfunctioned. They all believed, thanks to Eris, that it was an unusual asteroid. They call it Oumuamua, which in their language means messenger that reaches out from the distant past."

She grunted, "Irony at its best. The humans still believe that it is headed out to interstellar space towards the constellation they call Pegasus. Thanks to Eris, they can no longer see its projected trajectory."

As she said, "Thanks to Eris," I remembered how Eris had pulled that case from my team and how upset Max had been with her interference into our investigation of the actual truth about Oumuamua. Faith continued her lesson.

"Before the technology failed, its sole mission was to orbit the eleven planets in this solar system. It takes eleven years for Oumuamua to orbit all of these planets. Lucky for us, it is scheduled to arrive back into Earth's range next week. This is Plan B."

When Noach and I looked at each other, we spouted in unison, "Space! Fun!" Then we both began to shoulder bump each other back and forth.

Faith stomped her foot, a bit more playfully this time, and instructed, "Let's begin."

She led us to an orange door, which was her coat of arms color. The knob was shaped like an ox. Upon entering there was a dojo-type fighting platform. She moved to the center and bowed. Feeling confident and not wanting to waste any time getting started, I moved into fighting position and bowed at Faith. She bowed, said something I didn't understand, and disappeared. I promptly fell on my butt in shock.

Noach started to chuckle out loud. When I looked over at him, he winked at me, and declared with a heavy Jamaican accent, "Mi soon come." When he grunted really loud, like he was taking a big poop; he disappeared in front of my eyes.

Faith reappeared at the same time as Noach. She snorted twice with surprise.

"Very good. When did you learn this skill Noach?"

With a shrug, he explained, "Runs in my blood. Learned as a child. Thought I was weird. Kept it a secret." Then he gazed in my direction and crowed, "Surprise." Because I had just figured out how he had saved me from Eris without being detected. With this new knowledge, they both turned their focus to me. It was my turn to learn this skill. My life and many others that still lived on my planet, depended on it.

After six hours of grunting like I had to take a poop with minimal results, we called it a day, and Faith released us. Back at the cabin, I grabbed some of the food that was left on the kitchen table and crashed. When I emerged out of my cozy cave, I felt refreshed and ready to tackle invisibility training, one more time.

To my surprise, Max and Noach were casually sipping on coffee in front of a crackling fire. Max did a nervous wave.

"Surprise!"

After grabbing a cup of kape, myself, Max filled me in on how he had become part of the 11ᵗʰ Command, basically overnight. He shrugged his shoulders and blurted, "I guess I gots skills too. Although I have no idea how to talk to Henoch or Omah. They don't use words."

I remember shaking my head with great understanding of his dilemma.

"Yep, we will work on that. Using telepathy is how we can all speak the same language. In fact, projecting and reading thoughts is a big part of the communication process too."

Max looked like a deer in the headlights, as his thoughts spilled out over both Noach and I. He was literally wondering if we could hear him.

"No worries Max, we will work on that in the next day or so. I will help you open up that part of your sleeping brain, so you can actually understand what is going on."

Max shrugged off his doubt and turned to Noach.

"So should we fill her in on what we learned today?"

Noach nodded and telepathically projected to me, "I really like this guy."

Max proceeded to tell me that as I slept in, they had been briefed on the specifics of Plan B. His voice raised an octave with excitement when he squeaked, "Once you are fully trained all three of us will be transported to the actual observatory from Amartv's red planet." When I didn't give a vocal que of understanding, he pointed to the sky and added, "As in the actual floating Oumuamua, up there."

That's when I remembered to shake my head affirmatively, while Noach and I were having a complete conversation, as he spoke out loud. However, Max was oblivious to our private discussion and continued to babble.

"Noach's assignment will be to assist and protect us while we science and engineer the heck out of the alien technology that needs to be repaired." Max's eyes got huge when he remembered, "A scientific member of Amartv's lion community will also be present."

After I purposefully nodded, once again, he boasted, "Once fixed, I will use this alien technology to find the individuals that had been chosen for Amaranthine."

Noach finally jumped in, and vocally explained, "With Max being such a talented remote viewer and having a visual of the locations, we believe that the process will be much quicker. But the first assignment for Max is to locate the floating spaceship that the Earthlings called Oumuamua."

Max lit up.

"I knew it was alien. I can't believe Eris was in on this the whole time."

Moments later, a loud girl with flaming red hair burst through the door and announced the good news. They had been asked to stay and help with the mission in Washington. A few seconds later, Alaster popped through the doorway, as well. Davita was glowing when she pointed at Alaster and exclaimed, "Both of us. Together." Then they both squealed, just like on Evania, and started to jump up and down with celebration.

As Max took in my loud Scottish friends behavior, his thoughts betrayed him as he cringed, "I need to get out of here, I can't think with all of this noise. How will I ever find this asteroid with all of this commotion?"

Davita, overhearing all of the anxiety oozing out of him quickly responded, "I got you Max, follow me."

Without a second thought he popped up and followed her out the door. As they left, she informed us, telepathically of course, that she was taking him to Dublin. It would have been hilarious to see Max's face when they first arrived at the broken-down abandoned cabin. Or when Davita did the dance on the cobble stones to open the library for Max. However, I didn't have to be present to hear Max's thoughts as he took his first steps into the Long Room. All of us within a mile-range of the Dublin simulator could feel his excitement; through the air waves.

That afternoon, several Council members and their leaders departed from Planet #11 through Omah's special portal, behind the clutch of cedar trees, in preparation for the pending war and rescue efforts in their own worlds.

As for me, I went back into the training room with Faith to learn the mind-numbing and well-protected secret skill of invisibility.

34

THE NEW MISSION

THE NEXT DAY Max emerged from Davita's simulator with the answer we were looking for. He slid the coordinates across the community fire pit table and beamed, "I found it." Not having any discipline in how his thoughts could be projected and read, we all heard him say to himself, "Good job Max."

Omah grunted. Henoch tapped his head and did an alien eye roll. Davita and Alaster were grinning from ear-to-ear.

Since Max had not learned telepathy yet, I translated what Henoch and Omah were saying. Overall, the two ICC members were very pleased with his abilities. When Omah lifted up from his log and lumbered off, he mumbled, "I will tell the other Council members what he has found. I will make sure that Amartv gets his engineer ready for deployment. We will plan for departure in the next couple of days." As usual, he disappeared behind his cluster of magical cedar trees.

As Henoch floated off to converse with the remaining members of his kind, he sent me a request,

"Please work with Max on his communication skills."

After my lesson with Faith went really well, she allowed me to leave early. I was feeling confident with my new skill and I walked up to the cabin invisible. When I cracked open the cabin door, Max was wide-eyed and clearly overstimulated. Davita and Alaster had been enthusiastically filling in Max about the facts of our new lives. Noach was kicked back. I think he was high. Unnoticed, I went straight to the kitchen, grabbed a cup of coffee, and sat down in my favorite chair across from my friends. I watched them for a few seconds in cloaked introvert bliss.

When I released the cup on to the coffee table, all four of them yelped. Max slunk back into his chair after pushing off with his planted feet, and tipped over backwards. Noach, let out a loud, "Big up, Dariann."

When I let go of my concentrated hold on the part of my brain that allowed this weird skill to materialize; I yelled, "Boo!"

Max was speechless as I pointed to him and asked him to follow me outside. My Scottish friends were still laughing and pulling themselves together, when I heard Noach quietly say, "Nice job Kunoichi. I think we are ready to kick some ass."

Max still trying to figure out what had just happened, he followed me out the door in silence. Or so he thought, because his unprotected thoughts were shot gunning the back of my head. He was clearly quite glad to escape the clutches of my extroverted friends. His final thoughts were asking himself if I was an alien. It made me chuckle, because a few weeks earlier, I would have thought the same thing myself. When we arrived at the clearing where Sajan had taught me how to control my thoughts, I directed Max to sit on a log so he could hear my lesson.

"To be able to survive the next chapter of our lives, you need to start talking telepathically. Everyone does it Max. It is time to try it."

He rolled his eyes and grimaced like I was asking him to take illegal drugs.

"Okay, boss, show me what to do."

Knowing that Max was analytical, I described the scientific aspects of telepathy by saying, "Extrasensory perception starts with sound vibrations that can be converted to a universal language that all of the planet inhabitants can understand. And when I say planet, I mean all of the planets," as I waved my hand across the sky.

When he nodded, I added, "Direct transference of thought starts out like a hum. For me, I use the words of the Peacemaker song to help me concentrate. This song provides the focus I need to perfect the hum that I need to communicate with others that can't vocalize their words."

"Max, do you know the song?"

He looked down at his feet and shook his head no. I could tell that he was frustrated. He was thinking about how he screwed up with Eris and let her read his thoughts. When he saw me watching him he actually thought to himself, "You can hear this, can't you?"

And I shook my head yes.

I proceeded to sing the Peacemaker's song. I was surprised when Max started to hum with me, as if he did know it, but had forgotten it until that moment. Together, we sang the final verse. When I explained, "That hum, that you feel, is the energy within our minds. The song gives me focused energy, to tap into the lost parts of my mind. Humans use very little of their brains, because we have forgotten how to use our gifts. The song also reminds us of our purpose, as Peacemakers."

He shook his head with understanding, because as a remote viewer, he had tapped into one of those hidden gifts already. After a few tries he started to hear a few broken words coming from me telepathically. When his thoughts were unprotected, every time he said something in his thoughts, that I could read I started to answer. After about the tenth time, he started to protect them like a pro. When Max crinkled his forehead like he was trying to hold something back, he hesitantly asked, "Did you hear that?"

I shook my head and beamed at him like I was a proud parent of a child learning how to use the potty chair.

"You are really good at this. Maybe that is your gift. You can help the others that don't have this skill yet."

Happy with his progress we headed back to the cabin. When we arrived, without words, Max immediately projected across the room, "I am tired as hell, good night my thoughtful friends."

We all gave him telepathic kudos as he closed the door behind him.

In the morning, before I even got my kape, Omah was pounding on the door requesting our immediate presence at the community pit. All five of us rushed out after him. We could feel the anxious energy in his quickened lumber towards the social center of the camp. Henoch was standing on top of the table pacing back and forth. Amartv's engineer was sitting to his left anxiously tapping his long lion claws on the wooden surface.

Omah took his place to the right of Henoch. I couldn't help but crack-up, as I realized that Henoch, even though he was standing, was still shorter than the two creatures on either side of him.

Henoch impatiently projected, "Finally! We got problems folks."

All five of us quickly scooted around the table and focused on Henoch's thoughts. Luckily Max was keeping up, so I didn't have to translate.

"We believe Cozbi and Eris have ships in orbit around each of the eleven planets. They are declaring war by their actions. All of the commands have been deployed. A representative ship, with each of our leaders, will be headed to a different planet to try to get visual confirmation on these strong allegations."

After a few rapid steps he stopped.

"The technology that was deployed on Earth by Eris, has been duplicated across the galaxy. We have lost contact with our trusted partners in each of their governing bodies. The only way to contact anyone is through the secret portals that we put into place. Luckily, we were able to keep this location up and running, even after Eris and Dariann's technology was reinstated. This means we can only communicate with other sites that have done the same. We have blind spots."

Henoch put his long thin gray arm in the air and pointed to Earth's atmosphere, "We don't know what is happening out there."

When Henoch said my name, Max turned towards me and completely forgot what I had just taught him about controlling his thoughts. Without looking at him, I could hear him projecting, "Seriously Dariann! I thought you were on our side."

I turned and captured his gaze, physically touched my head with my index finger, just like Henoch always did when I needed a reminder that I had openly communicated. Then I whispered, "I am! Eris tricked me."

He cringed, squinted his eyes, and looked down at his feet before he looked back up into my sad eyes with deep remorse and mouthed, "I'm sorry."

After our exchange was done, I realized the other conversation had stopped. When Max and I looked up, all of the people, aliens, and sasquatch creatures were staring at us. Henoch tapped his foot with frustration.

"You done?"

But we didn't get to answer, because he jumped right back into the ICC's plan. As he laid it out for all of us to hear, I used Alaster's training techniques and sent an advanced telepathic message to just Henoch. I shared my frustration about being left out of the plan's creation. I was an ICC member, after all."

After a few seconds of ranting at my mentor, I added, "I get it, I'm new. I have known you all of my life. I totally trust you."

Henoch paused slightly, clearly hearing me, as he acknowledged my complaint with a nod.

Henoch explained that each of the planet's governing bodies had evacuation plans if needed. They believed that Eris and Cozbi's evil actions could potentially trigger catastrophic consequences. Maybe even planet annihilation. When he said this, Max openly and loudly gasped in his own thoughts, and then slapped his hand over his mouth like he had cussed out loud. Without skipping a beat, Henoch continued to discuss the number of war ships from each planet. He also mentioned that there were representatives from Planet #3, #6, and #9 in Earth's oceans.

"They are ready to assist with evacuation from the waterside of the planet as needed."

Omah took over the discussion and explained how Davita and Alaster would be going to the Eltopia safe house. They would be taking Atlantis. When Davita heard this part, she squealed with uncontrolled excitement.

Omah grunted, pointed at them and instructed, "You two will be helping Nesta and the others collect the remaining chosen and get them to the energy transport system that is located near each of the safe houses. Eltopia will be the control center to help all of the other safe houses. You two and Nesta are about to get a whole lot busier."

They both vibrated with excitement, as Omah turned his attention to Noach, Max, and I.

"You three will go with Lionel, Amartv's engineer, to Oumuamua. I will transport you there. We will leave in a few minutes." His gaze went to the clutch of cedar trees that I was dying to explore, after all of the coming and going of aliens, the last few days.

"Go pack."

We all practically ran to the cabin to pack for some kind of unknown adventure into space. I had no idea what to take. Max was frantic. His efforts to control his thoughts had completely vanished and Noach was trying to calm him down. Two minutes later, Omah was in the doorway, urging us to hurry. He scratched his head with concern and growled, "Let's go. Time is of the essence, people."

Without any time to think, we piled out of the house and followed Omah up the trail and towards the secret portal, that up until now, we were not privy to explore. Omah lumbered silently. When we approached the trees, Omah waved his hairy hand over an invisible keypad. When it appeared, he punched in some numbers, put his eye up to some kind of eye reader lock, and gave a grunt that must have been a sound activated feature.

Within moments, a round brown door appeared with bows and arrows as the door knocker. Omah grabbed the knob and turned. We walked into a tunnel like structure, similar to the ETT ocean transport that we took to get to our training classes on Evania. Except this transport had seats like you would find on a 747 commercial airplane. However, these seats were equipped with five-point shoulder harnesses. Omah directed us to quickly take a seat and buckle up.

"This will not be a pleasant flight."

When he said this, I thought Max was going to faint on the spot. I helped Max get his harness on and then I slipped into my own restraint. Within seconds we shot off like a rocket through some kind of lighted tunnel that looked a lot like one of those classic ever-changing colored wormholes that you see in those trippy science fiction movies. After several seconds of coming up to speed, I could tell that we were actually under water.

Max vocally shrieked like a girl several times. As the minutes under the ocean ticked by, Omah explained, "This is the same design as the ETT that Evania uses to get to the training facility, through its ocean." As he said this, we catapulted out of the deep blue ocean, thousands of miles from land, into space.

Omah announced to everyone, "This will be tricky. Usually, we have a carefully planned out flight plan to make the trip less bumpy, but here we go."

We barrel rolled and banked left and right to avoid the over 23,000 pieces of space junk that were floating in the lower Earth orbit. Noach and I just put our hands in the air like we were riding a rollercoaster at an amusement park. I think Lionel, the engineer, may have gone to sleep. Within moments, we shot out into dark space and hurtled towards Omah's home. We were immersed in a glow of lighted browns. When Max whimpered, "Should we be concerned about that brown light?"

Omah calmly explained, "My coat of arms color is brown, so this is also the color of my orb when out in space. It is a way to let others know who is coming. It is also our way to communicate with each other while out in space. Think of it like traffic lights in the sky." After a few quiet moments, he half-teased, "I just hope that the bad guys are not on our highway."

As things settled down, Max became curious about where we were going. He composed himself and projected, "So Omah, if I am understanding this correctly, we are going to your home planet? Why not straight to Oumuamua?"

"Good question Max, welcome back. My planet is called Kepler 69c. It is over 2,700 light years away. Our transport only goes to and from my home world to the training center. When we get to my home, we will get you loaded up on a spacecraft that can get you all over to Oumuamua by tomorrow."

Realizing this was going to be a long trip, Max raised his hand and said out loud, "Is there a bathroom on this thing?" And we all laughed. Even Lionel did a friendly little growl, just before he closed his eyes and went back to sleep.

Eventually, we all ended up napping, especially after Omah indirectly recommended it after saying, "It will be several hours before we get there." After eight hours of travel, we docked and were allowed out of the tube. I was shocked to find a lush forest outside. It resembled the Deschutes Forest training facility that we had left the day before. The trees were definitely bigger and taller, and the forest floor foliage was thick and wild-looking.

We were greeted by two bigfoot-looking guards that had similar armor as Omah.

Omah and the guards had words that none of us understood and then they directed us towards one of the large saucer-looking spaceships that was located in a clearing. The dense forest that surrounded us had alien sounds coming from the darkness. With no time to explore Omah's home world, we loaded back up and flew into space. After a few minutes Omah turned to us and said, "We have a few hours before we get there. Make yourself at home. There are sleep pods to the right. There is a kitchen with foods you will recognize to the left." He lumbered over to one of the doors, and disappeared.

Lionel chose to stay at the helm of the ship. He was concerned about unfriendly scouts that we might cross paths with.

Noach perused the well-stocked kitchen, grabbed a couple of rolls, and a couple pieces of cheese, yawned out loud, and headed towards a sleep pod. He mumbled just before the door closed, "Could really use some one-eyed Jamaican right now."

Too tired to laugh, Max and I grabbed some grub. While we ate, I pulled out my purple notebook from my backpack and peered at Max.

"So Max, remember when you helped me distract Eris so that I could find this notebook?"

He shook his head, as he shoved in a tuna salad sandwich.

"Well, I kind of did find something in it. Oops."

He rolled his eyes and sarcastically projected, "You are kidding. Really?"

That's when I said, in my best teacher voice, "Let's start with Planet #10. The leader's name is Intelligence. I first met her at Coffenbury Lake, when I was just a young girl."

We spent hours talking about the different worlds and their creatures. The different colored orbs. The different planets that all of the Conductor's creations came from. When I mentioned Amaranthine. His eyes almost popped out of his head.

When I whispered, "You have a spot there too, Max."

He was all in, of course. And I was so thankful to have him by my side.

35

OUMUAMUA

EVENTUALLY MAX AND I crashed in, what Omah had called, a sleep pod. It was actually an incredibly soft and comforting hammock-type structure. Each side stabilized with the ships movements, so once you climbed in, it felt like you were motionless. Following a several hour nap, I popped out into the main part of the ship, checked out the kitchen for a quick snack, and headed over to Lionel to ask if we were there yet.

He was still standing at the main console, focused on the monitors that were displaying the views from all sides of the ship. The stars were streaming by our ship as if they were streaks of lights. When he heard me shuffle up to the helm of the ship, he quietly purred, "Nothing new to report boss. Just your average everyday trip through the dark confines of space." When I looked over at him he had a kitty cat grin on his face that told me he was messing with me.

When I asked him his story, I was surprised when he started out with, "Well, when I was a small cub back on my home world my dad decided to make my life a living hell when he decided to be the leader of the 8th Planet of the universe."

When I looked over to see if he was messing with me again, he rolled his eyes and gave me a look that said he was telling the truth.

"Imagine how disappointed he was when I told him I wanted to be an engineer."

Feeling slightly embarrassed that I had not taken the time to study up on the council's kids. I stammered, "Wow, I had no idea of your royalty, Lionel. Why didn't you say anything earlier?"

He gave me a little growl.

"I prefer to not play the dad card if I don't have too."

When he looked up at the monitor he suddenly projected his thoughts, loudly throughout the ship.

"I see her. Wake up sleepy heads."

Within seconds the sleep pod doors started to pop open, and Omah and my team crowded around the large picture window to see Oumuamua. The well-hidden monitoring station looked like a cigar-shaped jagged rock. Just like before, when the humans had spotted this structure from Earth's telescopes, it was not generating any of the telltale signs of what constitutes an asteroid or a comet. That was why Max questioned it so many years ago. We could hear his thoughts sneak out of unprotected mode to let me know how he felt about that. "Told you so."

I just shrugged him off.

"We were both punked. What can I say?"

As Oumuamua quickly materialized in front of our eyes, Lionel hit a couple of controls and our movement slowed a few notches as we approached the slowly rotating object. Omah began to prepare a bag of tools and equipment for us to use once we boarded the flying red rock. He put it on a rolling cart that was beside the brown door that led out of the ship.

Lionel hit a few more buttons, and we were suddenly attached to the end of the long side of the alien observatory. On our side, Omah hit a keypad and it opened up. There was a red door on the other side. It had a lion's head engraved on it. Lionel swept his pawed hand over it, and it glowed red, faded, and then the door slid open like a pocket door. It made a classic Star Trek Door Swoosh #1 sound as it disappeared into the walls of Oumuamua. The air coming from Oumuamua smelled stale and musty. It was pitch dark, except for a few recessed running lights along the right-hand side of the smooth, metal walls.

Lionel had a skip in his step as he moved forward into the dimly lit tunnel. As he walked, additional lights turned on and then there were multiple bursts of a lion's roar. Lionel turned to us with giddiness, "It is in my native language. Unless you are a talented linguist you wouldn't understand it. It actually knows my biometric paw prints, so it knows it is me on board." Then he continued down the hallway.

When he said this, it made me wonder if Lionel's native language was part of the twelve languages that Sajan was fluent in. It made my heart skip a beat, thinking of him. I wondered where he was.

Everyone, except Omah, followed behind Lionel a few steps. Max was pushing the cart that had a variety of known and unknown objects that would be used to fix the ship. Omah stayed behind to monitor the space around us. Both Lionel and Omah had shared that they were worried that Eris or Cozbi may have thought that this could be something used against them. Especially since Cozbi had been privy to the latest ICC meeting.

When we reached the control panel room, Lionel didn't waste any time opening up the mechanical closet and reaching for the bag of tools on the cart. As he worked, he provided us a history lesson on the actual purpose of Oumuamua. Oddly enough Lionel reminded me a lot of my dad. If he could have, I think Lionel would have been whistling while he worked. Instead, he talked about his work.

"The technology, although older, still has its uses for monitoring planets that were not mature enough to join the governing bodies of the council. In the end, Earth was the only planet that had not joined and therefore in the last few hundred years it had only been monitoring Planet #11. Then it broke, and was discovered by humans. So, we abandoned it to float aimlessly through the universe." When he dropped a tool and growled out like he was cussing at it, I thought of my dad, again.

Lionel continued the history lesson when he started wrenching on the broken panel.

"The way it works though, is it can pinpoint certain coordinates anywhere on the planet and hear and watch activities on that planet. When intervention was needed, we would engage as needed to divert tragedy. That was why we developed different colored orb communication signals. The orb color would quickly tell all of us who was visiting the primitive human species."

He looked over his shoulder at the three humans in his

presence and nonchalantly said, "No offense to the humans in attendance." Then he did a quiet purr, which I think was a tee-hee-hee in lion talk.

That was about the time that Max slapped his forehead and said, "Like nuclear warhead capabilities and destroying our environment to the point that it kills off entire species."

Lionel nodded at him with agreement.

"Yep, just like that."

Lionel let out a heavy sigh and growled, "This is worse than I thought. Why don't you three go check out the simulator and get familiar with this place. It is down the hall, take a right, and go stand in front of the big red double doors at the end of the hallway. Your presence should open the war room, now that I let the ship know you are here in peace." He cocked his head toward the hallway.

Noach and I nodded at each other and found ourselves in front of the red doors of the war room. Max stood behind us, petrified. We could feel his nervous energy emanating in all directions. The door had an intricately designed lion head knocker. Like the one in my dreams. The doors were made of some kind of shiny metal rainbow-colored material that I had never seen before. As we stood there staring at the doors, Noach jokingly chimed, "Open Sesame."

And to our shock and amazement, it did. The room was a large circular room with at least 50-foot-high ceilings. Once we walked a few feet within the room, the doors disappeared. Max squealed a loud squeak, as the entire room became comparable to the large Omni Dome movies that I had attended as a young kid in Seattle. However, on this giant wrap-around movie screen, there were multiple screens that checkered the larger screen. Each of them were showing different events that were happening around the Earth.

On the left side of the room the screens were displaying burning high-rise skyscrapers in New York City. Flaming chunks of the buildings were falling down on the people in the streets. There wasn't one business owner that was safe from out-of-control rioters. Young children with torn and dirty clothes were standing over their hurt or in some cases, blood-soaked deceased parents.

Their soot-covered cheeks had tears streaming down them. The people walking by acted as if they were oblivious to the pain and suffering these young lives were experiencing. It was almost like the uncaring observers were heartless zombies. The horror of the scene was difficult to pull my eyes away from.

When I finally did and looked at Max and Noach, they were watching screens from their own hometowns. Max had big alligator tears falling from his eyes. When I saw the terror on their faces of the reality that they were seeing on the screen I projected over to them, "This isn't real. Lionel said this was a simulation."

Turning from the apprehensible horror movie that we were being subjected to, all three of us turned at the same time towards the right-hand side of the room. We were immediately bathed in peace and the power of doing good.

On one screen there was a red-haired man, in a tattered business suit, reaching down towards a black man in a hoodie and blue jeans. As they joined hands and the man on the street was pulled to safety on top of a building, zombie-like vandals screamed and shook their closed fists at them. The two men were joined by others who were actually joyously jumping up and down and singing something in unison. I started to look around the room to see if I could turn up the volume and hear what they were singing. You could tell they were so grateful to have found each other, in so much chaos.

Other screens in our multi-tiered simulation showed groups of men, women, and children of all cultures supporting each other. They were peacefully helping others with medical, food, or other life-saving needs. Several of them were whistling a song.

On the third screen, there were groups of young men and women walking by the Eifel tower that were braving the uncivilized parts of their cities to find those that wanted help. They were carrying swords, guns, or whatever weapons they could find to ward off the undead psychotic disruptors. As we watched them walk in a protective stance and collect a few frightened individuals into their fold, they were clearly chanting words, that we could not hear. That was when Lionel walked in behind us and growled, "Volume Up."

The song that they were singing, whistling, and chanting was the Peacemaker song.

Lionel turned to the three of us and quietly said, "Volume down." Then he whispered, "I'm sorry. I kind of fibbed," and as he turned back to the screens and swiped a paw in the air at all of the screens he revealed, "This is actually real-time. This is your mission."

Without even second guessing what he was laying out in front of us, we immediately cleared a table that was in the middle of the dome and created our plan of attack. Lionel provided the last known locations of the trained Peacemakers across our world, including Davita, Alaster, and Nesta. He handed each of us a wrist-type device that had a running list of coordinates and names attached to those coordinates. Lionel spent about twenty minutes with Max to show him how to use the observatory controls. When Lionel asked if he wanted to try it, Max immediately took the helm and tapped in the coordinates of the Eltopia safe house.

On the biggest screen, in front of where we were standing, we could see the farmhouse on the hill. Noach and I started to laugh out loud, when we saw Ally up on Henry the horse, plodding along the fence line. She was trying to get him to go faster than the only speed he knew, which was walk slowly. Max, on the other hand, sighed with relief when he saw her.

The zoom in and out features of the alien technology were amazing. Max flipped another button and immediately, we had crystal clear sound. We could even hear the cluck, cluck, cluck of one of Nesta's brown hens.

Lionel looked pleased when he reported, "Now that the cloak technology is in place, we are no longer detectable. In fact, now that I put in my newly created and approved upgrade to the code, even the rest of the ICC won't be able to find us. We will use this stealth to help the 11th Planet Peacemakers collect the rest of the good people."

When I asked Lionel how we could help the people of Earth, if Oumuamua was only a one way visual of our brothers and sisters, out in the field. He purred, some kind of unintelligible lion-speak, before explaining the process to us.

"We will be using a secure energy telecommunications system

to talk to them. So, you two," as he pointed at Noach and I, "will be using those two rooms over there." When he said "Those two rooms over there" two red doors magically appeared.

I looked at Lionel with a whole new level of respect and admiration, as I declared, "Lionel, I am so glad that you are on our side of this war. This is amazing!"

Noach and I quickly walked to the front of the doors, but feeling a bit anxious about what we would find, we both hesitated opening them. While pointing back and forth between the two doors, Noach started to say in a very thick Jamaican accent, "Eeny, meeny, miny, moe." Except for saying "catch a tiger by the toe," he replaced it with "catch a lion by the toe."

Lionel just growled and grumbled, "Funny boy. Ha ha."

"Like I was saying, before the kids rudely interrupted. Those two doors will provide the needed technology to project an energy signal that others can see." After several confused looks, Lionel grabbed his chin hair and finally shared, "Like a hologram. You will not be there, but there will be a representation of your energy signature there. They won't be able to see where you are, but you can see things in their environment. Capish?"

Without waiting for an answer, he jested, "Because I'm a hungry tiger." He padded out and left the three humans in an alien communication room, completely unsupervised.

Noach selected the door on the left and disappeared. So, I opened and closed the door on the right to see what was inside. Immediately, a woman with an Australian accent, emanated from the room.

"Welcome Dariann, what are the coordinates of your call?" I pulled up Nesta's farmhouse and tapped it on my watch.

All of a sudden, I saw Nesta standing in the kitchen. All of the ingredients for her world-famous jambalaya were scattered across the island. She was dramatically talking to Noach, who was shimmering in and out of my focus. Her gray dreadlocks were bouncing from one side to the other as she emphasized the events that were happening and how she was trying to keep her special group safe. When Nesta looked through Noach, she saw me appear behind him. She exclaimed in her strong Jamaican accent, "Hello Boonoonoonoos. Long time no see."

Noach and I quickly got Nesta up to speed, on the plan. We let her know that we would be dropping in and giving her updates each day. Since her safe house had connections to most of the other safe houses in the country, she was in charge of keeping them updated. We spent the rest of our call talking about the status of the collections of people that Davita and Alaster had been bringing in. She grumbled, "We are almost full here. Spokane too. There are so many good people to be saved."

When I asked if Davita and Alaster were at the safe house, she shook her dreadlocks back and forth.

"No they are out rounding up another group."

About that time, Ally walked in. She actually shrieked like she had seen a mouse. I am not sure if she thought we were ghosts or was just excited to see us, but the first thing she asked about, was Max. I playfully pointed up to the sky.

"He is having way too much fun. He is probably eaves dropping in on this conversation right now."

When it was time to end the call, we said our goodbyes, planned our next meeting, tapped our magical watches, and popped back into Oumuamua. After a few moments of trying to comprehend what had just happened, I pushed out of the communications room. Coincidently, Noach had pushed out of his own room at the same time.

He gave me his biggest Jamaican toothy grin yet, and boomed, "That was Wicked, Kunoichi. Let's do that again."

36

THE LOST WILL BE FOUND

NOACH AND I jumped back in our rooms and began tapping in coordinates. We touched base with the Peacemakers that we had met at the Dark Lake training camp, as our first priority. This included a quick check in on Davita and Alaster at the Spokane safe house. Unfortunately, they were not home.

By the end of the day, Max started to knock on our doors and transfer coordinates of lost souls that he had found on the big screens, flashing in the main dome room. We popped into these somewhat chaotic locations, introduced ourselves, and let them know we were there to help. Then we directed them to the nearest safe house. If they didn't trust us, we would sing the Peacemaker song to get them to believe us. At one point, I even practiced my hypnosis skills.

Exhausted, Noach, Max and I called it quits, long into the late hours. We found Lionel and Omah in the kitchen. Omah was kicked back on a red-leather couch and ottoman. Lionel was eating again.

When I asked Omah if we should be using the technology to find Sajan, Cozbi, or Eris, he shrugged his furry brown head and projected, "They are not on Earth. Plus, it would compromise our current mission. We have to stay on this course."

There was a sadness in his eyes when he added, "No word on Woola, either, sorry. We do have others looking for all of them though."

In between bites, Lionel did a frustrated growl.

"According to my father, we will be here probably another week until this mission is done. Then we can join that search."

With this new information, I panicked and ran out of the room. I immediately called Nesta. When she answered I cried, "Please Nesta, please save my family, Maddy, and Fanny."

Nesta crooned, "Oh silly Boonoonoonoos. We got your back. Davita just found Fanny and her kitty cat. They are safely hidden in the Spokane house. She and her little feline friend will be going to Amaranthine when the next train gets here. She wanted you to know that she was glad to finally get the truth. She was happy to hear you were okay."

Royally confused at the success of saving my somewhat paranoid and stubborn cousin, I had to ask,

"How did you know she would go with you? I always told her not to talk to strangers."

Nesta got a knowing look on her face.

"We had to do some convincing, before we could coax her out of her hiding place. Luckily, I took good notes when you were telling me about her and her experiences. I had Davita resort to retelling the stories about her daddy in Vietnam and explain that the green lights, that blew up the enemy ship, were the bad aliens." She chuckled, as she recalled the story.

"Your Fanny was very inquisitive and asked great questions. At one point she stopped being fearful and started to test our knowledge of your relationship. Davita said that Fanny actually asked her, 'If this is true, then what are blue lights?'"

"Davita went into great detail about the night that your Fanny and her daddy saw all of those lights over the ocean. She told Fanny that they had witnessed a private conversation between the good aliens, that they were not supposed to see. The final tipping point was when Davita shared that Intelligence did visit you through a portal, at the bottom of Coffenbury Lake. After that, she pretty much just handed the cat to Davita and said, 'Take me to your leader.'"

"She is so funny, Dariann."

After giggling about my cousin finally giving into the alien story, I looked up at Nesta and projected, "What about my dad and Maddy?"

Nesta looked down at her feet.

"So we are still working on those two. Eris's men are keeping an eye on them now. Her people are openly walking around with weapons and forcing people to camps, but not your dad or Maddy. I think they are trying to see if you will show up. We actually brought in a few others to help."

She took a deep breath, "Don't worry Dariann, we will get them, one way or another."

Before we hung up, I gave Nesta a list of my other family members that were spread across the planet, and a few other good people that I knew would fit into our new world. I knew that Nesta would make sure that they were saved too. When we ended the call, I headed straight to my sleeping pod and passed out.

At the crack of space dawn, I found myself around the sterile-looking kitchen table, drinking coffee of course. I let Noach know about the wonderful things that Nesta was doing to help me with my family and friends. He got a warm smile on his face and crooned, "De olda de moon, de brighter it shines."

Then he lifted up, patted me on the back and headed towards the dome room to get back to work. We spent hours contacting the other Peacemakers to locate and get those chosen individuals to safety. When I checked in with Nesta, she seemed exhausted, but grateful for our information. Just before we left the call she hesitated.

"Dariann, I forgot to tell you, Alaster picked up your Aunt Patty on his way to Spokane. She will be going to Amaranthine tomorrow. I have Peacemakers working on your sister and her family. Your brothers were both located, late last night."

When she provided this news about my siblings, I couldn't hold in my emotions and they spilled all over her. She nodded in acknowledgement of my feelings.

"We are, however, still working on your dad and Maddy. Eris is making the rescue efforts around those two very difficult. Those working with Eris are now in the open. The people of Earth are seeing aliens in broad daylight and their government is trying to keep control of the chaos. I'm not sure how long we can remain here."

When we hung up, I busted out of the communications room and found Lionel. He was literally eating again.

"Jeezum Pees Lionel, Planet #8 may need to be renamed, the eat like piggy race."

Feeling my frustration, he put down the sandwich he had in mid-flight to his large lion mouth and growled, "Sounds like we need to talk?"

With an exasperated tone I looked at his big brown eyes and explained my dilemma.

"As the newly appointed leader of the 11th Planet's Peacemakers I need to be down there, on the ground, leading my people. How do I make that happen?"

Lionel's fuzzy face lit up.

"You just had to make the request, boss. What is the plan?"

He immediately started to clear off the table, as he let out a growl. Underneath his piggy mess, a colorful map of the stars magically appeared. It showed where we were and how far away Earth was. A hum began to run through my mind, when I pointed to my planet on the map.

"I need to get to Earth, ASAP. I would like to bring Ally up here, to help Max find the others. He is a good teacher. He can help her with language translations."

With my finger still resting on my home world, I announced, "I need Noach with me down there. We have specific gifts that will help us move around Eris's people without detection." I took a deep anxious breath and peered at Lionel.

"Can you take my place in the communications room?"

Lionel gave me a 'no can do' lion look.

"Not trained, and your people would probably run away before I could say, "Hello Earthlings, I'm with the ICC. I am here to help you."

Realizing he was right. I thought about who, down on Earth, could telepathically communicate and that could come up to speed easily. As my mind raced for an answer, I must have inadvertently and openly projected my thoughts across Oumuamua, because Max and Noach busted through the red kitchen door, and at the same time, shouted, "Milo?"

Max added, "Milo would be our best bet. He is already at the safe house. He can already project and receive thoughts."

Noach shook his dreadlocks up and down in agreement. Then he flashed me one of his feisty Jamaican toothy grins.

"Road trip Kunoichi?"

As I rushed to make an interstellar phone call, I called over my shoulder, "If you are up for it my friend."

With the help of Lionel, we had Henoch and Intelligence on a three-way call. Omah was squished in the communications room with us. After pleading my case to them, moments later I had ICC concurrence to implement my revised plan. When we called Nesta to let her know what was happening and to prepare Ally and Milo for space travel, she uttered one word.

"Wicked."

And it made us all laugh. We told her to tell them that Max was coming to help them with the transition to their new roles.

Omah disconnected his brown spaceship from the Oumuamua, and we jetted off towards Planet #11. This time Omah broke council rules by not flashing his coat of arms color around his ship, to warn others that we were coming. The journey to Earth was under two hours. Omah used some kind of electromagnetic antigravity propulsion and cloaking technology, as we plunged through the Earth's atmosphere. I made a mental note to ask him about how that worked, someday.

We entered the western Pacific Ocean, somewhere near the Mariana Trench, into the Challenger Deep, which I knew was a few hundred miles from some of our military installations residing on Guam. It was ironic that this was where we would land. The area had been known for a variety of unidentified flying phenomena. Several groups had allegations about the UFO activity, but all of them had been debunked by Eris, through my team. As we dove down several miles, we turned towards a shimmering underwater city of lights.

"This is headquarters for our ocean-loving ICC members from Planet #3, #6, and #9. They have been helping with transport out to Amaranthine."

As Omah said 3, 6, and 9, Max, who had been very quiet, the entire time, suddenly yelped with excitement and whispered out loud, "Mermaids, sea monkeys, and octopi. Oh my!"

When we docked, there was a train looking type structure that was disconnecting. Within moments, it zoomed out the way we had come.

"They have been very busy getting as many of the three million selected souls out of here."

Omah's words made me think that things were at a point of no return with our beautiful planet. I wondered who was doing negotiations to save it, but I didn't have time to ask, because we were immediately escorted to a white train-looking transport. It looked just like the one that had just shot to the surface. From the outside, the white oval-looking ship appeared to have no windows.

It reminded me of the unidentified flying phenomena that my team had been investigating not too long ago. These were the high-speed, gravity-defying smooth white tic-tac looking things, that our military had kept seeing while conducting their secret ocean-based missions. They were, supposedly, never identified. It was hard to believe that I was actually boarding one with a giant hairy sasquatch.

Outside, we could see a couple of mermaids and a multitude of pink sea monkeys. They were busily swimming through the water and shoving different sized containers into outside compartments of multiple ships. Each of the cargo ships were docked to the platform, along the side of the enormous brightly-lit glass domed headquarters. Omah mumbled, "They are collecting sea creatures and preparing for transport to Amaranthine."

As we sped off, in our train-like-ship, the view out the window became pitch black. When we arrived, we unloaded into a cold tunnel that resembled the entrance to the training simulator from Omah's training camp. We shuffled a few steps to an elevator door that had a button that only went up. As we popped out of the elevator, Nesta bellowed, "Hello Boonoonoonoos. We missed you."

Ally jumped into Max's arms and gave him a strong embrace and a sweet kiss on his cheek. Max's cheeks immediately turned bright red. Milo was just standing there taking it all in. He playfully projected to me, "You have come a long way kiddo."

Remembering that Ally didn't understand telepathy, I said out loud, "Could not have done it without you, my friend."

That was when Ally tapped her head, and without words teased, "Ouch Dariann, why are you talking so loud."

Milo proudly confessed, "While you were gone, she learned the universal language from moi."

We shared a moment of levity and then Max, Omah, Ally, and Milo left, almost immediately.

Nesta pulled me along, through the hallway, towards the all too familiar kitchen. Sitting at the table was Maddy. She was nibbling on one of Nesta's chocolate dipped, shortbread cookies. When I saw her, I couldn't help but shout, "OMG" as I ran and gave her a great big bear hug.

"How did you get here?"

She pointed to Nesta.

"Imagine my surprise when an older Jamaican woman, dressed in ninja style clothing, showed up at my back door in the middle of the night and started to sing, 'The day before Christmas eve when Santa's working hard, the children write out lists to give to Santa Claus, the night is coming close, the children will rejoice, when you're asleep in bed, you'll dream of all the joys, for now it's Christmas day and you'll awake to see pretty presents wrapped in bows, and tied so naturally. We wish you a merry Christmas, we wish you a merry Christmas we wish you a merry Christmas and a happy new year.'" She caught her breath after singing our song.

"When my caroler explained what was going on, and that you were running late, I decided to follow her." Maddy gave me one of her classic girly grins.

"That song represents our trust and friendship with one another, forever."

After more hugs, we talked until midnight.

37

TETELESTAI

IN THE MORNING, Maddy prepared for transport to Amaranthine, with another ninety-nine passengers. We had one last hug.

"See you on the other side, my friend."

She gave me her icky kitty face, like my song choice sucked. As the lyrics from this Ozzy Osbourne song floated through my thoughts, I remembered that the song actually was about crossing over, after death. I followed up my well wishes with, "Energy is energy, no matter where we go."

She just playfully shook her head like I was crazy and waved goodbye.

Nesta and I immediately brainstormed our next steps. The first priority determined was to save my father. While nibbling on Nesta's homemade haystack cookies, we strategized how to get him out of his house without being noticed. Struggling with these plans we both sat back in defeat.

Noach nonchalantly shuffled in, flopped on to a cushy recliner, and suggested, "How about we just repeat what we did last time. Except this time, we go incognito." When he said incognito, he actually went invisible.

Nesta literally sucked in her breath with excitement.

"Oh Yes. We will take the UTV. I will get her ready."

Within minutes, Noach and I were headed towards the garage. But, before we reached the door, Henoch materialized in front of us with a frantic look.

"Oh good. You haven't left yet. We got more problems."

Without any warning, he proceeded to show us a holographic

image projected from his brain. Similar to drone footage, the image showed an aerial view of the area. Instantly, I recognized the facility that Eris had tried to imprison me.

There were at least a hundred off-road-type vehicles of various kinds, parked sporadically throughout the desert. Cars, that could not go offroad were lined up, along the one road that led to the facility. On one side of the barricaded facility there was a large group of humans, and to my shock and surprise, there were several armored Reptiles standing with them. Star, the winged mare that I met on Evania, was also standing to the back of the pissed off crowd. She was in full armor and stomping her feet and flapping her silver-tipped wings, up and down. In front of the group, I noticed another familiar face. It was Alaster. All of the human protesters were holding some kind of weapon. A few had altered automatic rifles strapped across their chests.

They were chanting, "Give them back. Give them back."

On the other side of the blockade, there were dark-tinted Humvees and sedans, parked in a way that was meant to stop the violent protest that they had sparked. I was surprised to see a multitude of Planet #12's race present on the other side of this dispute, as well. Their fully armored reptile heads were bobbing from side to side, protecting the silhouetted occupants of the black cars. When Eris slid out of the front passenger side of one of the Humvees and Cozbi stepped out of the driver's side, I gasped out loud and looked at Henoch, with wild eyes.

Henoch nodded his agreement, to my shock and surprise, of seeing these two together and on Earth. Eris pulled out a megaphone type device and looked up to the sky, like she could see us watching her. With a satisfied look on her face, she physically waved at the occupant in the back seat to get out.

As the passenger door cracked open, a robed figure appeared. He had a hood over his head, but you could see dark long unkempt hair, hanging out from underneath. His dark-skinned hand held on to the side of the door, as he steadied himself, to a standing position. I realized immediately that this was the same robe that he had worn the first time I saw him at Omah's training camp.

As Sajan stepped out into the last rays of the eastern Washington sunset, he held his palms down and walked towards the opposing crowd. The Reptile protesters and Star, dropped to the ground, as the humans began to roar with anger.

That was when I fainted.

When I woke up, Nesta was chanting some kind of Jamaican song and waving a white sage smudge bundle over me. I immediately started to sneeze, because like ganga, I am allergic to sage as well. When I looked around the empty room I practically shouted, "How long have I been out?"

"About 10 minutes, Boonoonoonas. They will probably be back in about an hour."

Not having any idea what she was talking about, and seeing my wild-eyed look, she trembled, "Noach and Henoch went to get your dad. They felt like the distraction at Eris's holding facility would allow them enough time to get your dad back safely. They took the UTV through the desert. They are hitting all of the back roads to your dad's place." Nesta stared into my watery eyes and whispered, "They have some kind of mind control over him. There is no way he is helping them, willingly."

But as she looked down, I could see the doubt.

When she left to get me a glass of water, at my request, I grabbed the keys to the Aston Martin and ran to the garage. Within seconds, I was out the gate and on the main highway toward the facility that Eris had taken me to a few days earlier. I knew it was a trap, but I had to help Alaster and the others. And if I could, maybe even get Sajan back too. After pressing all of the special Nesta car buttons to get there, as fast as I could, I covertly crept up on the facility behind the long line of vehicles.

While driving, I sang the Peacemaker song to give me strength. Just before I stepped out of my camouflaged car, I used the new skill that Faith had taught me. Hidden by invisibility, I ran the several hundred yards through sand and sagebrush towards the yelling that I could hear in the distance. As I crouched in the underbrush, behind a couple of all-terrain vehicles, I watched the angry crowd try to help my new alien friends get free from whatever spell Sajan had cast upon them.

Nesta, also invisible, popped in beside me, and quietly joked,

"Did you really think you could shake me that easily, silly girl? What's the plan."

By that time, Eris and her men in black had constrained Star and the human-friendly Reptiles. Eris's army was staggered around them. Sajan and Cozbi were no longer in sight, but Eris was on her megaphone-like device trying to calm down the angry mob. She was trying to convince them that they were on the wrong side. It didn't look like it was going as planned. The crowd looked more pissed off than ever.

I could tell that the angry humans were realizing that there was nothing they could do for their new alien friends. They had backed up and were about fifty feet away from the gates. They had formed a circle of protection. Based on their stance, it looked like they planned on holding their ground, as they pointed their guns out in all directions. Alaster was still up front and very visible. He was providing the protestors with encouragement. I looked towards Nesta.

"I think I see Sajan in that car, over there. I am going to pop in on him. See if I can break that spell."

Nesta paused, like this was a bad idea, but decided to offer instead, "I will wrap around the back and try to set Star and the others free while you do that."

Then she was gone.

With my mind focused on invisibility, I crept through the dark desert to the black car and lifted the handle. I was shocked when it opened. Inside was Sajan. He had a pained look on his face when he saw the door open and close. Cozbi was in the front seat, but he never looked back at us. It was like he was in a trance. Still in my disguise, I grabbed Sajan's hand and whispered, "Mahal Kita Sajan. Please come back to me."

He let out an agonized pant.

"She knew you would come. Please go Dariann. I don't want you here. I can't hold him off for long." He nodded towards Cozbi.

I violently shook my head, like a two-year old, and lost control of my focus. As if he didn't believe that I was actually there with him in the car, Sajan cried out when he saw me appear. Then he lost his hold on Cozbi.

Cozbi slammed his hand against the horn. Jolted back into action, I pushed open the door, and grabbed Sajan by the arm.

"I am not losing you again." I aggressively pulled him out of the car, and he fell to the ground.

Within seconds Eris arrived. She had a satisfied look on her face. Her lizard eyes blinked sideways, several times, from the joy of finally catching me, again. Two of her warriors surrounded me and tried to grab my arms. I quickly knocked them off and moved towards Sajan. At the same time, I unlatched my retracted Bo staff from my belt. I quickly shook it open and took a defensive stance against Eris's armored Reptiles. As they moved forward, I held them off with my Bo staff. Eventually they backed off and formed a large circle around both of us.

Behind their circle, I heard intensified screaming and gunshots. Nesta had successfully released Star and the others. Star was hovering in the air, looking for me. When she spotted me, she came straight down on the attack. Several of the Reptile guards began to fight her. She was able to kick one in the head, but the other swiftly maneuvered just as she was coming down for another attack and he sliced her in the side. She fell to the ground, bleeding. I could hear her suffering in my brain waves.

Eris's warriors came at me from all sides. I squeezed my eyes shut, ducked, and disappeared into an invisible cloak. They clashed into each other, where I had just stood. I watched, as Sajan palms down started to incapacitate the enemy Reptile race and they began to fall to the ground in submission. Sajan was struggling to keep upright.

Eris searched the empty air for me, without success. She cackled, "Come out, come out, wherever you are? There is no escape, this time, Dariann."

That was when I showed her exactly where I was. I rounded out a kick to her face and she fell to the ground. She maniacally showed me her bloody teeth, as blood ran from her nose, and hissed, "Gotcha now," as two men in black, grabbed me from behind.

As I struggled to free myself, my concentration was skewed and just as I was becoming visible again, Eris reached for Sajan and hit him in the head with her megaphone. He fell to the ground. Blood covered his face. No longer under his spell, all of the creatures regained consciousness and chaos erupted.

Alaster hacked his way through to me, as the friendly Reptiles went toe-to-toe with the enemy Reptiles. The crowd of humans began to shoot their guns and fight their way through the barricade to free their loved ones from the cages that held them. Several of my fellow Peacemakers led them into the green doors, towards their imprisoned family and friends within. They sang the Peacemaker song as they moved along.

As for the two men trying to hold me, I delivered a Gedan Barai followed by a Mawashi Geri. They crumpled to the ground after I delivered a Choku Zuki followed by a Mae Gen. In a split second, I thought to myself, "That was way too easy."

Eris and Sajan were surrounded by her army. Eris had called in reinforcements. There were too many for us to defeat. Eris and her warriors began to retreat, in a circle of protection, as they dragged my boyfriend's lifeless body across the sandy desert floor. Behind them, a set of black vehicles full of enemies, began to roll towards us. Alaster and Nesta caught up to me and pushed me back.

"Run, Dariann, Run."

After one last look at Sajan's limp body, I reluctantly did. We ran all the way to the Aston Martin. Nesta and Alaster left their rides and we all climbed in together. Nesta took the wheel and spun out. The dust cloud gave our position away and the black vehicles were suddenly hot on our trail.

Once out on the main road, we turned away from town towards the city of Yakima. Nesta hit the FSTR button, and we jumped into hyperdrive. The cars behind us disappeared. Nesta zoomed over the Vantage Bridge and cut through Othello, to get to the Eltopia safe house. When we pulled into the garage, I was in full blown snot-bubbling distress. Nesta and Alaster tried to calm me down, but I waved them off. So, they left.

Within seconds, the door opened, and my dad slid in. When he grabbed my hand, he playfully quipped, "So, just wanted you to know, aliens exist."

I sniffed up my snot and put my head on his shoulder.

"I guess so Dad. I guess so."

Then I added, "You will be happy to know I fell in love with a guy from Earth. Well sort of." And then I gave him a half-hearted grin.

That's when we both started to laugh hysterically, because our lives were almost too crazy to comprehend. When my dad finally coaxed me into the house and told me to get cleaned up, we found a quiet place to talk. When we got to the subject of his rescue, he started laugh.

"I almost shot up that Jamaican dude. Then that alien popped out. After almost peeing my pants, I heard a hum all around me, and then the next thing I know, that Noach fellow starts to whistle that song, that I always did, when we worked on your little house on Perkins."

When I started to hum, the "Whistle While You Work" song, he joined in. When we were done, we hugged, and he told me he loved me. Henoch interrupted our sweet moment and telepathically told me he needed me. With one final squeeze, I lifted up and shrugged, "Back to work for me."

As I walked out the door, my dad started to whistle.

Henoch was really upset. He was projecting deep sadness and I told him to spit it out.

He reluctantly floated over, "Star didn't make it. She is with the Conductor now."

Tears slid down my cheeks, as I replayed the last couple of hours and saw the sword that sliced through her side. I knew deep inside that she had not made it.

"We need to get your dad on the next train out. Our time is running out to save the rest of the chosen. We can't find Sajan. We think that Eris took him off the planet again. We are worried she might do something that will endanger all of us. We have lost contact with Planet #4. Aster can't reach anyone from his home world anymore. He is headed there now. We haven't told him about Star yet. I wasn't sure how."

Not quite comprehending what he was saying and being completely exhausted, all I could say was, "Okay."

Clearly upset, himself, he gave me an unemotional status report.

"Max, Ally, and Milo are finding and directing the Peacemakers and the chosen to the safe houses across the world. Nesta is getting reports of over two million souls already on their way to Amaranthine." When he finished, he walked away.

Over the next couple of hours, a continuous stream of cars arrived at the safe house. The protesters and their rescued loved ones showed up too. Alaster gave us a quick rundown on what happened after we left.

"When we broke in, they just left. No one stopped us. I have no idea where they went. And then, Star."

Alaster shook his head with sadness over her death, and then shuffled out of the room with a sobbing Davita.

Nesta spent most of her time shepherding the lost and confused people on to the next train. She was chatting away, as she handed them a goody bag, for their trip. When it was my dad's turn to go, he whistled all the way to the train station. He was so busy making new friends, he barely waved goodbye to me.

Eventually Noach, Davita, and Alaster, were assigned to a different train. Once again, they would become teachers to help the passengers transition to their new lifestyle to come. As the traffic slowed down to the hilltop farm and we didn't have any surprise visits from Eris's warriors, we started to worry about what she was up to. After another call up to Oumuamua, Max confirmed our suspicions.

"Eris has moved most of her evil army off the planet, except for twelve strategically placed ships. I recommend you leave immediately, just to be safe."

I helped Nesta load up her beloved animals and get them settled in the back compartment. The rest of the house occupants, strapped in tight, for the last train ride out of the city. Gary, Max's friend, had stayed behind in hopes of traveling with Max and Ally to Amaranthine. He had reluctantly loaded up his personal items after I told him, "It's time to go."

He sat quietly beside me, near the back, slumped in his seat.

Our ship backtracked down the dark tunnel and shot into the ocean. When we reached the headquarters for our ocean-loving Council members from Planet #3, #6, and #9, we transferred on to another ship. The docks were empty, but the lights were on as we shot out of the Challenger Deep, and up into the stars. Within minutes, our ship barrel rolled on its axis and spun out of the planet's atmosphere. We circled the outer rim from the pull of its gravity. The first timers, sat up straight in their seats, and gasped in unison.

"Is that Earth?"

Several others, that had seen this sight before pulled themselves out of their tired slumber and gawked out the small airplane-like windows too. I was one of them. There was a long chorus line of 'woahs,' and several loud cries as we all stared at our place of birth. Those that couldn't see the outside, shuffled out of their seats and squeezed together to see the remains of their beloved home. As the Earth wobbled, we could see large swirls of smoke and debris. The destruction extended hundreds of thousands of miles across its surface.

Henoch silently floated into the room. I was surprised to see him. I had not seen him board our ship. I could tell he was weighed down by the sorrow and anguish of the humans, as they witnessed their world burning. He was very aware, that leaving the only place we knew, was difficult to comprehend. Those who had not learned how to protect their thoughts, were freely sharing them with everyone on the transport ship. In his gentle, but firm way, Henoch pointed at my old home.

"I know this is hard, but this is what I have been preparing you for, all of these years. Dariann, your destiny is not to be a badass kunoichi, even though you are."

His unblinking blue almond eyes pulled me in. I saw the blues and greens of the ocean of Evania rhythmically rolling in and out from the pink sandy beaches, that I had seen in my dreams. As the waves gently washed in, I felt its calmness flow over me. Henoch blinked and it was gone.

"Your destiny is to lead the remaining people from Planet #11. You have been selected to help them find the truth about why they have been chosen. You have been given the responsibility to guide them, as they seek out a renewed purpose for peace."

When I couldn't think of any words to say, he continued.

"I just talked to Max. He is having visions now. If true, this next part is going to really suck."

Henoch walked over to the wall of the ship and waved his hand. The metallic wall suddenly dissipated. In its place the outside darkness seeped in. It was as if we were floating in space, unprotected. Several more vocal 'woah's,' filled up the cabin. Through my incomprehensible exhaustion and anxiety, my mind started to hum the song, "Radioactive," from the band Imagine Dragons. When I reached the verse about an apocalypse, those that could hear my thoughts started to chant out loud, 'Woah-oh-oh.' There was a strange levity in the room as we all screamed out, in unison, "Radioactive, radioactive."

Nesta sat in silence, she knew where she was going. She felt no woe for the planet she was leaving.

Henoch stood there, in stone cold stillness, as the humans grappled with their unstable and hysterical reaction to grief and shock of their new reality. But he didn't stay for long to hear our Earthly song. Instead, he floated over to one of the communications rooms and disappeared behind a closed door.

As if on que, at the end of the last verse, there was a deep grumble, as if gears from an unseen engine were engaging. We shot out into the deeper darker space, as the little blue marble of Earth began to get smaller and smaller. And even though there was no physical change in our momentum, several of us grabbed our seats to stabilize our vertigo, as we moved forward. The stars zipped by like a classic "Star Trek" warp speed scene.

When our attention turned back to the slowly shrinking planet, a blast from within its core shattered all parts of the broken world into a million pieces. The rings of the blast emanated out in brightly colored red, orange and yellow bands of particles. Like a déjà vu moment, my thoughts thrust me back to my past. I was watching old movie footage of a nuclear war head detonation. Being from the Tri-Cities, our little town was infamously known as a critical partner in the development of this kind of bomb. As a student, at Hanford High School, I learned it was secretly called, The Manhattan Project. The blast outside our window was something even worse.

The force of the waves eventually found our space craft. The energy released from the blast violently shook the train car. Fear and uncertainty rippled through all compartments, especially when we all realized that this was the final destruction of what had been our past. All we had now, was the promise of a new future in some faraway place, that very few of us had actually seen.

I noticed with horror, that a few of the departing trains were swallowed up by the Earth's explosion. Immediately, I knocked on Henoch's door. When he cracked it, and saw me, he whispered four words.

"Tetelestai. It is done."

After several quiet moments, he added, "According to Max, two of our ships were too close. We lost them. However, the four ships with your family and friends are safe. Omah is with the Oumuamua. He will transport them to Amaranthine when it is safe to do so."

With mixed emotions, I turned towards my seat. Just before I sat down, I quietly cascaded my thoughts and my voice over the ships frightened passengers.

"I'm Dariann, I am an 11th Planet's Peacemaker, and a member of the Interstellar Contact Council. I know this is scary, but please don't be afraid. It will be okay. Please rest."

Then I hummed the Peacemaker song. It's tone and rhythm, floated through the airwaves. Halfway through, others joined in too. When the sounds of the song ended, a peaceful feeling enveloped my new family. I could tell by their thoughts, that they understood that there was no turning back.

It was done and the entire room quieted down, as the tired and defeated remnants of the 11th Planet settled in for a long, but well-deserved space nap.

38

11TH PLANET REMNANTS

OVER THE NEXT few hours, the passengers all slept like they had been hypnotized.

While they napped, Henoch pulled me aside and explained that it would take a few weeks to reach our permanent home. He informed me that classes would be provided to keep everyone distracted and busy. There would also be training for those that had not learned the universal language. He suggested that I be part of that process to help build relationships with Earth's survivors. I, of course, was relieved to have an assignment to keep my mind off Sajan and Woola's demise. Henoch also explained that there were holographic communication lines between the different ships.

"If there are any passengers worried about others, they can actually find and talk to them."

He pointed towards two well-camouflaged communication compartments that I had not seen before. While everyone rested, I contacted my dad, Maddy, and Fanny. They were all doing amazing, considering the weird circumstances. When I spoke to my dad, he was beyond himself with enthusiasm.

"I just talked to your brothers and sister. They were on one of the last transports out. We should try to get together when we get to our new home."

Because the call was a hologram, I shook my head at him affirmatively as he babbled on.

"I am finally figuring out this ESP stuff. I even made a new friend. He said he would show me a good fishing spot on this new world that we are going to. He said the lake was purple. How cool is that?"

When he said purple, I knew exactly where he was going, and I told him I would join him when we got settled in. Fanny and her cat Lilly had also made some new friends. She was excited to start her new life, wherever that might be. She also let me know that she met up with Aunt Patty. They were on the same ship out of the shimmering city of lights. They were enjoying their time together and looking forward to their new future on Amaranthine.

After getting the assurance that my family and friends were okay, I rejoined Henoch, and he gave me a tour guide-type description of the ship. I think he may have been bored. His chattiness was out of character.

"The ship is equipped with comfy leather seats. Each seat has a five-point harness for space turbulence. Water and snacks for the first few hours of the trip are provided in the pocket in front of each of the passengers. Each ship has a host or hostess assigned to help with questions or concerns. On our ship, that hostess is Nesta."

As he said her name, I saw her leaning over a cute little kid and pinching his cheeks. She must have said something funny, because the little guy started to laugh out loud. Her gift of providing comfort was blatantly obvious as she cooed in her native language.

Henoch also showed me some of the cool features of the ship that were definitely out of this world.

Eventually, our travelers became more alert and active as the ship flew through deep space. One by one, the group started to slide out of their slumber and walk around to different sections of the ship. Nesta and I helped them get acquainted with the different elements of the ship's amenities – which were definitely alien-based.

Some of its design features reminded me of the technology that was on Oumuamua and I was eager to try some of it out. After a quick tutorial from Henoch, we realized that simulations of certain events could suddenly appear out of thin air. According to Henoch, the ship had been programmed for pretty much any scenario based on our dreams. When we entered the ship, its artificial intelligence knew us; just like how Oumuamua knew Lionel's roars.

The fascinating part was that proximity to other passengers determined what each of us would see. It was, as if whatever someone imagined in their minds, that set of thoughts would materialize in front of all of us. Like Henoch had said, it was a good distraction from the unknown that was ahead of us.

Like emotionally unintelligent school children on a field trip, many of the passengers took turns using their imaginations to create some kind of simulated scenario that we could all experience. Even Gary, finally snapped out of his catatonic state and joined in. He took us to the top of the Seattle Space Needle. We could see the city from all vantage points, as the observatory slowly spun on top. I could tell that his mind was blown by the experience. Especially when he practically screamed.

"This simulation capability reminds me of the movie "Star Trek," where they could create virtual holographic realities depending on the crew members memories. Oh my God, this feels so real."

Nesta even got engaged in the fun. After she shared a quiet moment of lapping waters against a beautiful tropical beach, in her deep Jamaican voice, she hooted, "This is wicked!" Then she proceeded to explain.

"The views from Mammee Bay Beach are amazing at sunset. We would dance naked around a bonfire all night long."

Luckily, we didn't have to see that part.

When it was my turn, I knew exactly what I wanted to conjure. As several of my compartment comrades circled around me, I closed my eyes super tight, like I was making a birthday wish, before I blew out my candles. I could hardly contain the vision within my head. The excitement bubbled up and out, as the room gasped at what had magically appeared in the room. A shimmering glass greenhouse full of lush tropical plants materialized in front of us, like magic. The environment surrounding us was warm and comfortably moist. Cute little bistro tables were scattered around the room. Brightly colored hummingbird-type creatures flitted around our heads. The air smelled like fresh honeysuckle and freshly brewed coffee.

A wide creek, full of crystal-clear water, snaked its way through the greenhouse and ultimately split the room in half. A wood bridge, with a white trellis, was wrapped in wisteria. Long purple blooms were cascading down each side. The pathways that zigzagged through the structure were made of iridescent smooth stones. When you stepped on them, they lit up in different colors. Orange and white Koi fish swirled around in the water. Several of them surfaced and puckered their lips on the water's edge, as if to say hello. Somehow, George, my green-haired turtle friend from Evania, had made it there too.

My companions literally skipped off to explore this newly created paradise. I found the nearest table and sat down to take it all in. Immediately, a foamy cup of latte appeared, just like the ones I used to have at The Coffee Bean. It had a picture of a hummingbird on top. With a sip of the coffee, I couldn't help but say out loud, "This is truly sublime. I just wish Sajan and my little dog were here too."

Henoch suddenly appeared at my table and gave me a little squint. "This is really nice, too bad I don't drink coffee."

After taking a big swig of my kape, I whispered, "Sucks to be you."

We sat there quietly, as I drank my coffee in peace. We had nothing new to say, except, just before he floated off, he forewarned me.

"Take your time. You deserve a break. But I wanted you to know, you are getting a visitor today. Their ship just docked."

With little control of it, my heart skipped a beat. I had been praying for Sajan's return. However, that dream was immediately crushed, when I felt Henoch's guilt. I knew that this was not the visitor I had been hoping for.

"We are doing everything possible to find him. I am as frustrated and angry, as you must be, with Eris and Cozbi's deception. As for your special guest, each of the ships were assigned with a hand-picked guide that is not from Earth. All of the planets had these individuals picked out and approved several years ago." When he paused, his tone changed to disgust.

"Except the 12ᵗʰ Command, of course. They are no longer part of this process, until we can thoroughly vet the good from the bad."

As we locked eyes, I shared my internal thoughts of how much appreciation I had for him and his abilities to communicate and understand the human-race. He truly was an amazing individual. Even if he was short and had a big head.

As expected, Henoch read my thoughts. He sent back a one-word response.

"Ditto!"

Which made me giggle. A few of the others in the room that had tuned into our conversation started to laugh out loud too. As the joyful noise drifted over the holodeck simulation, Henoch hovered down the smooth multicolored rock path that led out of the greenhouse. Each stone he touched lit up like a Christmas tree. As he passed through and out of the greenhouse, the double stained-glass doors slowly closed behind him.

For the next hour, I slowly strolled around my greenhouse paradise. With each step a new feature would appear, because my mind was remembering the creatures and flowers that I had experienced back on Earth and on Amaranthine. At one point, there was a cloud of white butterflies floating above our heads. Dinner-plate sized hibiscus blooms had sprouted out of the ground. When the brightly colored Salvia appeared, hummingbird-type creatures homed in on the blooms, like a well-organized swarm of bees.

I found myself walking along the stone pathway that spontaneously lit up. It reminded me of Davita's Dublin simulation and without even thinking, I found myself shuffling forward and backward, as the color changing rocks started to play a tune. My overimaginative brain had pictured a giant piano, just like the one found in the FAO Schwarz toy store. However, this time I envisioned Sajan happily playing the famous "Heart and Soul" song by Hoagy Carmichael, just before the broken-down cabin turned into Dublin. Part of me thought maybe he would appear.

When he didn't appear, that didn't stop me from euphorically dancing around the garden with my arms in the air, sounding out the notes of the 1938 song. On my third spin, the warmth of our first kiss under the mist of the triple moons of Evania snuck into my thoughts. I realized that this kiss was the one that had stolen my heart and soul, and at that moment, I could not have wanted him back in my arms more than if he had been there standing in front of me. As my mood shifted from joy to longing for his touch, there was a loud, uncomfortable snort from across the room. Startled, I realized that the visitor, that Henoch had warned me about, had arrived. I also realized that my thoughts had been projected across the entire holodeck.

Looking up from my shuffling feet, that awkward feeling that everyone was talking about me, became a reality. All present, in my greenhouse, had stopped what they were doing and were staring in my direction. Several of them had started to head for the stained-glass doorway, to escape my little fantasy, that had been concocted for all to see and hear. I uttered a simple, "Ooops," as the last of them left. I could feel that my cheeks were bright red, like an Oompa Loompa.

My visitor continued to stare at me from across the room. Somehow, he had slowly ducked in and entered the greenhouse unnoticed. He looked confused on who he was meeting here. He obviously didn't know who I was until that moment. We had never met, but when our eyes locked, he did not look amused by my immaturity on the projection of my thoughts on to others.

He had a thick stout snout with a bulbous, wet black nose. Unlike Faith, he had a small delicate nose ring embedded in his septum. It had sparkling garnets on both sides. This magnificent individual must have been over eight feet tall. He had two bright shining white eyes that looked like diamonds.

Just like Faith, focusing on his eyes was uncomfortable. Each of his arms were covered in shaggy black and brown hair that ended with an ox-type hoof. He had large brown wings stretched out behind him. Around his hairy neck hung three gold necklaces with dangling charms.

One of them read, "I Am #7."

Another one jested, "The New #12."

The third gold charm was a name, "Matthias."

After a few moments of staring at each other, Matthias ducked back under, and out of the greenhouse. When he disappeared, I realized that my arms were still in the air. When I lowered them back to my sides, I couldn't help but reprimand myself.

"Some ICC leader you are. You are such a dork."

Eventually, I composed myself and found my way back to the main train car. I took a seat and waited quietly with the others to see what this new visitor was going to say. He just stood in the corner of the well-lit room and observed the passengers with his shining eyes. We continued looking at each other for almost fifteen human minutes. Feeling the need to explain my earlier weird behavior, I mustered enough courage to slowly shuffle over to his side of the room.

"Hi."

Matthias slowly moved his gaze from the room, down to my level. His bright, clear, white eyes peered into mine. He had no visible iris to focus on. It was startling to not have the ability to distinguish any features, so I shifted my focus to his sparkly red nose ring and thought to myself, "Dang, that is so pretty."

Without vocalizing, he telepathically chortled, "Hey Dariann, what's up?" Then he snorted out loud.

The passengers jumped at his vocal snort and began to nervously talk amongst themselves. Startled by his friendly demeanor, I suddenly remembered that vocalized words were no longer needed. No wonder he didn't say anything at first, he was just waiting for someone to engage with him, telepathically. He shrugged his big burly shoulders and projected his message across the cabin of passengers.

"I bet you all got questions."

Anyone, that could hear him, raised their hands in the air like they were back in a traditional human classroom. The other half of the cabin looked confused and concerned by their behavior. And in that moment, I finally understood the true meaning behind the Bible verse that my mom had always told me about, when I asked how I would know if I had reached heaven. She would snuggle me in her strong arms and foreshadow where she thought she would go, when she died.

"Dariann, in heaven, there is nothing hidden that will not be found. There is no secret that will not be well known. Everyone will be kind, understanding, and you will be surrounded by the love of your family and friends."

As I pondered her wise words, I finally understood. It just took a spaceship full of good people, and couple of aliens, to get me there. I finally felt like I had acquired the wisdom to understand her teachings. I finally understood that no matter where we come from, if you have trust, love, and respect for each other, there is never a good reason to hide the truth. I finally understood that my mom was with the Conductor, above.

Matthias was very direct with his teachings, but hilarious. After a few exchanges, we both realized that half of the people on our transport could not understand a word of our conversation. On that day, I took Henoch's advice and became the true leader for the 11th planet remnants. I made it my mission to make sure they knew that they were headed to a place like Heaven. That there would be no more secrets and that what Matthias was teaching us, was the truth.

As he spoke, I translated his words to those that didn't understand. I made sure there was nothing hidden.

39

AMARANTHINE

THE NEXT MORNING, I started a class to teach the passengers how to telepathically communicate. The goal was to make sure that they could project and receive unspoken words from our alien teacher. Taking a page from Davita's classroom setup, I decided to have our learning sessions in my simulated greenhouse. We sipped lattes and practiced this new skill set surrounded by butterflies and flowers.

Gary was picking it up much faster than the rest, and he offered to help me teach. We split up the class, and by the end of the night, most of the participants were fluent enough to at least understand the basic concepts. I was overwhelmed with introverted joy that I didn't have to translate the universal language anymore.

For the next week, Matthias shared the history of all of the different planets that were part of the ICC collective. He was an excellent storyteller. Many of the topics he taught us about were subjects that I had learned before, either through my dreams or at Omah's training facility. However, due to the way that he presented the facts and evidence about our creation, I was just as engaged as the newbies. In addition to his telepathic language transfers, he also used the simulation room to actually show us what each world looked like. I was glad that Matthias skipped over Planet #12's visual history.

The story that was of most interest to me, of which I never really understood, was the story about the Conductor. Matthias explained it in a way that provided the clarity that I needed.

"Like the Biblical stories that most of you are familiar with, the scripture that I grew up with, proclaimed that our Conductor was the One that created all things. The Conductor did this millions of years ago. Our Creator designed twelve different planets, with twelve different types of His creations. The Conductor's intent was to enable an Eden-type world for all of the types of races, and creatures, that He envisioned. Then, He placed those creations on that particular world."

Matthias took a quick look around the room to see if there were any questions. When no one raised their hand, he continued.

"The Conductor saw that some of the creations that He had developed, were doing lawless and cruel things to others. Planet #12, in the beginning and the end, has been the poster child for bad behavior." He grunted at his wisecrack and kept going.

"After observing what was happening on the Grays planet, the Conductor decided to recruit help from them. This was because the Conductor saw them as good. He chose the kindest and most righteous individual to help pull together a council. This individual's purpose was to make sure that all planets understood the Truth, and to help the ICC monitor progress across all of the planets." He stopped his lesson and looked directly at me.

"Who do you think that might have been?"

Without even thinking about it, I blurted out, "Henoch. It had to be Henoch."

Matthias grunted out loud and then followed up with a telepathic, "Yep, Henoch was the first member of the council. This is why he is #1."

The football lover section of the ship started to chant, "He's #1. He's #1."

As the passengers started to get revved up. Matthias stomped his hoof on the floor of the space ship, and playfully retorted, "Yeah, yeah. He is #1."

"Speaking of Henoch, he worked hard to bring the other planets into the Interstellar Contact Council. The ICC was supposed to include an approved leader from each planet. There were certain Golden Rules that had to be followed. He was patient with us, though. He provided the incentives and the warnings about following the Golden Rules. He warned us, that the Conductor would provide obvious signs if we didn't follow the rules. He even told us that the Conductor would put in safeguards to save the chosen few." Matthias waved his hand from one side of the ship to the other and took a dramatic pause.

"Also known as, you!"

"Some of the planets took time to convince. But eventually the Conductor's creations gained enough wisdom and understanding to follow those rules. Well, at least most of them did."

Matthias stopped to take a mental break, before adding, "This is when the ICC decided to start interchanging the critters between planets for sustainability. They also began to populate Amaranthine with each of these different creatures. Amaranthine was part of the Conductor's back up plan for the chosen few. At this same time, Henoch and the ICC activated the other half of His plan. This is when the directive to find 12,000 Peacemakers, per planet, was put into place. Henoch and the other Council members were in charge of contacting and conducting extensive interviews with each Peacemaker to determine their worthiness."

Matthias gave a deep sigh of defeat.

"Then they set out to train them, just in case all hell broke loose. We really didn't think we would have to activate them."

I let out a breath that I didn't know I was holding. Without stopping, Matthias added, "We thought that Planet #11 was ready to join a few years ago, until they started to create weapons that would ultimately destroy themselves. After that, Henoch visited your planet back in the 1950's and created agreements that would have provided the path to Amaranthine. Your government secretly took that privilege from you, when they created technology to block the ICC from observing their progress."

When he said this, many of the passengers actually hollered out loud, "I knew it."

As for me, I felt sick, because I had unwittingly helped develop that technology that led to my beloved Earth's demise. Luckily, Gary raised his hand with a question.

"So why wouldn't we be Planet #12, if we were the last one to join the Interstellar Contact Council?"

Matthias nodded his head, as if to say, "Great question."

"You are correct, Planet #12 joined the ICC before your planet did."

"The truth is, we thought Earth would join before the Reptiles.

The Reptile planet kept breaking the rules and were under, what humans call house arrest, after they started eating animals from other planets, including from Earth. After the ICC went into negotiations, on what was in and out in regard to sustainable food sources, they quicky complied with the new requirements. We had already named Earth the 11th planet, and therefore, they made a decision to name the Reptile planet as #12."

Then Matthias did a disgusted snort and added, "However, as you all know, the leaders of the 12th planet broke those rules again, and are directly responsible for pulling all of us into this war. They have disrupted everything the Conductor had envisioned for his creations."

He paused, as if he was having an internal battle with himself. When he nodded to the air and looked across the attentive and horrified audience, he added, "I do hope that you know, there is good and bad on all planets. Some of the individuals on Planet #12 took the Conductor's creation towards a bad place, but there are good souls there too. We are trying to sort those out and include them in our future plans. However, #12 is no more. Like Earth, their world has been destroyed. We have also found out that the Pegasus world, known as #4, was destroyed yesterday. We have lost one of our most committed and kind Interstellar Contact Council leaders."

When he said this, I let out an uncontrolled, "What?"

Everyone turned towards me as I said a little too loud, "OMG, did Aster not make it?"

Matthias gently shook his head and looked down at the ships floor.

"He did not make it. We just found out this morning. Aster was firing on Cozbi's ship, because they were attacking Aster's home world. We thought Aster had won that battle, but just before Planet #4 blew up, we lost contact with Aster and his crew. There were no survivors on either ship, that we could find."

When Matthias said this, there was no way I could control my grief. Not only was there deep sadness for the loss of my flying horse friend, but I also knew that there was a high possibility that Sajan was on the ship, with Cozbi and Eris."

Matthias heard my unprotected thoughts and gently said, "We were unable to confirm who was on the enemy ship."

Gary raised his hand again and asked Matthias to describe Amaranthine. He must have thought that we all needed a distraction and some good news. Matthias squeezed himself into the nearest unoccupied chair and let out a deep breath.

"Amaranthine means infinity. It is like Heaven, but it is not. It is a place that is only envisioned in your wildest hopes and dreams. It is a place that the Conductor created for all of us to live peacefully together until he calls us to what you all call Heaven."

Gary raised his hand, high in the air. Matthias tried to ignore him, but Gary started to project his question across the room, anyways.

"So even though Amaranthine means infinity, it's not?"

The entire room erupted into laughter. It was definitely a thought that was easy to overanalyze. Matthias snorted, too.

"Yes! However, on Amaranthine you will find that life is simple. Each of us choose a lifestyle that favors our gifts. He pointed to his big hairy chest and explained, "Those that want to teach, teach. Those that want to dabble in technology, join the science and engineering team. Those that like physical activity and warfare, become warriors. Those that just want to help grow and distribute food, have farms. It is truly a harmonious and peaceful place full of love and kindness."

The passengers smiled warmly, as he said these amazing words.

"Amaranthine is a self-sustaining garden, like the Biblical Garden of Eden. We don't have money. We don't embrace greed. We help each other to be successful. We give honest feedback to each other, openly, without judgement. When you arrive, you will find that there are twelve sections that represent the twelve different planetary environments. The track's path connects all twelve sections. We call it the Eight Train." Then he grunted, because he knew that infinity, was sometimes represented, by a sideways eight by Earthlings. After his own privately projected joke, he elaborated.

"The train's tracks symbolize, and remind us, that we are all connected and that our love for each other is never ending.

When we get to Amaranthine, you get to choose which of the sections you would like to live in. There is ultimate freedom on where you decide to live, but you must follow the Golden Rules of the Conductor to make it to Heaven." As he raised up, out of his chair, he suggested, "Let's take a break and pick this up tomorrow."

Then he walked out of the room, leaving us with our thoughts.

40

COMMAND AND TEACH THESE THINGS

AS THE WEEK crept by, Earth's remnants were ready to get off the train. Matthias's teachings had come to an end, and he exhibited a restlessness to escape as well. We were excited to hear him announce that we would be arriving to Amaranthine by the end of what he called, a 'human day.'

As our 24-hour clock timer ticked down to zero, Matthias finally informed us, "If you look over there, Amaranthine is now coming into view."

Like a bunch of tourists, on a bus to a country they had never experienced before, we all raced to the windows to see our new home. At first sight, the planet looked a lot like Earth. It had the telltale signs of blues and greens of land and ocean; however, it also had a variety of other colors swirled in too.

As we zoomed into the atmosphere of Amaranthine, we dropped down to a track of the Eight Train. The transition was seamless and silent, except for a small exchange of technology that helped capture the floating ship and propel us forward down the tracks. Matthias pulled me aside.

"As discussed, each of the passengers decide where they want to go. They just need to pull the colored cord and step off the Eight Train. Someone will be there to greet them and get them settled. Some of these folks will need some additional guidance and support."

That was when he indicated I would be that person. Shortly after this news, he gave me a shoulder bump, that made me lose my balance. Then he megaphoned his voice over the train's passengers, and imparted, "It was a pleasure being your teacher. I wish you all the best of luck. I leave you in good hands." Then he pulled the orange cord and walked off the train.

All eyes watched him disappear down an orange-colored, concrete-stamped path that looked like the yellow brick road from the "Wizard of Oz" movie. In the background, you could see a city of strange buildings and lights on the horizon. As the train started back down the tracks, they all focused on me.

Luckily, I was finally ready to lead my weary companions. I helped each of my new friends maneuver through the decision of which country on Amaranthine that they would like to resettle in. I was surprised at how quickly they had adapted to their new situation. It was a good litmus test of their faith in the stories that we all had been told as truth – even when we didn't' have the physical evidence to actually see this new world. They readily believed in our Conductor's great plan, and through this faith, they found peace and purpose on their paths going forward.

After the Eight Train did a full circle around the track, the passengers began to collect their Earthly belongings and calmly pull the colored cord. For some odd reason, I felt a sense of loss, as each one stepped down and out to their new country. When the last passenger left the compartment to start their new adventure, the joy that I had held for others' happiness, quickly turned to sorrow.

I tried to hold back tears, but eventually they spilled out the corners of my eyes and streaked down my cheeks. I rode the Eight Train through all of the countries several times. At one point, I started to argue with myself.

"Why can't I pull that cord? All of these countries are amazing in their own unique way. I would love any of these."

But I never pulled the cord. All I could think of was Sajan, and how much I missed him. I didn't want a life without him. On the last loop of this reoccurring nightmare, Henoch was suddenly sitting beside me. He had floated over and sat down without disturbing me. I could feel his calming presence beside me. When I finally had the courage to look into his endless, sky-blue eyes, he whispered, "Don't be afraid. It will be okay."

Jokingly, I cried, "Hey, those are my words."

And if Henoch could have, he would have given me a big toothy smile, because he knew what he was doing when he said those words. He was reminding me of the blessings in my life. He was reminding me to have hope. As I stared into his blue eyes, I began to see the ocean. The waves rhythmically washed up on sandy pink beaches. In this vision, Henoch reached out with his hand and guided me up a steep path. At the top of the dune there were acres and acres of waving multicolored pasture grasses. There were no fences. There were no other structures in sight, except for a small bench, that had been placed at the end of the trail. When we reached the weathered wood bench, we sat, and watched the vastness of the ocean in front of us.

In this vision, Henoch looked up at me and whispered, "This is Evania. It means peace."

When I snapped out of my reminiscent moment and looked out the window of the Eight Train, I saw a young horse-type animal, quietly staring at the passing train. Without hesitation, I quickly reached up, and pulled the thin red cord. Henoch walked over to the door and reached out his long thin fingers. When I placed my hand in his, the door slid open. As I stepped off the train, the foal-looking creature shifted its focus to me and enthusiastically whinnied.

"Hi Dariann, I'm Nova."

Shocked, I looked at Henoch to see if he was messing with me. The only Nova I knew, was the one that Aster and Star were having almost fifteen years earlier. Oddly enough Henoch was still holding my hand.

He stood there in telepathic silence, as his memories played out in my head like a movie. The scene, in my mind, looked like a funeral type of procession. I recognized a few of the creatures in attendance, like Intelligence, Amartv, Gyaan, and Faith. In front of the crowd of supporters, was Aster and Star. They were pulling a small cart that was decorated in a plethora of flowers. The cart held a lifeless premature foal.

When the reel of my telepathic movie moved forward, there was another cart, with another lifeless premature foal.

By the time Henoch's memory showed me a third foal in a

cart, I actually started to cry. I finally understood, the little foal, standing in front of me, was Nova. She was the first of their line, after all of these years of her parents trying.

When Henoch let go of my hand, and as that scene melted away, the dancing foal in front of me, meant so much more. She was prancing, back and forth, like an impatient toddler wanting an answer to all of her impulsive questions. I managed to sputter, "Hi" to the adorable black and white creature with big blue eyes.

Clearly pleased with my acknowledgement, she let out the cutest horsey trill. Then she unfurled her bright white wings and flapped them behind her. After a failed attempt to fly, she squealed.

"Intelligence told me you would come. I have been waiting a long time for you."

Still in a bit of a stunned state, I stammered, "I am glad to meet you too, Nova."

Henoch clasped my hand, once again, and pulled me along a pink sandy path. Just like my dream, it was surrounded by waving sea grasses. Nova quietly trailed behind us. There were strange and unusual looking plants that I had never seen before. Some of the flowers that waved in the gentle breeze had red winged butterflies flitting around them. To my surprise, I noticed that they had the number 88 etched into their wings. Without even thinking, I yelled, "Ah ha, that is the butterfly that was under Eris's desk."

Henoch pointed his big head towards it and confirmed my new knowledge.

"That was one of our first critter transplants to Earth from Evania. That is why it is marked with a double infinity symbol. It did very well on Earth and was able to survive in Central and South America. It was even found in Texas a few decades later."

Before I could put together another question about that thought, a transparent thin-bodied butterfly floated in front of me and landed on a giant gold flower. It looked like it was made of glass. Only a thin outline of a wing could be seen. It was truly something that could only be found in science fiction movies, but I knew better, by now, and looked at Henoch for his tutelage.

"That is a Glass Wing butterfly, it was found in Earth's rainforest."

After a dramatic pause, he snickered, "You really didn't get around much, did you?"

Before I could come up with a witty response, he let go of my hand.

"I'm going to let Nova mentor you from here on out."

Nova started to flap and skip beside me like a charged-up energizer bunny. I remember letting out a long-held breath of relief. I had finally found the place that I had defined as "Heaven" in my dreams. It had been Evania, the entire time. Henoch nodded his head with approval at this thought. Then just before he disappeared into one of his tractor beams, he waved his long fingers at me, and called out.

"Makita ka, Dariann. Sana ol."

Then he was gone.

When he said it, my heart dropped to my stomach, because I had learned in Sajan's language, it meant, "See you Dariann," followed by an expression that means, I hope for your success. However, I didn't have time to dwell on what he said, because as it turned out, Nova talked my ear off.

I found out that she was, in fact, the foal of Aster and Star. She had been born a few months before they were asked to fight for righteousness in the planetary wars. She knew that both of her flying parents had lost their lives, in what her kind were calling, "The Eris Battle."

After a little pause, she quickly said with hope in her thoughts, "But Intelligence has been caring for me until you arrived. She has told me so much about you. I am so glad you are finally here."

She trilled a horsey celebration and popped up a few feet off the ground, as her wings fluttered erratically.

Although the loss of her parents was tragic, I was surprised at how well Intelligence knew my heart. She knew I would adopt Nova immediately. She knew how much I loved magical horses. Especially talking ones. That first day with Nova, was the beginning of my new life on Evania. All day we wandered around the dunes and through forest areas, while Nova showed me the different areas and creatures that lived there. Thanks to Sajan's tutelage, I had met a few of the residents already, like the fuzzy pink armadillo and the big-mouthed Potoo.

We eventually forked on to a familiar trail, that led down to a house surrounded by every flower you could imagine. There was a cobble stone pathway leading up to the door. The front yard was surrounded by a short white fence. The door and the shutters around the windows were hot pink. When I looked down at Nova, she gave me a toothy horse grin like she knew I wasn't fond of the color pink, then she trotted off down the path. Her tail was held in a high prance position, as it flipped back and forth.

When I walked through the pink door, I was pleasantly surprised to see that the inside was designed similar to Davita and Alaster's cottage.

Nova explained, "Intelligence and several of the other members of the ICC built the little cottage that overlooked the ocean, just for us. They even put in a magical country-style kitchen that provides all the food we could ever want to eat." She gave out a high horse pitch neigh and flapped her little wings up and down.

Then Nova clasped my shirt with her little flat teeth and guided me to one of the bedrooms. A shimmery net elegantly draped each of the poles. Soft satin sheets and fluffy pillows called my name. But before I jumped in, I walked over to the fountain that flowed into the pond, and there on the bottom, was George, my green-haired turtle friend. He poked up his head and gave me one of his beaky grins.

Later that night, when we cuddled up into the bed, just like Woola used to do, Nova curled up at the end of the bed. Her head was tucked under her feathery wing. With one last stroke of her soft little neck, before I faded off to sleep, I had decided that my purpose was to help others settle in and find their special place. I had to help them find their happy place here in Amaranthine. Even if, I couldn't fulfill all of my own dreams to be with Sajan and my little dog too.

Just before I faded off to sleep, I hummed the Peacemaker song and gave thanks to the Conductor above for the opportunity to have purpose once again. No matter how hard Sajan's loss was, I knew that this was what he would have wanted me to do.

In the morning, with Nova by my side, I traveled the same path that Sajan and I traveled the first time we visited Evania. When we arrived in front of the ocean transport, Nova nudged me on to the ETT and told me to have a great day. When I arrived at the hallway of doors, I already knew that I would be very busy. I was greeted by an exhausted Arisanna, the ancient historian, and she clued me in.

"Many of the over two million transfers from Planet #11 need guidance and support maneuvering through the new worlds. Your door, to your section, is right over there." When she started to laugh, I got suspicious about what I was going to find.

Befuddled by her behavior, I looked over her shoulder. A door that I had never seen in all of my dreams, shimmered at the end of the hall. It was, of course, hot pink. When I walked over to examine it, it had the #11 embossed in the middle of it. The doorknob was shaped like the waves of the ocean. When I pushed through the bright pink door, the sun was shining and the sky was blue. The Homo sapiens section of Amaranthine looked a lot like Earth. I chuckled when I saw a table with an empty chair, and a stack of hot pink sticky notes. There was a long line of humans patiently waiting in line, looking at me. I made a mental note to ask Henoch about how this world materialized, without me knowing it.

Luckily, my new job kept me busy and distracted, which was a blessing in disguise. If it had not been so time-consuming, I would have settled into deep sadness about the lack of Sajan and Woola in my life.

Days turned into weeks, and eventually I had memorized each twist and turn of the path that led to the hallway of doors. I knew that along certain stretches of the path I would probably see a friendly saber-toothed deer or an occasional Pooty bird. On the ETT, I often saw the Japanese spider crab armies and the graceful Glaucus Atlanticus that gave Sajan so much joy.

When I did get a break from the business of my new responsibilities, I would go visit my dad, my siblings, Fanny, or my best friend. They had chosen different countries to live out their lives and it was always a good distraction to see what new and exciting things they were discovering.

However, some days I got lost in my thoughts and I could not help but wonder what evil the 12th Command was doing to my beloved. What kind of torture were they putting him through? I never found the strength to accept that he might be dead. But with a little help from my alien friends, I never lost hope that I would see him again.

Intelligence visited often to check up on us. After Nova's parent's untimely deaths, she and the little foal had developed a strong bond, and you could tell Intelligence loved her very much. One night during one of these visits, as Intelligence stroked Nova's baby stubble of a mane, she excitedly updated me on that day's war and rescue efforts.

"Evangeline, my top warrior, has found a new lead. She is researching it and will get back to us in the next day or so. Please don't lose hope Dariann. We will find him. And if they are still alive, we will deal swiftly with Eris and Cozbi too."

After a week, no news materialized, and the sadness was starting to creep in and take away that glimmer of hope that she had planted in my heart. To top that off, that afternoon I had helped the last of Planet #11's transfers, that were behind the hot pink door, to find their special gift. My mission was coming to an end. And once again, I heard a reminiscent whisper of Henoch's final words, after Earth blew up.

"Tetelestai. It is done."

It was a bittersweet accomplishment, but fortunately I had Nova. She made sure we celebrated the good things that came out of that day. Per her request, we set out a blanket to watch the sunsets. We ate strawberries dipped in chocolate and I finally found the strength to tell her how Sajan and I had met. As the evening progressed, she curled up beside me and was quietly snoring. I gently stroked the soft feathers of the wings tucked up on her back.

In my other hand, I held a glass of bubbling champagne, and as the last rays of light dissipated to darkness and one of Evania's moons took its place, I quietly called out.

"Good job Dariann. Way to go. Far out!"

That is when white wings and the silver-suit of a visitor flashed in front of me. Intelligence and Henoch appeared from behind my home. When they floated over to where Nova and I were sitting, Intelligence did a crisscross applesauce stance in front of us. Henoch stood behind her. I could barely see the top of his chin.

Intelligence had an angelic look on her face and her blue eyes were sparkling. Henoch, on the other hand, was keeping his thoughts close to him. He wasn't showing me any air wave emotion, one way or another. I put down my glass and straightened up, just as Nova woke up, squealed and jumped into her lap. After a few moments of cooing and love, Intelligence abruptly stated.

"Cozbi is alive. We caught him. He was in an escape pod floating through space. Oddly enough, he was happy to finally be in our custody."

A renewed hope bubbled up and out, as she expressed this exciting news. With double protection, I safely thought to myself. "If Cozbi is alive, maybe Sajan is too."

Henoch gave me a hopeful nod, while Intelligence continued to tell me the news.

"That day, when the members of the ICC discovered that Eris was the Nero, we spent most of the day and night trying to figure out how to defeat her. Rather than staying to strategize the next steps, Cozbi said that he had to get back to his ship to protect Woola. This is the claim he made, as to why he left without a word and returned to his ship. He said that he fell in love with that little black dog of yours."

When my mouth popped open, with surprise at this news, both of them pushed out a telepathic chuckle, before Intelligence responded.

"He knew Eris was going to use Woola as bait to capture you, or hurt you, because she had mentioned that plan before he knew that she was the Lawless one. When he got back, he had convinced several of the crew to cover for him by starting a couple of diversions. Then he grabbed your dog and hid him. He claims he was going to go back for Sajan, too."

With great doubt, I blurted, "Aye. Right!." Because I had a hard time believing a guy whose name meant, "Liar sliding away," would be telling the truth.

Intelligence paused and gave me a little nod of understanding.

"Cozbi told us that Eris was furious that the dog could not

be found, when she arrived unannounced that day, and before Cozbi could warn Sajan, she captured Sajan instead."

As she collected her thoughts she whispered, "Cozbi claims that he had been trying to get away from Eris since the conflict back on Earth began. He claimed she had put some kind of control device under his skin that would not allow him to escape. We found it. We removed it."

As she talked, my mind was a whirlwind of thoughts and emotions, as I tried to piece all of this new information together. I wasn't sure if I should throw up or shout-out with joy.

"So, is my dog alive? OMG, is Sajan dead?"

Intelligence gently shook her head as if she wasn't sure.

"Cozbi says he moved Woola to a different planet for safe keeping. Which is why Max and Ally couldn't locate him. Cozbi also insisted that he eventually earned Eris's trust and was able to get close to Sajan. That was when he realized that Eris had some kind of control over him, too. Cozbi thinks she hypnotized him and made him think that her side was the right side. When Sajan saw you on Earth, he broke free from her control and when they returned to the ship after the chaos at the facility, she locked him up."

I shot up off the blanket and started to pace back and forth in the grass.

"Is Sajan dead?"

Intelligence peered into my now tear-filled eyes, and confessed, "We don't know. Cozbi said Eris decided to blow you and the rest of the human race up on Earth rather than trying to capture you. She started to lose herself to emotions and began to yell at everyone. That was about the same time that all of the other planets started to join forces. When Aster was chasing down Eris's ship and tried to stop their engine capabilities, Cozbi claims that Aster was successful. Aster thought they could get them to surrender."

She paused before sharing any more details. Henoch was pacing back and forth behind her. Nova's eyes were as big as dinner plates.

"Instead of surrender, Eris found a way to shoot down Aster's ship and it was destroyed. Eris did a self-detonation of her own ship, so it looked like Aster had blown her up. When the rest of the fleet caught up to the location of her ship, it was destroyed. However, Cozbi believes that Eris and most of the 12th Command, under Eris's control, made it to escape pods."

Frustrated that Intelligence was not giving me the answer I wanted, I demanded.

"Intelligence, what happened to Sajan?"

Then I cringed inside, preparing for the answer that I thought she was going to give me.

Feeling my pain, she winced.

"With all of the chaos, Cozbi was able to grab Sajan and they escaped in one of those pods together. Cozbi claims that he left Sajan with Woola on the same planet together."

Without thinking, I thought out loud, "I need to go find them."

Both Henoch and Intelligence shook their head no.

Then Henoch explained, "We have to keep you safe. You are still in danger. The Conductor has indicated that there are still important things that you must do. Saving Sajan and Woola is not one of those things. We must trust His plan."

Intelligence, feeling my anger for being stifled, offered, "I have sent Evangeline to investigate, but she informed me that most of that planet was destroyed in the war. She has sent in search parties, Dariann. If he is there, she will bring him back. Please don't lose hope."

Henoch gave a heavy mental sigh.

"We will keep you apprised of any new developments."

Intelligence nodded and silently lifted the sleepy foal from her lap and handed Nova to me. Nova took her little wings and gave me a hug, just as Intelligence and Henoch left the same way they had come. She grabbed my shirt with her flat teeth and dragged me to our room. I was so thankful to have little Nova there to keep me company on that lonely night, while I waited for updated news.

In the morning, to help with my anxiety I decided to take a walk around the garden. Nova quietly followed me. I found myself at the little wooden bench that overlooked the outside pond where George lived. He was happily eating some kind of purple leafy plant at the side of the pond, with his pointy turtle beak. As I tried to relax, the noise of the waves of the ocean floated through the air and gently rocked my sadness back and forth. Nova had somehow worked her head into my lap. Her white wings were furled up on her back. Several bright colored Earth-like hummingbirds hovered in front of me. They were twisting and turning, as if they were in danger, and at first I thought they were in trouble and needed my help.

When I finally gave them my full attention, they flitted off into the distance to lap up the nectar from the fields of brightly colored flowers I had planted for them. They followed the pink sandy path that led down to the ocean. As usual, Nova was right there in the middle of this scene and watched them fly off as well. Her big blue eyes were focused on their every move.

Suddenly, Nova straightened up and unfurled her wings. I followed her gaze of intensity. At first, all I saw were the birds hovering about and thought she was just being curious about the little birds' activity.

Then I saw it too.

Behind the busy little hummingbirds, on the sandy path, there was a slight figure briskly walking towards me. A black and white pug-nosed dog, with big brown eyes, was trotting behind him. Its tongue was hanging out from the brisk walk on the sandy pathway. Its little bear paws were splaying out on the sand, in all directions, as he paddled along.

I abruptly stood up and desperately cried.

"SAJAN?"

His answer floated above the sounds of the crashing waves on to the wet sands below.

"DARIANN! OMG! Dariann!"

With his answer, I ran as fast as I could on the gritty and slippery sand. I jumped and crashed into his warm strong chest. We fell to the sandy ground and rolled a few feet off the path. When he grabbed my face with his weathered hands and looked deep into my eyes, he quietly whispered, "Oh, Dariann!"

The pain and the anguish that he had been through flashed through my mind, and I cringed at the trial that he had to endure to come back to me. He had a fresh purple scar that ran along his cheekbone. His dark muscled forearms hid deep scratches and bruises from his hardship. He was thin and weak.

However, there was no holding back, and all I could do was place my hands over his, reach down, and gently touch his lips.

Woola jumped in between us, and started to whimper, and shake. I grabbed his sweet little smashed face and gave him a smooch too. Then, I cooed to my furry friend, "Hello sweet boy. Where have you been?"

Nova was bouncing off the sand and flapping her immature wings, excitedly above us. The joy of the realization of this new beginning with Sajan was overwhelming for her. All three of us knew it, at that very moment. We had just become a family with a cute little Earth dog named Woola.

When we got back to the cottage, Sajan cleaned up and ate his beloved balut. Woola got a bath and one of his favorite bones. Nova and Woola became fast friends, and she immediately decided that he needed to sleep in her room. When she announced this, my heart filled with happiness, because it was the first time she wanted to sleep in her own room after losing her parents.

Sajan and I cuddled on the couch most of the night. He told me everything about his last few months. There was good and bad in all of his stories. We spent several hours incoherently sobbing in each other's arms. When he finally got to the topic of Eris, with deep exhaustion and defeat, he whispered, "She is truly pure evil. She has to be stopped."

Then he gave me a firm bear hug and sputtered, "When things got really bad, it was the thought of you that got me through." After a few moments of silent embraces, he quietly chortled, "Well and that little dog too."

Just before he passed out in my arms he whispered, "Mahal Kita Dariann."

And I whispered right back, as fast as I could, "Mahal Kita Sajan."

As he quietly slept in peace, one of the last memories of my mom being alive floated through my thoughts. It was of course, on Earth, back on the farm. I remembered how she was tucking me into sleep after watching a series called "The Time Traveler's Wife." It was a thoughtful and mind-bending episode, where the little girl had finally realized that the man that kept popping into her life, was actually her soul mate. Time was not a barrier in their love story. As my mom and I said our usual nighttime prayers, I remember asking her, "What would you change or do differently if you could change time momma?"

And she whispered, "Each of us gets the choice to choose, good or bad. I have taken both paths and personally my time seeking righteousness provided me with more joy than I could ever imagine. I would not go back and change anything. I choose to learn from it and then teach it to others."

She gave me a sweet peck on the cheek and moved my long bangs out of my eyes. She hummed a familiar song about the grace and love of her God above. When she slowly struggled to rise up and leave, she said under her breath, "Command and teach these things."

When she said it, I had no idea what she was saying or that it was from the human-based Bible. Looking back, I realized the Conductor was telling me my future, through her words. That moment with my mom, although just a small fraction of a second of time, packed a lot of wisdom. It is something I would take with me into eternity. It was my turn to teach others the truth about acquiring wisdom. It was my turn to command and teach these things.

Lucky for me, I was in the right place, because I had literally landed in infinity. I knew that there were new adventures and challenges ahead, but I was ready to tackle those over time. There was peace in my heart knowing that just like those that went before us, like Aster and Star, and even my mom, we would all meet the Conductor, some day. It was just a matter of time.

While holding my sleeping mo anam cara in my arms, I reaffirmed my oath to the Conductor to always seek Him. I promised Him when it was the right time, I would find and take-down the Nero that was currently on the loose somewhere in the universe.

However, at that moment in my timeline, I was planning on soaking in the love of the man of dreams, raising a flying horse named Nova, and petting a little black dog with pointy ears, named Woola.

Blessed is the one who finds wisdom,
and the one who gets understanding.

Proverbs 3:13

ACKNOWLEDGEMENTS

AS ALWAYS, I acknowledge and appreciate the blessings of the gaggle of understanding and supportive key contributors to this book's review, editing, and marketing process. Special thanks to Andrea, Cousin Fanny, Sandy, and Tracy for pushing me to be a better writer by providing honest feedback.

This book is dedicated to the real-life Darian. Just like the main character of this book, her strength and perseverance to pursue good in all things makes her a bad ass kunoichi and one of the kindest people I know.

May you find the strength and courage to command and teach the wisdom that you acquire about all things good in this world.

ABOUT THE AUTHOR

ALETA MAREE WAS raised on a farm in a small-town community in Washington State. She has a degree in business management and is an avid student of quality assurance, project management, operational controls, and continuous improvement.

Aleta married her high school sweetheart over 32 years ago. They have two children that also live in the Tri-Cities area with their families.

After working over 30 years at a government-run research and development laboratory, she decided that writing books was way more fun and retired in 2020 to continue her dream of authoring science fiction novels.

Please visit her website for more information about her other books, as well as, new developments about book two of the 11th Planet's Peacemaker series.

Please visit me at:
www.aletamaree.com

www.ingramcontent.com/pod-product-compliance
Lightning Source LLC
Chambersburg PA
CBHW021231310726
48971CB00006B/1768